IT'S ALIVE

Warily Gath glanced at her, then at the flames crackling around the bridge. Suddenly they lowered, as if in obedience to her silent command, and the bridge, smoking and spattered with small remnants of fire, lay open to the prize.

"Take your time," Cobra murmured. "Stand close, look into its eyes and you will know that all I say is true. Meanwhile, I will be in my chambers ... waiting for you ... to conclude our contract."

He shook his head. "I will test it first." He slung his axe on his back.

"Wait!" she gasped. "What are you doing?"

He pushed past her and started over the bridge. The bubbling lava boiled and a flame shot up, licked his legs in warning. He jumped forward, dashed of the flaming pit.

Cobra shrieked. "No! Don't!"

The room shook. Thundered. Parts of the bridge broke away under his feet. Rocks fell from the ceiling, crashed through the skull, knocking Gath to his knees. The flames were again enclosing the helmet. It was only a vague shape crackling within the red fire. He jumped up and plunged both hands into the flames, growling at the searing pain, and came away with the horned prize. The hair on his arms was curled and smoking. He lifted the horned helmet above his head, then lowered it carefully, engulfing his head in its brutal blackness.

Also by James Silke
published by Tor Books

Frank Frazetta's Death Dealer Book 2
Lords of Destruction

JAMES SILKE

Frank Frazetta's Death Dealer

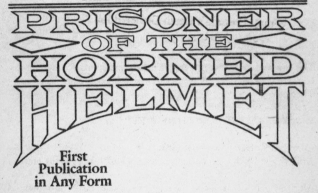

PRISONER OF THE HORNED HELMET

**First
Publication
in Any Form**

A TOM DOHERTY ASSOCIATES BOOK

PRISONER OF THE HORNED HELMET

Copyright © 1988 by James R. Silke
Artwork and Death Dealer character copyright © 1988 by Frank Frazetta

A TOR Book
Published by Tom Doherty Associates, Inc.
49 West 24 Street
New York, NY 10010

Cover art by Frank Frazetta

ISBN: 0-812-53823-4   Can. ISBN: 0-812-53824-2

First edition: February 1988

Printed in the United States of America

0 9 8 7 6 5 4 3

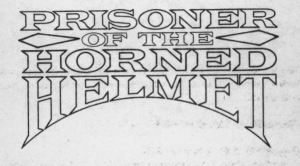

PRISONER OF THE HORNED HELMET

One
INVADERS

They came out of the sunblasted desert. Tiny dark specks wagging a tail of billowing yellow dust at the yellow sky. Occasionally they glittered metallically; otherwise they were shaggy, the color of dirt when it was in a mood to be filthy. All of which meant they looked their best, like tarantulas with their hair combed.

It was a mounted detachment. Nine riders with crossbows in their saddle holsters and sheathed swords, quivers and daggers riding their belts. Scouts. Probing fingertips of the nomadic empire which dominated the southern lands from the Dark Continent in the west, all the way across the lands of Yellow Faces to the Islands of the Rising Sun in the east. The Kitzakk Horde.

Their horses were small, scarred, with braided manes and tails. Durable. The riders were more so, leather-skinned veterans of the desert campaigns. They were Hunters, members of one of the three Chel Regiments under the personal command of the warlord, Klang.

Helmets, arm bands and breastplates were black-lacquered bamboo striped with steel bands. Skirts were wide leather thongs mounted with steel studs. Crescent moons of precious silver glittered on the tops of wide-brimmed helmets shaped like overturned shallow bowls. Their weapons were carved with the figures of butterflies and inlaid with a patina of gore and grime gathered from

1

uncounted battlefields. There were the inevitable dents and stains, but each carried a story of violent, painful victory.

Their flat brown faces carried similar stories, stories of themselves. Men wearing steel and death.

They rode north to the dry cataracts where Sergeant Yat reined up and halted his command. He was short, thick and sun dark. His squad numbered seven veterans and one rookie, a boy they called Young Hands, who brought up the rear. They stared down at the cataracts like performers about to step onto a stage they had not played before, a dangerous one.

The massive shelves of rock, splintered by bottomless gorges, descended in almost regular steps then vanished amid low-lying clouds. Like a staircase for the gods, the large variety who use trees for toothpicks and urinate lightning.

Soong, the wrinkled one, said, "Not a regulation border, is it?"

Akar nodded agreement. "The regiments will be one large target crossing this, and so will we."

Sergeant Yat grunted as if the cataracts were of no more concern than an unpolished belt buckle and moved his squad forward with a circular motion of his hand.

They turned west, rode until they came to a steep trail descending into the cataracts. Soong put up a trail marker, a red flag embroidered with a rising sun, the sign of their Butterfly Goddess. Akar removed a map, bamboo pen and ink from a metal cylinder and noted the trail on the map. This done, Yat led them down the trail into the uncharted, savage wilderness.

As the scouts descended, the iron chains and slave collars dangling from their saddles echoed pleasantly among the stone chasms. These instruments were beautifully made, hand carved with images of entwined flowers. The soldiers made no attempt to mute their metallic song.

It brought terror to their enemies, was music to their ears. A proud reminder that they no longer used barbaric ropes or crude leather collars, but hard steel. They were civilized. They even drank their blood from a cup.

Two
COBRA

Beyond the cataracts, deep within the Great Forest Basin, the tiny Glyder Snake slithered under dense ground cover, came to a stop at a wild scarlet rose graced with flickering sunlight. The reptile was in a section of the forest called The Shades. Vast. Uninhabited. Primeval. Dense with fir, spruce and hemlock rising from the embrace of creepers and sword ferns, and carpeted with needles, leaves and moss. A land with a roof of leaves penetrated by a few scattered shafts of gold light. A world of shadows. The perfect place for a snake at work.

The reptile's gold eyes hunted and came to rest on a black cavelike opening amid the exposed roots of a massive spruce. Its nostrils widened. Its black tongue tasted the air. It had found what it hunted.

It slipped out of the concealing ground cover, wound its way up onto a dead fir tree lying on the ground, and slithered into a pool of flickering sunlight. The slim olive green body, the length of a forearm, coiled, then lifted in an elegant arc and pointed its stabbing tongue at a shadowed cave at the base of an outcroping of overgrown rock. Within seconds, sunshine turned its body yellow and its tiny scales began to radiate golden light, like a glowing trail marker.

There was the sound of something large shifting its weight within the shadows of the cave, then silence.

A spread of man-high sword ferns swayed behind the reptile, then parted, held by two hooded faceless spearmen crowded in the shadows. An opulent female figure emerged robed in emerald velvet. Small pearl-white hands clutched the heavy garment about her, their red nails hot, sharp. She stepped into the pool of light beside the glowing Glyder Snake. For a brief moment her draped body shimmered, reflecting the colors of the sunlight and the scarlet rose, then it flickered brightly and turned to scales of glittering gold. She slowly pushed her hood back and gazed intently at the shadowed cave.

Her grey-and-gold, almond-shaped eyes were heavily rimmed with kohl, and glistened in the deep alcoves of her finely wrought skull. Thin arched eyebrows. Wide full cheekbones. Lips narrow but fleshy above her finely pointed chin. Her skin was flawless, translucent, cream tinted with rose madder. Her hair was hidden beneath a shoulder length skullcap of metallic scales crusted with tiny jewels and cut like a serpent's hood. It glittered with wealthy abandon. This was the sorceress called Cobra, Queen of Serpents.

The shadow within the root cave shifted.

Cobra's cheeks rose with the trace of a confident smile. She parted her robe to reveal a lush body ripe with curves. Wide hips. Narrow waist. Full breasts swelling above the restraining gold cloth of her garment like soft prisoners. She spoke in a tone that was playful, in the manner of fingers stroking a naked thigh.

She said, "I bear a message, Dark One."

A voice from within the cave said, "I have no use for messages." It echoed softly, as if the speaker were imprisoned in a hole at the center of the earth. Yet strong, holding back thunder.

"You will have use for this one," she said, abruptly changing her tone. "It carries a warning. Great and terrible events are traveling towards the Forest Basin. Events more horrible than even you can imagine. The armies of the great Outland empire in the south are coming, Dark One, and they wear armor and bear weapons stronger than the earth has ever known before."

A grunt escaped the shadowed cave.

A smile spread across her mouth then died at the corners. "Contempt will not blunt their weapons. These Outlander champions are stronger than any you have faced. No fire you stoke can soften their metal, no weapon you hold can penetrate it. You will not be able to stand against them, unless you arm yourself properly."

She waited, got no response, and continued coaxingly. "I do not insult you, Dark One. I am certain that you will die grandly, in a manner that will be spoken of with praise around the campfires for many years. But if you are of a mind to remain Lord of the Shades a little longer, hear me out."

Silence.

"Listen to me! Go to the bridge called Lemontrail Crossing. Today! There you will find armor and weapons of hard metal, tools which can be yours if you have the will to take them."

She waited again for a response, got none, and her smile coiled restlessly in the cool beauty of her face. For a moment it was naked, then suddenly flashed hotly, all rouge and painted lips.

She said, "Understand, Cobra seeks no payment for her words. Not of you. What I will have of you is far more than a mere tuft of your fur or a cup of your urine could provide."

She turned, moved back through the parted ferns with the Glyder Snake following at a respectful distance, then the ferns closed, and they were gone.

Three

LEMONTRAIL CROSSING

It was midday before Sergeant Yat's squad reached the lowest cataract and descended a twisting, shadow-filled gully out of which blew a welcome cool breeze. Its walls were as pockmarked with caves as the skull of the nine-eyed crab. A perfect place for an ambush. They rode on, not breaking stride.

They were confident with reason. The Kitzakk Horde had not known failure in one hundred years, and the scouts had helped enslave tribes, nations and continents with the routine indifference of camels dropping manure cakes. As members of a Chel Regiment they were among the Kitzakk elite, handpicked by the Warlord Klang who commanded the armies, tent camps and skintowns of the Great Desert which formed the western third of the Kitzakk empire.

For the last nine years Yat's squad had found and mapped the trails and villages of the desert tribes so the Invader Regiments and commercial Companies of Chainmen could follow with ease and efficiency. But now the deserts were mapped, and the merchants in the skintowns were complaining because their customers were becoming bored with desert merchandise, with dusky-skinned women and lean, truculent men. They wanted new produce, and the high priest of the Temple of Dreams had said the time was right. It was summer, the Time of Harvest. So the first year of a nine-year campaign against the barbaric forest tribes had begun.

Emerging from the gully, the scouts reined up. In front of them was the last bridge, a crude, sun-bleached wooden structure spanning the wide, deep gorge which separated the steep cataracts from the edge of the forest. Flayed ropes and sagging timbers barely held it upright, and it swayed in the light breeze, showing a definite inclination toward falling down. This was Lemontrail Crossing. But the scouts were looking beyond it, their eyes transfixed by a seemingly endless sea of green which spread in all directions behind a stand of mist-filled trees. This was the Great Forest Basin. The Land of the Barbarians.

Only the sun and moon can remember now how it looked then. Lush, rich, tangled. Savage. Shadowed. A world populated by demons and serpents, by wild men and proud, sensual women. A world of mystery. Magic. Music. Murder. Here and there in the distance beyond their vision, islands of rock rose like massive citadels out of the verdant green, islands which would one day be called Malta, Sicily, Majorca.

Beyond the sea of forest was the land mass which would become the continent of Europe, its northern half now buried under blue ice. In time, a long time, the ice would melt and the oceans would rise, break past the massive pillars of rock far to the west, and drown this fabled land of legends. But that is a story of another time, another age.

Now, warring, laughing, lusty tribes lived here. Independent men and women given to changing their chiefs with the season. Bickering, fighting people who could not agree on laws or borders, or raise an army larger than a marauding outlaw band.

Even though facing the land of the enemy for the first time, the faces of the scouts showed little concern. They knew that in the coming campaign there would be no organized defense. No armies to overwhelm. No citadels to storm. The work should be easy, like scraping flesh from boiled skulls.

Soong said, "The companies are going to be short on

cages, I'm thinking. There are as many people out there as there are leaves on the trees.''

Akar, the second in command, nodded. ''Not enough cages or time. Nine years won't do it this time.''

''Fine by me,'' Yat said. ''There's nothing like steady work to keep the regiment sharp.''

They dismounted, watered their horses and themselves, stretched in the sunshine, remounted and walked their horses forward. Reaching the bridge, they suddenly reined up, and their eyes darted furtively, hunting, bodies cocked. What did they hear, sense? They plucked crossbows from saddle holsters, mounted finely pointed steel bolts and waited.

Beyond the bridge a wide dirt trail ran east and west alongside the deep gorge. Another trail joined it at the intersection with the bridge. It ran north through a scattered stand of lemon trees, then into the forest. A thick grey mist covered the ground at the edge of the forest. Suddenly a huge grey timber wolf emerged from it and studied the scouts with narrow yellow eyes. Then it casually strolled back inside the mists as if the scouts were meatless creatures not worth his trouble.

The scouts glanced at Sergeant Yat uncertainly, then turned sharply as a screeching flock of sparrows erupted from one treetop, a hawk from another. The scouts watched the birds. As they did, they made magic signs on their groins and foreheads. Then they started forward again. Suddenly a wind blew up out of the trees, gathered the clinging gray mist in its embrace, and swept it through the lemon trees and across the bridge.

It was as if some silent, unseen Lord of Nature had sneezed. The scouts quickly covered their faces with their neck cloths and the fog swirled over them. When it passed, they looked back at the bridge and relaxed. This they understood.

The wide, ragged, black shape of a helmeted man carrying a shield and axe was advancing through the mist still swirling on the bridge. When it drifted off, the sun revealed a thick body layered with slabs of muscle which rippled under burnished flesh, glistening as if only he had the right to wear the sunshine. A massive Barbarian as confident as a continent, but seemingly without reason to be.

His armor consisted of stained black hides. Dark bits of fur were strapped to his feet and waist with hide thongs. His axe was the kind called elephant killer, too heavy headed and long handled for close combat, despite its size. His masked helmet, like his small circular shield, was of wood belted by metal bars. The axe blade and belts were of crude iron.

The Barbarian stopped a third of the way across the bridge and waited. His eyes, deep within his helmet, blinked as shafts of sunlight ricocheted off the Kitzakks' armor and splashed across his body.

The scouts, moving with disciplined habit, spread out in three units and studied the Barbarian as if he were dead game to be skinned and boned.

Soong spoke first. He said thoughtfully, "I think he thinks he's defending the bridge . . . maybe even the whole forest."

Yat said, "Maybe, maybe not. But he surely wants a fight."

"The fool," Akar cackled. "He's meat now."

"Perhaps more than meat," Soong said. "In that forest some still mate with serpents and cats. Even demons."

Yat nodded. "Akar, let's look at the color of his blood."

Akar, still cackling, edged his mount forward, leveled his crossbow casually, fired from the hip.

The dark figure settled slightly. A flick of white heat showed within the eye slits of his helmet as he watched the steel bolt drive towards him cutting the air with a faint whistle only the coyote or owl could hear.

At the last moment, the dark Barbarian lifted his shield

and caught the flying bolt with the corner, just above his
heart. The impact made a loud clang as the bolt imbedded
itself in one of the metal belts and shoved him back two
steps.

The scouts shared wary glances, then Yat barked,
"Ching! Wei! Clear the bridge! Boy, you watch the
horses."

Ching and Wei holstered their crossbows, dismounted,
giving Young Hands their reins, and stepped forward
rolling their shoulders. They were agile, sober soldiers.
They drew their swords, holding the grips of the slightly
curved blades with both hands, then, with their weight
centered on the balls of their feet, advanced in scattering
side to side movements.

The Barbarian watched thoughtfully.

Suddenly the two scouts stopped and, moving like
dancers, positioned their swords behind them, tips down,
nearly touching the ground, as if in surrender. It was a
mocking stance. There was no sign of any real concern on
their faces. No sweat on temples or under the eyes. No
movement at all. They just waited, cold as stone.

The Barbarian trembled with outrage, and without
warning erupted like a flung rock. With sudden quick steps
the scouts shifted their weight forward, and their swords
flew off the ground, came at him in measured strokes from
opposite sides. The Barbarian did not break stride. He fed
one sword a bite out of the handle of his axe, let the other
cleave the top off his helmet, then was between them. They
stepped back to make room for second blows. Too late. The
Barbarian jabbed Wei ten feet back with the butt end of his
axe handle, pivoted and swung the flat of his axe at Ching's
chest.

The Kitzakk's grip on his sword went wet in his hands as
he saw the flat axe head swinging for him, its metal spitting
light back at the sun. Then his mind went foolish and he
covered up with his arms, like a schoolboy. The flat axe
head crashed through his arms, hammered him to the floor

of the bridge, crushed him against it with such force that the air in his lungs and the blood in his veins exploded, ripped him apart inside so that he ballooned at his shoulders and neck.

Sergeant Yat and his scouts sat motionless, momentarily stunned before they opened fire with crossbows. But the Barbarian had planned wisely. He had turned to face Wei so that his shield faced the scouts and now caught their bolts. Wei, with his estimate of the Barbarian's threat dramatically altered, had backed away. He now waited, sword dancing in front of him.

The Barbarian charged. Wei struck. His sword took off a piece of the wooden shield as the Barbarian swung his axe head in an arching uppercut. It caught Wei under the chin and took off his head.

Wei's headless body stood motionless for a moment, as if it were about to object. But his head betrayed him and tumbled to the bridge where it looked up dumbly while spewing blood on the bare calves of the scouts charging past. Then the body fell, and hit the head which rolled off gathering splinters.

The scouts, with swords and shields working in front of them, surrounded the Barbarian. He did not appear to mind. Turning quickly from side to side, he watched them from behind his shield with the eyes of a man who had worked crowds before.

He choked up his axe handle, as if expecting the scouts to work cautiously in order to avoid striking each other. But they showed no hesitation and attacked in a bunch. They cut up his shield, nicked his axe and cracked his helmet. In the process, bridge posts were hacked apart, floor beams splintered, and supporting ropes severed to fly skyward, their tension released.

The dark Barbarian's blows clanged majestically against steel breastplates and helmets drawing blood from panting lips and removing one of Yat's ears. But his success was limited. The scouts deliberately allowed him to attack their

steel armor, and it resisted his blows. No matter how great
his effort and cunning, his axe could not reach their vital
parts. Finally his axe head tangled in Yat's fringe skirt, and
the Sergeant threw himself down, using his body weight to
yank the axe from the Barbarian's grip.

Instinctively, the Barbarian swung around, hammering
with the flat of his shield, and bought himself a little room.
As he did, the bridge sagged under him. He leaped back
and the planks splintered. His legs and body crashed
through them, then came to a sudden stop as his shield,
too wide for the hole, caught against the floor of the
bridge.

He dangled under the bridge, hanging desperately to the
shield's handle. Below him the jaws of the gorge, a
thousand feet below, waited. Above him his shield concealed him from the scouts.

Sergeant Yat, the area of his missing ear spitting blood,
moved over the Barbarian's shield and began hacking at it
as he shouted, "Crossbows! Crossbows!"

The scouts, limping and trailing blood, retrieved their
crossbows and loaded them, then struggled back onto
the bridge and peered over the side. They could not
see the Barbarian, so they joined Yat as his blade splintered the shield. It crumpled apart, tumbled through the
hole in the bridge, and dropped into the gorge. But it was
making the trip alone.

The Barbarian, by swinging back and forth on his
shield's handle, had been able to propel his gasping body
onto a supporting beam. He now straddled it as he looked
up through the hole at Yat.

The Sergeant, snarling and spurting blood, drew a
dagger from his belt. He flipped it once, caught it by the
blade, and raised it to throw. Abruptly, the fountain of
blood spurting from his ear lost force, sputtered, and
became a dribble that spidered down his chin. It was the
only color on his face. His expression was even less
communicative. His knees buckled, and he folded up like a

rope, pitched forward, crashed through the hole, and dived for rocks far below still holding his dagger.

The Barbarian did not watch him fall. He scrambled over the cross beams toward a cliffside ledge from which the bridge's main support beam protruded.

The scouts dropped to their knees above the hole just in time to see Yat hit the rocks and explode like a flung tomato. They winced audibly, immobilized for a moment, then leaned into the hole aiming their crossbows. But they held their fire. The Barbarian was out of sight.

Akar growled, "Mother of Death!" He squirmed over the hole, shouted, "Hold my legs!"

The scouts took hold of his knees and feet and lowered him into the hole.

When Akar saw the Barbarian, he was sitting on a cliffside ledge beside the main support beam. His legs were raised and he was leaning back against the cliff. The rocks were cutting into his meaty back, tearing his flesh, but he did not appear to notice. Suddenly he kicked with both feet, hammered the main support beam and splintered it.

Akar was still leveling his crossbow when he heard the loud crunch of tearing wood. He looked up, white eyed. The entire bridge sagged, groaned, then crumbled apart and fell into the gorge taking Akar and the scouts with it. They fell like soldiers, with faces snarling, and arms and legs flailing against the air. As silent as the timbers and splinters which fell beside them.

Young Hands, who had remained at the south end of the bridge with the horses, trembled in his saddle as he watched, then looked across the gorge.

The Barbarian was gasping with relief, then a falling timber caught him in the back and another across the shoulders to knock him off the ledge. He dropped five feet, hit a piece of protruding cliff, slipped another ten feet, then clawed his way onto another ledge and lay there gasping. He lifted slightly, as if he would have liked to turn and watch the scouts hit the ground, but collapsed instead. His eyes were glazed, as if thunder had taken up residence in his brain.

Young Hands tied the horses in a string, then again watched the Barbarian as his head lifted dizzily. The big man stood, looked around, then dragged himself back up to the road and sat down tiredly in the dirt. The top of his helmet was severed and dangled at an angle to his broad shoulders. He looked around, then across the gorge and into the rookie's eyes. The lad drew his crossbow and loaded it, but the Barbarian did not move. Young Hands angrily raised his weapon to fire. But he quickly reconsidered, turned his horse and rode off the way the scouts had come leading a file of eight horses, their saddles empty.

Four
NEW TOOLS

It was sundown before the Barbarian reached the bottom of the gorge. A family of vultures was already at work on the bits and pieces of bodies protruding from the wreckage of the bridge. The birds eyed him angrily, screeched and flapped about making a show of their gore-specked beaks and neck feathers. He kept coming and they took flight, winged back up the narrow gorge, almost beautiful in the fading orange light.

The birds came to rest on the remnant of bridge, then looked back down, their beaks dripping.

The Barbarian found his axe and picked it up. The handle was broken off a foot short of the head. He moved to the first body, drew a knife, bent over, then hesitated as if sensing life. Then he saw it.

Twenty feet away, a serpent colored with gold, brown and black diamonds slithered down a large rock towards a dead arm protruding from a pile of fallen timbers. A Sadoulette, the mother breed of the python. It was not yet fully grown, but big enough to have a squad of Kitzakk scouts for supper.

The reptile approached the arm, saw the Barbarian and coiled back, nostrils flaring. It appeared more than willing to wrestle for its dinner, then suddenly lost all confidence, slithered up the rock and tumbled awkwardly out of sight.

The Barbarian listened to the sounds of crunching gravel and breaking grass made by the retreating reptile, grunted with contempt, then glanced around again. Nothing moved. Nothing made a sound. He searched through the rubble of the bridge, shoved timbers aside, found the source of what he sensed.

Soong lay on his side, jackknifed over a rock. He still lived, barely breathing with short, wet gasps. One eye was smashed closed. The other watched fearfully as the Barbarian lifted his short-handled axe and moved for him. As the shadowed face of the Barbarian loomed close, Soong's eye opened wide, white with wonder, and the axe struck.

The dark savage checked the other bodies, but they were dead. What remained was work for vultures and ants.

He stripped each body and made a blanket from their leather tunics. He heaped their armor and weapons along with his broken axe and helmet on the blanket, tied them in a bundle. He drank from the stream in animal fashion, and washed most of the dry blood and gore off his body. Then he picked up the bundle, heaved it to his back, and started down a narrow trail beside the stream.

The family of vultures watched until the man-animal had vanished around a bend, then glided down and came to rest on broken timbers beside the naked dead bodies. They eyed them warily, then the largest screeched, leapt on Yat's back driving his claws into the flesh, and stabbed his pointed beak at a shoulder muscle.

The other vultures screamed and moved for the meat. There was a loud crack of breaking wood. The vultures, screeching, took flight. Above them, a heavy timber broke loose from the remains of the bridge. It tumbled through the air, hit the side of the cliff and dislodged several large rocks. A small avalanche followed, and covered the birds' dinner.

Reaching the sky, the vultures looked down and cried out in rage, then flew off, still complaining.

Five

BROWN JOHN

The three men riding the wagon had not intended it to be a shy vehicle. Its flatbed, side boards, driver's box and shaft were as red as a harlot's lips and trimmed in a pink and orange so bright they would have made the same harlot blush. The men were Grillards, a clan of outcast and outlawed entertainers. Their wagon was designed to serve as a traveling stage, but at the moment it was on its way to do, hopefully, some serious hauling.

Heading south, it danced through the tall pines at the southern end of the Valley of Miracles, crested the mountain, and raced across a glen that was a riot of greens in the early morning sunshine.

Old Brown John sprawled in the bed of the wagon, and despite the clattering wheels and bouncing boards, dozed comfortably on a pile of ragged blankets beside a clutter of coiled ropes. He was the *bukko*, the boss and stage manager of the Grillards. He wore a ragged brown tunic with large patches which, in addition to covering holes, were the clan's sign. He was short, wiry and bandy-legged. At first glance he appeared no more impressive than his patches, but on closer examination, even in his prone and snoring position, he had a surprisingly alert, in-charge and genial manner.

His bastard sons rode the driver's box.

Bone, the older, held the reins. He wore bright red patches, was big all over and proud of it. Regardless of the role his father cast him in, on- or offstage, he played it as a swaggering, braggart soldier whose brain was just slow enough to make him suspicious of everyone and everything. Dirken, the younger, was short, lean, and favored deep umber patches. He picked his own roles, was always on stage, and cherished playing vile, treacherous villains, so long as he could play them well groomed.

All three men wore leather belts hung with pouches and short swords. Not stage weapons, but working tools which protected them during the cold wet season when they had to survive as thieves.

The wagon rolled clear of the forest, skidded to a stop where Thieves Trail met Lemontrail Crossing, and Brown John glanced over the side board.

His white hair fell in smooth silky slopes down over his large ears and bristled with feathered tufts at his neck. His tangled white eyebrows, rising at sharp angles, gave his face a slightly satanic expression. It was deeply cut with all varieties of wrinkles, but they only gave a vague indication of the complexity of his wrinkled mind.

Seeing the crossing, he chuckled with far more amusement than any bridge, particularly one which had been destroyed, deserved.

Father and sons got down from their wagon, moved onto the battle-scarred remnant of the bridge, and peered down into the gorge at the pile of dirt. The tips of splintered timbers protruded from it.

"There they are," Brown John said with exhilaration. "Go to it, lads."

"Now just a minute," Bone said with grave caution. "If the Dark One and his axe did all this work by themselves, it's something a man should think on some before messin' about with it."

Dirken, barely moving lips as thin as fork blades, asked in a theatrical whisper, "How many did he say he killed?"

"He did not say," their father said in an instructional tone, "because I made certain there was no discussion of bodies. It would have made him suspicious. I simply inquired, while your brother traded our wine for his meat, as to where he got his new armor. All he said was, 'Lemontrail Crossing.' Two words."

"Then where are the bodies?"

"If you were more interested in the work, Dirken, and less in the drama, you would have noticed by now that the hyenas and jackels have already been at work on one of them."

He pointed at the bottom of the gorge about fifty feet to the east of the wreckage where a gutted rib cage rested among rocks. It was black, and the blackness moved vaguely. Ants.

"Well now," Bone announced, "that sure enough used to belong to something that drank from a cup, and it sure enough is dead."

"Not completely," Brown John corrected him. "His Kaa is exceptionally strong."

Bone and Dirken hesitated, then nodded thoughtfully. They knew that the Kaa, the spirit of the victor, could be infused within the bones of his victims at the moment of death. It could live there for days, weeks, even months, depending on its strength, and they normally did not question their father's evaluation of anything. Brown John had "vision." He saw many small, insignificant things and put them together into great and important things that common people like themselves could not see. Nevertheless, they were wary. Brown John had told them the Dark One's Kaa just might be strong enough to be contagious, and that kind of strength usually only lived in legends.

Brown John, ignoring their hesitation, pointed at the dirt pile. "You will more than likely find the bodies under that rubble. I'd say you'll find five, perhaps even six Kitzakk scouts."

Dirken put two sharp, black, skeptical eyes on his father.

Bone blurted, "That is a whole mess of muscle and metal for one man to murder, to say nothing of it being Kitzakk!"

"That, lads," Brown John glared at them impatiently, "is precisely why we are here."

Bone scowled with his entire face, two chins and both ears. "Well, if there are five scouts down there, the Kitzakks are coming for certain."

"Yes," said Brown John solemnly. "It is no rumor this year. They've been sighted in all the passes. So get to work. The kind of magic we now trade in can not be made by tossing dancing girls about a stage. It's man's work. Best done unseen and fast. We don't want the Dark One, or anyone else, to know what we do until it is done."

Brown John and Dirken glanced up and down the crossroads to make certain they were unwatched. But Bone stared at the dirt pile.

"Now just a minute." He put his fists against his hips, looked at his father and brother. "If they've been down there two whole days and nights, they're going to be nasty ripe."

Dirken grinned darkly. "We'll bring them up in pieces. If you forgot your spoon, you can borrow mine."

Bone winced.

The old man said, "Bone, you bring up the large pieces. Let Dirken handle the arms and heads, we don't want to lose any fingers or teeth."

Bone grimaced sickly, but obediently helped Dirken drag blankets and ropes out of their wagon and down into the gorge.

Late that day, when the Grillard's wagon was rolling west on Border Road, Brown John sat between his sons in the driver's box. Silent. Grave of expression except for a faint flicker of pride behind his eyes. His sons were filthy with dust and blood, exhausted, and grim faced. Their expressions had not been fashioned by their theatrical training, but by the day's work. Today they had played roles they had never played before, roles they were going to have to master, and had taken to them nicely. The colorful wagon had also taken to its new duty: It now hauled the slimy, swollen cadavers of eight Kitzakk scouts tied down under a blanket on its bed. It was doing a real wagon's work, and doing it in style, sporting a nauseous perfume.

Six
===
COBRA AGAIN

In the midnight darkness of The Shades, the Glyder Snake was as black as a buried stick, as invisible as a creek meandering through the ocean depths. It hid at the edge of an open track twenty feet wide and many miles long which ran in a straight line through the tall spruce, hemlock and pines. Faint moonlight cast a glow on the track's ground cover of fallen leaves. The snake wiggled into the moonlight, lifted into an arc of a cold blue and pointed across the track.

The glowing blue light revealed the jagged stone about

two feet high supporting the tiny snake. The sounds of crushing leaves and twigs came out of the forest behind the Glyder Snake, then a massive blackness the height of the stone appeared beside it. The blackness had two fist-sized yellow eyes. It was the head of a full-grown Sadoulette python. Its body receded into the darkness for forty feet. The Glyder Snake was not big enough to serve as its tongue.

A graceful figure emerged from the forest, stopped in the yellow glow of the python's eyes. The Queen of Serpents.

Her enveloping black robe was travel stained. Her almond eyes were cold and calculating. She studied the opposite side of the track. There spruce and hemlock rose to towering heights supported by thick exposed roots taller than herself. Between the roots were shadowed caves and passageways.

When Cobra's eyes found what the Glyder Snake pointed at, they flickered with the first satisfaction she had felt since having sent the Dark One to Lemontrail Crossing seven days earlier. It was a wide section of roots grown together to form ribbed walls that were covered with moss, vines, plots of grass and beds of needles. These walls rose nearly thirty feet to vanish into black shadows cast by the branches of the trees they supported.

Cobra bent and stroked the Glyder Snake. "Well done, small one," she whispered. "You may go now."

She pulled her hood over her face and stepped into the moonlight, moved like a drifting shadow across the track. The python followed, a serpentine blackness as thick as a young pine. Reaching the wall of roots, she crept up one of its natural trails, and the giant snake slid up the roots into the darkness of the trees overhead.

The moonlight had left the sky by the time the Queen of Serpents found the cluster of hanging vines which concealed a recess big enough for a crouched man to enter. She felt around inside the recess, touched the edge of a man-made door, a string latch. She pulled it, pushed quietly on the door, but it resisted. She lowered the latch, placed her fingertips on the door, then moved them about until she sensed the thickness of a locking beam on the other side.

She took a breath, blew on the tips of her fingers and placed them carefully against the spot. She closed her eyes. Her body began to tremble. When the trembling reached her fingertips, she slid them across the door, and the sound of the sliding locking beam came from within. There was a dull clack of something falling to the floor beyond the door. Her eyes snapped open. She held still, listened for a long moment. No sound. Her tongue darted eagerly between her scarlet lips. Then she slid the unseen locking beam clear of the door.

When she tried the latch again, the door swung inward, and a faint glow of firelight emerged to illuminate the sculpted whiteness of her face. She stepped out of the recess, looked up into the shadowed branches overhead. There the large yellow eyes of the python watched her. On guard. She dipped her hooded head, glided across the recess and through the door.

Thick roots formed the walls of a shallow entryway. The dark mouths of crawl holes opened among them. A larger hole in the floor opened onto a stairwell hand carved from a single root. An orange glow came from somewhere below.

Leaving the door open, Cobra silently descended the stairs until she could see the lower room.

It was hewn out of living roots. Irregular seams climbed the sides of uneven walls where the roots had grown together. The floor was hard dry earth, a deep red ochre. A stone fireplace and chimney had been built within the cavity of the roots. Beside the fireplace stood a woodpile, an anvil and assorted tools: hammers, tongs, a barrel of rainwater. The floor was cluttered with empty earthenware jugs, wooden cups, broken crockery, and bones recently chewed clean of meat.

At the center of the room was a table. On it were several cups, a wine jar. The far wall supported a wide, deep shelf with a washbasin, a dirty cloth, a pitcher and barber's knife. Beside the shelf wooden pegs held assorted black furs, a helmet, and armor and weapons stolen from Kitzakks.

The helmet was strange: the bowl of a Kitzakk helmet, a mask of crude iron, and reinforcing belts of Kitzakk steel bent around both to attach them. The belts had been crudely bent by fire and hammer and fit badly. One had sprung loose and dangled awkwardly.

Cobra smiled knowingly and edged down the stairs to the floor, hesitated. In the shadow beside the helmet was a huge axe with a new handle which belonged to the Dark One called Gath of Baal.

She trembled slightly, and glanced about at the deep shadows of the many recessed areas, then at an alcove around a corner. It was heaped with furs covering a large mound. Her breath raced. Color flushed her face, throat. She drew a tiny dagger from a sheath strapped to her forearm.

Its blue steel glistened like wet ice. The blade was needle sharp, just long enough to plunge into the heart of an onion. The cutting edge was finely honed, sharp enough to trim a baby's lashes without the baby noticing.

Moving like a melting shadow, Cobra crossed to the bed of furs, stood over it, her bosom heaving, dagger in hand.

With reptilian grace, she sank silently beside the furs, lifted one gently and gasped audibly. Underneath were only more furs. She crouched over the furs, explored them with delicate fingers and recoiled. They were warm.

She closed her eyes, gathered control, then spoke without moving, distinctly and carefully.

"Do not kill me, Dark One. I come as a friend."

She opened her eyes, waited. From the shadows came a low growl, then a ragged grey timber wolf emerged. He was large for a wolf. Three feet tall at the shoulders, six feet long. His head and neck hair were erect. Yellow eyes were lethal. His teeth showed as another low growl moved past them.

Cobra lowered her lids, held her place without moving.

A low harsh command came from a shadow somewhere behind her. "The wood beside the fireplace! Put it on the fire."

Cobra rose carefully and walked slowly to the fireplace. She covertly returned the tiny dagger to its hidden sheath, then stoked the glowing embers into a flame with an iron poker, and placed four logs one by one on the fire. A moment passed before they burst into flames, filling the root cave with flickering orange light. She warmed her hands, then sighed, a faint whistling sound.

"Be quiet and turn around," said the voice.

Turning slowly, she said, "Forgive me, I have traveled alone a great distance to see you. I am weary."

Gath of Baal's head and part of his bare chest glowed in the firelight across the room. The rest of him was hidden in inky black shadow. His chiseled head, sculpted by moving shadows, had a harsh savage beauty. Wild, knife-cut, black hair fell to brawny neck. His lips were wide, flat, and sensually sculpted, while his nose was square. His eyes hid in the dark shadows of a blunt brow crusted with thick eyebrows. A thin smooth scar ran from the left corner of his mouth to his chin.

The color in Cobra's cheeks flamed. Her voice became a husky whisper. "Thank you . . . for sparing me."

His eyes seemed to look off at nothing, yet see everything. He listened, then shot Cobra a brutal glance. "You lie."

He strode out of his concealing shadow and moved, not toward Cobra, but to the stairwell. There he stopped short, and the firelight probed his muscular flesh. He was naked except for a loin cloth. A long thick dagger protruded from his left hand. His right was balled in a fist.

Cobra gasped sharply with sudden fear.

The head of the huge Sadoulette dropped down out of the stairwell and floated in the air with its yellow eyes level with Gath's grey. It hissed, spread its jaws wide showing Gath fangs no longer than the blades of a pitchfork.

Gath's cocked body exploded with rippling muscle and his balled fist drove up at the snake's head. Its hammer end caught the reptile's left jaw flush, drove the head up at an angle, crushed its skull against the sharp edge formed by the end of the stairwell and the wall of the cave. There was a loud crack.

Cobra winced.

The head of the dazed python dropped onto the stairs, its body convulsing. Gath kicked it out of his way, moved up the stairwell to the landing. There he hauled the dying snake up and threw its tangled body through the doorway. It was too large and stuck in the doorjamb. Gath kicked it the rest of the way out, then closed the door, slamming the locking beam shut. He then picked a yellow stone off the ground, placed the stone in the open shaft which cradled the locking beam at a position between the end of the beam and a hole carved out of the bottom of the shaft. When he turned, Cobra was standing at the base of the stairwell watching him.

She said, "You are a careful man."

He said, "You are careless."

He moved down the stairs, took her by the elbow, guided her roughly to the fireplace. There he took hold of her black velvet cape, ripped it open breaking the tie thongs and revealing a tunic of gold cloth. She did not protest or struggle. He stripped the cape off her, then shook it out. Finding nothing hidden within, he tossed it aside, looked at her. The jeweled handle of the tiny sheathed dagger glittered on her forearm. The whites of his eyes became cold within the shadows of his brow. Firelight danced there, as if it came from within rather than without.

Cobra took a step back trembling and said accusingly, "He would not have hurt you. He was only for my protection on the trail. You had no need to kill him!''

He muttered with a low, thick coarse voice that made words unnecessary.

The metallic petals of her scaled skullcap and cape shimmered wetly with fear from her toes to her flushed cheeks. Her breasts heaved.

"Take them off!" He spoke as he moved to the fire. He picked up a large stick, thrust it into the fire. She did not move. When he turned to face her, the stick burned like a torch.

She smiled uncertainly, and unbuckled the clasp at her throat saying, "Whatever you wish. I have nothing to hide . . . not from you." She pushed her skullcap back, let its cape drop off her arms, and her long hair cascaded down her back like black rain. She made no movement to remove her gown.

He growled, "The gown."

She whispered, "The cloth is thin. You will have no trouble seeing what hides under it." There was a teasing warmth in her tone.

He passed the torch around and behind her. The gown glowed hotly, then the scales slowly dissolved and the cloth became a shimmering transparent amber. She was naked underneath. He grunted contemptuously.

She stiffened sharply, insulted. Then, seeing that his cheeks had taken on a ruddy flush, a playfulness moved into her eyes.

She asked, "Would you be happier if I had a tail? Or fangs?" She smiled widely, displaying perfect teeth.

Scratching a naked hip, he studied her thoughtfully. The wolf rose, made his way toward Cobra sniffing the air, mane bristling and fangs bared. Growling.

She said, "I do not please your pet."

"Sharn is not a pet. This was his home before it was mine."

His eyes stayed on Cobra as Sharn made his way across the room to the stairs. The wolf looked back once with cold eyes at Cobra, then bounded up the stairs into one of the crawl holes between the roots.

Gath muttered, "He'll see what other pets travel with you." His nose twitched, and he pawed it with an open hand more in the manner of a cat than a man. Then he stared at her, naked of expression.

She appraised him openly. As she did, her lips parted, her breathing quickened. The rose tint in her cheeks spread to her chin, and the scarlet of her lips brightened. Abruptly she turned away, moved to the fire and sat in front of it. She looked into the fire, hiding her face from Gath. Slowly her gown regained its scales and gold color.

He shifted uncomfortably, moving sideways to see her face and suddenly stopped.

Her body had altered slightly under the gown. Her curves, which had been supple and sensual, now only looked pleasingly comfortable. When she turned to Gath, there was no color on her face except that made by sunshine and good health. Her smile was still playful, but in a manner that made fun of herself, not him.

She said, "I should have known better than to try and sneak up on you."

He ignored her moved to the table, leaned against it and drank from the wine jar.

She started to say something, stopped herself. She turned back to the fire, then spoke in an even, modulated tone.

"I know that it angers you to have me, a mere woman, find and enter your hidden lair as easily as if you had put up signs showing the way and given me a key. I know the pains you take to avoid the outside world. But I had no choice. I can change my appearance . . . but not my nature. I use the darkness and certain powers I have to enter where ever my desires lead me. Often," she laughed, "with dark intent." She turned to him, void of guile. "But I meant you no harm. You are far too valuable just as you are. Alive. Powerful. And so . . . so savage." The color was back in her cheeks before she finished. Feeling it, she looked away.

His voice was low. "What do you want?"

"Please, allow me to finish," she said to the fire. "You must understand, I have a thousand eyes. Ten thousand. And they have watched you for many months." She turned to him. "But I had to see for myself, with my own eyes, that you came away from the battle with the Kitzakk scouts unhurt."

"You lie," he said. His tone was harsh, wise. "If your thousand eyes can measure the man, they can measure his wounds."

Cobra flinched, looked away. A moment passed. Her shoulders lost strength, rounded. Her voice lost its music, became weak, shrill. She said, "I have been too long in human form. My natural skills have deserted me . . . at least with you." She hesitated. "That . . . that is why I was afraid . . . and called for my friend. I . . . I shouldn't have. It's my fault you killed him."

Gath studied her back, took another swallow, studied her some more.

She turned to him, looked him directly in the eye, said, "You are right, I lied. I knew you were hardly wounded. The entire forest knows it. The Grillard minstrels tell your tale at every road crossing, in every village square." She hesitated, laughed quietly at herself. "Oh yes, I knew. The scouts were child's play for you. They taught you nothing . . . were no test at all." She turned back to the fire, softened her voice. "My true reason for coming is your strength. Because I . . . I need your help . . . your protection."

He took two swallows of wine. Between them he muttered, "More lies."

"I don't blame you," she said. "I have become so human, I now find it hard to trust a serpent myself." She picked up her cloak, stood, smiled with self-mockery as she looked at him. "I'll go now. I won't bother you again."

She moved for the stairwell. He watched her, then stepped into a shadow, came away with his axe and flung it.

The blade buried itself in the first step, brought her to an abrupt stop. She looked at him. There was a hot, challenging glint in her eyes.

She said, "If you are asking me to stay, I accept."

"Who sent you here?" he demanded sharply. "Who is your master?"

"I believe I have already told you that," she said. There was a reckless abandon in her throaty whisper. "You are, Gath. You are my master."

Seven

SERPENT'S KISS

Cobra waited for Gath's reaction, but he showed nothing in reply to her declaration of servitude. Taking a circuitous route, she paused to warm her hands at the fire and idly fondle a wine jar on the table, then sauntered toward him. She looked up into his eyes, and he looked away. After a moment she said softly, "They tell me that the forest women blush like little girls and giggle hotly when they say your name."

His jaw was clenched. He seemed no more interested than the underside of a rock.

The playfulness left her. "I don't blame you. You are different." Her breath quickened. "All the others were afraid of me."

His dark mysterious eyes turned on her and blood suddenly gorged his cheeks. She lifted fingertips, touched one. His wide lips parted. His breathing became harsh, brutal. She moved close. Her breasts, stomach, thighs touched him.

She whispered, "You will let me go . . . afterwards?"

He put an arm around her, pulled her gently but firmly against him until her feet dangled above the floor. She coiled her arms around him, purred. He kissed her throat, the lobe of her ear.

She moaned with pleasure, pleading, "Oh, yes."

He carried her to the alcove, spread her on his bed of furs with forceful but strangely gentle hands, like she had no more will than a blanket. She started to rise, feeling obliged to protest, and his lips met hers, forced her back down into the furs. His hands moved inside her garment, kneeding her flesh, and the cloth surrendered, ripping away. He rolled her over slowly, fingers and lips invading naked swell and hollow. He could have broken her like a twig, but his tenderness was more powerful. It enslaved her, and she surrendered, gasping into the furs. His hands took hold of shoulder and hip, turning and lifting her body to his, then joining them. Her body arched back gasping, and her eyes came open with wonder and awe and love. Out of control, her body convulsed against him in serpentine passion, as if her bones were made of butter.

When they had finished, he kissed her florid cheek, and returned to the main room. He opened another wine jar, sat back against the edge of the table, and drank, watching the firelight play on Cobra's flushed, moist body.

Slowly her breathing came back under control, and she stood. Arranging her torn garment about her, she moved to the table and poured water from the pitcher into a bowl. Dipping her hands in the cold water, she held them against her burning cheeks. Then she sat on a stool in front of the fire, opened her pouch, removed a mirror and arranged her mussed hair under her skullcap. Using a vial of red paste taken from her pouch, she applied fresh color to her lips with the tip of a little finger. Finished, she glanced over her shoulder and acknowledged Gath with a big dark eye saying, "I'd like some wine."

He removed a cup from the shelf behind the table, and

filled it as she joined him. Lifting the cup to her lips with two hands, Cobra stared past the rim at his brutal male flesh. Moist. Curls of soft black hair glistening like a panther's on his chest. She sipped the wine, then murmured, "You have surprised me once more, Dark One. You live and feed like an animal, but you do not make love like one."

"You are disappointed?" There was a subtle mockery in his tone.

She chuckled throatily, and said, "Hardly." She moved close, her body again touching him, and her eyes holding his. Color rushed into her cheeks, and the sound of her breathing filled the room. A soft, vulnerable woman, yet proud, demanding.

"I want you again," she whispered. "Now."

Gath could not look away. She pressed against his chest, her lips slightly parted, her fragrant breath on his throat, cheeks. His lips lowered to meet hers. Without warning her eyes turned dead yellow, her cheeks ballonned like the cobra's hood and venom spat past her wet red lips.

The poison splashed across Gath's open eyes, sizzled in his hair above his ear. Blinded him.

He grabbed for Cobra. She was gone, had recoiled, or jumped away. He did not know which. He roared, lunged about, kicked the table over with his thigh splattering cups and wine jars in all directions.

Cobra backed against the wall near the stairwell, watched. There was pain, fear in her wide-open eyes.

Gath reeled, ran into a wall and it punched him to the floor. He lay dazed on his back for a brief moment, then rolled upright onto all fours, growling. He started to rise as the poison hit his spine, spread into his nerves. By the time he tottered to his feet, the best he could do was fall back down.

Cobra watched him flounder on the floor for awhile, then said coolly, "Do not fight it, Dark One. There will be no permanent harm. You will not be able to move for a few hours . . . but then you will be fine.''

He replied by rolling over on his back and twitching violently, then he lay still. His eyes were glazed. He could see nothing, feel nothing.

Cobra removed a small empty turquoise jar from her pouch. She unplugged it, kneeled beside Gath, set the jar on the floor. Then, using her tiny dagger, she trimmed his fingernails and cut away a thick tuft of his pubic hair. These she placed in the jar. Using the edge of the blade, she gathered spittle from his lips, put it in the jar, then plugged the jar, put it in her pouch, and removed a brown earthenware vial. She uncorked it, lifted Gath's head, poured the contents into his choking throat saying, ''This will ease the pain while you recover.''

She crossed to the alcove and came away with a fur blanket. She kneeled beside him, covered him tenderly, then took his hand in her hands, pressed it against her. Heat came to her face. Her garment glowed under his hand until the scales dissolved and it cupped a naked breast. A moan of pleasure escaped her lips. Then she kissed his hand, smiled warmly and whispered, ''Until next time, Dark One.''

She stood, picked up her black cloak and put it on. She crossed to the stairwell, climbed it and went out, closing and locking the door behind her.

Outside Cobra found her giant python sprawled in the open track at the base of the root house. It was shuddering in the moonlight, dying slowly. She moved down to it, confronted the thin slits of its yellow eyes, and said coldly, ''Fool!''

She turned, hurried off into the night. She was a half mile away before she could no longer feel the python's shuddering in the earth beneath her feet.

Eight

THE DARK ALTAR

Lava staircases climbed the side of a black active volcano, the largest in a range of volcanic mountains. Smoke rose in spires from their craters to form a thick layer of black clouds below a blue afternoon sky. This was the Land of Smoking Skies far to the west of the inhabited parts of the forest.

The domain of the Queen of Serpents.

Cobra climbed polished steps cut out of the black lava toward a cave with golden doors. She was stained with dust and perspiration from the three-day march, but exhilarated. Her stride was strong, triumphant; her hand clutched the small turquoise jar as if it were a weapon.

Reaching the shimmering entrance, Cobra did not break stride and the solid gold doors swung open. Beyond them, in a corridor of shiny obsidian, two soldiers knelt with their foreheads to the ground. They wore dark green tunics belted with swords and daggers. Jewels glittered on their fingers and earlobes. Traces of scales crusted the backs of their hands.

With a silent nod, Cobra marched past them down the torch-lit corridor, then past a barracks cave to a tavern room at the end of the corridor. Oil lamps hung from beams casting flickering light over wooden tables, benches and a large red interior door at the cave's deepest point. Soldiers, both male and female, who had been sitting and drinking, prostrated themselves in front of Cobra as she strode regally through them. She pushed open the red door, closed it behind her.

She had entered a corridor of black volcanic rock. Torches and incense lamps lighted it. Some distance below, the tunnel leveled off to become a polished obsidian hallway. Cobra descended it to a shallow stairway at its far end.

At the bottom of the steps was a short length of level floor, then a second flight of steps rising to heavy silver drapes through which passed slivers of golden light. In the center of the ceiling was a hole six feet in diameter. The hole opened onto a tunnel which passed horizontally above. Cobra passed under it and swept through the silver drapes.

She stood in a large circular cave with a dome ceiling of hammered gold. The floor was silver. The furniture was lacquered black. Highlights raced across the sharp edges like shooting stars at midnight. A massive circular bed of black furs dominated the center. The bedroom of the Queen of Serpents.

She dropped on the bed clutching the turquoise jar to her breast and sighed with relief.

Silver columns sculpted as giant serpents circled the room at four-foot intervals. The tails were coiled against the silver floor. The bodies wound up around the columns to the ceiling where their jaws, spread wide, supported the rim of the golden dome. The columns fenced off an outer corridor just large enough to contain a monster snake which lived within it. It was over five feet in diameter, and three times the length of the python Gath had killed. Its scaly skin bore diamond patterns of emerald green and gold.

The tail of the reptile flopped contentedly to the left of the curtained entrance. The body ran around the room, passed over an interior stairway opposite the entrance, then circled back to the front of the room. There the diamond-shaped head of the snake was feeding on a dead ox. Its jaws were just short of the entrance. The hole in the stairway ceiling provided the giant snake access to the polished obsidian hallway and bedroom when its services as a sentry were required. The reptile swallowed, then its eyelids drooped reverently, but the eyes glowed sensuously as they observed their queen.

Cobra rose, set the jar carefully on a stand beside the huge reptile's head, then shed her garments, and poured a pitcher of water over her naked flesh. She shivered splendidly as a tongue big enough to pull off her arm shot out between two columns and licked her from knee to hip.

Cobra laughed easily, toweled off with a cloth, then removed a black garment of glittering obsidian scales from a silver chest and stepped into it clasping the hood over her head. Only the creamy white of her face and hands was revealed; the rest was black elegance. Picking up the turquoise jar, Cobra lifted her head regally and descended the interior stairway which led to a tunnel.

Alternating between gentle inclines and steep steps, the tunnel descended in a circular pattern toward the center of the mountain. Smoke was gathered against the ceiling. As she went deeper it thickened and the rock walls became warm, then hot.

The tunnel led her to the cone of a living volcano. Flames shot up out of holes bubbling with molten lava to cast active black shadows and moving red light over thousands of flickering forked tongues which protruded from snake holes pockmarking the walls. The devout were at worship.

Cobra genuflected, then moved towards a dark altar rising out of the largest fire-hole at the center of the cone.

It was a living altar. The most sacred shrine of Cobra's god, the Lord of Death and Master of Darkness who provided life with all its appetites. It was a death's-head altar which served as the god's mouth. Here he could speak directly to those devout supplicants who were privileged to comprehend his language of flickering flames and growling thunder.

A mammoth saurian skull formed the altar. It stood on an island of black rock protruding from a pit of bubbling and smoking lava. Its jaws were spread wide to reveal flames flickering within the skull, rising like fingers around a dark object so that it appeared to float in the brain cavity. A narrow stone bridge emerged like an ancient crusted tongue from the jaws, arched invitingly over the bubbling lava and came to rest on the edge of the pit.

Cobra's almond eyes darkened noticeably as she approached and gazed hypnotically at the dark shape within the flames.

It was a horned helmet, hammered from a dense black ore, carved ornately. A spike stood erect at the crest. Dark horns protruded from either side in slow, cruel curves to point almost back at the masked face. The mask was unadorned except for eye, nose and mouth holes.

It was stark in its beauty, made starker yet by the power emanating from within it.

Reaching the bridge, Cobra prostrated herself, touching her forehead to the hot stone floor. Then she stood regally, triumphantly held up the small turquoise jar containing the fingernail clippings, pubic hairs and spittle of Gath of Baal, and offered it to the altar with both hands.

A flapping of rising flames and a roar of thunder shook the room.

Cobra knelt, dipping her head, the perfect image of sensual supplication.

"Thank you, Master, I am privileged to please you." She rose with anticipation glittering in her dark eyes. "I will now prepare the ingredients . . ."

A slap of thunder brought her to a startled choking halt. She blanched. "Forgive me, my Lord, I did not mean . . ."

The thunder came again, a hard repetitive clap.

Anxiety filled her eyes and she protested, "No! I would

never let any desire for him interfere with my judgment. I swear it."

Flames rose up out of the pits, reached for the ceiling in towering walls, filled the cone with a blinding illumination until she was only a tiny vague shadow. She gasped and dropped to one knee, humbled by the power and majesty of her deity, thrilled and empassioned by his invincible strength.

"I understand and will obey." She spoke with reverence and obedience. "I am to have the totems delivered, by my most trusted servant, to the high priest of the Kitzakks, Dang-Ling, who dwells in their desert city of Bahaara."

Thunder rumbled quietly and steadily from the bowels of the earth. Cobra nodded repeatedly as she listened to it, then replied, "I will not forget. The secret of the high priest's service and devotion to you will not be betrayed. It will be his task, not mine, to use the totems to humble and educate Gath of Baal, and convince him that he must align himself with you, my most holy Lord of Death, in order to satisfy his honor and pride."

A slap of thunder echoed through the cone with a peculiar ring of approval.

She rose obediently, and said respectfully, "Thank you, Master, I understand now. If Gath of Baal is killed by the high priest's efforts, then he is not the man I have claimed him to be. But if he is that man, then only the threat of death can now instruct him."

The altar rumbled like a thousand well-fed stomachs, and Cobra, bowing low, backed slowly out of the room.

Returning to her chamber, she sent for Schraak, a small, devious, grey-skinned alchemist with perpetually blinking eyes who sidled into the room like a favored pet. She reluctantly handed him the turquoise jar and told him to deliver it promptly and secretly to the high priest Dang-Ling in the distant desert city of Bahaara.

When he had left, Cobra paced her chambers frantically without relief. She threw herself on the bed and writhed in

an agony of rage and frustration, then surrendered and
moaned hungrily as a craving to feel Gath's human power
again possessed her. It would be days, perhaps weeks,
before Schraak could deliver the jar, and Dang-Ling could
prepare his magic and act. And all she could do was wait.

Nine

BAUBLES & BONES

A new sound came from Rag Camp. The daily jangle of
tambourines, thumping drums, singing flutes and children's laughter now mixed with the music of tinkling
silver. The Grillards, whose specialty was low farce, had
been thrust into the high drama of good fortune.

The camp was situated at the northeastern edge of the
valley where the river called Whitewater formed the natural
border between the territories of the lawfully established
Barbarian tribes and the Valley of Miracles. Outlaw territory. A massive grey rock, Stone Crossing, straddled the
river which passed through a natural tunnel at its base. The
trail called the Way of the Outlaw passed over Stone
Crossing then came to an end in a spread of bald dusty
ground which formed the center of Rag Camp, a name
derived from the Grillard dependence on and preference for
rag patches.

A scatter of women, children, big young country louts,
intinerant peddlers, traveling merchants and charlatans
were coming down the trail. Their pace was anxious. Their
manner was both excited and furtive. They were doing
something that was at least suspect, if not downright

punishable, and were having a fine time doing it.

Wagons and horses, belonging to strangers as well as recognized members of various nearby tribes, were already parked at the edge of the clearing. The occupants were moving about the camp excitedly. No lords or nobles were among them. They were common folk with tight pockets and tight minds. But their normally country-sharp and forest-wise faces reflected no suspicion. Instead they were giddy and gullible. Eager to be amazed.

With *oohs* and *aahs*, they shopped along a row of homespun blankets spread in front of eleven house-wagons which formed the body of a camp. Displayed on the blankets were the carefully butchered and brightly painted bones of the dead Kitzakk scouts: totems which were assured to make the child safe and the sword arm strong. They were arranged according to anatomy and size. Wrists and anklebones began the line, and boiled and scraped skulls mounted on poles and painted with macabre blacks, indigos and blues, ended it.

The buying was active, and, as the Grillards had been instructed by their *bukko* to take nothing but silver, the sound of it was loud and constant.

Dowats, being the largest tribe of the forest, were the most numerous and outstanding in their traditional bright persimmon tunics. A careful people, they bought quickly and left immediately, avoiding the main trail over Stone Crossing. Savage Kraniks from the north were numerous. They were still ruled by women, and wore loincloths, white clay markings and had wide dazzled eyes. They had arrived the day before, showed no sign of leaving, and haggled over the relative strength of each totem they examined. There were also Cytherians from Weaver in white tunics, and small groups of outlaws in bushy furs and as many weapons as their belts and chests could display. Also among the crowd were traveling vendors and charlatans selling rejuvenating waters, painkillers for toothaches, racy jokes and love philters.

At the end of the village the Wowell witches from Bone Camp offered their talents as surgeons, cut hair, pulled teeth and appraised totems for a price. They had done the butchering for Brown John and were proud of it. They had not washed since doing the work so everyone would know it. Old blood clotted their dark bony arms up to their elbows. As payment for their work they had been given Sergeant Yat's body, and had carefully reconstructed his bones. Displayed on their wagon bed were two complete hands, feet, legs, arms, and a pelvic region, chest and skull. Expensive totems, but capable of spreading their magic throughout an entire household or small outlaw band.

At the middle of the clearing, children battled with swords made from twigs and branches. The largest wore tattered black furs and swung an axelike stick with a ball of rags tied around its working end. The smaller children, boys and girls alike, fed their small bodies to this weapon with abandon and went reeling about to roll in the dirt and die in spectacular fashion, with terrible gagging, prolonged choking, and howling screams.

The music for this occasion was provided by tambourines and flutes of Grillard players who sat or squatted at the front of the large stage at the opposite side of the clearing from the wagons. Behind the stage was a two-story, red house-wagon which served as a backdrop for the stage as well as being home to the *bukko*. At the sides of the stage were two yellow wagons which were used as stage wings, dressing rooms and homes for the dancing girls. They also made convenient brothels during the cold season.

At midday the players put down their flutes and tambourines, gathered up drums and beat out a strident drumroll to announce the main entertainment.

A small crowd gathered in front of the stage, and Brown John stepped out of the red wagon to greet them with open arms. He bowed with great respect to their scattered ovation and, with sonorous voice and elaborate gestures, informed them they were about to see a tale performed that was so daring and realistically portrayed that it was only for the stouthearted. This increased the size of the crowd substantially, especially with children. He stepped aside, the performers arranged themselves on the stage, and a young boy with a soaring tenor voice delivered the song with which the Grillard minstrels had been attracting customers to Rag Camp.

The ballad sang the praises of Gath of Baal, his axe, his strength, his black furs, his hot blood, and his brave heart and magic powers while telling the blow-by-blow story of his defense of Lemontrail Crossing. The refrain was lyrically even less modest. It sang of a great Lord of the Forest, a Defender of the Trees, a mighty one named Gath of Baal who had arisen from The Shades to strike down the evil invaders and defend the forest tribes.

As the boy sang, the players performed in the same spirit of modesty.

Bone, in the role of Gath, wore a black fur cloak and black helmet, and stood at one end of a shallow bridge defending it with a wooden axe as the Kitzakk scouts attacked. Dirken, in the role of Sergeant Yat, looking as dark and sinister as possible, led the Kitzakks. Bone wheeled about, slashed and hacked. The Kitzakks, upon being hit, spit up mouthfuls of red syrup, then rose up shuddering terribly and announced their impending deaths with prolonged screaming. Then they pitched off the bridge and died acrobatically.

Brown John, who had staged this drama, had, of course, embellished it. There were now sixteen scouts instead of eight. Among them were two clowns and a barking dog, who managed to get mixed up and do each other more damage than they did Bone. In addition a large cage had been erected at one end of the bridge. Inside the cage five dancing girls clung to the bars and screamed almost musically for the Dark One to save them.

At the climax of the story, Bone broke open the cage, and the girls leaped alluringly around the stage. As they did, they managed to lose most of their clothing to artfully placed protrusions of the cage and bridge. What was left was pillaged from their tawny, oiled bodies by the clutching fists of the dying Kitzakks. Naked, the girls circled the bridge as Bone hammered it down. He was helped in this effort by a mechanical lever which made the bridge collapse in two. Dirken, of course, was standing at its center when this happened and plunged three feet to a howling ignoble death which he would have prolonged indefinitely if the impatient dancing girls had not run over him to swarm around the proud, magnificent Bone and drop at his feet in prone adoration.

The audience cheered, howled, clapped.

Bone, grinning widely, was bowing for the fifth time when Brown John strode abruptly on stage, raised his arm and shouted for silence. The players and audience, startled and suddenly afraid, looked around, then off at Stone Crossing, and went silent.

Six armed riders on large groomed stallions were coming over the crest of the crossing in a steady, determined pace towards the camp.

The main body of the crowd stepped aside, making way for the riders, while others fled with their precious totems clutched to their breasts. The Grillards gathered up the blankets and carried them out of sight.

The performers edged back to the yellow wagons, their eyes moving back and forth from the riders to Brown John. Bone and Dirken, who remained at the front of the stage with their father, now held real swords in their hands.

The riders reined up in front of the stage. Their large, chesty horses pummeled the ground with their hooves, raising clouds of dust which billowed around them, and swirled over Brown John and his sons as they bowed slightly in recognition.

The three lead riders were powerful Barbarian lords. The

following trio were their men-at-arms. One of these held the lead rope of a pack horse with a wicker cage mounted on its back. It held a large, smokey-grey she-wolf.

Golfon of Weaver, chief of the Cytherians, had the middle position. He was a wine-flushed, fatty piece of meat in a scarlet tunic and too much brass armor for a man with a weight problem. Vitmar, lord of the Barhacha woodmen, rode at Golfon's right. He wore fur and hides, had lots of muscular sunburned flesh, and displayed the mild expression of a man who killed without emotion. Sharatz of Coin, Lord Master of the Kaven moneylenders, was the third chief. He wore a violet tunic and jewels. His narrow face was as pious as a religious relic.

Brown John let the dust clear, then bowed again in greeting and in a generous tone said, "Welcome, mighty lords of the forest. How may I . . ."

"Shut up, clown!" Golfon spat the words. "Tell your bastards to drop their weapons, then get down off that stage. We're not going to sit here looking up at the likes of you."

"Ah," murmured Brown John, "your business is serious." He glanced at his sons. They dropped their weapons, and the three carefully climbed down to the ground to face the riders.

Golfon glared down at Brown John. "We want Gath of Baal, and you will tell us where he is . . . understand?" To make their relationship perfectly clear to everyone watching, he spit on Brown John's shoulder.

Brown John flinched, but answered politely. "I do not understand. No one knows where he lives, so how can you expect me to know?"

Golfon darkened. Vitmar leaned forward and said levelly, "Because everyone knows you and your bastards have traded with him for years, because your minstrels sing of him, because your miserable tribe grows rich on the totems of the dead Kitzakks . . . and because we know you helped him murder them."

"Lord Vitmar, you tell a splendid tale," Brown John said. "So splendid that I can assure you that we, being the poor powerless characters we are, are not even the smallest part of it."

Vitmar nodded without a trace of agreement, said quietly, "Be reasonable, *bukko*." He glanced at the sons, then back at Brown John. "You are a proud family—I understand that—and as outlaws obliged to lie. But we cannot allow it now. Any day the Kitzakks are going to come seeking the bones of their dead scouts so they can give them a proper burial . . . and in the process they will seek revenge. But we do not intend to suffer for your foolishness and greed . . . so show us his hiding place. Now! It is a small price to pay for bringing the wrath of the Kitzakks down on all of us."

"I see," said Brown John with a ring of alarm in his voice. "You . . . you intend to negotiate with the Kitzakks?"

"Exactly. And you should be grateful for it. It is much better for you if we give them the head of the man who killed their scouts . . . rather than the heads of all those who stole their bones."

"But, my lords, surely you know that the last nation to attempt to negotiate with Kitzakks concluded its discussions from the interior of Kitzakk cages."

"Tell us where he is, you Grillard scum!" Golfon blurted. "And tell it quick, or we'll gut the lot of you!" This time he made his point with the butt end of his spear and knocked Brown John to the ground.

Bone and Dirken started to go for their swords, but held their places as Vitmar edged his horse forward. He looked contemptuously at Brown John as he slowly got back up, and said again, "Be reasonable, *bukko*."

Brown John nodded. "To see the Kaven, the Cytherian and the Barhacha in the same riding party inspires nothing if it does not inspire reason, but I cannot help you."

"Lying outlaw filth!" Golfon struck Brown John with

the butt end of his spear, drove him back to the ground.

Dirken and Bone moved for Golfon. But Vitmar spurred his horse into them, and they went down ducking and rolling away from the animal's hooves.

Brown John motioned for his sons to stay put, then, holding his collarbone, rose onto an elbow, and addressing Vitmar from that less than lofty position, said, "I am afraid, Lord Vitmar, that the Lord Golfon has a poor opinion of reasonable discussion."

By way of agreement, Golfon spit on Brown John again.

"Give us directions, old man," Vitmar demanded.

Brown John, looking from Golfon to Sharatz, said, "I do not know where he is. Mere chance led my bastards and me to the sight of the massacre. Due to its amazing proportions, it was not difficult to determine that a spirit bordering on the magical had been the cause." He looked at Vitmar. "Consequently, we choose to share, for a small price, given our efforts, that spirit with all the tribes of the forest. And, I dare say, we have done a decent job of it."

"You were there! You helped him!"

"We were not. We only saw the results of his work, and I will tell you, I have never seen better work done by man and axe."

"And just how, *bukko*," demanded Vitmar, "did you know it was the Dark One's work?"

Brown John squinted up and muttered, "I . . . ah . . . I see things. In entrails. Clouds. That sort of thing. He . . . he was one of the things I saw."

Golfon grunted with foul disgust, lifted his spear.

"Wait!" Sharatz intoned in a devout register. The Kaven waited until every head turned toward him, then dismounted with regal solemnity. He leveled a long finger at Golfon and Vitmar, and said, "If you choose to soil your weapons by killing this trash, you will ride without my company."

"You have a better idea?" grunted Golfon.

"Naturally," Sharatz said with quiet disdain. He advanced to Brown John, smiled down at him so pompously he was in danger of falling over backward. Then, ceremoniously, he unbuckled his leather codpiece and urinated on Brown John's hip.

The Grillards gasped. Vitmar, Golfon and the men-at-arms grinned, then laughed out loud. Here and there suppressed titters erupted from the crowd.

Sharatz buckled up, then said to Brown John, "We do not need your help, clown. We have the Dark One's wolf." He indicated the caged wolf on the back of the pack horse. "With the beast's quite involuntary cooperation I can guarantee you that your benefactor, Gath of Baal, will be dead before sundown. That, of course, means your totems will then be totally useless."

The Grillards, shocked, made signs on their bodies while the customers looked at the totems they had purchased with distrust.

The three chiefs chuckled, remounted and rode out the southern end of Rag Camp in a whirl of stifling dust. They were headed in the direction of The Shades.

Brown John, the red flush on his cheeks spreading as low as the backs of his hands, rose onto all fours. He stared after the departing Barbarian chiefs, muttering, "Idiots!"

Bone and Dirken jumped up and, with the aid of some Grillards, helped their father up. Over the babble of the outraged, humiliated, sympathetic clan, Dirken spoke to Brown John. "You know what they're going to do! They'll make his wolf howl like the lord god of Pain himself. And when it does, Gath will come fast. He'll be wearing their spears before he even sees them."

Brown John, still staring at the departing riders, said flatly, "It's not his wolf."

The Grillards grinned with relief.

Brown John turned to them. He wasn't smiling. "But it will make no difference. He'll go to it anyway." He turned to Dirken and Bone. "But this will all take time, perhaps time enough to warn him. Get the horses. Quickly!" The reckless twinkle was suddenly back in the old man's eyes.

As the two bastards hurried off, the Grillards crowded around their *bukko* and gaped at him with astonished eyes.

Brown John was standing in the sunshine. The dark wet spot at his hips steamed. He smelled of urine. And he was laughing.

Ten
CALLING ROCK

Brown John, Bone and Dirken rode south through the spare trees and green glades of the Valley of Miracles. Two miles from Rag Camp they reached Summer Trail and headed west. It was a wide dusty avenue between the trees, filled with summer sun. An hour later they entered The Shades. Here the trail narrowed, and the soil became dark, moist. Shadows populated the dense foliage of the rain forest, and the undulating ground rose and fell as the trail twisted between massive firs, hemlock and spruce. The three men had not seen the six riders, nor any sign of them.

They plunged on, leaping over fallen trees, ignoring the pain as their suntanned faces whipped through overhanging ferns.

Summer Trail became muddy; small creeks cut across it, murky ponds hid it. It almost vanished altogether within clusters of elderberry before it widened again and rose toward Calling Rock, a massive stack of house-sized boulders which stood several hundred feet above the tops of the trees. Creepers and shrubs crowded the base of the rock at the eastern end. Gulleys and cracks cut up into the rock, twisted under overhanging rocks and over fallen boulders as they thrust towards the heights.

The three Grillards rode across the wide clearing of bald earth at the southern side of the rock, then left the trail moving north along the western side. They turned up a wide, open gulley which rose almost two-thirds of the way to the top of the rocks. They whipped their horses up into the gulley until their mounts bogged down in loose earth, then dismounted and scrambled forward on foot. They cut their way through rope-thick cobwebs, reached a turn in the gulley and bulled up it through a tangle of fallen boulders five times their size.

Reaching the heights of the rock they stood gasping for a moment. There, boulders, shrubs, and trees surrounded an open flat shelf of rock. At its far edge stood a naked, black thorn tree. Its branches, burnt to sharp points, thrust like giant spears at the belly of the pink-gold sky. The three men hurried across the clearing to the base of the tree. There was an oval opening in its charred shell.

Brown John muttered, "Hurry! Hurry!"

Bone poked around inside the tree with his club. Satisfied that no spider or snake lay in wait, he reached in and came away with a bullhorn as thick as his thigh. Hurriedly he dropped his club against the tree, took the horn in two hands and, taking a deep breath, blew. Two long, resonant, shrill blasts, one short. Bone waited as Dirken counted to one hundred, then repeated this short performance.

They sat down to wait.

Time passed.

No sounds of breaking branches or rustling leaves. No flurry of birds to indicate someone approaching silently, and no sounds of the six riders in the distance. Only the quiet steady drip of dew and the wind singing through the trees.

More time passed, then a sudden terror-fed howl of pain

pierced the peaceful murmur of the rain forest, then again and again.

Brown John, Bone and Dirken jumped to their feet, raging.

The howl came once more, terrible and prolonged. From the south.

Brown John led the way back across the clearing. Reaching their horses, they mounted on the run and bolted down the gulley kicking up dust and rubble. They headed south, following no trail. They plunged through openings in the forest, rode down ferns and shrubs, twisted through thick fallen trees, jumped others. The distant sounds of battle, cursing men, the clang of metal, spurred their reckless charge.

Their mounts faltered, but they drove them on through thornbushes and across vaporous ponds tangled with creepers and possibly quicksand. Then the clamor stopped as abruptly as it had started.

Brown John reined up hard. His sons found their way through the thick undergrowth to his side and consulted him silently.

"Wait here." It was a whispered command.

Brown John prodded his horse forward, cautiously picking his way through the rain forest.

Eleven

FOURTEEN PIECES

Reaching a sun-drenched clearing, Brown John rose in his stirrups, astounded.

Gath stood at the center, his axe in one hand, the door of Sharatz's cage in the other. The cage rested on the ground in front of him. Inside it the wounded she-wolf trembled and bled. Her left foreleg was broken. There were cuts about her eyes, hide hanging in strips from her throat, and mangled bloody clumps of fur on her rump.

Suddenly the she-wolf leapt out of the cage, stumbled, rolled fitfully and struggled upright on three legs. She circled wildly, spinning with her wounds bubbling red. Abandoned to her agony, she lurched in one direction, then in a second. Fear still hard in her, she picked a third direction and dashed on three legs past Sharn into the surrounding dense shadows.

Sharn, sitting on his haunches, watched the she-wolf without moving, then looked back at the new intruder. Head erect. Steam furling from his mouth. A thin strip of pale violet cloth which had obviously belonged to Sharatz's violet cape hung from a fang.

Brown John sighed in relief, dismounted and started towards Gath. The whites of his eyes bulged under brows climbing for the top of his head.

"Holy Zard!" he gasped. This was appropriate as it was in reference to the God of Blood.

What had been six hard, angry riders that morning now

lay about in the shade at the edges of the clearing in peaceful silence. The scatter of gore and limbs was so spectacular Brown John could not refrain from measuring it. He estimated ten pieces.

Golfon accounted for five. The severed stump of his right hand still clutched his spear, which was stuck at an angle in the acid green grass. Beyond that lay his body. It had wandered into a tangle of exposed hemlock roots and tripped on one. He had lost his way because his head was fourteen feet further off. He had bitten off his tongue, which lolled on the ground beside one of his teeth.

Vitmar had lost only an ear and thumb. He was facedown in the grass, limbs spread wide, still brown and warm in the sunshine. The three men-at-arms had died intact, except for one who had lost a chunk of shoulder.

Brown John wagged his silver head, toddled over on shaky bowlegs to a rock rising out of matted green grass, sat down and counted again. The total this time was twelve.

Sharn rose, held the strip of cloth stuck on his fang to the ground with a paw, then pulled his head back, ripped it loose.

Brown John's eyes were puzzled. Where was the owner of the violet cloth? He stood, edged towards Gath to ask, and a drop of hot blood splattered on the back of his hand.

"Holy Zard!" he gasped again, and looked up.

Sharatz was stuck among the high branches of a fir tree. Both pieces of him. They were approximately of the same size and weight. That made fourteen pieces.

Brown John stumbled out from under the dripping corpse, looked at Gath.

The sharp frenzy of battle was still as fresh as budding thorns in his young eyes. He spit his words, "You sent them."

Brown John started to deny it passionately, but stopped himself, and instead spoke in a slow, thoughtful tone. "No, I did not send them. But in a way I am responsible. My sons and I took the bodies of the Kitzakks you killed and had them butchered into totems. These chiefs,'' he indicated the dismembered bodies, ''in their fear and cowardice, had hoped to appease the Kitzakks by returning the bodies for proper burial. As they were not able to do this with the parts now spread throughout the forest, they rode into Rag Camp and demanded that I tell them where you live. They foolishly hoped to negotiate with the Kitzakks by offering them your head. I, of course, did not help them. I have not the faintest idea of where you live. Nor do I wish to find out. And, believe me, if I had known, I would not have been so shortsighted as to tell them and earn your anger.''

Gath waited, then deliberately tossed the cage door aside. It landed with a brittle crack, and Brown John jerked nervously. Some play appeared behind Gath's shadowed eyes. He moved to Brown John, lifted the bloody blade of his axe, wiped it on the tunic covering the old man's trembling belly. As he did, his low, coarse voice demanded, ''What else?''

Brown John answered anxiously. ''I, and my sons as well, tried to stop them and they beat us brutally.'' He indicated his wounds.

Gath ignored them and moved to Vitmar, squatted over him with his back to Brown John. As he unbuckled the dead man's dagger belt, he asked indifferently, ''And?''

Brown John shuffled uneasily. ''Only this. I regret that they found you before I could warn you. You did hear the horn?''

Gath slung Vitmar's belt over his shoulder and stood, turning slowly to Brown John. The axe rode his fist as easily as the eagle rides the sky. The veins on his chest and arms stood out as if gorged with fluid stone. Dappled sunlight and shadows played about his face, adding mystery and a shimmering savage light to his brawny menace. His wide, flat lips, spread in a sardonic smile, allowed a low mocking laugh to escape. When he spoke all the play in his eyes and voice was gone.

"You are right. You are responsible. Your minstrels sent them."

Brown John flushed. "Yes," he said weakly. "That is a fair conclusion, but I assure you, that even without our vulgar songs and antics, the tale of your heroics would have soon spread throughout the forest."

"No, you bandy-legged *bukko*!" His tone was a threatening whisper. "You took a great risk making me the clown of your stories. If I were not so fond of your wine, my axe would have talked to you about it long ago. Now your foolishness brings these arrogant chiefs who want my head and hurt my friends . . . while you sell what you call my magic to weak and gullible fools."

"I assure you," Brown John pleaded, "there is no mockery in our tales, nor the least desire to cause you displeasure or discomfort. Only praise. Glory. I . . ."

"Do not flatter me, *bukko*," Gath interrupted with an ugly whisper.

"Forgive me." Brown John dipped his head in a slight bow. "I am accustomed to dealing with dancing girls and jugglers who require an excess of praise and protection from hard truths. From now on I will attempt to keep my language simpler and to the point."

He moved gingerly around the blood dripping from Sharatz's stumps, parked himself on a rock and spoke with a semblance of confidence. "How may I call you?"

"By my name."

"Of course. Then let me tell you, Gath of Baal, why I have involved myself, my family and the Grillards in your business." He paused, wet his fingers, slicked his hair away from his eyes. "I have created the totems and sold them for a more serious reason than even you, with your keen sense of observation, might suspect."

Gath's eyes hardened in warning, and he scratched his kneecap with the flat of his axe blade.

"Ah yes, forgive me, the words of flattery come habitually. But allow me to continue, please. The silver I have collected is to be used to employ a war master, a champion, to defend Rag Camp . . . to keep my people from having to sing their songs and tell their jokes from behind the bars of Kitzakk cages. To put it as plainly as I can, I am offering you a job.''

Not waiting for a response, Brown John untied a heavy pouch from his belt and tossed it to Gath. The Barbarian did not bother to catch it; it dropped in the tall grass at his feet, breaking open to spill silver on the bloody ground.

Taken aback, Brown John, not daring yet to meet Gath's gaze, peered at the coins saying, ''I intend, of course, to hire other mercenaries from the Soldier's Market in Coin to serve under you. The best in the forest.''

Gath said in his low thick tone, ''We in The Shades do not use silver . . . or mercenaries.''

Brown John looked up, smiled lightly, then said just as lightly, ''That, then, will change. With the Kitzakks riding this way, you will need better weapons, stronger armor, and the strongest men fighting beside you.''

''I have what I need.''

''Yes,'' said the Grillard quickly, ''I can see you seriously believe that.'' He hesitated, then stood facing Gath. ''But there must be something I can offer you? More wine? Women?'' Gath did not reply. Brown John edged forward hopefully. ''If it is women, I dare say, I can supply the most beautiful and eager girls ever to lie on a blanket.''

Gath eyed him with disgust and slung his axe on his back.

Defeat washed across Brown John's flushed face, but he forced a warm smile. ''Then . . . then all I can do is ask you to help us . . . my people . . . out of friendship.''

''Friendship!'' Gath grunted with a harsh thick growl. ''I have no friends who stand on two legs.'' He moved across the glade, stopped and picked up the strip of violet cloth then looked back. ''But I will still buy your wine.''

Brown John smiled lamely.

Gath studied the Grillard a moment, then marched into

the forest, Sharn at his side.

Brown John started to follow, but gave up. He mumbled unpleasantly, then shouted recklessly, "Barbarian, if you think your pride and arrogance will protect you from the Kitzakks, you are sadly mistaken." Defying the humiliation which had turned his bumptuous cheeks apple red, Brown John advanced to the edge of the clearing, propped a fist on his hip, raised the other over his head and shook it with the bravado of a commander standing at the head of forty regiments of foot and ten of horse. "Do you hear me? Your pride is not enough. You, the tribes, none of you can survive alone."

The sounds of undergrowth being crushed by booted feet were the only response he got.

Brown John had an answer for it. He shook a scolding finger and shouted louder, "And do not think I will quit! Not for a moment. Just because I have been beaten, peed upon and rudely rejected, do not think I am unable to see past these trifling humiliations to the greater truth. I may not have your animal power, Gath of Baal, but I have a different gift. I see things coming. Yes! And I can assure you I have not failed to measure the import of the fact that today, for the first time, the Kaven, the Cytherian and the Barhacha rode together. Don't for a minute think that I am blind to that miracle, or that I fail to recognize it for what it truly is, a portentious omen of an even greater unity to come! Perhaps even a triumphant one!"

Brown John stared at the forest shadows. Only silence answered him now. He muttered to himself, then the bravado went out of him. It shortened him by half a foot. He glanced about at the scene of slaughter, moved to the spilled silver, got down on his knees and began to pick up the coins.

A short time later, when he rejoined his waiting sons, he was leading his horse and deep in thought. When the bastards started to inquire as to what had happened, he silenced them with a lifted hand and thought some more.

After a long while he looked up, said, "You will find some bodies, six to be exact, in a clearing about fifty yards up ahead." He pointed it out. "Bury them, so that no man or animal will find them. Ever. Bury their armor with them, and make sure you find all their parts. There are, I think, twelve or fourteen, perhaps more. I do not remember clearly."

Bone and Dirken gave each other a sober glance, then mounted and rode off leaving their father alone.

Brown John stood silently, thinking again. As he did, he smoothed his hair with a hand and tucked it back over an ear with a thumbnail, but this failed to groom his troubled mind. The furrow of wrinkles creasing his forehead dug so deep they grew dark. His brow drooped so low that his bushy white eyebrows tickled his cheeks. Feeling their touch his scowl grew even deeper. Then the words came to him.

It was a line of dialogue from *A Fig for the Ice Queen*, a line he had delivered on countless occasions on countless stages. But now, as he said them aloud to no one, there was no trace of fiction in the words, no trace of the actor in his tone or in his suddenly boyish smile.

He said, "I've got it. I'll get the girl."

Twelve

ROBIN LAKEHAIR

The Dragon Lizard sprawled lazily on a flat grey boulder in a manner that made hard rock look warm and comfortable. The boulder rested atop a stack of boulders which formed the bend in the river.

He looked contentedly at blue-green water flowing around a rocky bend some fifteen feet below. It rippled over half-submerged rocks, formed ponds at the edges of a pebbled beach until it widened into a large pool. Cascading on, the stream churned itself to white water on a scatter of small boulders and flowed on.

The lizard obviously liked the view.

His sun-drenched body lay just out of dappled shadows cast by a scrub oak. He was the length of a child's forearm, the color of the stone except for shiny gills reflecting greens of the forest trees and the gold of the morning sun. His eyes flickered closed, then one suddenly popped back open.

The girl, carrying her sandals in one hand and a walking stick in the other, was coming fast, leaping barefoot from rock to rock as she moved along the shaded side of the river. She wore a belted tunic, her pouch slung by a strap over a shoulder. A sheathed knife dangled from the belt.

The lizard dashed down a narrow crack. A moment later it reappeared in the company of three little things a third its length. They scurried to the lip of the rock, lay down, eyes wide.

The girl waded through the water just below, then

climbed onto a large rock rising about three feet out of the water. The top of the rock descended in gently rolling swells to the water's edge. Here and there puddles the size of footbaths glistened in its smooth natural recessions. The girl, splashing through each puddle, moved to the water's edge, set down her sandals and walking stick, and stretched luxuriously, letting the morning sun bathe her face.

It was a small, triangular face framed by a cascade of red-gold hair that parted at the center and fell sideways in natural waves to the tops of smooth tan shoulders. It had gently arched eyebrows, a small straight nose. The upper lip was as straight as a delicately sculpted knife cut, and appeared even straighter over a voluptuous lower lip the color of a budding rose. There was a hint of the same color in the tan cheeks. The delicate clarity of her features heightened the contrasting lushness of her firm flesh. Her hazel-green eyes were big and active, with brilliant whites surrounded by long dark feathery lashes.

Her name was Robin Lakehair. She was a Cytherian from the village of Weaver, a Sacred Maiden who, like all virgin Cytherian girls, worked spinning the sacred cloth for which Weaver's temples were renowned. She was an orphan. Since her parents had died of the black death that passed through the forest when she was three, she had been raised by temple priestesses until she was fifteen when, being of adult age, she took a room by herself. She was seventeen.

Robin lifted her leather satchel and emptied its contents on the warm rock: a collection of corked vials carved from colored stones, a bone comb, a crust of bread, a tangle of colorful ribbons and her sacred wooden whorl. After carefully arranging her precious collection, she stood, unbuckled her leather belt and dropped it beside her satchel. Taking hold of the hem of her plain grey square-necked tunic, she lifted it over her head. She folded her tunic neatly, set it beside her things and again stretched, giving her nude body to the luxurious, warm embrace of the sunshine.

The great ball of fire in the sky painted her a golden nutmeg with loving strokes, as if the great orb of endless fire knew well that rarely was there a human animal created to wear only garments made of light.

Robin was no taller than a full-grown deer. Her breasts stood high on her little barrel chest, as smooth and firm and plump as river-washed pebbles. Her arms were short, her hands small, her waist tiny, and her legs long muscular arrows ending in sturdy feet. As young and vibrant as a new blade of grass, as strong as a bowstring.

She looked up and down the river, into the forest, then up at the top of the outcropping of rock topped by the scrub oak. Spotting the lizards, she smiled and made a soft clicking sound. She opened a pouch, scrambled up the rocks and sprinkled a spoonful of dried insects on a shelf of rock. As the lizards scurried down to the meal, she hopped back down to the edge of the water and watched them feed. Robin laughed with delight, then strode into the water and with a joyous shiver sank into the cold blue-green current.

She floated on her back letting it carry her out into the middle of the pond, then rolled over on her flat tummy so that only her head and round firm bottom protruded from the rippling blue water. She arched up, dove, vanished under the water. A long moment later she surfaced some way down river. She turned and swam back with strong strokes, climbed out.

She shook herself like a frisky colt, and beads of water shot with sunlight flew in all directions, like a riot of wet jewels. Kneeling on her tunic, she uncorked a vial and poured its contents on her hair. She scrubbed until a thick lather formed, spread the lather over her body, rubbing vigorously, then plunged back into the water.

The lizards stayed and watched, and a shadow crossed over them. They promptly bolted in all directions and disappeared.

Brown John, who had been concealed behind the scrub oak, had edged forward. The look on his face was bawdy, flushed, and profound. He also liked the view.

Robin floated back downriver, playfully flopping about and diving, then swam back to her rock and climbed out. This time she wore not only a slick coat of water, but a handful of soap bubbles.

It was the kind of wardrobe Brown John admired.

Robin shook and wiped herself dry, then kneeled on her tunic. Using a rose ointment, she economically annointed her face and body, then rubbed her lips with rose vermilion. She selected a bright yellow ribbon, set it aside, put everything but her comb back in her satchel, then sat down cross-legged on her tunic. With her hair to the sun and her back to the scrub oak, she began to comb her hair.

Brown John's fingertips drummed the air in time with the stroke of Robin's brush. His head bobbed to the same tune.

When Robin finished with her comb, she picked up the ribbon and, laying it flat across the top of her head and joining the ends at the base of her neck, bent her head forward and tied her hair back. As she did, Brown John moved down and across the rock to stand behind her.

Suddenly, seeing his shadow, she gasped and rolled upright in one movement, drawing her knife. She waved the blade at the stranger using one hand while the other tried to cover her nudity. It was a beautiful and energetic effort, but futile.

Brown John smiled and said, "Robin Lakehair." It sounded like a title rather than a name.

Robin hardly heard him. She was gasping and tugging at her tunic with her free hand.

Brown John said politely, "Perhaps, child, if you lifted your foot."

She looked down, groaned, and jumped aside, snapping up her clothing. Turning her back, she slipped into her tunic with three wiggles and a yank, while watching him over a shoulder. Then she turned back, deliberately smoothing her tunic with one hand, while the other held her knife aimed at Brown John's belly. Her straight brow was lowering over angry eyes. She seemed to be frowning but it was difficult to tell. Her firm smooth forehead was barely cooperating, and her cheeks were too busy blushing. But her tone helped.

"You snake! Were you watching?"

Brown John sat down on a flat rock, said, "To my great good fortune, yes."

Groaning, she glanced away, then looked back at him sharply. Her eyes were large beautiful wet wounds. "That was awful of you. Mean."

"Not mean, child, simply lucky. Extraordinarily lucky to have chanced to pass this way. The sun, the lizards and I will not only carry your lovely image to our graves, but far, far beyond."

She hesitated, then asked, "Do I know you?"

"I believe so," he said with a slight tone of mystery. "I, at least, have seen you many times."

"Really? Where?"

"Well, once I saw you standing on top of a barrel and laughing in the village of Coin. And last summer you were watching the performers on the stage in Rag Camp."

Robin, unconsciously lowering her knife, gasped, "But . . . but no one knew I was there!"

"I thought as much," he said. "Then, of course, you are always in the front row when we perform in your village."

"Oh!" Robin blurted. "You're the *bukko*! The wizard-master!"

He bowed extravagantly. "I am called Brown John."

"I know! Everyone knows!" Robin exclaimed. She picked up her belt, sat down cross-legged on the rock facing him, and buckled it on. "But you remember me? You know my name?"

Brown John studied her smile as it performed about her face, as varied as the song of the robin after which she was named. He said quietly, "Indeed I do."

She stiffened slightly, and suspicion returned to her eyes.

"You . . . you came here to find me . . . didn't you?"

"Yes. And you are right to be angry with me. When confronted by a scene more dazzling than any that could be created on a stage, the manners of performers are inevitably rude and inadequate."

"Oh."

"Nevertheless," he continued, "my spying on you was not intentional. The fact that you selected this extraordinarily beautiful pond, and were bathing in a wardrobe made of sunshine and bubbles, was all quite by chance. But to look away would have denied my nature, and I would be lying if I said I regretted it."

She blushed, and shook her hair vigorously to hide it. Beads of water flew about sparkling. She eyed him warily. "You're too clever. You make me forget what I'm saying." She hesitated, collecting her thoughts. "Why did you come to see me?"

He considered her thoughtfully. "Because your virtues are well-known, and because I have seen in you a brave heart. And an appetite for chance, adventure."

Her big feathery eyes scolded him more gently now. "You're trying to confuse me again . . . not really answering my question."

He chuckled. "You are right, Robin Lakehair. Let me put it this way. I have a role which I believe you, and only you, can play."

"Me?"

"You."

"But I . . . I'm not an actress."

"Indeed not. In fact it is well known that you are incapable of anything false or artificial . . . and can hear all that is false in others."

"But then why . . ."

"Because the role is real," Brown John said interrupting her.

She cocked her head boyishly, her eyes glistening with sudden curiosity.

"If I am right, the spirit of the open road already makes your feet itch." He leaned forward, lifted her chin slightly with a finger. "In fact you remind me of a former traveling companion, a girl who joined us when she was just about your age. I can't recall her real name. We called her Ansaria, after the wild root which enchants children. She was the embodiment of beauty and adventure. They loved her everywhere we went. Even named their children after her." He sighed nostalgically. "Oh, we were respected then. Invited to carnivals and castles to perform for kings and queens."

She looked at him from under her straight brows. "You're playing with me."

He shook his head. "I do not play, it only sounds that way because you are not accustomed to hearing someone speak seriously of dancing girls. And because the nature of your, and Ansaria's, attraction is difficult to explain. Elusive. Like trying to cage a shooting star. But then, it is not required that you understand." He looked directly into her eyes intently. "Tell me, which of our acts do you like the best?"

"Oh, I loved them all," she said enthusiastically.

"Of course." His eyes twinkled. "But think now. I am certain you have a favorite!"

"Well, last summer, there was a dancing bear and a clown . . . and a beautiful dancing girl. She was small and dark, and wore red scarves and all kinds of baubles and beads. They were wonderful."

"Ahhh," murmured Brown John. "Nose, the rubber man, and Lale."

"That's it! But what was the bear's name?"

"They called him Sir William."

Robin chuckled, "Sir William. How wonderful." She became dreamy. "The girl was so beautiful."

"Yes . . . she was," he said with a touch of nostalgia. "In a way she was also like yourself. She could not hide. There was no distance between her and her audience. No matter how she cluttered herself with jewels and gaudy cloth, her deepest feelings were always on display. One night she would be so brazen and frenzied in her dancing that she would drive Nose wild with jealousy. The next night she would jump into the audience and try to plunge her dagger into a girl for winking at him.''

"Really?'' Robin whispered.

He nodded. "They no longer dwell in Rag Camp. One morning they were just gone. They are what we call followers of the wind. Sometimes they're like a storm, sometimes like a breeze. But always moving.''

"It sounds frightening,'' Robin said with a shiver. "But wonderful too.''

"Yes,'' Brown John said thoughtfully. He looked off at the water swirling down over rocks, gathering in eddies, turning white as it crashed over logs and boulders. "I miss it,'' he sighed, "but I no longer have the temperament for the road.''

She nodded, waited. Eyes wide and impressed.

He looked at her. "What others did you like? What skits? *The She-Ass*? *Chums*? *The Gelded King*?''

She blushed. "Well . . . they were funny . . . but very bold.'' She hesitated, then said with a rush of excitement she could not conceal, "There was one story! I've seen it every time, *The Lizard Song of Ting-Gad*!''

"Ahhh yes,'' said Brown John. "And the part which you liked best was, of course, where the lizard turns into the handsome outlaw chief?''

She blushed.

Brown John threw back his head and laughed out loud. Just as abruptly, he became subdued and serious. "The transformation is a very difficult piece of stage business to perform. It has a touch of magic to it, but a very, very fragile magic. The performers who play it must be totally involved and dedicated, as well as skilled. Its effect comes a long time after the performance. Sometimes it is years before its subtle power takes hold, and transforms the audience with its dream.''

Robin leaned forward excitedly. ''Is . . . is that how . . . how your magic works? It takes that long?''

''Not always, but sometimes longer. Generations.''

''But . . . but, I don't understand! Everyone says that the only magic a *bukko* can make is with dancing girls of low character and strong wine, and they laugh when they say it.''

Brown John chuckled. ''Some of that is true, but do not think unkindly of me or my girls. Sometimes they can be as enchanting and profound as *The Lizard Song of Ting-Gad*.''

Robin nodded as these new ideas whirled behind her eyes. Then he abruptly changed the subject.

''Do you truly love your tribe?''

''Of course,'' she said with sudden show of hard pride.

''Would you try to protect it, if you could?''

Her eyes became startled. Her voice trembled. ''Is . . . is that why you're here?''

He studied her intently. ''Yes. I need a messenger . . . one who will not act . . . who can not lie.''

Her teeth took hold of her lower lip.

''Yes, you. But do you know that soon more Kitzakks will come, and invade the forest?''

Robin gulped.

''Listen carefully. You have heard our song of the battle at Lemontree Crossing?''

She nodded.

''It is true. The song does not lie.'' He lowered his voice to a conspiratorial whisper. ''The defender of the bridge lives in The Shades, a man of incredible strength! And spirit! He, and only he, has the skills and power we must have to defend the forest, but he distrusts all men.''

''Gath of Baal! The Dark One!'' She trembled.

His head bobbed. ''He alone can stand against the

Kitzakks, and save the tribes. I do not know if he will, but I know he can. And I can help him do it. But he will not cooperate with me. He does not trust my motives or see the value in my imagination. But you . . . you understand?''

She nodded, her breath racing.

"He must be made to understand the immense size of the danger, of the horror of the Kitzakk chains and cages. And he must be made to understand that they endanger not only the freedom and lives of the forest tribes, but his freedom! His life. Once he knows these things he will realize, as he is a man of keen intelligence, that he can not prevail alone. And that I can help him, provide him with the metal and weapons, and the army, he will need." He looked off at the river. "I have tried to tell him this but he will not believe me." He looked back into Robin's eyes and smiled wisely. "But he will believe you."

She grabbed a quick breath, stammered, "But . . . but how can I find him? And if I did, would . . . would he listen to me?''

"He can be summoned. And your beauty, your innocence, and honesty, they are powerful weapons of persuasion. When he finds you helpless and vulnerable in his domain, a place of beasts and demons, and for no other reason than to speak to him, you can not fail but to gain his attention. And hold it. At least for as long as it will take for you to deliver my words.''

She gasped. "And then?''

He hesitated, then said flatly. "I do not know.''

She shuddered, looked off at the flowing river. After a moment, she glanced back over her brown shoulder at him and said weakly, "He'll hurt me, won't he?''

Brown John shifted uncomfortably. "I do not know. I don't think he will.''

Her head dropped so all she could see was the rock between her legs. From that position, she asked, "You're certain he can save my people?''

Her head lifted. The question glistened in her eyes, but

also a tenative commitment. Seeing it, an excited tremor shot through Brown John as he nodded. When he spoke it sounded as if he were the Lord God of Imagination.

"Child, the extreme, the immeasurable power of this man is beyond our feeble contemplation. This is a man who can not only overcome the Kitzakks, but become the sword of justice itself. A man, Robin Lakehair, who can be the savior of our land, our people. Who can drive the nightmare from the children's sleep . . . and fill their minds with soaring dreams worthy of the dreaming."

Her lips trembled.

He lowered his voice. "The Kitzakks are not the future, child. We are. A time is coming when there will only be masterless men and women. When there will be no barriers across the trails except those placed there by the limits of our imagination."

Robin began to glow.

"Soon, if we dare to make them so, all things will be possible. You and I, at this very moment, can take the first step into an age of adventure, into the childhood of a time made for legends. And he, Gath of Baal, he can be the first to walk them." Her hands trembled as they held her knees. He placed his hands over hers, held them as he spoke. "But he is a prisoner of his pride. He is caged by it. And you . . . Robin Lakehair . . . can open the door of that cage. Set him free."

She gasped, "Is . . . is this truly possible?"

"You be the judge of that. Have I lied?"

A rush of feeling left her breathless. Light leapt into her face. There was joyous surrender and resolute commitment in her voice.

"No."

Brown John took her cheeks in his hands, lifted her to face him and looked into her eyes with an honesty that almost hurt saying, "I was right. You, little girl, are the one." She nodded within his hands, and he continued. "Tomorrow morning, at the third hour, my sons will be waiting for you outside Weaver's western gate. They will guide you to Calling Rock which is deep within The Shades, but they will not stay with you." She nodded again. "There is a large blackthorn tree at the top of the rock. Concealed in its hollow is a horn we use to call him. You will blow it three times, two long and one short."

Robin, whose eyes had not left his, nodded once more. "Two long and one short."

Thirteen

RED DANCERS

A distant note, like the cry of an elephant, rose above the sounds of the wind in the trees and the dialogue of the crows and sparrows. Gath, standing in the clear track in front of his root house deep within the southern part of The Shades, heard it clearly.

His dark brow furrowed and his sweating face lifted slightly, but he did not turn in the direction of the sound. He was busy.

In front of him Sergeant Yat's helmet was wedged over the stump of a root. Its wide brim had been hammered off. All that remained was the steel bowl. Attached to it by two bands of Kitzakk steel was his own crude iron mask. The iron was blunted and black. The new steel was grey-blue, bristling with highlights in the afternoon sun.

Gath looked down at the helmet, spread his feet.

He was wearing Yat's forearm guards and chest- and back-plates. Like the helmet they had been hammered to raw steel and refitted to the Barbarian's thick-muscled chest and back. Holes had been drilled through the sides of the plates, and hide thongs joined them. The plates, being too small, left wide unprotected areas at his sides.

He edged sideways to get the best angle from which to deliver a blow and test the helmet, then raised the axe high over his head. Determination drew down the sides of his upper lip, making short vertical lines. He struck, putting no more muscle into the blow than would be required to end the careers of three men and a wagon.

The axe caught the curved steel of the bowl, glanced off, buried itself in the dirt up to the haft. Gath shook from the impact. He rubbed numbed fingers, took hold of the axe and pulled on it. He had to wrestle with it some before the dirt was willing to let go.

A second distant note came out of the north but quickly lost force, sputtered to silence.

He glanced to the north, wiped the sweat off his lips with the strip of violet cloth which was now tied around his left wrist. Setting the axe aside, he plucked the helmet off the still-shivering root. The iron bands sprang loose from the bowl and fell to the ground.

That brought a scowl. He studied the steel bowl, found only a slight dent in it, and a grin replaced the scowl. He picked up his axe. A portion of the axe blade's cutting edge was flattened, wide enough to reflect a bar of sunshine and a piece of clear blue sky. That brought the scowl back.

Gath put the helmet back over the stump, repositioned the iron bands. Using the blunt end of the axe like a hammer, he beat the bands down over the steel bowl until their studs locked in small holes rimming the bowl. This done, he sat down beside an uncorked wine jar, slid a thumb through the handle and held it in the cradle of his arm as if it were a girl instead of a piece of cold crockery. His eyes were steady, judgmental, as uncompromising as grey slate. Staring at his new helmet, he lifted the jar to his mouth and poured. Suddenly he lowered the jar.

The trumpeting sound had come again, a long note. It

was now followed by a long wavering note, then by a short one. A stranger was blowing the bullhorn, and knew the signal.

Gath stared north, then whirled toward a subtle movement at the vine-covered entrance to his root house. It was the wolf, ready to go for a walk.

An hour later Gath and Sharn spotted the brown boulders of Calling Rock above the treetops. They moved warily to the clearing at the south side and stopped in the concealing shadows.

Thirty strides across the clearing, beyond Summer Trail, the sheer southern face of Calling Rock rose fifty feet. Creepers and vines fought against fallen rocks and dirt spilling out of crevices to embrace the lower boulders. Above this foliage, the late day sun caressed brown stones with an orange glow. In the gullies, caves, jagged cracks and crevices of the rock were deep shadows, black places of mystery designed for demons and unseen hands to hide. But they were not responsible for the brightness that entered Gath's eyes.

A small figure at the top of the rock knelt over a smoking fire at the base of the blackened thorn tree. It looked no more vulnerable than a bite of meat on the end of a fork.

Frowning, Gath looked around. At the eastern end the rock broke apart in a tangle of massive boulders penetrated by three deep crevices. They zigzagged and grew narrower as they approached the heights. There they vanished among shrubs and thorn trees. Except for an unusual silence there was no sign of anyone hiding among the crevices or within the surrounding forest.

The man and wolf shared a wondering glance, and looked back up at the figure. It was a girl. She had moved to the thorn tree, and, climbing halfway into its burnt-out shell, came away with the bullhorn. It was as thick as her waist at the bell end. She wrestled with it until she had the bell propped on a branch, then took hold with two hands, inhaled deeply and blew hard. A clear strong note left the horn, and a covey of crows lifted out of the trees to the east to spatter the gold sky with black-winged specks. With resolve, she blew again. The note started strong, then lost force and whined like a lonely dog.

Gath grinned, then laughed as the girl, gasping for breath, collapsed in a lump against the tree, bringing the horn with her. It banged her knee, escaped from her hands, and defiantly rolled out of reach while the girl held her knee and rocked painfully in place.

Gath, with his eyes on the girl, stuck his leaf-bladed spear upright in the ground, lifted the waterskin slung on his back along with his axe, and poured a long drink into and over his grinning mouth. The girl glanced at the bullhorn as if it were deliberately picking on her, and he laughed again and choked.

Sharn looked at him with critical eyes, as if he were suddenly a stranger, then turned to leave. Gath drew in his grin, whispered, "Hey!"

The wolf looked back at him as if he were as useless as a dead leaf dancing on the wind, then vanished behind shrubbery.

Gath glared after the wolf, but the amusement was still at play behind his eyes. He ripped his spear out of the ground, glanced down their back trail, then headed for the eastern end of the rock keeping to the forest. Reaching the eastern end, he quietly moved up through one of the crevices to the top. There he found a shadowed recess in the sprawling boulders. From its shadows he peered through shrubs, saw the girl sitting quietly under the tree about thirty strides off.

She was dressed simply in a bone-colored tunic, a cloak of harvest yellow. Her walking stick rested on the ground beside her. The girl looked like she had neither the will nor the strength to stand. Then she stretched and sat up with renewed vigor, as pleasant and as promising as a budding daffodil.

Gath found a spot behind some shrubs and watched as the girl placed rocks around her fire, then removed a hen from her shoulder pouch and prepared and cooked it. She drank from her waterskin, dined on the hen, and cleverly made herself a cozy bed of needles between the exposed roots of the thorn tree. When the daylight died, she rebuilt her fire, covered herself with her cloak and a blanket, and lay down to sleep. When sleep did not come to her, he watched her scratch her nose, raise her eyes to the first star in the night sky, then count the needles in her pillow, smelling each one. He watched her get up, pace around the tree, haul the bullhorn back to its hollow, then try to sleep again. This time she drew her knife from its sheath and held it tight in her small fist.

Gath continued to watch.

When sleep came to her it was fitful. She twisted, rolled onto her back, arched her soft supple neck, exposed a length of thigh, twisted and rolled again until she was a ball of soft shadows exposing only a pink earlobe, warm, tender and inviting.

The moon was high in the night sky when Gath emerged from his hiding place. Making no sound, he moved through shadowed boulders, then across to squat beside the sleeping girl.

She was cradled between the thorn tree's roots. Her fire glowed with red hot embers at her feet. Greasy stains marked the circle of rocks surrounding the fire. Bits of fat and bones from the hen clung to them. Her leather fire pot, walking stick, belt and pouches, and waterskin rested on the ground beside her. Her knife had fallen half out of her sleeping hand. The fire's orange glow stroked her sleeping form, and cast deep shadows which hid her face.

Gath inspected her walking stick and knife. He opened her pouches. One carried several tiny corked vials of stone and clay, and smaller pouches holding pungent herbs. Another held an apple, raisins and the remains of the roasted hen wrapped in a cloth. The third held coins, and a small, wooden spinning whorl painted gold. This he knew. It was the sacred sign of the Cytherian maidens who wove cloth in the temple at Weaver. Gath set her belt and its pouches back beside the girl and started to rise.

The girl shifted restlessly, and her small red mouth with its plump lower lip emerged from the concealing shadow. She yawned slightly, and the vermilion flesh of her lips glistened wetly in the fire's glow. Then she sighed in musical surrender, the prisoner of a sleep fashioned by dreams.

Gath's eyes warmed within the deep shadows of his brow. The brutal glint was gone. The pupils were large and brilliant reflecting the fire. The eyes of a hard, savage man, but one who refused to forget his childhood, a time which had held a dream distant and supreme, like those clung to only by boys raised in cages.

The girl's lips massaged themselves, then a pink tongue emerged and tickled a corner until it glistened wetly. The lips closed and, to the accompaniment of another soft sigh, danced back into the darkness and were gone.

Gath unconsciously lifted his spear and scratched his knee with the haft. He took a breath, waited. When the two red dancers failed to reappear, he reached with the spear tip, caught the blanket with it and lifted it away from Robin Lakehair's face so the orange glow of the dying fire could stroke it with moving color.

As her beauty knifed into him, he did not turn away or move. Then he lowered the blanket and took a step backward out of the firelight.

He glanced about furtively, suddenly aware again of the night and its sounds: the crickets' song, the hoot of an owl, the scattering feet of nocturnal lizards. He looked back at the sleeping girl.

The soft rise and fall of her shadowed form had a subtle, compelling strength, a power which stretched time, proportion, size. It was as if her lips were a perch where a soldier could stand guard, her red-gold hair ropes to climb, the upper slope of her breasts rising and falling above her square-cut collar a place to lie down and sleep. As if she were an inviting landscape where gods rode on white chargers, and goddesses wearing chains and luxurious virtue were held captive in the towers of shadowy castles.

Gath forced himself to turn away, then retreated across the clearing and through the boulders and shrubs to his hidden recess. There he picked up his axe and waterskin, and slung them on his back. He started down the crevice, but paused hearing a slight, vague sound. He edged back to see.

The girl was sitting up, stretching languidly in the warm firelight. She stood and put twigs and branches on the fire so it glowed brightly. She watched it for a moment, then glanced around at the shadows and sighed with defeat.

Gath uncorked his waterskin, drank.

The girl settled back, pulled her covers over her and sank into the shadows.

He corked his waterskin and strode off into the shadows. A long moment passed during which the black night gave up no sound and betrayed no movement. Then he reappeared wearing a scowl no natural force could have removed. He moved down through the boulders to a shadow under a shelf of rock. There he sat, folded his arms across his knees and waited.

Fourteen

SAVAGE LULLABY

The intruder did not arrive until the moon had gone and The Shades was roofed by a black star-spattered sky. It was the grey she-wolf tortured by the chiefs.

The animal had limped from behind a boulder at the

north edge of the clearing and stood just within the glow of the fire sniffing the air. The smoke, riding a low breeze, swirled around the tree and across the clearing to her dilated nostrils.

Head low, the she-wolf dragged forward with a halting limp. Her left foreleg, broken and gashed, was drawn up under her.

Sharn, who had joined Gath earlier and now lay beside him, lifted slightly as curiosity glowed in his yellow eyes.

The she-wolf halted short of the tree and again sniffed the air, her ears moving from side to side. Her last meal appeared to be a long way down her back trail. Her coat was filthy, and clots of fur were gone from her bloody neck. A three-pronged, scabbed trail ran across her back.

The animal started around the tree, saw the sleeping figure, and circled away, then approached the flames from the side opposite the girl's feet. Settling low, she inched forward, flicking her foamy tongue at a greasy hot stone. The tip sizzled, snapped back inside her mouth. She tried this again with the same result, then a third time and came away with a hot fatty scrap of meat. She savaged the morsel hungrily as thick white foam showed on her gums, and pushed her muzzle forward for a second bite. Suddenly the sleeping girl shifted.

The she-wolf rose abruptly on three legs, snarled. Her mane bristled.

The girl's eyes popped open, and she rolled up on all fours, her hands grasping for her stick. She jerked it up with its pointed end aimed at the beast, and planted the butt end against the heel of her right foot. The whites of her eyes were large enough to cover a bed.

Gath watched, chin on folded arms. Sharn waited.

Snarling, the she-wolf backed away from the fire. Her efforts made the blood drip from her left foreleg, and a bright red puddle formed on the ground below it.

The girl winced. "Oh nooo!" Her eyes moved from the blood to the she-wolf's eyes, then over the battered, panting body. A maternal warmth showed in the girl's eyes. Her voice held the same warmth.

"You poor thing. Let me feed you . . . please." She squatted and a smile moved into her rose-tinted cheeks. "You might as well, you haven't the strength to hurt me, you know."

The animal drew back her lips, snarled.

The girl gently lowered her eyelids, drew the corners of her mouth into her cheeks. The she-wolf's snarl slackened, and she lowered the stick.

In the nearby shadows, Gath's head lifted off his arms.

Moving with a slow fluid motion, murmuring softly and rhythmically, almost chanting, the girl sat down and crossed her legs. From one of her pouches, she removed the breast of the roasted hen, tore off a chunk and held it up for the she-wolf to smell. Then, with maternal sternness, she said, "I'm only going to give you a little bite to start with. So you won't make yourself sick. Do you understand?"

The wolf's head dipped lower. Her ears laid back, but she did not move.

The girl leaned forward extending the meat, cooing, "Don't be afraid. It's all right now. We're getting to know each other." She gently wagged the meat at the animal.

The wounded animal snarled, edged back, and blood spouted from her foreleg.

The girl, keeping her arm extended, lowered her shoulder to the ground, rolled over on her back and let the meat drop. She withdrew her arm, then waited, lying perfectly still.

A long time passed. Eventually the animal glanced around and advanced slightly.

Gath rose in place silently raising his spear to strike. Sharn, with his eyes tight and narrow to contain their astonishment, moved silently around to the left side of Gath. From there things appeared no more normal than they had on the right side.

The she-wolf advanced to within two feet, looked suspiciously from the meat to the girl three times, then snapped up the meat.

"Not so fast," the girl whispered sternly. She tore off another piece. The animal looked at her hand from three sides, sniffed it, then snapped the meat off her palm, chewed and swallowed.

She fed the wolf the rest of the meat in this manner, and lay still as the she-wolf licked her hand clean. The animal sniffed the girl's arm and hair, then her ear and nose, and the girl returned these courtesies of the wild, sniffed the she-wolf's muzzle, touched the animal's nose with her own nose. The animal licked her eye then stepped back, whimpered slightly.

The girl sat up slowly, took more chicken from her pouch and fed the wolf from a sitting position, face-to-face. Intermittently she offered the animal water from her waterskin. Before long, the wolf was chewing and swallowing at a reasonable pace and she was petting it at will.

Gath had watched with the corner of one eye, as if it were unsafe, or unholy, to watch with both. Now he kept one eye averted as he and Sharn crept down to a dark shadow at the base of a boulder not seven strides from the thorn tree.

When the she-wolf finished feeding and lay docilely beside her, the girl drew her knife and held the animal's broken leg in her left hand. She trimmed the bloody fur away, doused the wounds with water, and gently licked the wounds until they reopened and bled cleanly. She then massaged the bones until they were loose and pliable within the body of the foreleg. As she did all this, she continued to murmur softly.

She tore lengths of cloth from the hem of her tunic, and broke two straight sticks off the tree. They were slightly longer than the broken portion of the leg. She removed a tiny jar from her shoulder pouch, and poured its pastelike contents over the open wounds. Then, with a sudden, precise jerk, she pulled on the foreleg, reset the bones. The she-wolf shrieked and started to bolt upright. The girl, petting her, held her down. She bound the medicated wounds with cloth, then positioned the sticks as splints and tied them to the foreleg. The animal tried to get up, but she gently pressed her down whispering, "Not yet."

For a long time she leaned over the wolf, kissing the animal repeatedly about her whiskered face and whispering into her ear.

Suddenly the animal bolted upright, and the girl sat back smiling with warm pleasure. The she-wolf tottered off, stopped, sensing something, then trotted haltingly off into the night.

The girl watched the animal until it was gone. Humming to herself, she put her things away and stirred the fire to life. She sat down, drawing her covers around her, then stared dreamily into the fire.

The distant bay of a wolf rode through the night's silence. It was strange and beautiful as it mixed with the wind's song in the trees. The girl lay down contentedly. A moment later the savage lullaby had rocked her to sleep.

In the concealment of the nearby rocks, Sharn stared with a profound intensity at the sleeping girl. Beside him, Gath uncorked his waterskin, took a long drink, pouring some over his flushed face, then whispered, "Sorcery."

Fifteen

A TOAST

The same star-spattered night sky which roofed The Shades also cast its faint light on a narrow trail through the cataracts miles to the east. There mounted soldiers moved north down the pass, an undulating blackness glittering metallically where starlight touched it.

A Kitzakk regiment. Filthy. Deadly. Nearing the end of a three-day march from Bahaara. It consisted of sixty-six men; two companies of light-horse Skull soldiers armed with crossbows and scimitars. Their faces were painted black to resemble skulls. They were raiders, not invaders, equipped to spread terror and take revenge.

Two commanders, mounted on heavy black stallions, led the regiment. Working soldiers. Metal clad. Cluttered with the totems of dead enemies. Wearing enough grime and sweat between them to fill a wine pitcher.

Two wagons followed the commanders. The first was lacquered black and had a cagelike carriage on which rode three hollow-cheeked, black-robed guards of the Temple of Dreams. The second was a supply wagon heaped with spare weapons, saddles, and food.

The first dim light of day tinted the night sky as the raiders reached the bend in the trail where their two scouts waited for them. Up ahead, still a half-day's march away, the regiment could see the gorge which formed the natural border between the cataracts and the forest basin beyond.

The commanders dismounted, strode to the edge of the

79

road and looked down at a length of the gorge where three natural bridges of earth and stone crossed it. The bridges were partially closed off by unfinished gates. Beyond the gates a village sprawled over a dirt hill, Weaver at Three Bridge Crossing.

The commanders' names were Trang and Chornbott. They were experienced raiders, champions of the Kitzakk Horde. Trang was short and thick, with a jaw big enough to eat table legs. He wore battered pieces of armor and a red helmet with heavy steel bars caging his face. An axe rode on his back; it was big enough to be his brother. Chornbott was a head-and-a-half taller, encased in a suit of polished steel chain mail, and arrogantly bareheaded. He carried a sheathed sword in his right hand; it was as tall as Trang.

The two men studied the village, then returned to the lacquered black wagon. Two temple guards opened its side door and the commanders bowed to the shadowed opening.

A small, rounded man daintily emerged from a shadowy heap of red and orange pillows within the cagelike carriage, descended three iron steps to the ground and stretched without removing his arms from his garments. He wore a black robe over an orchid tunic with an allover pattern of tiny black and yellow butterflies. A red skullcap with long, pendulous earflaps covered his round head. He had a narrow neck, soft-boiled eyes, the milky flesh of the albino and pink baby lips. As the two commanders waited with the confidence of tombstones, he bowed with a servility that could only be matched by a throw rug.

The commanders shifted with embarrassment and uncertainty. They were obviously unaccustomed to being treated with such formal courtesy by a man who was their superior, the second highest ranking Kitzakk in the Desert Territory.

The man they faced knew this and privately enjoyed their discomfort. This was Dang-Ling, a high priest of the Butterfly Goddess's Temple of Dreams and the secret servant of the Master of Darkness.

The high priest sauntered to the edge of the road and looked down at Weaver. When he spoke it was as if he were reading.

"The village is called Weaver. It holds approximately five hundred residents, among which are between one hundred-and-twenty and one hundred-and-forty able-bodied warriors. No more." He turned to the two commanders. "Your regiment will steal its nine most beautiful maidens from the temple and burn the village to the ground. You two will kill this annoying Barbarian who is so partial to black."

The commanders bowed low. When they looked up, Dang-Ling said, "Please forgive me, but I must ask you to remove your clothing." His tone was soft, considerate, nevertheless commanding.

The two champions shed their metal and undergarments, stood expectantly in front of the high priest. Their bodies were sun dark, mostly callouses, with large patches of white scar tissue grown over old dirty wounds.

He removed a red earthenware jar carved in the shape of a butterfly from his robes. He uncorked it, extended it to the two commanders. "Apply it liberally. It is a very old and potent formula whose magical powers are assured. It is made from his own living totems. You will not even have to look for this dark Barbarian. He will find you."

Trang and Chornbott dipped their fingers into the jar, came away with a grimy, pungent, green ointment, and eagerly applied it to their genitals. It went on easily. The fingernail clippings and pubic hairs which Cobra had stolen from Gath of Baal had been ground to a fine pulp along with his spittle and other ingredients. When they finished, the two large men whispered prayers to the Butterfly Goddess, and got dressed.

An amphora of temple wine called Bwong was then removed from the supply wagon and served by the temple guards. When the cups or helmets of the regiment were filled, all present raised their vessels, gave the required toast, then downed the Bwong in one gulp.

They drank to murder.

Sixteen

SPIDER'S WEB

The morning sun splashed over Calling Rock, flowed through its crevices and gullies, and spilled across the flat clearing at the crest to annoint Robin's sleeping, tousled head with a cool gold light. She was not alone. A yellow-eyed, ten-foot python dangled out of the thorn tree. It was awake. Its tongue flickered inches from her face. She stirred, brushed a hand sleepily across her eyes and blinked at the warm touch of sunshine. She rolled up on an elbow. The python spread its jaws with a rasping hiss that did not exactly say good morning, and, to let her know what kind of day it was going to be, displayed glistening rows of sharp teeth and two cold, black eyes set in a green scaled head. Robin screamed.

The python gathered to strike, and the leaf-shaped blade of a spear drove into its skull with a sharp crack, nailed it to the trunk of the tree.

The body of the huge reptile dropped out of the tree and coiled violently around the offending spear, collapsed when the spear was pulled out. Its tangled weight hit Robin's legs as she scrambled away and knocked her flat. She screamed again, kicking at the writhing, thrashing serpent, finally rolled free and sat up on her haunches still screaming.

A shadow moved over her body. She stopped, looked up, screamed again, and buried her face under arms and elbows.

A huge, dark Barbarian stood over her. The bloody, leaf-shaped spear dangled from his right hand. His face was flushed. His dark eyes gleamed intently under the threatening bulk of his forehead. His helmet, tied to his belt, bulged at his hip like an unnatural growth. His armor, glistening on his chest, rose and fell ominously. The movement made the black fur under the armor appear to be growing from his oak-brown flesh.

Robin peeked from under an elbow and saw an arm reach for her. Its hand looked big enough to send to school. She gasped and scrambled back.

He put a foot on the hem of her tunic and brought her to a sudden stop. Frantically, she hid behind her arms again as the hand advanced like a siege weapon. It hesitated, then parted her arms until it found her face. She watched its thumb hover in front of her mouth, a breath away from the trembling curve of her lower lip. Then it gently stroked the lip.

Paralyzed, she closed her eyes, felt the thumb work her lip, then opened her eyes to see the veins cording along a thick metal-clad arm, moving each nick and hair, and surging with the taut muscles of his shoulder and thick neck. Her lids fluttered, then her head tilted back, and she looked into his shadowed face. Dark stubble of beard. Bright hard white teeth. Eyes that hid under a shaggy brow. Grey animal eyes of the predator ruled by the laws of claw and fang, yet black wounds opening on to a haunted past, to the child long buried within. Eyes proud of their mysteries. Eyes that had hidden his feelings too well and long, but which could not hide from her.

A rush of empathy pulsed through her, bringing color to her cheeks. Her smile was not far behind.

He touched her curved cheek, then studied her smile so intently it seemed he thought it had a life of its own.

Boldly she asked, "Are . . . are you Gath of Baal?"

His dark brow lifted as if he had never heard his name before.

She tried again. "You are?"

His eyes moved to her eyes and quickly withdrew. He turned to the tree, kicked the shuddering python aside, picked up her things and handed them to her. She took her belt with its dangling pouches, slid her knife into its sheath. She tied her cloak and blanket into a bundle and hung it on the end of her walking stick. She did all this with her eyes on Gath and speaking rapidly, in short breaths.

"I . . . I'm sorry," she said. "I was wrong to scream. I should have thanked you . . . and I do thank you. You saved my life."

"Go," he said quietly. "You should not be here."

She nodded, pleaded, "But . . . if you are . . . Gath of Baal, I must talk to you."

He took hold of her elbow, guided her toward the trail at the north rim.

"Go! You do not belong here."

With a willful strength she yanked free and confronted him bravely. "I will not go! Not yet! I have a message."

"I have no use for messages," he said curtly and pushed her forward.

She staggered, then stood her ground. "It's important! Brown John sent me."

"Go!"

"But I can't." Tears choked her words. "Not until . . . oh, please listen."

Tears welled in her eyes; the corners of his mouth drew down hard. Gath's eyes lost all expression, and he started back toward the eastern rim leaving her behind. She stared in disbelief, watched him stride casually past a massive grey timber wolf that was staring at her as if she were a disobedient pup. The wolf barked. Robin gasped, and hollered at the man.

"Wait!"

Gath kept moving, vanished among the boulders.

Robin started after him, then at the wolf and sank with defeat. A large cat howled somewhere nearby. She looked around wildly, the color gone from her cheeks. Warily she started for the trail at the north rim. After five steps she was trotting, then running.

She tore through shrubs and boulders, reached a crevice filled with loose rubble, and dashed down. She did nicely for ten strides, then slipped on the loose earth, pitched forward, hit the ground and rolled and slid for thirty feet raising a cloud of dust. The decision to stop was made by a flat wall, a painful decision to which Robin replied with a thud and a groan. When she opened her eyes, she was bruised and bloody, smothered with dust, sweat and sunshine. The crevice now angled west, and she was looking directly into the blazing ball of white gold still low in the morning sky.

The light, streaming through billowing dust, blinded her. Shading her eyes with a hand she started forward, blinking, trying to see the ground. Suddenly a rubble of rocks came loose under her feet. She staggered forward trying to keep her balance. The loose ground was not of a mind to help her. It abruptly dropped away at a steep incline, and she went racing down, arms flailing, into the dusty golden light.

This time she came to a sudden standing halt, arms spread, and bounced, but snapped back. Her body was stuck flat against a wall of light. All except one leg. It dangled helplessly, like a noodle just before it is swallowed.

Dazed and astounded, she wrenched wildly at whatever held her, but could not get free. She pulled her head back, looked down, and a spasm of horror tore through her. Just below her chin was a hairy, thick rope, coated with a sticky wet substance which glistened in the golden sunlight. Her hands, arms, and body were glued to a huge spider web. It spread like a target to the sides of the crevice. Her right leg, from the knee down, hung loosely over the open center of the web.

She thrashed helplessly against the gooey threads. The effort only secured her more firmly to the web.

Her strength ebbing, Robin hung in place like the last bite on a plate. Tears welled up under her lashes, but she fought to see the source of a grating sound below her. At the base of the web, a circle of ground three feet across was lifting. She screamed. Her body shuddered, shaking tears loose from her eyes.

Staring down into widening darkness, she watched spellbound as hairy clawlike legs grasped the rim of the dark hole. The legs flexed, then lifted the dark umber body of an enormous spider out of the darkness. It was a Chupan, about forty pounds, the color of dirt and in bad need of a haircut. Its body was all belly. It was mostly mandible, except when the curved mandibles were open, as now. Then it was all bad intentions. A meat eater.

Robin flailed, and long strangled cries leapt past her trembling lips. Music to the Chupan's ears.

The spider watched Robin's right leg flail wildly at the open center of its web, then started for it, but reconsidered, as if the leg were too great a bother. Instead it moved sideways for the other leg. That sandaled foot was securely stuck to the web.

Robin wiggled furiously and managed to twist her head under her shoulder until she could see the hairy creature nearing her foot. She yanked frantically on her left leg and freed it slightly so that its sandled foot sank even closer to the advancing mandibles.

The Chupan lurched upward, snapped at Robin's trembling foot and came away with the sandal.

Her eyes sliding back, Robin sank, semiconscious.

The spider chewed on the sandal for a while, then its pea-sized brain seemed to decide there had been some kind of mistake, and it spit the sandal out in pieces. Seeing the pinkish underside of Robin's bare foot, it started up the web again.

When the spider was positioned to dine, with a choice of five perfect toes as appetizers, spreading jaws crashed over its pulpy body.

The jaws belonged to Sharn. He was still in midair when they snapped shut, cleaving the spider in two. He landed cleanly on all fours ten feet beyond the web, then calmly spit bits of its chitin and hairy pulp from his mouth as he watched the two oozing pieces of the Chupan roll past him and down the crevice. Calmly the wolf began to pick off the bits of web which had caught in his fur.

A short time later, when Robin's eyes flickered open, Gath's shadowed body blocked out the sun. He was cutting her free of the web with his dagger. She whimpered, looked into his dark face and found his slate-grey eyes wandering across the rise of her breast, the turn of her neck. His cheeks felt like flames against hers as they brushed past.

Leaning her head against his cheek, she moaned, "Gath!"

Ignoring this inadequate effort to restart their conversation, he continued to cut at the web. Suddenly she dropped and landed hard on her backside at his feet. She groaned and pushed herself up onto her hands, and looked at him. Did an amused glitter pass behind Gath's eyes? She was too dazed to be certain.

She caught her breath, then dragged herself to the side of the crevice and let her exhausted body sink back against it. Her mouth trembled. "I . . . I thought I was going to die."

Her dark feathery eyes grew wet. He squatted facing her. A cheering grin lifted the corner of his mouth, defying her to cry. She dropped her dusty head in her hands and began to sob.

The grin went away, and he stood abruptly. "You are not hurt."

She looked up past her hands, startled by his abrasive tone, and stammered, "But that . . . that thing almost killed me."

"In The Shades one is always almost dead."

She flinched, glanced at the wolf then back at him, and saw no opening in the armor of his eyes. Had they been watching the whole time? She indicated Sharn, said uncertainly, "You ordered him to . . . to save me."

"No. No one orders him to do anything."

She nodded and looked off at Sharn gratefully as she pulled at the sticky residue on her cheeks.

He picked up her walking stick and extended it to her. "You are too far from home."

She nodded. "I know, but I believed you would listen to me."

She passively accepted the stick, and he lifted her off the ground as if she weighed no more than a basket of peaches. She staggered slightly and caught herself against his arm. He did not pull it away. A smile leapt back into her cheeks and her eyes lifted to his, but the armor was still in place. She withdrew her smile.

"Go," he said quietly.

She nodded, removed her remaining sandle and tucked it in the bundle hanging from her walking stick. She sighed, then barefoot moved down the crevice towards Sharn. As she came alongside the wolf she stopped, kissed him on the head before he thought to protest, then continued on down until she was swallowed by the sunlight.

At the bottom of the crevice, she looked back up at the two predators standing in the dusty glow. Massive. Impressive. As one with the rocks and forest.

She turned and started through the forest. After traveling over a mile, she could still feel Gath's presence, and see him in her mind. Held there by the fingers of her imagination.

Seventeen

HOME

Robin Lakehair traveled Summer Trail heading east. She crossed through The Shades and the Valley of Miracles to Thieves Trail, which she took south until she reached Border Road at Lemontrail Crossing. There she paused and drank greedily from her waterskin. As she did, she gazed across the gorge and her heart sank.

Just beyond the remnant of the bridge, a heavy Kitzakk spear stood upright in the ground in plain view. Impaled on it was the fresh cadaver of a Wowell witch.

Robin's mouth gaped open. One hand covered her mouth, the other held her stomach as it convulsed. She grabbed up her things and scrambled back to her feet.

Hurrying east along Border Road, and passing only occasional travelers, she soon reached Amber Road. It was the main merchant road. It started far to the north in the Empire of Ice, stretched across the forests, then south through the cataracts and across the deserts to the jungles. There was some traffic to the north, but none coming from the cataracts to the south.

Robin's eyes darted about suspiciously as she dashed across Amber Road and hurried on. An hour later she rounded a bend and stopped to catch her breath. She had been traveling for four hours, but now, in the distance, she could see Three Bridge Crossing and her Cytherian home, Weaver. It waved in the midday sun like a giant, multicolored flag. She dropped to the grassy ground, leaned back against a rock and sighed with relief. She was no longer too far from home.

The village stood on a reddish hill cleared of trees except for occasional clumps. It was shielded on three sides by forest. The border gorge guarded the southern side. Sheep and herders cluttered the wide clearing which Robin knew surrounded the village. Past it rose a palisade wall with a gate at the northern corner. The wall stopped just before reaching the southern end of Weaver. There the village fell apart and ended in rubble just short of the gorge spanned by the three bridges where workers were building gates. The village's three main interior streets crossed over the bridges of Three Bridge Crossing, then joined together and moved south up into Weaver Pass.

Weaver itself rose above the palisade in irregular tiers. Mud and wood houses crowded the lower tiers. They were well-made structures with outside shutters on the windows and the stone chimneys rising from flat roofs exhaled white smoke. Clean-clothed and freshly scrubbed residents were active here sorting wool, cleaning and washing it, and combing and carding it into fluffy readiness for spinning.

On the upper tiers were rows of steaming wooden vats of dye the size of small houses. Workers, male and female, stirred the fabrics in the vats with long, heavy, wooden paddles. Golds, yellows and mustards made from safflower and fustic stained their naked bodies and loinclothes, as did reds, rusts and oranges made from madder, and the roots of Teima, Arrashad and Fantell berries which had been harvested and dried in spring. The Cytherians dyed the huge squares of finished cloth rather than the spools of thread. Consequently, there was considerable spillage and the heights of the village, as well as many of the residents, tended to change colors with the seasons. Even the supervising priests in their formal tunics of spun gold and silver sported red and yellow stains.

Above the steaming vats was a level space, circled by unpainted wooden buildings, and a wooden temple. Weaver Court. In its sunny yard the children of Weaver were taught the village trade by the elders. Within the temple the virgin maidens of Weaver spun cloth to the music of their own voices.

Weaver Court was surrounded on three sides by sheer bluffs called the Heights. They rose twenty feet above the roofs of the temple and formed a large, irregular spread of flat ground fed by many footpaths. Here the wet dyed cloth was spread to dry on poles. The resulting effect was a single multicolored patchwork flag of yellows, oranges and reds, the gigantic banner of a fairy-tale village.

Robin picked herself up and half-skipped toward the village. Nearing it she drank in the familiar scents of the hot, moist steaming dyes that mixed with the pungent odors of lye, lime and the fresh urine used in the washing. Reaching the clearing she heard footsteps behind her and turned around to see Gath coming down the road. The wolf waited behind at the edge of the forest. Neither looked at her.

Gath's eyes were fixed on the frantic activity at the bridges. Groups of men, half-hidden by dust, were noisily working on the gates with hammers, nails, saws and curses. When he neared Robin, he looked up at Weaver Pass and tilted his head slightly, listening to something she could not hear.

"What are you doing here?" she asked.

He looked at her as if he had not realized she was there, and said, "Nothing." He glanced at the village. "Is this your home?"

"Yes," she replied proudly.

He looked at her warily and said accusingly, "You are a sorceress. You brought me here?"

"What?" she exclaimed. "Me? A sorceress!" She almost giggled. But, seeing he was deadly serious, she stopped herself and spoke evenly. "I didn't bring you, honestly. I'm not magic, not at all! I only weave cloth."

He scratched his shin with the shaft of his spear, then

growled, "Tell me your name."

She blushed, averted her head slightly and watched his eyes with the corners of her own. "Robin . . . Robin Lakehair."

She waited, but no other question came. With artless sincerity, she said, "I want to thank you again. I owe you my life, and I won't forget it. If there's anything I . . ."

"We are finished now," he said abruptly.

She hesitated and her lips curved up slightly. "Then why did you follow me?"

He said, "You healed the she-wolf," as if it explained everything.

She nodded solemnly, then tried again to communicate. "Can . . . would you let me explain now? I'll only take a . . ."

He shook his head.

She dropped her eyes, turned without speaking and headed directly across the clearing toward the Forest Gate. But her feet betrayed her, and dragged. She felt, for the first time in her life, as if she were doing something absolutely and terribly wrong. But there was no explanation for it.

At that moment Dirken and Bone emerged from Border Road behind Gath. They were wheezing and grumbling. Robin, then Gath, turned and saw them, and they, humiliated, edged back out of sight into the forest.

Robin hesitated thoughtfully, then turned back toward the gate and wandered directionless through women herding goats and spinning wool not seeing their welcoming smiles. She passed through a crowd of boys battling with stick swords, reached the gate and suddenly stopped, looked off at the cataracts.

A distant thundering was coming out of the massive shelves of grey rock. It grew louder by the heartbeat.

Spellbound, Robin looked back across the clearing at Gath.

He stood facing the cataracts, head lowered. He unbuckled his helmet from his belt, lifted it above his head and lowered it into place, waited. A predator scenting blood.

Robin shuddered, looked back at the cataracts.

Dust billowed up out of the pass, and mounted Kitzakk raiders erupted from its mouth, plunged toward the three bridges screeching.

An alarm gong clanged inside the village. The women in the clearing screamed as they drove the children and animals toward the forest. In the village women cried out and raced to find their children, scurrying through men who scrambled for their weapons.

Robin, shuddering, looked back at Gath as he slipped his axe off his back, then turned sharply, hearing the sharp cries of children coming from Weaver Court. She plunged into the flow of bodies spilling out the gate, fought her way through them and ran into the village.

Eighteen

PLUNDER

Gath started after Robin, then stopped short and turned toward the charging raiders, slowly, like a nail being bent by a crowbar.

Two metal-clad commanders led the screaming, skull-faced raiders. The pair carried huge weapons that glittered, and they themselves radiated streaking spears of white light from an eerie glow at their groins.

Gath blinked. His breathing became deep, racking and noisy. A vast heat filled his world. Light obliterated sound. Nothing moved for him except the two illuminated, metallic champions. They seemed to plunge slowly as if galloping through a sky of blood. He started for the raiders in a slow steady march, his feet plodding like those of a condemned man. The piercing screech of women cut through his enchanted world, brought him back to the real world of dirt, panic and the smell of fear.

He looked back at the Forest Gate. Animals, men, women and children were spewing out, heading for the safety of the trees in wagons and on foot. Gath's face became hard and expressionless behind the mask of his helmet, then he again turned back to the raiders, as if held in the grip of an invisible demon.

The Kitzakks had split up into two groups and were plunging across the two closest bridges. The structures shuddered and shook under the pounding hooves dislodging heavy chunks of their earthen bodies into the gorge.

Cytherian defenders, spears in hand and snarling, met the charge at the bridges. Neither their weapons nor attitudes were sufficient. All but two panicked and ran before the steel-shod avalanche reached them. The two remaining took crossbow bolts in their foreheads and dropped in place. Their fleeing comrades died soon after, catching flying steel bolts with their backs and necks.

Hefting his spear and axe, Gath forced himself to turn away and march to the Forest Gate, pushing through the thin remnant of fleeing bodies. Inside, panic had sucked the life out of the village. He could hear sounds of clanging steel and cursing at the opposite end of the village where Cytherian warriors were fighting the raiders. Ignoring the inviting noise, he passed a wagonload of unshaven, leather-clad mercenaries who apparently considered fighting Kitzakks not part of their contract to protect Weaver. He continued through deserted wagons jammed at a cross-roads, passed a man holding his dislocated jaw with both hands, and saw another with straw held against the bleeding stump of his wrist. The incessant clanging of the alarm stopped abruptly. He hesitated, listened, then strode on passing open windows and open doors. From the shadows beyond them came the silence of empty rooms, empty beds and empty chairs.

He climbed a zigzagging deserted street at the north side of the village until he was two tiers below the Heights. There he went up a staircase siding a building. It led to a flat roof where a ladder rose to a higher roof. From there he could see the battle unfolding at the south end of the village.

Cytherian warriors, in scattered, unorganized groups, were meeting the Kitzakks' charge amid the rubble and streets. Their long spears, twice their height, splintered uselessly against the raiders' steel. The Kitzakks closed with them, trampled them firing crossbows at point-blank range with brutal accuracy. Steel bolts impaled staring eyes, speared open mouths. Farther off, the main body of Cytherians, some forty strong, were gathering at Weaver Court to defend the temple and its sacred maidens.

The Kitzakks joined forces in the Market Square, dismounted and split up. A small detachment ranged through the now almost empty lower tiers of the village, mopping up stragglers. A few remained in the Market Square guarding their horses. The main body, led by the two commanders, charged up the twisting street connecting Market Square to Weaver Court. Huge dye vats stood like massive sentinels along the street's high dirt walls. At the top of the street the Cytherian defenders met the raiders with swords and daggers, and demon war drank deep of blood.

All Gath could see was the back sides of the wooden buildings surrounding the court. From beyond them came the sounds of hysterical young girls and the clang of steel on iron. Gath leaped down to the lower roof, then into the empty street below. Up through twisting alleys he charged to the Heights.

He wound his way through ranks of drying yellow, gold and orange cloth, heading towards the bedlam of sound. Stepping out from behind a yellow cloth, Gath came across

a Skull soldier who failed to notice his arrival. The soldier
was preoccupied. He had a half-naked Cytherian maiden
pinned under his kneeling body. Handfuls of her blonde
hair were clenched in his sweating fists, and protruded
between his fingers. Her big eyes were muddy pools
bubbling with mindless terror as she stared past the
soldier's metal-clad shoulder. Her expression told the
soldier he had company, and he turned to see who it was.

Being a civilized man, the soldier had removed his
helmet in order to more fully enjoy his pleasure, but he had
not bothered to remove his dagger from between his
clenched teeth. It was a poor place to keep a dagger.

Gath kicked the soldier flush on the mouth. He flew off
the woman in one grunting piece, landed with a metallic
crunch, and rolled five feet clawing down orange bolts of
cloth. When he stopped, his head was turned far enough
around to look down at his buttocks. Three inches of
dagger blade protruded from his left cheek.

Gath stepped over the girl, moved through the sheets of
cloth, and stopped in the concealing shadows near the edge
of the sheer bluff. Below him was Weaver Court.

The battle was over.

Brutal eruptions of lust, murder, torture and pillage were
breaking out spasmodically about the white marble courtyard. The raiders were taking the payments due victors,
rewards best collected when the blood was still hot with the
kill and the mad terror of death was still fresh on the flesh.

Upended, spread-eagled Cytherian women were being
raped both in the shadows and in the sunshine. Nails raked
naked backs. Hands groped. Spines were bent over stairs
and barrels. Mouths were gorging themselves on wine,
cheese, fresh fruit and raw meat. Intransigent prisoners
were being kicked to death slowly, while the reasonable
were being drowned just as slowly in the well. The dead
and dying, sprawled among the living, added to the hellish
celebration by spewing fountains of blood and emptying
their bowels into the slippery, stumbling chaos. The stench

perfumed the rioting passions, and the large wooden temple provided appropriate music. There the screaming was a chorus.

Gath's stomach bubbled and churned. His muscles throbbed, eager to throw his body into the Kitzakk hell. But he remained motionless.

A group of Skull soldiers burst out of the broken doors of the temple herding bruised and bloody young girls, many with their tunics torn away, clutching the shreds to their naked bodies.

Gath leaned forward, eyes steady and patient.

Robin was at the center of the group, framed by five of the smallest girls, young things from nine to thirteen. They clung to her tunic and arms, sobbing and hiding their faces against her. Robin held them close covering their eyes. Her legs wobbled, but the pressing weight of the girls kept her upright.

The soldiers prodded the girls across the yard toward a lacquered black wagon parked facing the main access street. When the girls reached the wagon, a small, fat priest emerged and greeted them with an unctious, openmouthed smile. He probed their breasts, teeth, buttocks and flat stomachs with shameless fingers, mindless of their cringing and sobbing. Reaching Robin, he had the young girls driven away from her, and clapped his fat hands in relish.

Robin reeled back, as if confronted by a serpent. Two temple guards promptly seized her arms and held her in place. The priest took hold of her tunic, ripped it open exposing her breasts, then looked at them as if they were pretty peaches. With a lewd laugh, he turned to the guards and spoke to them, his voice lost amid the constant screaming.

Robin, struggling and sobbing, was forced into the wagon, and the priest proceeded through the whimpering, shuddering girls making additional selections.

Gath watched all this without showing any sign or taking action, then scanned the activity in the court, and again saw the two metal-clad commanders.

They sat on the steps of the temple consuming cheese and wine, aloof to the bedlam around them. Every so often one lifted his head, looked off at a shadow or alley as if he were expecting someone. Sitting beside their weapons, they looked like a party of four.

Gath's world again filled with blood and light, and became devoid of sound and reality. But he shook the enchantment off and looked back at the lacquered wagon.

Robin sat in the front left corner. Her small fists trembled as they clung to the bars. Her head was down, and red-gold hair trembled in tangles over her face.

Past the wagon was the narrow street by which the vehicle must depart. High dirt walls cast deep shade on the street. The shade was filtered with steam which drifted down from huge dye vats positioned along the top of the walls.

Gath hesitated thoughtfully and stepped back into the concealing red cloth. He dodged through the bolts of cloth at a steady, quiet trot, circled around the bluff above the court, and emerged from the opposite side. In front of him were two of the massive steaming vats that lined the narrow road. They were wooden with iron bottoms heated by fire pits. Gath moved between them to the edge of the dirt wall. The narrow street below was empty. A racket of unholy pleasure and misery came from the upper end of the street, then the tramp of horses' hooves moving slowly and the creak of wagon wheels joined the racket. He waited and a team of horses emerged around the sharp turn pulling the black lacquered wagon.

Gath settled in place. His armor heaved and glistened as his chest swelled with his racing breath. The thrill of battle slashed through his nerves and muscles. The time to abandon patience was at hand. He hefted his spear over his head, arm cocked and biceps throbbing.

The fat priest sat beside the driver of the wagon. The temple guards rode on seats built at the sides of the wagon.

When the wagon cleared the turn, the driver rose to whip the team of horses and a leaf-shaped spear blossomed on his chest, slammed him back into his seat. The whip and reins spilled from his hands, and he pitched forward, fell among the traces.

The priest's soft-boiled eyes bulged and rolled. His head bobbled helplessly on his feeble neck as the wagon jerked to a sudden stop, then he whimpered, something he did superbly, and with reason. Gath was standing beside the lead horse, holding its bridle. The priest wheezed low in his throat, grabbed the reins and flicked them frantically, squealing at the horses.

The lead horse started to bolt, and Gath hit the animal flush on the jaw with his fist. It fell sideways, driving the horse beside it into the dirt wall. The rest of the team panicked, rearing and bucking forward, each in a slightly different direction. The wagon lurched and crashed from side to side crushing itself and the screaming temple guards against the narrow walls.

The priest struggled back over the roof, falling and crawling most of the way, then dropped off the end and dragged himself back up the street toward Weaver Court.

Gath, ignoring the priest, moved for the jolting wagon where the sounds of screaming captive girls and splintering wood mixed with the crackle of breaking bones. Nearing the wagon, a horse butted Gath against a wall. His head hit the dirt and the iron bars of his helmet sprang loose. The steel bowl flew off, and the mask fell to his shoulder. He tore off the mask, bullied the horses to a stop, and hauled himself up onto the driver's box. From there he climbed to the roof and, working with his axe, made a hole in its front left corner.

He had figured accurately. Robin was looking up through the hole with big wonderous eyes and splinters on her face.

Gath reached into the hole and pulled her out as if she weighed no more than a leather belt. Carrying her in his arms, he jumped from the wagon roof to the top of the dirt wall, and they vanished between the vats.

The lead horse, recovering from Gath's blow, got back onto its feet and plunged mindlessly forward. The other horses followed, and the wagon full of screaming girls plunged down the street as a crowd of Skull soldiers came charging around the sharp turn and raced after it.

As the last soldier jumped over the fallen body of the driver, a vat fell away from the dirt wall above him and spilled a steaming yellow bulk of water the size of an elephant into midair. The water caught the soldier in the back, drove him facedown into the ground, scalding his arms and legs to the bone. Then it sluiced forward leaving his steaming body behind with raw exposed bones and pulpy muscles dyed a bright yellow.

Gath, who had pushed the vat over, stood heaving in place on the wall above the street. Robin trembled behind him. He laughed once, a dry rasp, and moved to the next vat. Flexing and straining, he pushed it over into the vat beside it. Both broke apart, then lurched into the third and fourth vats, and all emptied their contents into the street. Robin shuddered in his shadow, her eyes as terrified of her demon rescuer as of the Kitzakks.

A vivid-colored flood slewed down between the high dirt walls taking away parts of it, then caught up with the charging soldiers. Most of them ran faster. Several foolishly slowed and turned to see what was happening, and the gaudy fluid splattered over their startled faces, then hit them with its entire weight and carried their scalded, screaming bodies down the street.

The steaming liquid traveled the length of the street gathering mud, and spilled into Market Square depositing scalded and blistered bodies in all directions. Then it slewed sideways, washed down alleys and over the southern side of Weaver putting out the fires which the Kitzakks had started there. It was now a dull bloody brown.

Gath watched all this with pleasure, then took Robin by

the wrist and pulled her into the rows of hanging cloth. Reaching the Heights, they looked over the village. The black wagon had crashed into a mud wall at the edge of Market Square and turned over. Three girls, who had crawled out the hole in the roof, were limping into shadowed alleys. Five were still pinned inside.

At the south end of the village, Cytherian warriors, who had been hiding in the village, now came forward and began to butcher the blinded, scalded, brightly stained Skull soldiers.

The two commanders, the priest, and a group of Skull soldiers were racing down a footpath. Reaching Market Square, the two commanders helped the priest onto the supply wagon, and the driver took off toward Weaver Pass with five mounted escorts. The commanders then led their men toward the sounds of battle at the southern side of the village. By the time they reached the area, the Cytherians had vanished and the scalded, stained soldiers were all dead.

Gath growled with satisfaction, then dragged Robin back through the ranks of colored cloth to the north edge of the Heights, and they looked down at the village and forest beyond. The smell of blood and steam hung heavily over Weaver. Below, to their left, beyond tiers crowded with alleys and buildings, they saw an open yard at ground level. At the far side of the yard footpaths angled through low buildings to the tall Forest Gate. Gath pulled Robin down off the Heights, then into the tangled alleys heading toward the open yard.

Nineteen

FIGHT AT
WAGON YARD

At the intersection of two alleys, Gath and Robin stopped.
The alleys appeared deserted. One descended through
shadows to ground level, then twisted toward the open
yard. The other came from the direction of Market Square.
Through it they could see dust swirling above the southern
side of Weaver where it met the bridges.

He led her quickly across the open intersection and down
through the shadowed alley to the edge of the open yard.
There they stopped again, still concealed in the shadows.

The irregular oval of the open area was filled with
sunshine and the familiar odors of warm dirt and straw.
Stables and stalls surrounded the yard. At the opposite side
of the yard two footpaths angled through the low buildings
toward the high Forest Gate beyond. The stalls and stables
were empty of everything but shadows. The dusty ground
was cluttered with straw, stacks of buckets and several
unharnessed wagons.

Gath started forward, but paused at the sound of iron
tinkling against a metal bucket somewhere. It made Robin
shudder, but to him it was a strangely pleasing sound, as if
belonging to another time and world, like tiny silver bells
tied to a child's ankles so he cannot get lost.

Gath pushed Robin back up the alley a stride, and held
her against the wall listening. The sound of the bells was
replaced by the distant snorting and stomping of the
retreating Kitzakk soldiers and the faint unintelligible
chatter of their voices.

Gath's body heat became so intense it made Robin's cheeks flush, and she cringed. When he turned to her, she gulped. His eyes held no more warmth than a tomb. His cheeks were dark pulsing hollows. Black vertical gouges cut into them, drawing the corners of his lips down low.

He found a side door nearby. He opened it quietly, peered inside, and pulled her in closing the door behind them.

They stood in a small, dirt-floored room with saddles, tack and blankets hanging from the log walls. Crossing it, they moved through a doorway into an empty stable. Its roof was low, forming a hayloft above. Shadows filled it. The front doors were open, letting light from the sun-filled yard partway in. Staying in the shadows, Gath crossed to a ladder lying on the ground below an opening into the loft. He drew Robin close, pointed up at the loft. Avoiding his eyes, she nodded docilely. He leaned his axe against the wall, raised her over his head, gave her a slight toss, and she landed on the hay in the loft. He picked up the ladder, handed it up to her, and she looked down at him.

An unnatural battle hunger glittered in his eyes, and his breathing was like a starved panther cat's. But, as she took the ladder, his hand embraced hers with a gentle but firm reassurance.

He picked up his axe, crossed the stable and the small tack room, and moved back into the alley. There he looked out into the sun-filled wagon yard and waited.

What came was the strange pleasant tinkle of metal brushed by the wind. This time Gath knew where the faint, mysterious music originated. From somewhere in the yard where there was nothing but dust and sunshine.

The first thing that informed Gath that there was indeed someone else in the area was the scent of a hardy male body odor. His nostrils wrinkled at the scent, and his eyes widened with another mystery. He recognized the smell. It was his own.

The hair on his neck stiffened. Then the world of silence, blinding light and bloody sky again consumed him. It filled the open yard. He snarled silently, feeling his blood gorge through his arms and thighs.

He shortened his grip on his axe, and marched deliberately out into the sunshine to the heart of the magic world, stopped, and the real world returned. The yard was empty. But he was on killing ground. He knew it. Every tissue in his body wanted it.

He glanced about the emptiness, body cocked and eyes wary, and peered into the shade of a covered stall. Two vague silhouettes of figures were crouched just beyond a shaft of sunshine spilling through a crack in the roof. Slowly they stood, to become two massive figures which turned toward Gath, as if he had called out to them. The spill of sunshine caught their shoulders, made one burn bright red while the other glittered as if made of coin silver. The rest was shadows.

They picked large objects off the ground, then moved out of the stall into the sunshine. They carried axe and sword. The two commanders.

One was short and thick, big jawed, and wore a red helmet with a cagelike mask of steel bars. The other was close to two hundred and fifty pounds of trouble, not counting his full-length suit of chain mail which undoubtably outweighed most men.

The two commanders looked at Gath almost with pleasure, as if he had come to polish their metal. But there was no amusement in their weapons, or the steel studs which decorated their knuckles. As if they had a single mind, each put a foot on the top rail of the stall, pushed it over slowly and stepped into the yard.

Gath moved for them, and they separated. Gath kept moving, got between them, and charged the steel suit. He blocked the giant's sword with his axe and jabbed him with the butt end driving him back. Using his momentum, Gath pivoted and swung an arching blow at the red helmet. But Red Helmet's axe deflected Gath's blow, momentarily bringing him to a stop. Gath bolted sideways, but not before the tip of Steel Suit's sword had buried itself in the meat of his left shoulder.

Gath reeled with pain, then suddenly stepped in again bringing his axe around in a backhand blow aimed at Red Helmet. The blade landed with a terrific clang flush on the steel cage, drove the owner fifteen feet back, and left Gath's axe vibrating in his hands. The center of its cutting edge was caved in leaving a wide half-moon-shaped gap.

Gath snarled and backed up to a wall. Blood ran down the back of his arm, and dripped off his wrist in measured beats.

Red Helmet had recovered, was moving for him. The sunshine made a slight new scratch across the steel bars of his cagelike mask glitter.

Steel Suit was also advancing with a heavy plotted pace, holding his sword in two hands in front of him. He tilted it so that the blade caught the overhead sunshine and reflected it.

The bright bar of light caught Gath in the eyes, blinded him briefly. When his vision returned, both champions were bearing down on him, weapons raised over their heads. He stepped in under the blow of the sword, deflected Red Helmet's axe with his own and again drove Steel Suit back with the butt end. Butting Red Helmet in the chest with his head, he spun and drove a shoulder into the wooden wall of a stable, splintering it, and fell through the hole into the darkness beyond.

The two commanders shared an annoyed glance and moved for the hole, but stopped short as Gath emerged from the adjacent stable. His left arm now carried an old circular wooden shield belted with iron bars. The Kitzakks grinned, then moved for him hard, weapons working.

Gath caught their blows on his shield with his arm slightly relaxed. This softened and deflected them, but the blades bit chunks out of the wood while their impact drove him backwards, allowing no counterblow.

Without breaking stride, they rained blows on him from

right and left, gave him no time to do anything but block, duck, and bleed. Finally Gath's back slammed into a wooden stable wall. He worked there awhile, blocking blows as the wall rubbed his shoulder blades and elbows raw, stitched his flesh with splinters.

Methodically Red Helmet trimmed Gath's shield down until half the wood was gone and the iron belts looked like chewed meat. Steel Suit, with a malignant grin, let his mammoth sword play with Gath's axe head. His blows mangled the blade and sent reverberations up the shaft, through the Barbarian's grip and into his arm and shoulder. Numbness spread back down his arm and into Gath's grip. Sensing this, Steel Suit discarded his grin and struck Gath's axe where the head joined the handle, ripping it out of the Barbarian's numbed grip.

The huge Kitzakk chuckled huskily, shifted his weight and brought his sword blade down at Gath's unguarded right side. Gath let it come, then squatted in place. Steel Suit's sword sliced into the wooden wall behind him and came to a sudden shattering stop inches from the Barbarian's hair.

Gath charged forward, drove his head into the huge man's gut and knocked him to the ground. He kept driving, stepped on the Kitzakk's thigh and chest, then tripped and fell into the middle of the yard.

Red Helmet leapt over his fallen comrade and raised his axe, but Gath rolled onto his back, threw dirt in his face. The Kitzakk was not blinded long. Seeing the metal of the Barbarian's shield through the dust, he brought his axe down on it. The blade sank into the shield, split it, then buried itself deep in whatever was under it. Red Helmet almost laughed but snarled angrily instead as his vision cleared. His axe was buried to the haft in dirt.

Gath was now five strides off, backing away in a low crouch, eyes moving from one commander to the other. His dagger was in his hand.

While Red Helmet tried to remove the remnant of Gath's

shield from his axe, Steel Suit ripped his sword free, then backed Gath up to a shallow door. There the huge glittering man laughed out loud and began to play more seriously with his victim. He hammered the dagger from Gath's hand, kicked him in the chest spinning him around. Then, deliberately using the flat of his blade, he struck him across the back driving him face first into the door and laughed again.

Gath, stunned, hung against the door supporting himself on the latch handle. The impact of the huge Kitzakk's blow had popped the leather thongs holding his armor in place. It dripped off him like old flesh and fell to the ground. Steel Suit spit a rope of blood, and, without a trace of play in his small eyes, raised his sword over his head with both hands.

His sword blade glittered in the sunlight, slashed down. At the last moment Gath reeled backward, opening the door and bringing it with him. The sword cut into the top of the wooden door and did not stop until it had cleaved it in two.

Gath, finding half of a door in his hand, swung it at the mass of glittering steel. The door caught the Kitzakk flush from the base of his skull to the base of his spine and drove him back into the yard, mouth spread wide, gasping for breath. It did not come. Steel Suit dropped his sword and grabbed for his throat. This also did not help. He hit the ground hard, shuddering and heaving.

Gath, gasping and crusted with dust, splinters and blood, gathered up the Kitzakk's sword in two hands and turned on Red Helmet as the short, thick Kitzakk commander finally ripped his axe free of the remnant of Gath's shield.

Gath and Red Helmet, two-handing their weapons, moved for each other. Their weapons met with a resounding clang, then kept on meeting until they were more than well acquainted. Then the Kitzakk got in low and scooped out a cup of flesh from Gath's side. Gath replied by bringing the sword around in an arc and caught the Kitzakk flush on the mask of his helmet. The helmet did not give, but the man inside did. A little. He dropped his axe and staggered back in a low crouch fighting for balance. He caught it about fifteen feet off, then started back for the axe he had left behind.

Gath's eyes were thin slices of disbelief. The blow should not only have pulped the Kitzakk's helmet, but his head. Instead, it had only exhausted Gath. He staggered over the fallen axe blocking the Kitzakk's path. Red Helmet kept coming. His march was unsteady but relentless. He kept his head low. When Gath swung his sword, the Kitzakk deliberately fed the blade his red helmet. The blow drove the Kitzakk back five feet, but he kept his feet and started forward again. Gath growled low in his throat and struck again. In this manner he drove the Kitzakk around the yard, hammering the defiant red helmet. Ropes of blood erupted from the cagelike mask with each blow. Spider trails leaked from the neck rim, trailed down the commander's armor, turning its dull red color bright.

When it appeared that the Kitzakk carried more of his blood outside his flesh than inside, Gath sagged back gasping and dripping sweat. Mindlessly, Red Helmet charged without a weapon. Gath let him come, then lifted the sword, and the Kitzakk ran himself onto the point of the blade. The blade cut through his gut, drove in hard, jammed itself into the corner of the pelvic bone.

Glaring at Gath from behind the caged mask of his helmet, the Kitzakk staggered back. His weight ripped the sword out of Gath's hands, and he went over on his back with the sword sticking upright like a steel flag. Blood puddled under him. Struggling, Red Helmet unlaced his helmet, pushed it aside, then attempted to rise but only managed to twitch.

Gath squatted and leaned back against the wall gasping. He looked about for something to staunch his wounds, and through half-closed eyes saw Steel Suit rise off the ground slowly and uncertainly, as if he had never done it before. Gath was stunned. So was the Kitzakk; one eye was filled with blood, the other blinked. When it found Gath, the huge man cursed fouly and staggered toward him.

Gath drew a deep breath, erupted off the ground, caught the giant around the gut and drove him back into the side of a parked wagon. The side board splintered and they fell half onto the bed, grappling without much effect. Then the Kitzakk's hands found Gath's neck, began to throttle him. In desperation, Gath buried his fingers in the first things that came to hand, Steel Suit's wrist and armpit. But they were of little help. Gath could not breathe. His mind grew dark, then again swam with the blood red world of howling death, and a terrorized surge of strength went through him. He spun in place swinging the huge Kitzakk around in the air, then, with an animal roar, threw him across the yard. Steel Suit hit the ground with a clang, rolled over, and came to a limp stop.

A moment passed before Gath realized he had not let go of Steel Suit's left arm. It dangled from his right hand by the wrist. Gath lifted it uncertainly, then discarded it like an apple core.

Twenty
ROLL CALL

The supply wagon of the Kitzakk regiment was parked several miles up Weaver Pass on a knoll overlooking the village. Five chained maidens from Weaver were tied to the rear end of the open bed. Behind the wagon the surviving

Skull soldiers sat their horses in a line as a sergeant called the roll.

Dang-Ling sat among the spare weapons, blankets and saddles at the front of the wagon bed. He had recovered from his terror and was cooly assessing his situation. He was certain his warlord, Klang, would be humiliated by the defeat, and he would have to appear to also be shamed even though he felt no shame. The scouts he had sent back into the village had verified that the Barbarian had met Trang and Chornbott in combat, and that the commanders had been killed. But the champions, even though unable to conquer him, had undoubtedly taught the Barbarian the lessons of false pride and mortality. Consequently Dang-Ling was certain he had served the Master of Darkness well. Now, if the Barbarian survived his wounds and was the man the Queen of Serpents claimed he was, he would be ready, even hungry for the extraordinary opportunity she would offer him.

Dang-Ling smiled to himself, then turned to hear the sergeant's report. There were twenty-seven present. Thirty-nine Skull soldiers, three temple guards, and two champions remained in Weaver. All dead or not, it mattered little to the priest.

Dang-Ling conducted a prayer for the deceased, then ordered the sergeant to proceed quickly up the pass and settled down for a nap.

Twenty-one

GOOD-BYE

Robin, who had watched the fight through a knothole and passed out at the sight of Gath ripping out the Kitzakk's arm, now revived to find her face buried in tangled straw. Remembering gradually what had happened, she pushed herself up and peered out the knothole. A scatter of people had gathered in the yard. Villagers. She hesitated thoughtfully, and clutched fearfully at her throat. Hurriedly, she pushed the ladder down through the hole, climbed down and rushed out of the stable.

Several Cytherian warriors, and a scatter of women who had reentered the village, stood at the edges of the yard watching the mighty victor stagger toward a footpath. His stagger was impressive, but his entrance into the path was not. He missed the opening by a foot, hit the corner of the wall with a shoulder and spun around, taking down barrels, awnings and a stack of buckets before hitting the ground.

Robin raced to him. When she reached him, he was trying to get off the ground without much success. He was crouched face down, shaking, blinking with one eye. The other was swollen closed. Tears swam in Robin's eyes as she kneeled beside him. She offered him her hand. He took it, obviously without knowing whose it was or even if it was a hand. His nerveless fingers spent a long time before they found a grip.

Using her hand for support, he tried to stand and this time made it to his knees. This put him face-to-face with

Robin, and he hesitated, recognizing her. She murmured, "We must stop the bleeding!"

He was taken back for a moment, as if the resonant truth in her words was too much to bear, then said weakly, "We are finished."

He pushed her away, staggered through the alley brushing its sides, and reached the clearing beyond. He shuffled through Forest Gate and started for the forest. He fell to his knees twice before vanishing within its greenery.

Robin slumped in defeat against the wall in Wagon Yard and several women moved to comfort her. Before they reached her, she jumped up and raced into a side street.

When she reached the small wooden building on the first tier where she had a room, she luckily found her horse and flatbed wagon parked in the stall behind it. She fetched satchels, fire pot and blankets from her room, threw them on the wagon, and hitched up the horse. Leaping into the driver's box, she shook the reins and clicked her tongue, and the animal trotted down the street toward Forest Gate.

Robin was driving recklessly out of the gate just as Bone and Dirken entered it. They saw her and ducked out of the way, staring in dismay as the wagon plunged across the clearing to the edge of the forest. There Robin reined up only a moment, then whispered to her horse and the animal moved into the forest following a trail of blood.

Twenty-two

CELEBRATION

It was late afternoon when Brown John's colorful wagon burst out of the forest into the clearing outside Weaver. His team, frothing and steaming, pulled up short of a cluster of empty, parked wagons as he reined up hard. A crowd of Grillards tumbled out and hurried through the wagons into the village, where the wailing of the grief stricken mixed with music and dancing. Brown John, head erect, remained in the driver's box.

The wagons wore the marks, colors and totems of local forest tribes, and their owners crowded the terraces of Weaver. There were left-handed Wowells in furs, lean, round-faced Checkets, plain-looking Barhacha woodsmen, and Kaven money changers from Coin in three-belted robes. There were even savage Kraniks and Dowats, who had come all the way from the high forest.

The southern edge of the village still smouldered amid large puddles of spilled dye. At Three Bridge Crossing a group of Cytherians were hurriedly raising a finished gate to block the western bridge. Other villagers labored with shovels and picks, demolishing the other two bridges.

Brown John chuckled wisely and turned as Bone and Dirken came running through the wagons to him wearing proud smiles.

"We saw it all," Bone said triumphantly. "And up close."

"Splendid," said Brown John, "I want to hear every

113

detail, but first, tell me . . . did the Dark One play a part?''

"A part!" Bone blurted. "He was the whole bloody thing.''

Dirken indicated Weaver with the back of his head. "There are thirty-nine dead Skull soldiers in there, three temple guards and," he hesitated for effect, "two commanders. Champions. And all dead. He drowned and scalded most of them by pushing over dye vats, the rest was hand work.''

"He tore off one of their arms," Bone added with a grand gesture. "Ripped it right out of the shoulder.''

Brown John grinned. "Your sense of the dramatic is comendable, Bone, but when telling a tale, do not stretch the truth beyond its endurance. You'll lose your audience.''

"It's absolutely true, it is!" protested Bone.

Dirken nodded. "The commanders were the strongest bastards I've ever seen! But Gath was stronger. You couldn't have staged a better show yourself.'' Then with a whisper resonant with impending horror, he asked, "Want to see it?''

"Yes, I would." Brown John laughed and dropped lightly out of the wagon.

The brothers led their father into the forest to a stand of birch trees surrounded by alder shrubs. They moved in among the bushes to a pile of fresh cut brush from which Bone removed a large branch. On the ground under it was a folded blanket of green moss. Dirken unfolded the moss, and showed its contents to his father. A very large left arm.

"My, my," whispered Brown John truly impressed.

Bone pushed the rest of the brush aside as Dirken went on.

"The Cytherians laid claim to all the Kitzakks killed inside their village, but before they got around to it we had already hauled off the best of the bunch. If things keep going like this, we'll be the richest men in the forest.''

Dirken helped Bone pull off the last of the brush to

reveal the dead bodies of three men. They were short and thin, shrouded in black robes.

"Guards of the Temple of Dreams!" Brown John's smile twisted strangely. "Now that is an intriguing sight."

"We've got better," Dirken said. "One of their commanders." He removed another shrub, revealing a tall massive man glittering in a suit of chain mail. He lay facedown beside a huge sword and axe. A bloody hole at his shoulder and his other wounds were packed with moss.

The old stage master chuckled, "By Kram and Bled! This will send a message to the very corners of their empire!"

"And we've got a wagon load of weapons," Bone added.

"Splendid! Absolutely splendid." The old man gingerly lifted the empty, scalloped sleeve of the chain mail suit. Its arm had indeed been pulled out.

"Amazing," he said. "Truly amazing. And fortuitous. Tonight, around the fires, and in the coming days, many will speak of the events of this day, and you and I will play principal roles in their tales. Count on it! We placed the central player on the stage." His arm swept elaborately over their grim trophies. "It is we, the Grillards, the ridiculed and outlawed, who now stir the pot!"

He turned intently to his sons. "Now tell me, slowly and accurately, each detail. It is critical that I know everything. How did you convince Gath to come to Weaver? How did you know the Kitzakks would strike here?"

Bone and Dirken shared a sheepish glance, then Dirken said flatly, "We didn't."

"Didn't what?"

"Didn't know when the Kitzakks would strike."

"Then how did you get him to come here?"

Dirken hesitated. His face reddened, then he grinned. "We didn't. The Lakehair girl brought him."

"That's right," Bone added quickly. "He followed her here, all the way from Calling Rock."

Brown John clapped his bony hands excitedly, then beckoned with long fingers to his sons. "Of course! Of course! She gave him the message. So what did he say to her?"

Bone and Dirken shrugged. Then Dirken whispered, "We don't know. We didn't talk to either of them."

Brown John's wrinkled face surrendered to gravity with alarming speed.

"We're sorry," Bone blurted. "But we never got the chance. We waited for her on Summer Trail just like you said, but she just marched by us. Gath and that wolf of his were following her, so we hid 'til he went by. We followed them, you know, real careful like, and they came all the way here. Then all of a sudden, out of nowhere, came the bloody Kitzakks. You should have seen the people run and scream!"

"Enough!" Brown John's arm cut the air like a sword. He closed his eyes with deliberation. When he opened them they were on Dirken and his voice was modulated.

"What precisely are you telling me? Why did Gath of Baal choose to defend this village?"

"He didn't, not really," Bone said, then Dirken explained.

"The Kitzakks tried to carry off the Lakehair girl in a caged wagon, and he killed a good half of 'em to get her out. Then after it seemed to be all over, he fought the two commanders alone. In the Wagon Yard. Nobody knows why exactly. It was weird. Sort of like a couple of kids going out behind a barn to see who's toughest, but without the laughs."

"I dare say," muttered Brown John with a mocking laugh. "So, the pot surely does bubble, but we, just as surely, do not stir it . . . or even know what is in it." He chuckled ironically, looking from Bone to Dirken. "I presume, then, that the tribes have not annointed the Dark One with flowers and offered him their jewels and their daughters?"

His sons shifted uneasily, then Dirken said, "Nobody knows where he is."

"Or the Lakehair girl either," said Bone. "She went after him. In a wagon. He was bleeding bad."

Brown John's mouth sagged grimly. "He's dying?"

"Or dead," Dirken said. "I say sell off the armor and weapons, then pack up the village and go."

The old man considered this, looking at the ground, then replied with surprising assurance, "No. Not until we know."

"Know what?"

"If Gath of Baal is alive. It is a frail hope, but Robin Lakehair has the gift of healing. And perhaps, if she finds him . . ." He raised his eyebrows in expectation, then turned away. More for his own ears than theirs, and with a ring of amused fatalism, he added, "It always comes to this and no doubt always will. Our hopes, our joys and our dreams, everything that a man holds as necessary and pleasurable in his life, eventually depends on a woman."

He shook his ragged head, sat down on a stump and laughed outrageously. His sons watched him stupified. Finally, he addressed them mockingly. "It appears that the fortunes of we three brave and cunning heros, and the future of our tribe lies in the small hands of a mere girl."

"You picked her!" They both shouted the accusation.

"Indeed I did," said Brown John, then he said it again.

Twenty-three

DEAD MAN'S EYES

Caution moved behind the wolf's yellow eyes, as Sharn forced himself to edge out of the dense shade and stand in a spear of sunlight like a target.

Robin's face lit hopefully. She reined up and jumped off her wagon onto the narrow, unnamed trail. The horse snorted and pawed the needled ground cover nervously. They were deep in The Shades, surrounded by a jumble of birdcalls, clacking and purring, and the trickle and dripping of water over rocks and moss. Green tangled growth and shadows were everywhere. It was cool and moist. Visibility was diminishing quickly as the late daylight faded. Robin looped the reins around the seat of the driver's box and glanced around.

Every shadow seemed designed as a hiding place. Every sound was a mystery. She had no time to care. She raced back to the spot where she had seen the wolf.

Sharn was still there. He stood in a shallow mossy glen surrounded by walls of fern. He backed away and pushed through the ferns, stopping once to look back at her.

Robin followed him through the tangled growth and across the glen.

They emerged from the ferns to face a shoulder-high ridge of ground. A gnarled oak grew out of the ridge, casting black shadows on the thick moss covering it. A big-boned, limp hand stuck up out of the deep moss. Thick spider trails of blood ran down the back of the hand, across the little finger and dripped off a torn nail.

Robin climbed hurriedly up onto the mossy ridge, then stopped short. Gath lay on his back, half buried in muddy, torn-up moss. His mud-streaked face was the color of a peeled potato. She kneeled and pressed an ear to his matted chest. His heartbeat was faint, but he was alive. She removed the muddy moss. The deep gouges in his ear, jaw and neck had clotted. His chest and legs were bruised and cut, and there was a deep wound in his side. It bled slowly but steadily.

She removed her waterskin, uncorked it and rubbed some water on his lips. He opened his mouth slightly, enough for her to squeeze a few drops inside. Sharn licked his bleeding knuckles. She gently took the hand away from the wolf's tongue whispering, "Just let me have it for a moment, then you can have it back. We have to be a team now."

Robin, holding Gath's right wrist with both hands, sat down and placed her feet against his left side. She pulled until her body weight almost levered him onto his left side, then he began to sink back. She struggled, pulled with her arms and pushed with her legs. Blood pumped from his gouged knuckles, flowing into her grip, and the wolf growled. She did not look at the blood or the wolf. She grunted and strained, levering him over until he finally dropped facedown on the moss at the edge of the ridge.

The impact drew a groan from him, and he tried to rise. But the effort made the dark fluid pump fast out of the deep hole under his armpit, and he collapsed again.

Robin mumbled urgently, "We have to work fast. He's losing too much blood."

Sharn gave her no argument.

By tearing away ferns and plants, Robin made a path back to her wagon which was wide enough for the wagon to pass through. She untied the reins, then led the horse down the path. The wagon crushed down shrubs and bounced over boulders, then pulled alongside the ridge. The flatbed was about two feet below Gath's body.

Flushed from the effort, Robin climbed onto the rise, sat down beside Gath and placed her feet against his right side with her knees drawn up. She gathered a deep breath, then pushed with all her strength. He did not budge. She crawled over him and carved away the earth under his body with her knife and fingers until he sagged slightly. Then she climbed back to his other side and tried again. She was gasping and sweat soaked. Suddenly he rolled away and crashed on his back with a heavy thud, to lie still on the wagon bed. His eyes were open. All they showed was disinterest, like a dead man's eyes.

Robin whimpered fearfully, got on her hands and knees and looked down at him. She could smell—but only vaguely see—the fresh blood welling from his wounds. Night was taking command of The Shades.

Robin quickly gathered a pile of leaves and sticks, and piled them on a ridge beside the wagon. From one of her leather pouches she removed a warm folded lump of moss, unfolded it, and, taking brass tongs from her satchel, removed a glowing coal and placed it on the kindling. She blew on the pile until it broke into flame, then returned the coal to its pouch. From green palm leaves and pitch, she made a torch, lit it and set it in an embrasure on the wagon so that it cast light over the wagon bed. By this time the fire was blazing. She placed her dagger in its flames.

When the blade was red-hot, she pushed Gath's arm across his chest and without a blink placed the flat of the knife against the hole under his armpit. It sizzled, and he cried out hoarsely, then collapsed. She reheated the knife then pressed it against the wound in his side. Smoke incensed with burning flesh swirled into her face. She turned her head away, but not her eyes. With those two wounds closed, she went to work on the one in his thigh. It persisted in bleeding after her first attempt, so she sealed it twice.

When she finished, night had defeated day. The world

around her was black, and she felt suddenly cold and sticky.

Sharn growled, a low, almost inaudible, warning.

"I know," she answered. "We don't dare stay here."

Robin climbed up into the driver's box and started to flick the reins, but shuddered instead as a searing bolt of fear shot through her stomach. She looked around frantically. There was no sign of the trail, no indication of which way she came. Then she saw the wolf waiting up ahead and gasped with relief. Fear subsided, and she called to him, "I'm lost. It's up to you now."

Sharn trotted slowly forward, moving west, deeper into The Shades.

Robin twitched the reins, and the horse obeyed. Blindly they moved into dense shadows. After forty paces the horse balked. Robin tied off the reins and jumped down from the driver's box. Plucking the torch from its embrasure she hurried to the horse. Moving her hands gently over his eyes and around his muzzle, murmuring steadily, she led the animal forward casting the torchlight on the trail ahead.

It flickered on Sharn's yellow eyes, then the eyes vanished and were replaced by a brush of tail.

As Robin followed the wolf, she glanced into the shadows. She could not see them, but knew the night creatures were there, watching silently. The great horned owl, the jackel, and the bat-winged moth. She wondered if they had seen such a sight before, and if they would remember and someday tell of it. Of the night when wild wolf led tame girl.

Twenty-four

ALDER, HOPS, IRIS

Sharn hesitated short of the open track. Robin's torch was only a flicker now, but the moon was high in the sky. Its pale light filled the clearing between walls of lofty trees.

Robin stared awestruck at the cathedrallike corridor. The clear track stretched as far as she could see, with cool, blue moonlight gracing the smooth floor. It was as if large gods had marched this way in single file.

At the opposite side of the clearing, the giant roots of spruce and hemlock trees clustered, making shadowed passageways between their massive, gnarled bodies. Entrances to the underworld.

Robin trembled, took a deep breath, and followed the wolf across the track leading the horse and wagon. Sharn hesitated and eyed her over a bristling grey shoulder, then dipped between two thick roots and vanished. Robin stopped short in dismay, but promptly scolded herself and led her little caravan into the shadowy passageway.

Pulling the skittish horse and following the occasional padding sounds of the wolf's paws, Robin moved through a corridor of roots. Soon the air lost its wet grassy odor, and they moved into a large, dry dirt tunnel. It twisted through thick, buried roots to a crossroads joining three narrower, shallower tunnels. The wolf had vanished.

Robin dropped the reins and entered the largest tunnel. It ended a short way off in an underground room which could be closed by a low door made of logs. The back of the door had thick iron rings to hold a locking beam. There was hay scattered about the floor of the room, a water trough to one side, and rings buried in the dirt floor to which animals, or perhaps people, could be chained.

Robin hurried back to the crossroads. The wolf had not returned. She groaned and looked about frantically. A grating sound came from within the underground room. She pushed herself back against the dirt wall, held still. It came again. She shivered, edged sideways along the wall and peered into the room.

A semicircular outline of dim orange light emanated from a corner of the roof. It widened, throwing a faint glow on a ladder leaning against the dirt wall below. A trapdoor. It slid away from the hole, and a shaft of glowing firelight melted down into the darkness. Out of it appeared Sharn's head.

Robin smiled with relief and dragged the horse and wagon into the room, closed and bolted its door. She looked up at the trapdoor. The opening was not big enough for Gath even if she could have carried him. She turned to Gath, touched his forehead and frowned. He was burning hot. She replaced her torch and hurried to the ladder, but hesitated. Sharn's whiskered face was a threatening black silhouette against the orange glow. He backed out of sight, and Robin climbed the ladder.

She emerged in a narrow tunnel of tangled roots, and followed the wolf through a maze of tunnels to the entrance foyer of a root house, then down a staircase lit by a faint orange glow. At the bottom of the steps the wolf waited in the hot glow of a dying fire. Reaching the animal, she smiled in wonder, like a child.

Embers in a large fireplace of living roots illuminated a large room. It held meager furnishings, broken wine jars on the floor, and weapons and armor mounted on the root walls and heaped beside an anvil.

She moved about touching things thoughtfully. If this was Gath's home, then how strange that the fire had not died. Did someone else live here? There were no answers in the room.

She stirred the embers in the fireplace, added logs, and light quickly filled the room. A dragging sound came from the staircase, and Robin looked up, gasped.

Gath was standing in the hollow of the staircase, filling it with his dark sweating bulk. His eyes were tight and hot. He smelt of dirt and blood and pride, reeked of it. Suddenly he sagged against the wall of the staircase, bleeding again from thigh and shoulder, and glared at Robin and Sharn. His voice was a dead echo.

"Fools."

Robin smiled bravely and said, "You are probably right. But that should not make you angry. You would be dead now if it wasn't for us."

Gath watched her with the corners of his eyes, as if remembering vaguely what had happened, but it did not change his tone. "You are still a fool," he growled. "Sharn may have led you here, but he will never let you leave." He slipped lower and muttered darkly, "And neither will I."

He pushed himself away from the wall and stood with legs spread in the middle of the staircase blocking it. He looked impressive, but starting down the stairs was a bad decision. His first step dropped him to his knees and he pitched forward, descended with all the control of a baby emptying its bowels. He finished facedown at Robin's feet.

Undaunted, Robin fetched furs from the alcove and spread them in front of the fireplace. She helped Gath to his feet, guided him to the furs, and he sprawled there gasping.

Robin placed her knife in the fire, and removed her many vials from her satchel in preparation for a long night's work. After cleaning and closing his wounds again, she made him chew on the inner bark of a birch tree, then cooked him a broth using meat and vegetables from his larder.

Gath, between short, fitfull periods of sleep, spent the night glaring at her, eating, and passing out.

Sharn's night was spent on the fourth step of the stairwell where he sat like a sentry. He ignored Robin's attempts at friendship, but did not decline the food she served him.

When morning came, Gath was sleeping soundly. Robin had the room clean and orderly, and was heating water in a brass pot over the fire. As the water simmered, she found a partially concealed alcove, stripped and sponged herself off with a pan of water, then got dressed again, tied back her hair and rouged her lips. She added some herbs and a pale violet powder to the simmering pot, approached the wolf, and spoke in an uncompromising tone.

"I am going out. I need alder and iris roots to clean his wounds. I need clover to keep his spirit strong, roses to clean his blood, and more birch bark to ease his pain. And I need hops to make his sleep peaceful. I will come back, but if you do not believe that, come with me. Now please get out of my way."

The wolf snarled at her in the manner belligerent men reserve for bossy women. When she started to mount the stairs, he made an extremely unpleasant expression, but got out of her way.

Robin unlocked the front door and went out into the dawn light. Her tenseness melted as the green glory of the primeval forest greeted her. She breathed deeply of its clean, sweet air, then descended a path through the roots and began her search with renewed strength.

She did not have to look far. The forest was a storehouse of magical supplies. A short time later, when she reentered the dwelling, she not only carried the needed medicines in her many pouches, but a skirt full of berries, mushrooms and vegetables. Her expression was buoyant.

She spent the day in much the same way she had spent the night. She redressed Gath's wounds, fed him, and exchanged smiles for frowns and twinkling eyes for hard glares. When he slept, she slept in a blanket near him. Once she woke up to find him watching her intently, as if she were about to perform some magical feat, and she sat up to ask what he saw. But he looked away, and she withheld the question.

When the forest again surrendered to the night, she prepared a vegetable stew. She filled a bowl, laced it generously with hops, then sat down to feed it to him. Waving her aside, he sat up and fed himself. She fetched herself a bowl, one without hops, then sat down facing him and showed him that she could also feed herself, and far more efficiently, as he dropped generous portions on chest and floor.

Finished, he tossed his bowl among the broken crockery with an air of independence and deliberation. He told her again that she was a fool, and his prisoner as well, then lay back down with an expression of satisfaction that was not the least satisfied.

She smiled at him playfully and replied quietly, "We will see."

Robin finished her stew, cleaned their bowls, then wrapped herself in her furs. In moments both were sound asleep.

When the fire died down to an orange glow, Sharn also slept.

It was not until well into the darkest part of the night that the animal heard the warning sound of the yellow stone dropping to the floor. His mane bristled. His nostrils dilated. Abruptly, he stood and stared narrow eyed and growling up into the darkness of the staircase. Suddenly his tail dropped between his hind legs and his murderous growl faded to a whimper. He backed numbly down the stairs and into an alcove. His head wagged, and his gut sagged so low it spread out on the floor bringing the rest of him with it. His red tongue lolled out, then his body and head fell over, and he slept.

A moment later, Cobra emerged from the darkness of the stairwell, and her beautiful hypnotic eyes appraised the sleeping wolf. They glittered briefly with amusement, and she stepped out of the shadows, descended. The glow of the firelight played among the deep folds of her emerald robe, touched her metallic skullcap with flashes of red and silver.

Her gold eyes shifted under thin arched eyebrows, and came to rest on the sleeping figures in front of the fire. Kneeling between the Barbarian and Robin, she delicately lifted the furs away from Gath's body and studied his bandaged wounds. She softly placed her palm across his forehead, held it there, and the corners of her plush red lips made sharp creases in creamy cheeks.

Robin's eyes suddenly opened, and she sat up. She lunged for her knife, resting on the floor beside her, but Cobra snapped it up. Robin drew back in a crouch, breathing hard, and demanded, "Who are you?"

Cobra answered with her eyes, and their intensity forced Robin back against the hearth. As she stared at the glowing almond eyes, her own eyes took on the expression of clouded glass. She was unable to move.

The Queen of Serpents said almost tenderly, "Do not be afraid. I have no desire to harm him, or you."

Cobra stood and crossed to the stairwell, then looked back with curiosity. Resentment touched her eyes, then a hand played at her queenly throat, rode down over the thrusting pressure of a full breast, and across her stomach to her hip. Her hot scarlet lips brightened against her cool skin. A dazzling, fleshy temple as proud and sensual as her voice. "He was not made for a mortal like you, child. Only I can give him what he needs."

Cobra started up the stairwell, stopped, glanced over a supple shoulder at Robin. "You will go back to sleep now. Tomorrow, and during the days that follow, you are going to need all your powers. He must be healed completely. And quickly! Death hunts him now."

She moved up the stairs and was gone. Robin yawned and slumped over, certain now she was dreaming. She just made it back under the blanket before falling asleep.

Sharn's sleeping head rose slowly. He yawned, then stood and looked across the room at the stairwell with confused eyes. His head low to the floor, he sniffed about the room retracing his steps several times and growling quietly, then returned to his position on the steps. The frustration in his eyes was cruel. The hair at his neck was erect. At irregular intervals he shuddered.

Twenty-five

THE DOLL

Bahaara, the capital city of the Kitzakk's Desert Territory, was a blunt, massive rock mesa which rose off the flat, endless body of the desert like a jagged scab. It was the active center of all military, religious and commercial activity. Here all the caravans from the desert "skin camps" came to deliver their living merchandise. Its everyday sounds, along with the sounds common to all cities, were the rattling of chains and an incessant moaning punctuated by shrieks of terror. This clamor usually peaked at midday when the flesh markets opened. Yet now, as the midday sun baked the dirt-brown body of the city, there was silence except for the occasional bray of a camel or yap of a dog.

Earthen breastworks, manned by small brown men in glittering steel and enameled bamboo armor, formed an irregular circle around the city. Beyond that was an open clearing heaped with cages, and occupied by drill yards, stables and caravan camps. Beyond the clearing itself was the mesa, an eruption of jagged earth and stone. A maze of streets, alleys, footpaths and passageways twisted up, over and through its many levels. Mud buildings rose in stacks and clustered along the thoroughfares which rose to the flat plateau that dominated the city. At its eastern side were the red buildings of military headquarters. On the western side were the black and orchid buildings of the Temple of Dreams, the sacred brothel of the Butterfly Goddess. Between the two clusters of buildings was a mutual courtyard called the Court of Life.

Bahaara's principal thoroughfare was the Street of Chains. It was named after its merchandise, as were the other streets which featured butchers, blacksmiths, bakers, soldiers, and all varieties of slaves. As the people went about their business, they did so silently. Every so often they would cast troubled glances up at the Court of Life.

Nine days had passed since the Kitzakk raid on Weaver. The remnant of the Skull raiders had made a three-day forced march to reach home. The next three days had been spent cleansing them of the contamination of defeat. During these three days a wave of panic spread throughout the city, and frenzied fanatics emerged making loud demands. A few called for total surrender to the demon Barbarian. The majority demanded that the warlord Klang cancel all plans for harvesting the forest flesh, and blockade all the passes to the Forest Basin to contain its contaminating magic.

Klang reacted decisively. He ordered the twenty-seven survivors of the raid, with the exception of the high priest Dang-Ling, to prepare a final offering to the Butterfly Goddess, in order to assure her help in the destruction of the Barbarian demon.

Today the Skull soldiers were waiting in the Court of Life to make that offering. They formed three straight lines of nine each. Eyes to the front, they were perfect soldiers on parade, but each was kneeling with a red cord binding his hands at his back.

At the front of the formation, in a teakwood box, was a

sword and a soft white towel. The sword's steel was mirror bright. It was a conventional military model but heavier, with a straight back and slightly bowed cutting edge.

An audience of the generals of the regular army, the commanders of the personal regiments of the warlord, and a swordsmith stood at attention. Otherwise the yard was empty. The streets opening onto it were blocked off. The shutters on the windows of surrounding buildings were closed.

The red oval doors of the Temple of Dreams opened, and Dang-Ling ceremoniously appeared. He wore his orchid and black robes and scarlet skullcap.

The rims of his wet eyes were a florid pink brilliantly contrasting with the dark rings under them, the result of devout sexual excess heightened by drugs. Frothy ringlets of dark brown hair crowned his round milky face. Pink, flowerlike ears, nestled in the froth, twitched as hidden emotions agitated his flabby cheeks.

A gong struck three times, and Dang-Ling flinched with each ringing note as he watched Klang stride through the iron gate of the red buildings and march directly to the teakwood box.

He was naked except for black leather loincloth and black calf-length leather boots polished to a glasslike finish. A cool, sorrel-skinned, handsome animal with massive, sharply cut muscles. The sweat from his warm-up exercises formed glistening beads on his oiled skin. He toweled off his hands with the cloth, and dropped it in the dirt.

His expression said clearly that he was not a man who was stopped by military setbacks, inadequate magic or frenzied fanatics. He was the muscle of the Kitzakk Empire. If cold, calculated murder had a face, it was Klang's. And it was imposing. Compelling.

Drums began a steady cadence somewhere within the military buildings. As their reverberations spread throughout the city, people dropped to their knees in the streets, in their homes and on the battlements.

The drums stopped. Klang removed the sword from the teakwood box. He stroked the cutting edge, and bowed to the swordsmith.

Approaching the head of the first kneeling Skull, he shook out his shoulder muscles, looked down at the naked neck. He set himself, then whipped the sword up and brought it down, striking off the head with a single cut. He stepped around the spurting blood and addressed the next head. He went through the first two lines without pausing. Then he rubbed his sore fingers and forearms and appraised the last line. Big, thick-necked brutes, they were rank with fear. Klang growled, and angrily proceeded with the execution, deliberately missing their necks and striking heads and shoulder blades. Only partially decapitated, the soldiers died slowly and painfully.

The drums rolled again. A squad of soldiers assigned to cleanup duty raced into the Court of Life with baskets, wooden carts and buckets of sand. The officers were excused, and the city returned to its normal noise and activities.

Klang joined Dang-Ling on the steps to the Temple of Dreams, and the priest bowed deferentially. Klang's thin, flaring eyes studied him suspiciously before he spoke.

"You failed me, priest. Your magic was inadequate." His whisper was rich with foreboding.

Dang-Ling dipped his head and said respectfully, "I regret this terrible misfortune as much as you, my lord. But I must differ with you. The formula was not designated to harm him, only to draw him out, and it did that. It was your commanders who were inadequate."

Klang darkened angrily. "Do you think I have forgotten it was you who suggested Trang and Chornbott?"

"No, my lord, but I only did so because I believed they were the strongest."

Klang nodded, but his anger did not abate. "Listen carefully, priest. In eighteen days the regiments will attack the forest village and the harvest will begin. Before that time I will have the head of this irritating Barbarian nailed to the northern gate.''

"Then I am certain it will be," Dang-Ling said with exaggerated servility.

The warlord continued. "I have employed bounty hunters to fetch it for me." Dang-Ling's smile became wary. Klang nodded. "I realize they will be no match for him, so they must be armed with magic that will assure they can find and strike at him without being seen."

Dang-Ling spoke carefully. "There would be no greater honor for me than to be able to assist you in this murder, but, regrettably, there is no formula for such magic."

"Find one!"

"But . . ."

"Make this magic," Klang interrupted with a harsh whisper, "or I will find the weakest one-armed man in Bahaara and order him to saw off your head with a bamboo sword."

Dang-Ling hesitated, then bowed low and said, "My humblest apologies, my lord, for failing to measure the extreme importance of his death. Rest assured, your bounty hunters will have the required magic or . . . I will cut off my own head with the same sword."

Klang smiled darkly and strode across the yard toward the red buildings. Dang-Ling watched him for a moment, then entered his temple, closing the doors behind him.

He passed through a maze of enameled black corridors and stairways, moving casually, acknowledging the bows of priests and inhaling the scents of burning incense and jasmine mixed with the strong smell of heated female flesh which flowed out of the sanctuaries. Once in his private quarters, he locked his door. At one side was an altar featuring a marvelous swallowtail butterfly of gold and teakwood; it was perched on a dying serpent with its wings spread. Dang-Ling pushed the wings together and a stone rose at an angle out of the floor revealing a secret staircase lit by oil lamps. He descended the staircase, and the stone lowered back into place, the wings of the butterfly again spread wide.

He stood in a small room deep in the heart of the mesa, one of several hidden chambers he had secretly built under the Temple of Dreams. It was paved with dark red tile. Black plush divans framed three sides; a drowsy lynx on a gilt chain lay among red pillows on one of them. The fourth side was a cluttered workbench and a door. Incense oil lamps provided a deep orange light and the heavy aroma of sandlewood. Smoke clung to the ceiling. The only sound was the purring of the cat.

Dang-Ling sat at the workbench for an hour downing drafts from a bottle of clear amber Harashiid. The lamps burned low and the room got dark. Numb and wobbly, he locked the bottle away in a drawer under the bench, then sat still. Suddenly he erupted wildly, screaming, and swept flasks and bottles off the bench. They crashed to the floor. Breathing hard, flushed and momentarily appeased, he sat back down at the bench. With trembling fingers he carefully cleared away the clutter of knives, carving tools and shavings of stone. Then he set his elbows on the bench and held his white face with white fingers and thumbs. Their trembling made his oily ringlets flutter.

His florid mind conjured forth the vivid image of death by bamboo sword, then judged its relative merits against some unnatural torment which the Lord of Death would administer if he did help Klang's bounty hunters find and destroy the "chosen one." He scolded himself for letting fear make him foolish. He had no choice but to fulfill his warlord's request, and do it diligently. If he failed, his position within the Kitzakk Empire, a position which was of invaluable service to the Master of Darkness, would be wasted.

He sighed and reached to open a small cabinet at the back of the bench. He withdrew a small totem doll carved from a black stone called Kaitang. It was a crude, blunt

likeness of the Dark One. He knew its magic would serve
the bounty hunters well.

Knowing the bounty hunters also could be of service to
him as well as Klang, he opened a second cabinet,
withdrew a doll carved out of Paitang, a white stone. It was
the figure of a girl and sculpted with immaculate artistry,
by hands inspired by desire for the living model. The hands
belonged to Dang-Ling. The doll was an extraordinary
likeness of the Weaver maiden the Dark One had rescued.

Twenty-six
ROSEBUDS

Robin and Sharn stood in the shade of the forest at the edge
of the clear track. Sunlight filled the track, and touched the
petals and leaves of a wild rosebush at the forest edge.

Cutting a rose just short of the branch, she lifted the bud
to her face. Its scent made her smile the way the sun smiles
at break of day. She added it to her pile, folded a cloth
around the bouquet and picked it up.

The wolf watched each move, then followed her back
into the root house. Reaching the main room, Robin's
straight brow lowered.

Gath stood over the anvil, naked except for a fur and
hide loincloth. His wounds had scabbed over, but several
cracked open as he hammered a piece of Kitzakk metal
which glowed red within exploding sparks. He stopped,
looked at the face of his hammer and growled with disgust.
The edges were being mangled by the hard steel.

Robin said quietly, "Maybe you can do some of your

work outside today, in the fresh air and sunshine.''

She moved to the side table, and arranged the roses in a wine jar. Gath frowned at her. Feeling it, she tilted her head playfully.

"There," she said. "Fifteen roses, one for each of the fifteen days I've been here. So you won't forget me.'' Her smile had some fun romping about her cheeks. "At least not right away.''

Gath did not comment, but his expression softened.

Robin turned from his eyes and began to move about the room touching the armor, furs and root walls. She moved slowly. His eyes followed her like leashed pets. When she reached him, she looked up solemnly. "I'll never forget being here. It's like something in a minstrel's tale. So full of hiding places and tunnels and . . ." her wistful eyes locked with his, "and mysteries.''

Still no reply.

She grinned, lifted a hand and touched the scabs on his jaw as her voice scolded. "You know, if you're going to keep getting in fights, you really should wear a helmet.''

He grabbed her hand as if to throw it aside, but instead cradled it in his pawlike hand. Lifting it, he breathed in her fresh warm scent, a bouquet of roses and leaves and air and Robin. When he looked at her, there was wonder in his eyes.

Robin trembled slightly with a rush of uncertainty, and looked away in confusion. He let her hand drop, and turned back to the anvil. Robin glanced over a shoulder at him and his head turned slightly toward her. The glowing metal cast deep shadows in the sockets of his eyes. They were intense and alert, yet strangely young, like a child grown old and hard before his time, before enjoying the years of laughter and the thousand nights of dreaming. She could not tell if he had lived thirty summers or twenty.

After a moment, Robin said quietly, "I will be going soon, but there are some things I must tell you first." He turned away again and she moved to his shoulder. "Will you listen now, please? It's very important.''

Without turning he said, "Because you saved my life does not mean I have to listen to your jabber." He positioned the glowing metal, raised his hammer, then suddenly gave up, shoved the metal back into the fire and set his hammer down.

"Thank you," she said primly. She fetched a wine jar and gave it to him, then gathered a fur and sat down. He took a long drink and sat down facing her, his back against the hearth.

Robin repeated her message carefully. "I came to Calling Rock to tell you what you now know better than anyone, that the Kitzakks are coming, in great strength. And to . . . to ask for your help."

"Why? The forest tribes have hidden from raiders before."

"This isn't the same. There are thousands of them, and they'll come again and again, and keep coming. It's the truth. Brown John knows them. He lived among them. They're organized and relentless. They will march through each village one by one, kill the men who resist, and carry off the women and children in chains and cages. No one will be spared. And Brown John sent me to tell you . . ."

"To do what? Conquer this horde?" He grunted brutally. "Does he think I am a magician?"

"He thinks . . . he knows you are strong."

He nodded. "Strong enough to take care of myself."

He lifted the wine jar to drink, but did not. He stared over the lip at her, watching her enthusiasm and confidence waver. She did not avoid his eyes, but her voice became quiet.

"How can you hide when you know what I say is true? When you know we need you?"

"It suits me."

"But you can't ignore them forever. They'll come here too."

"Let them," he whispered, and drank deep.

"Gath," she begged, "you must believe me. No one can hide from them. Particularly you. You've defeated them twice now. Shamed them. They won't rest until you're dead."

"My trail is set," he blurted harshly. "I have taken an oath. I work alone."

"But surely the god of these trees," she pointed at the root walls, "or whatever god you swear by, will understand?"

"I did not swear to a god. I swore to myself." His tone had the finality of a driven nail.

She sat back defeated. "Then you leave us to die . . . or live in cages."

He studied her, his eyes impenetrable. "What do you . . . no . . . what does Brown John think I can do?"

"Oh, Gath!" She sat forward with a sudden rush of renewed hope. "You can unite us! Be our champion! If we have hope, everything is possible. And with you and Brown John working together, we'll have it."

He smiled mockingly.

"Don't look down on him," Robin begged. "I know you think he's only an entertainer, but entertainers can be smart, and they can inspire. Look at what he's done already!"

"I will tell you what he has done, small girl of the Weavers. He has pestered and annoyed everyone, particularly the Kitzakks. He is a foolish troublemaker! An actor and maker of lies who trades for silver, things which are not his."

She started to argue, but stopped as he stood up and hovered over her. His voice was hollow.

"Look at yourself. He tricked you with his fancy talk and tall tales, compelled you, a helpless girl who weaves cloth, to come here and feed yourself to the dangers of The Shades, to find and enter this house which no other mortal has left alive."

The sudden sharp truths made her falter. They were

different, new, but unalterably true and she swayed beneath the understanding of them.

He turned to the anvil, and looked down at the metal in the fire.

"I see," she whispered, "you . . . you're not going to let me go?"

"I should not," he said, "but I am going to, so you can carry my message to Brown John. Meat for metal, that is all I will give him. Tell him that. I need a helmet, and body armor made of this outlander metal." He turned to her. "Now we are finished. I saved you, and you have healed me. So you are free to go."

She sighed with relief. "I swear I'll tell no one of this place."

His expression remained impenetrable.

She nodded, then stood and said bravely, "Well, I don't understand you any better than you understand me. Least of all why you saved my life. But you did. And you saved my village, my people. I am grateful to you for that, and I always will be. But . . . well, I am finished also. I have given you my message, so now I will return to Rag Camp with your reply. Will you take me there?"

He nodded.

"Thank you." She slung her pouch over her shoulder, moved to the stairs and Sharn, sitting on the fourth step, stood abruptly and growled.

"Wait!" It was a command.

Robin stopped short and turned to him. "It's all right," she said calmly, "Sharn won't stop me. He knows me now."

She moved up to the growling wolf, stroked his head and gave it a kiss, then ascended the stairs and went out. The wolf and man remained motionless, staring at each other, their expressions as identical as a matched pair of fools.

By late afternoon, Gath and Robin were moving east along Summer Trail in the Valley of Miracles. He walked.

She drove her wagon. When they came in sight of Rag Camp, Gath turned back. Robin reined up, sighed, and watched him for a long while. Then she headed her wagon toward the camp.

Twenty-seven

NIGHT SOUNDS

On his return trip Gath, parched and dry, was forced to stop and water frequently. When he reached his root house, he was exhausted and feverish. His bandaged wounds were seeping. He looked around outside, then inside for Sharn. The wolf was not there. He moved to the table, noticed the rosebuds had begun to blossom. He swore, lay down on the furs in front of his fire with a wine jar and began to drink. After two cups he was asleep.

He woke fitfully during the darkest part of the night. His mouth was again dry and his lips parched. He took a drink of wine and put more wood on the fire, then looked around. Sharn had not returned.

He went outside and stood in the cool moonlight, listening. The shrill clutter of nocturnal melodies soothed him. Then another sound rose above them and cut into him painfully.

It was the distant howl of a wolf. Not the normal night cry of that breed, but the sad, forlorn howl of an animal without a mate.

Twenty-eight

DAWN

The colors of the gaudy wagon were muted by the cool grey morning light that was spreading over Stone Crossing. Bone sat in the driver's box folding a blanket on the seat beside him. Dirken sprawled on the flatbed snoring.

Brown John stood a short way off under an apple tree, his hands on Robin's shoulders, and his lively eyes looking cheerily into hers. Her forlorn little face blinked back. He cupped her cheeks fondly in his gentle hands, rubbing away the moisture with his thumbs, and said, "You've done well, child. And I will hear no more words of defeat and failure from your lovely mouth. All that was asked of you was to deliver a few words, and you did that and more. A great deal more. You led him into battle against the Kitzakks, you saved his life. And he showed you his secret dwelling place, allowed you to leave with no more guarantee of silence than a small promise. These are truly extraordinary achievements, and totally unexpected."

"Thank you, Brown John," she murmured. "It's kind of you to put it that way."

"Kindness, dear child, has nothing to do with it." He wagged a pedantic finger at her nose. "I merely speak the truth. And the most promising thing of all is that he sent you to me with a request for weapons and armor."

"Really?"

"Yes, really. Because it reveals many things. Not only that he now understands the strength of the Kitzakks and their metal, but that he begins to understand himself. Believe me, Robin Lakehair, the stage is now set. His time is at hand. Soon, very soon now, he will be more than eager to deal with me in order to assure his superiority over other men.''

He laughed out loud, hugged her and it brought a smile to her cheeks. "Go now," he said. "Bone and Dirken will see you home so you can get a well-deserved rest.''

She nodded and started for the wagon, but shyly turned back and kissed him on the cheek. Then she scurried to the wagon, climbed up and sat down beside Bone. The big man rose up proudly beside her with a grin on his face big enough to carpet a castle, then flicked his whip, and the wagon rolled forward.

As the wagon crested the top of Stone Crossing, the sun's rays spilled over the horizon and the Grillard wagon blossomed in all its scarlet, pink and orange glory.

Twenty-nine
WET SCARLET

The Glyder Snake arched up out of mossy soil and pointed a flickering black tongue at the green wall of leafy ferns. Beyond the ferns, harsh sounds rose above the music of dripping dew, trickling water and insect songs that filled the deep shade of the rain forest. Booted feet were crushing dead undergrowth.

As the footsteps came closer a delicate, red-nailed hand stroked the snake's head. It arched up languorously against the pleasing pressure of the fingertips, then looked up at the owner of the hand. Suddenly the fingers snapped up the snake, held it tight behind the head. Its jaws spread wide, gasping for breath, and its nine-inch glowing body flailed around the wrist in agony.

It was Cobra's hand. She held the imprisoned snake up to her black-rimmed gold eyes. "I am sorry, small one, but I have no choice."

Holding the writhing snake within the concealing folds of her robe, she moved through the wall of ferns toward the footsteps, and emerged at the edge of a small shaded glen. She was nearly invisible, part of the vegetation. Her robe had taken on the color of the ferns. Her silver skullcap, like the tips of the ferns, glittered green-gold where the sun touched it. Her bosom rose and fell matching the rhythm of the feathery green leaves fluttering on the damp breeze.

The small glen was no bigger than a private room at an inn. A deep bed of moss carpeted the ground. It was surrounded by ferns except for the side opposite the sorceress, where two birch trees framed a doorlike opening through which could be seen an infinity of flickering black shadows. The roof was leafy branches. A shaft of golden sunlight pierced that roof, made a golden puddle of light at the center of the mossy bed.

The sounds of footsteps beyond the two birch trees grew louder.

Her narrow lips parted slightly in anticipation, and she stepped into the warm column of sunlight.

The advancing sounds hesitated, then moved forward again, angry with snapping twigs and breaking bushes, and Gath stepped out of the enveloping darkness, like a sword drawn from a scabbard. He was darker than she remembered. More brutal. Hard dry scabs were turning to scar tissue. His fur loincloth bristled slightly in the breeze. A new suit of chain mail, his belt and a Kitzakk helmet were slung over his shoulders. A bright steel axe rode his right fist. His chiseled features were mottled with dark shadows, and wore an expression of dark invitation. To a bed of murder.

Cobra trembled involuntarily, and her robe shimmered in the sunlight, began to change. Yellows faded to orange, vermilions to hot scarlet. When she parted her robe, the golden cloth surrendered to its prisoners and flushed flesh revealed itself at breasts, stomach and thighs.

Gath sneered at this invitation. He shrugged the belt, helmet and suit of chain mail off his shoulders, and they dropped with his axe to the ground. His only weapons were his hands, more than enough.

Cobra shuddered, took a step back, lifted the writhing Glyder Snake in front of her and held a thin dagger at its throat. "Wait!" she pleaded.

Gath did not break stride.

Cobra slit the Glyder snake's throat, and its head tumbled away. She held up the spurting throat and gasped, "Wait! Your secret is safe now. Only the snake knew where you lived. I can not find you anymore."

He knocked the bloody reptile out of her hand, and backhanded her hard to the ground. She went down in one soft piece, sprawled on her back. There were streaks of blood across her cheek. Her dagger lay five feet off.

He glared down at her, a hot shadowed mass of muscle pulsing with death.

She gasped for breath, rolled onto a hip and gaped up at him as he dropped on her. He took hold of her head and turned her face away from his, slowly began to twist her neck. She gagged and shuddered under his body sending warm waves of heat through his hand, thighs and groin, and he hesitated. When she spoke, it was very carefully.

"Don't kill me! Let me talk first." She gasped for air, begged, "Please, let go. I can't breathe." She looked at him over a shoulder. "There's no danger. I'm alone."

He let her drop back gasping on the moss, and glanced around warily, then back at her.

She drew herself from under him, and rose on her elbows, whispered, "The Kitzakks send men to hunt you, bounty hunters who kill from shadows and great distances."

"And you will tell them where to find me."

"I can't. Only the snake knew the location of your cave. But they will find you just the same."

"Again you lie."

"No," she said firmly. "I have no reason now, you have passed the test."

The corners of her mouth reached into the lush hollows of her cheeks. She indicated his new tools. "You must have better, far better! A man who has the kind of enemies you have needs better metal than any 'man' can provide."

He studied her thoughtfully, then said quietly, "I did not know there was better."

She nodded. "There is always better if you know where to shop . . . and have the price."

He studied her for awhile. Her scarlet robe brightened, took on an almost hypnotic glitter. Her heat wafted across the moss and caressed his chest. Ignoring it, he said arrogantly, "I have the price, if you can get the metal."

She crooned, "I have it now. A helmet. One like no other. It was worn by the legendary Shalarmard, and the demon tyrants, Barbar, Karchon and Geddis. A helmet made from an ancient formula with steel smelted by the fires of the underworld, and hammered on the anvil of the gods." She waited. "You are interested?"

He nodded.

Realizing he had agreed more quickly than he had intended, her teeth flashed briefly behind the moist scarlet of her smiling lips. They stood slowly, appraising each other. Then, with confidentiality, she murmured, "The helmet is in my dwelling. In the Land of Smoking Skies beyond the Land of Toofar. Come, visit me there, and it will be yours."

He said, "A long trip!"

"Yes," she replied evenly. "One most men do not dare to take."

"With reason." His tone challenged her. "You spoke of a price?"

She started to reply, hesitated. Color flamed on her cheeks. Her garment glowed wet scarlet, then turned transparent revealing the dark accents of her body, lewd living jewels. She covered herself with her robe, and held her right shoulder gently with left hand. Her right arm hung loosely.

She said, "Dark One, I am not made in the normal manner, but in the manner of the ancients. My passions and my nature were formed during a time when women sat in judgment over men, a time when woman was the hunter and man the prey. So forgive my boldness." Her eyes became almost imperceptible. A husky whisper exhaled her words. "You are the price. Come to me, be my consort, and you will have paid in full."

He responded sharply, "A whore's price."

"No," she said with force, "a king's. Once you wear the helmet no creature will be able to approach you unannounced, no venom poison your blood, no man defeat you."

He ran a thumbnail across a scab on his forearm then back again and shook his head. "I would rather kill you."

"No, you wouldn't," she said in a low throaty whisper. "Not, at least, until you find if I speak the truth."

Cobra used a finger to tuck a disobedient strand of black hair back in place, then stiffened elegantly, regal in manner and tone. "Take your time. Wait until your wounds are completely healed and your strength is what it was. Rebuild your new armor until it suits you. There is no hurry." Her tone became low and husky. "Believe me, I will wait. Men like yourself, my friend of the shadows, are rare. Very rare. And I can make you unique . . . release all the power that boils in your blood. Make you invincible." She took a sharp breath. "Do you know what that means to me? No.

You could not. You have no idea what it means to a woman, or how she would feel, holding that kind of power in her arms.''

His body replied with a flush of desire.

She smiled hotly, moved to him confidently, and allowed her voluptuous curves to press against him.

His hand took hold of her neck and he demanded, "Name the landmarks. I will find my way."

He let go of her, and she staggered back. Her breath caught in her throat, then she told him the way. He picked up his things and strode past her, disappearing into a fluttering wall of ferns.

She did not watch him go, but listened to his footsteps fade away. Relieved, she let herself sink slightly with exhaustion and the natural colors of her clothing returned. She glanced at the headless body of the Glyder Snake sprawled awkwardly on the moss. It had lost all of its beautiful electric colors, and was as dark as a wet stick.

Thirty

THE JOURNEY

At first light, four days later, Gath left his root house wearing the mended suit of chain mail. It was now blackened except for scattered glitters of raw metal. Two jars of wine, a blanket roll, sword, two daggers, a satchel and a leather fire pouch rode his back and belt, and he carried Red Helmet's axe in his right hand. His clean-shaven face wore the color of good health, and he was bareheaded, moving west with a hurried stride.

By the time he reached Trail's End, at the farthest edge of the Shades, he slowed to a reasonable pace. His face was flushed, and the wounds on his shoulder and thighs were hot and chafed under the chain mail.

A crowd of bleached skulls mounted on sticks marked Trail's End. Beyond it was Toofar, and beyond that the Land of Smoking Skies.

Gath picked his way through the skulls, weaved through the tangled vines beyond, and found a dusty path apparently formed by big-footed, wide-shouldered beasts. It took him to Noga Swamp, a seemingly endless spread of mangroves whose mammoth roots rose out of murky green slime to form house-sized structures roofed by leafy trees. Amid the shadows, a scarlet dragon-lizard sunned itself in a scrap of sunlight.

It was sprawled on a bald rock about a foot from the spot where Gath's boot landed with a crunch. The lizard popped an eye open, spread its toothy jaws in a silent scream, and fled leaping and dashing over a highway of branches into the swamp.

Gath grinned at this show of comical flattery, then splashed to a stop. The cacophony of insect sounds that swarmed over the swamps was swelling in volume. Then all about him there was a multitude of slithering movements, as if the enormous swamp were a single living creature. A pandemonium of splashing and bubbling followed, then silence. The sudden void of sound gave the wet land a strange compelling aspect, and a thrill shot through Gath, as if he were a boy again feeling that first hunger to see the other side of the mountain.

He high stepped his way along the edge of the swamp, and as Cobra had said he would, came to an ancient, raised dirt road that wound its way through the mangroves. At irregular intervals along its battered broken body, vine-covered bridges rose above the water to pass over deep ponds and the tallest roots. He followed it and moved west deep into the swamp.

As he passed over the murky ponds the sounds and movements slowly returned. They started behind him, then came rolling around him, waves of tiny, clacking voices washing him forward.

Large, slime-coated eyes watched him from the root shadows. He felt a thousand others on his back. But the road in front of him seemed strangely lifeless. He shortened his grip on his axe.

At a bridge spanning a wide canal that linked two lake-sized ponds, Gath stopped warily. At the center of the ponds the green slime dissipated and feathered out in webs of yellowish foam, then gave way to patches of blue-green water. Splashes of sunlight, finding passage through the thinning tree cover, made them glitter, and graced the skeleton of a man dangling from a high tree branch. He hung by his own chain neckpiece. His legs were missing, but he still looked as tall as Gath. An ancient giant who had had his stature severely reduced by some enterprising swamp creature.

Gath's eyes hunted through the murky wetness, stopped and turned cold. A mammoth crocodile floated on its belly in the shade below the skeleton. Its scaly hide was the color of the swamp and crusted with warts, scars, sores. Its blinking eyes, dense with thick yellowish cataracts, had obviously seen centuries of the primordial world's suffering. The creature's teeth, rotted to sharp jagged stumps, had no doubt contributed a large portion to that agony. Its best days were long gone, but with jaws big enough for three men to wrestle in, it was still Lord of the Swamp.

Gath rolled his shoulders and moved arrogantly across the bridge giving the mammoth reptile his back.

At the western side of the swamp the road consisted of rotting wooden planks mounted on wooden stilts as tall as trees. A floating bridge that passed narrowly over giant Tubb plants, spined cannibal flowers shaped like pitchers with rounded lids that poured forth beckoning tongues.

Beyond the swamp was more forest, then Panga Pass, a

narrow dirt trail through brown foothills of stacked boulders of uncanny sizes and shapes. It was as barren of plant life as the swamp was dense. Beyond the boulders the pass twisted between two mountains. The yellow-orange ball of the sun dipped below their rugged horizon in glowing invitation.

Gath traveled west until the light was gone, then made camp under an overhanging rock and ate. When night came threats came with it; the vicious roars of strange, prowling demons, the hiss of everything that slithered. He did not try to sleep.

The next day he was on the march again.

Deep within the rising pass he found a swinging bridge, another landmark. It was built of ropes as thick as tree trunks with wooden planks serving as the roadbed. A few hundred feet beneath the bridge, the turbulent Nualna River crashed over the huge, blunt boulders of the gorge. Here the trail turned north while the river cascaded down steep waterfalls flowing east. Beyond the falls to the west he could see only blue sky.

He left the trail and moved west to a cool shaded area near a waterfall. He had heard, but not seen any living creature for a day and a night, no bird, insect or beast. Here the river water was no haven for fish, frog or dragonfly, and the sky looked as if it had never served as a highway for bird or butterfly.

He peered into a still pond at the base of the waterfall, expecting to see his own reflection. But refractions of sunlight distorted his image so he could not tell who or what he saw. He started to kneel and drink the water, but stood instead and urinated on his rippling reflection.

It was dusk when he reached the top of the falls. Rain started drizzling down through thick mists. It was impossible to tell direction. Mists lay low, enveloping the ground. All he could see were thick, grey places of moving mysteries.

Gath found a dry perch under a shelf of overhanging

rock. When night came clouds of moving blackness swirled over him. Moon and star were invisible. He could not see the axe in his own hand. The sounds of the unseen crashing water blotted out all other sounds and dominated his senses. Again he did not sleep.

Morning arrived as a pale grey glow behind swirling fog. But the rain had stopped.

With burning red-rimmed eyes, Gath stalked out from under his shelf wearing an expression as temperate as a flung spear. He could not see trail or landmark. He growled, groped for his belongings and started off into the mists blindly. Ten feet of this, and he stopped short. An emerald and gold lizard poised on a black rock was staring at him audaciously.

Gath took a stride toward it and his eyes widened with curiosity. The arrogant lizard was wearing a thin gold collar. He grabbed for it, but it scooted off and vanished among the rocks, only to reappear on a flat bare area a short way off. An escort? Why not? He, more politely, moved after the lizard and it turned, led the way scittering forward.

Gradually the mists burnt off, and the midday sun spilled light down through blue sky to grace distant black clouds with crowns of dusty gold. The clouds clustered over the flaming mouths of several volcanic craters, the largest of which rose directly in front of him. The Land of Smoking Skies.

As he advanced, Gath spotted guards standing at the mouths of caves on the sides of the volcano. Coming closer, he saw a small troop of soldiers carrying game into one cave as another troop moved out. They saw Gath and seemed to hesitate and consult each other. But then they went on about their business.

He reached a rock staircase leading up to the two enormous golden doors Cobra had described. Upon arriving at the landing he found the golden doors slightly open and two soldiers in green leather waiting for him. Music and the scents of jasmine and strong, sweet liquor drifted out of the dark corridor behind them. The soldiers were heavy boned, with jewels on their fingers and in their ears. They welcomed Gath using the common language of barter, and told him that the Queen of Serpents awaited him in her quarters. Their tone was one of hardy warmth, but Gath found it difficult to trust. Their tongues were forked.

Thirty-one

THE HORNED HELMET

The two escorts led Gath slowly down a corridor of polished black rock. As they passed the open barracks door, Gath glimpsed men coiled with serpents, heard hissing sounds and pleasurable groans, and disgust crawled down his back.

Reaching the long tavernlike room, the escorts hesitated and soldiers, both male and female, stopped their drinking and conversations to look at Gath. They all had blackened, lewd eyes as cold-blooded as last year's dead. By contrast, their faces were vivid and hot. Glittering scales showed on the backs of their hands. In a corner a young naked girl, a Dowat, was chained to the wall playing a flute. Seeing Gath, she stopped and a flicker of hope touched her eyes. A soldier stood abruptly, kicked her, and she resumed playing.

The two escorts asked Gath if he wished to eat and clean up before being presented to their queen. Without looking at them, he snapped, "No."

He tossed his backpack in a corner, then, with axe still in hand, strode past the tables and preceeded his startled escorts through a blood-red door. Before the door shut a burst of bawdy laughter followed them out.

The guards led Gath down the tunnel of volcanic rock, through a corridor of polished obsidian and into a wide staircase. He noticed a large hole in the ceiling and paused, scrutinizing it intently, before proceeding up the opposite stairs. The two escorts had hurried ahead to part heavy silver drapes revealing a room spilling with gold and silver light. Gath entered alone, and the drapes fell closed behind him.

Cobra stood at the center of the silver floor, a figure of cascading diamonds and glittering light in silver scales. Regal. Magnificent. She stood perfectly still yet seemed to be constantly moving, like a liquid jewel being poured from a goblet. For a breath of time she softened and radiated rosy light from a voluptuous body of powdery rose-pink flesh, then the gown returned to behaving like the formal tunic of ornamental majesty which it was.

"Greetings, Dark One," she said with throaty emotion. "You are a welcome sight indeed. But you look exhausted. Your new armor must be very heavy."

He hardly heard her. Everything about her and the room emanated a discomforting elegance and heady sensuality that made his flesh crawl, yet brought color to his cheeks. Regaining his composure, he admitted, "It was a long trip."

"You didn't sleep, did you? I was afraid of that."

"That is my business."

"But it's my fault, and I am truly sorry. The creatures of the swamp and mountains did their best to ease your trip, but it is difficult for them to be quiet at night."

Gath's eyes impatiently searched the bed of black furs, the ebony cabinets, and the silver drapes which circled the room. "Where is it?" he demanded.

"There is no hurry. If you would like to eat and sleep

first, you are welcome to.'' She indicated her bed.

''I have no need of sleep.''

The corners of her full mouth drew down slightly, but then, with a subtle show of confidence, she nodded graciously and said, ''Then come with me.''

Cobra's glittering form glided to an internal stairway and down into it. Gath followed, taking note that it did not have a hole in the ceiling but was decorated artfully with ancient spears, swords, shields and pieces of armor.

The stairs descended in a steep circular fashion through a rough-hewn tunnel of basalt. Gath could feel himself approaching the center of the mountain. Black smoke hovered at its ceiling. As they descended, it gathered around their heads and the walls became hot.

Gath's face reddened, and he began to sweat. Cobra's movements showed no change, but the gleam of excitement in her eyes was not completely sane.

The base of the tunnel clouded with a smokey red glow. Gath squinted under the glare, his pupils retreating to inky points, then followed her blindly into a searing, enveloping light.

When his vision cleared he saw they stood in the cone of a living volcano. Its hard basalt floor was penetrated by holes bubbling and flaming with molten lava. The flames cast moving red light over the smoke-filled room, and crackled and bubbled with sounds of eerie aspiration. Then, as if the mountain itself were drawing its breath, the smoke was sucked away to reveal an altar over the large central hole of bubbling lava, a huge reptilian skull mounted on a rock. Flames filled the massive brain cavity. They alternately hid and revealed a glistening dark object, fondling it in their torrid embrace.

Gath, his eyes fixed on the altar, muttered, ''What place is this?''

''A sacred place,'' Cobra answered reverently. ''The only living altar of my master, the Lord of Death, whom we also call the Master of Darkness.''

He turned to her sharply, amazement and disbelief flashing behind the reflections of fire in his eyes.

"Do you doubt me?" she asked without concern.

Without warning the room shook. Thunder cracked. Pieces of rock fell from the ceiling beside Gath, and tongues of flame roared out of the nearby lava pits to lick his shins and drive him back against the wall.

Gath's boots were smoking. His chain mail was smeared with black smoking soot. When he looked at Cobra his expression was a long way from doubt, and showed signs of total conversion. The room grew quiet again.

Cobra's exquisite eyes shone with pride. "My master resides far below in the world of fire within the bowels of the earth, but sees . . . understands what we feel . . . what we think."

Gath did not argue.

She studied his face with satisfaction and continued, "The Lord of Death designed the helmet I spoke of. It is he himself who has selected me to make the choice of who shall wear it."

Gracefully she wound her way through several small flaming pits and stood before the stone bridge. Its tongue-like body arched through the flames of the large central fire pit, passed over the lower teeth of the monstrous outspread jaws and into the flame-filled brain. She beckoned Gath who had not moved. "Come, you can see it from here."

He moved cautiously through the fire pits to her side. She arched her long neck proudly and looked up reverently into the cavity. Gath, his head slightly averted, did the same.

The flames within the brain cavity lowered fitfully to reveal the dark metal of a magnificent horned helmet outlined sharply against billowing grey and yellow smoke. A tongue of flame held it erect at the center of the brain cavity. Its masked eyes glowed directly at Gath.

The Barbarian swelled as the thrill of anticipation surged through him. A reckless glint flickered across his eyes.

Cobra caught his glint and smiled. "It is beautiful, isn't it?"

He nodded.

"You can feel its power even from here."

He nodded again.

She turned to the helmet. Her voice came from a distant place, as if disembodied. "It is made with magic. From the spirit of a thousand tyrants and warriors, and from metal which has drunk so deeply of conquest it has assumed its own spirit, its own nature."

She turned to him, and her voice became intimate again. "Its steel is like no other, Dark One. Go look at it, see for yourself. It's alive."

Warily he glanced at her, then at the flames crackling around the bridge. Suddenly they lowered, as if in obedience to her silent command, and the bridge, smoking and spattered with small remnants of fire, lay open to the prize.

"Take your time," she murmured. "Stand close, look into its eyes and you will know that all I say is true. Meanwhile, I will be in my chambers . . . waiting for you . . . to conclude our contract."

He shook his head. "I will test it first." He slung his axe on his back.

"Wait!" she gasped. "What are you going to do?"

He pushed past her and started over the bridge. The bubbling lava boiled and a flame shot up, licked his legs in warning. He jumped forward, dashed for the brain cavity.

Cobra shrieked, "No! Don't!"

The room shook. Thundered. Parts of the bridge broke away under his feet. Rocks fell from the ceiling, crashed through the skull, knocking Gath to his knees. The hot rocks burnt his hands. The flames were again enclosing the helmet. It was only a vague dark object within crackling red fire. He jumped up and plunged both hands into the flames, growling at the searing pain, and came away with the horned prize. The hair on his arms was curled and smoking.

Cobra, screaming hysterically, retreated to the tunnel.

Gath, bobbling the hot steel, started down the bridge. More rocks fell. They crushed the center of the bridge, and it fell away, hit the lava and exploded. He ducked back into the protection of the brain cavity, avoiding the spewing lava, then leaped forward and sprang across the wide opening in the bridge.

The floor of the cone greeted him by splitting apart in large jagged cracks and spewing sheets of flame to wall him in. He charged through them. The room was quaking, lurching. Thunderclaps roared up out of the bowels of the earth. The entire floor of the cone buckled and threw him down. When he rolled upright he was isolated on an island of rock with lava bubbling in wide trenches surrounding him. Twenty feet away Cobra stood with her back to the entrance tunnel, arms spread, pressing against the sides of the tunnel. Defending it. Her voice was brutal, desperate, hoarse.

"You're mad! It will destroy you!"

Gath gloated at her in wild defiance. He unslung his axe from his back and rested it against his knee. Raising the helmet in both hands, he brought it to his face, held it there as he glared past its horns with savage reckless fury.

Cobra reeled. "You fool!"

He lifted the horned helmet above his head, then lowered it carefully, engulfing his head in its brutal blackness.

Cobra, shuddering, blocked the tunnel with her shimmering, hypnotic body. Her eyes were wet and vivid.

Gath watched her through the eye slits of the helmet. His blood coursed through him like thick hot ropes. His chest, neck and thighs heaved against the chain mail, stretching it. He crouched warily, gripping his axe in two hands. The hunger in his eyes was ravenous.

Cobra had advanced into the cone and was smiling at him. But her teeth extruded strangely and there was a queer, sickly tint to her face and eyes. The whites turned dead yellow, and fangs appeared at the corners of her hot red lips.

She hissed, "You will not escape. The helmet won't let you. But if you honor your contract . . . you will deal in death like no other man has ever dealt before. You will become the champion of the Master of Darkness . . . the Lord of Death's executioner."

Gath growled and leapt off his island. Flames shot up at him. The room again shook and thundered. Rocks came hurtling down, and knocked him to the floor.

Cobra, writhing in a whiplike fashion, screamed, "Go then! Go and learn! You will never know rest again! The Master owns you now! You're mine!"

Gath rolled up, raced for the tunnel, and the floor split apart under him. He leaped to the side, crashed against the wall.

Cobra spread her jaws and spit at him. Her venom sizzled against his chain mail as she plunged into the tunnel.

Gath rose with his back against the wall as the ground started to collapse under him. He swung his axe high, buried the blade in a shelf of earth overhead, then climbed the handle as the ground gave way under him.

He clambered onto the shelf of rock and headed for the tunnel. Flames tongued him and scorched his metal. Ahead a huge protrusion of earth and stone blocked his passage. He ate into it with his axe desperately to cleave a crevice. Then he turned his shoulder to the rock and drove it into it. A dusty rubble dribbled through the slim fissure and fell into the bubbling lava below. He drove his shoulder into the rock again, and it sagged with a loud wrenching crunch, hung motionless with dirt and pebbles trickling loose, and dropped in one lump to the floor of the cone, smothering the nearby fires and filling the cone with dust.

Gath picked his way across the ridge until he was above the tunnel, jumped down, and raced into it.

Thick black smoke engulfed him as he raced up through the passage. Thunder from below shook it. Reaching the stairway, he plucked a heavy spear off the wall, and advanced up the stairs with axe in one hand, spear in the other.

Convulsions of smoke and flames and thunder boiled up out of the stairwell into Cobra's chambers, then out of the demonic breath appeared a black horror. A spiked, horned helmet with its eye slits spitting flames of fury.

Thirty-two
THE SENTRY

The horned helmet faced huge spreading jaws. Saliva as thick and green as wet grass dripped from teeth as long as table legs. They protected a raw purple throat which vomited a forked tongue, about three hundred pounds of red meat. The jaws belonged to a snake as thick as a full grown pine tree. The silver drapes of the Queen of Serpent's bedchamber were drawn back to reveal its body behind the surrounding silver columns. Its head rose up out of the entrance stairway completely blocking it. Its lower jaw rested on the floor of the chamber. Cobra stood beside it, only a foot taller than its largest fang.

The monster hissed. The floor shook from its trembling weight, and several silver columns fell knocking Cobra aside. She staggered back, and stumbled down the entrance stairway out of sight.

Gath's metal-clad body hurtled out of the smoke. His spear was leveled at the reptile. The blade drove between two white teeth and buried itself in the pulpy meat of the tongue. The tongue convulsed, cracked the spear against the jaw's upper teeth and whipped the holder into the air. He twisted in midair, landed on all fours, and leapt up, bringing his axe with him. He caught a tooth with the blade, and cracked it off. But the impact flipped him tumbling back across the room empty-handed.

He rose slowly in the middle of the black swirling smoke, the helmet's eyes glowing. His body, fed by battle, swelled. The chain mail bulged at his chest stretching the links from circles to ovals. The hides under the metal pressed through the small openings as if the steel was growing fur. Sweat dripped from the rim of his helmet, sizzled on his mail and ran in bright rivulets down his pulsing arms.

He backed down into the interior stairway and vanished within the smoke. A short time later he reappeared carrying a brass bucket of bubbling lava and marched for the mouth of the reptile. The snake obliged by spreading its jaws in a mindless repetition of what normally worked best for it. Gath charged through the gap he had made in the snake's lower teeth and heaved the lava, bucket and all, into the throat.

The lava splattered over the wet purple flesh. The monster mouth sizzled, foamed. Its tongue shot forward, caught Gath in the chest and drove him out as the upper teeth clanged down with shattering force.

Gath hit the ground, kept rolling and came up facing the writhing creature, dodging the flaming, smoking spittle, his axe back in his hands.

The reptile's body thrashed and convulsed, knocked over columns and bulged out into the room with its mouth vomiting bits of teeth, chunks of tongue, and the gore of throat and brain tissue.

As Gath started forward, axe raised, the snake whipped forward, knocked him down, and rode over him. There was a dull smoky haze over its yellow gold eyes. It was blind.

The lava had reached the brain cavity. Then the head collapsed on the floor, spitting up melon-sized glands and a river of steaming blood.

Gath clawed through the gore and found the body blocking his escape. He climbed the reptile's convulsing back, stumbled along it toward the entrance stairway. The last convulsion carried him up to the ceiling. He dropped flat and, axe in hand, slid down the slick wet back of the snake into the stairway. He dropped to the floor, squeezed past the undulating tail, and raced up the polished obsidian passageway, not seeing Cobra's unconscious body partially buried by rubble.

Thirty-three

THE PRISONER

Gath stepped through the red doorway into the tavern.

It was empty. Everything was silent except for the distant thunder of the Lord of Death raging within the earth. Furniture had been thrown down and shattered by falling rocks. Ceiling beams were splintered and broken. Dirt trickled down from cracks in the roof to make neat conical piles on the floor.

Gath moved through, passed the cluttered empty barracks room, and reached the golden doors. He kicked them open, and strode out into the sunlight.

There was no one in sight. The caves and the mountainsides appeared deserted. The volcano was spewing smoke at the sky, turning it black. A strange unquiet emptiness permeated everything. Sensing threats everywhere but seeing none, he descended the stairs and trotted down the trail heading for the swamp.

By nightfall he made the waterfalls and found an overhanging shelf of rock. He made a camp under it and built a fire. Falling to the ground more than sitting, he leaned tiredly against the rock and unbuckled the strap under his chin to remove the helmet. The helmet would not come off. Its chain mail cowl had somehow become tangled with his body armor. He sat up and worked at it for awhile, but, without any sort of mirror and in the dim light, he could not free it. He sagged back, sighed, then closed his eyes. But he could not sleep.

Thirty-four

BUTTERFLY MORNING

The Kitzakk fort was situated on the heights of the cataracts at the mouth of the main pass, The Narrows. It was built of wood and designed in ancient fashion, like a butterfly. The head was the main gate, with the mouth opening on the pass. The front wings spread forward along the sides of the pass then fanned out backwards forming the main body of the fort. The hind wings formed forked fortifications to guard the rear gate.

At the very center of the fort, on a rectangular earthen rise, a red lacquered box rested on a shallow black altar.

Behind the box General Yat-Feng sat on his bamboo campaign stool watching the eastern horizon where the cool glow of dawn light promised to deliver the sun. Beside him, mounted on a red pole, two horsetails fluttered on the morning breeze, the insignia of his rank as field commander. Standing beside him were six greybeards, old campaigners wearing battered, unfashionable armor from forgotten wars. They also watched the horizon.

The faces of the old warriors were set with proud expectation. They had reenlisted to consult with Yat-Feng on the organization and training of new raider regiments and the tactics of the raids which were about to commence.

About the fort all human life stood waiting. Some at attention, others scratching, whispering: the regiments, mule skinners, drivers, animal and slave wranglers, cooks, skinners, armorers and general scavengers. Horses, oxen, mules, buffalo and camels, momentarily masterless, drifted about inside the stables and corrals, and wandered loose among a formation of large wagons, chewing grass and tent ropes.

A hush fell over the still camp as the white-gold eye of the sun appeared. When the light touched Yat-Feng's flat brown face, he chanted, "Let the butterfly free," and the others present echoed the chant three times.

The eldest greybeard kneeled reverently over the red box and removed the lid. Within the black interior poised a large yellow and black swallowtail butterfly. It remained motionless for a long moment, then fluttered, lifting itself out of the box into the white-gold light on wings of weightless beauty.

Gasps of exaltation ran through the crowd, then cheering broke out.

The communications sergeant in the wooden signal tower which stood at the highest point of the camp, lifted a huge yellow and black butterfly flag mounted on a long black pole. It danced with rhythmic sweeps in the air, and the thrill of proud memories played among the wrinkled features of the old campaigners.

The message, passing from the fort to the first flag tower, then from flag tower to flag tower, was carried across the high cataract, then down through the three selected passes.

The Hammer Regiment waited in Wowell Pass to attack Bone Camp. It was the home of the left-handed totem people called the Wowells. Among them were the witches who had manufactured the totems from the dead scouts.

The Spear Regiment was positioned in Snake Pass above Pinetree Bridge. Beyond the bridge was a log village of the Barhacha Woodmen.

The Black Hand Regiment waited in the pass above Short Crossing to hit the village called Coin, the home of the priestly Kavens, the money changers.

When the commanders of these three regiments saw the signal flags, they ordered their mounted troops forward, and they plunged, with trumpets blaring, down the three passes. As they did the first of two innovations which had been made in the day's order of combat took place.

A desert people called the Feyan Dervishes had been enlisted as irregular troops in the Kitzakk Army. They were a tattered group of wanderers who were converts to the cult of the Butterfly Goddess. They had a fetish for pain and, when half-mad on drugs, an insatiable appetite for sacrificial death. These dervishes were to strike first from within the target villages where they had hidden themselves.

On hearing the regimental trumpets, the dervishes erupted from their hiding places screaming and waving daggers and torches. They were stark naked. Their flesh was stained with carmine from toe to forehead, and their hair and flesh glistened with translucent pitch. Noses bled, and trickled blood over foam-flecked lips. Their eyes were mad with drugs and death.

They grabbed the first available chief, magistrate or priest and stabbed them, then set their own bodies on fire. The thick pitch ignited instantly, turning them into living torches, and they raced screaming throughout the three villages setting fires and spreading terror. Before the villagers could kill them, the dervishes flung themselves onto the nearest child or aging woman and clung on with teeth and nails. Both assassin and victim burnt to death before they could be pried apart. The grotesque beauty of the carmine bodies and the earsplitting discord of shrieking voices turned each village to mindless pandemonium.

Next came the attack, and here the second innovation in tactics occurred. Each soldier wore a regimental flag in the old style, mounted on the back of his armor. This added height, color and fluid, flashing movement to the regiments as they galloped down out of the cataracts toward the awestruck, disorganized villagers. Before the Barbarians recovered, the Kitzakks had crossed the gorge and dashed through the gaps in the unfinished walls of the villages.

The battle at each village was a routine Kitzakk job-of-work. At the points where the Barbarians were able to initiate significant resistance, the Kitzakks surrounded and contained them. Then, while the main body of Kitzakk soldiers swept into the village to bottle up the children and young women, a Company of White Archers was brought into action. Each soldier carried a long composite bow made of bone and bamboo that stood two heads taller than himself. Each was a veteran sharpshooter. They set up on rooftops and with deadly rhythmic accuracy shot down the small pockets of resistance.

The result was screaming surrender.

The women, children and surviving men were then herded into a long line stretching out of the villages and across the bridges. At the same time the Companies of Chainmen with their wagons of chains and cages rode across the bridges into the village to form two parallel lines. The Kitzakks chained and caged their living booty, then turned about and left in the same orderly manner in which they had arrived.

The remaining Barbarians were driven into the forest, and Companies of Engineers entered in large wagons. With fire, exploding jars of pitch, and rake, shovel and hoe, the engineers then leveled the mud, brick and stone villages of Coin and Bone Camp, and the log structures of the Barhacha.

The commander of each regiment entered his conquered village and measured the rubble of its body with his black ceremonial rope, knotted in three equal sections. No structure remained above its length.

The commanders folded their ropes neatly, tucked them inside their armor, and surveyed the scenes of slaughter and destruction with satisfaction.

Later, as the raiding parties retreated through the passes, the slavers forced their prisoners to shake their chains. Each chain was made with tuned metal, so an eerily beautiful harmony swelled like a chorus of temple bells and was carried by the wind back to the forests where the huddled, beaten barbarians heard them and wept.

Bounty hunters lying in wait also heard the music of the chains, and crept covertly into the forest on separate trails.

Thirty-five
RED JAW

Brown John sat in the driver's box of his colorful wagon at Pinwheel Crossing, where the roads to the border villages joined Amber Road, and several other roads leading to different sectors of the deep forest. The wagon was parked in the afternoon shade on the western side of the crossing. The old man was watching refugees from the demolished villages flow north in a steady stream in hope of finding safety from the Kitzakks.

He had tried to count them, but it was impossible. The Barhacha, the Kavens and the Wowells were in full flight, and among them were Barbarians whose villages had not been raided: groups of Cytherians from Weaver and outlaw bands. The homeless traveled on wagons and drove pack animals and surviving livestock. Only a few weapons could be seen, and no warriors.

Brown John's head drooped dejectedly. The Kitzakks had reached across continents to harvest flesh. To reach a little farther into the forest would not inconvenience them.

Across the road, under a spreading oak, the tribal chiefs were meeting. They paced and sat on tree stumps talking animatedly. Bone and Dirken stood at the edge of the group. After a moment, the chief of the Dowats, a man called Jathh, with a patch over his eye, turned to the two Grillards and spoke to them. They listened, intently, nodded and dodged through the fleeing multitude to Brown John.

Bone leaped up beside him. "It's you they need now, it is, and they've finally figured it out. They want you to sit with them, and be a member of the Council of Chiefs."

"Is that so?" Brown John replied slowly. Ideas tumbled behind his troubled eyes, and he turned to Dirken. "Whose idea was this?"

"I don't really know," Dirken said with a theatrical whisper. "Someone not so dumb would be my guess."

"They've got no leader," Bone added. "Not a real one. All they can agree on is to argue."

With only a trace of the bitterness Brown John felt, he said quietly, "Yes, they would ask . . . now that it is too late for so many of their kinfolk. They probably believe I will negotiate with their new hero for them. But . . . they will have to do the waiting now."

The brothers liked that, and it showed.

Brown John turned to Dirken. "Go back to them. Thank them for their invitation, and do it with sincerity, and tell them that I have pressing business elsewhere this afternoon, but that I may be available this evening."

Dirken nodded, and pulled at Bone.

"No," said his father. "He will stay with me. And,

Dirken, talk slowly and courteously, but with pride, just as you did in *Up by Lamplight*. Go now, and don't run, but leave as soon as you have their answer."

With a slow, easy manner, Dirken nodded, got down off the wagon, and paraded back through the flowing refugees toward the waiting chiefs.

As they turned to welcome him, his father spoke to Bone, "Take the Weaver Road. We're going to talk to Robin."

Bone, grinning with pleasure, cracked his whip, and the wagon lurched forward through the refugees and rolled onto Weaver Road.

Dirken delivered his father's message. The chiefs huddled briefly, then Jathh approached Dirken stiffly and told him that the council would welcome his father's participation at the evening meeting. Dirken bowed graciously, walked jauntily to the wagon and climbed aboard as it continued to roll slowly down Weaver Road.

There was only a scattering of elderly people coming up the road. Those were the last people they saw until an hour later when they approached a stretch of apple trees.

A man was sitting on a grassy knoll with his back against the greyish trunk of a tree laden with green apples. He was neatly slicing an apple into sections and eating them. He wore plain leather boots and a leather tunic banded by several buckled belts that carried a wide range of different sized and shaped daggers. A leather skullcap with long, dangling earflaps covered his square head, and he wore a necklace of brightly colored beads interspersed with human finger bones. His eyes were grey and empty, unmemorable. What was memorable was the brilliant red stubble on his enormous chin.

As the wagon lumbered by, Brown John studied the man with the corners of his eyes. When the wagon was well past, he motioned to Bone and his son reined up. The brothers looked at their father with questioning eyes. Before they could speak, Brown John silenced them with a raised finger, picked up his walking stick and got down off the wagon. With a jerking limp and leaning heavily on the stick, he started back toward the stranger.

Brown John stopped a good fifteen feet short of the big-jawed man, and waited respectfully. The man carved and ate three more sections of his apple, then lifted his head slightly, measuring the old man with thin, squinting eyes.

Brown John dipped his head courteously, and asked meekly, "Excuse me, sir, but perhaps you could do a tired traveling player a favor?"

"And perhaps not," the stranger replied indifferently.

"I understand," the old actor agreed. "Nothing is certain in these tragic times. Nothing at all." His deliberately artless eyes met the stranger's stare. "I am afraid we are lost. I am trying to reach the village called Coin, which I hear has been attacked by Outlanders. I . . . I have relatives there. Could you tell me if this is the right road?"

"This road leads to Weaver."

The old man signed tiredly, and sank a little. "Then we are surely lost. Do you, perhaps, have a map?"

"You think I'm a rich man? That I can afford a scribe to draw maps?" His red jaws snapped impatiently.

"No, no! It is only that I can see that you cut your apple with great care and skill. I thought that, perhaps, such a precise and well-organized man might also have a map!"

The man slid the last section of his apple past his pale lips, chewed it slowly, his eyes regarding the old man curiously. He swallowed, and said, "You have sharp eyes . . . for an actor. Perhaps we can help each other." He unbuckled a pouch, and removed a folded parchment.

Brown John leaned forward on his stick, but did not move closer. The stranger looked up at him sharply. "You'll never find out where you are standing over there."

Brown John nodded. "I know, it is just that a man of my age and physical infirmities must move with care."

The stranger offered what he considered a smile. It did

unpleasant things to his face. "You can die just as suddenly over there as you can over here," he said. He lifted a small loaded and cocked crossbow from behind a grassy rise and leveled it playfully at the tottering figure. "Come on over and talk to Red Jaw."

Brown John mumbled meekly, shuffled over under the tree and sat down placing his walking stick across his knee. The bounty hunter handed him his map. Brown John studied it making appropriate murmurs of discovery.

"Humm! Oh yes, here it is. Thank you."

He looked up to return the map and nearly dropped it.

Red Jaw was holding a black, hand carved doll in his hands. It was a likeness of Gath. Brown John needed all his craft to hide the jolts of shock that went through him.

"Cute, isn't it?" Red Jaw said conversationally. "Ever see a life-sized version? Or heard words about anyone who might look like this?" He pushed the doll closer to the older man. Brown John hesitated, then nodded, once. Red Jaw, with sudden animation in his empty eyes, drew the map from his limp hands. "My map tells you where your village is, your words tell me where he is. Fair?"

Brown John shifted nervously, glanced back at his wagon, then muttered, "The Shades. He lives somewhere in The Shades."

"Shades?" Red Jaw's forehead gathered in folds.

Brown John pointed at the parchment. "It's on your map. The large forest to the west there."

Red Jaw, squinting, raised the map to his eyes.

Brown John grabbed his walking stick with two hands, and drove it through the map into the bounty hunter's chest bone. The blow drove him against the trunk of the tree, pinned him there, gasping. Brown John shouted over his shoulder, "Hurry, lads! Hurry!"

Bone and Dirken leapt out and raced for their father.

Red Jaw, fighting for breath, tried to wrestle the stick aside. The old man held him in place with grunting, sweating effort. Red Jaw drew a knife from his belt, and raised it as Bone and Dirken jumped him. They pulled his arms back and stretched them around the tree until he dropped the knife.

Brown John, without letting up on his stick, bellowed, "Don't play with him!"

Bone and Dirken blanched at the ferocity of his tone. Dirken dropped on Red Jaw's head and, using his body weight, slammed him back over an exposed root and Bone drove his sword into his bulging chest with such force that it splintered ribs and backbone. The blade went four inches into the earth before coming to a stop.

Brown John, heaving from the exertion, clutched his chest and sat back. Bone, hands numb from the impact, tried to remove his sword, but couldn't budge it. His father waved him off, still panting. "Leave it for awhile . . . you never know . . . when his kind are truly dead."

The old man stared at Red Jaw's bulging eyes. When he got his breath, he whispered, "Bounty hunter."

The brothers stepped away from the contorted corpse, bodies cocked. The man hunter continued to bleed.

"How can you tell?" whispered Dirken.

"The knives. There's one for every bone in the body," Brown John said with recovered energy. "We've done well."

He lifted the doll and map off the ground where they had fallen, held them up. "This is a Kitzakk map, and this is a totem made by the hand of someone very skilled. I would advise you not to touch it. Its magic may be strong."

They did not argue.

Brown John looked musingly at the black doll and murmured, "Incredible. What detail! As if the doll itself had once been alive."

He looked up and snapped, "Search him."

His sons did the work quickly, searched Red Jaw's many satchels as well as his boots and tunic. Bone came away with a handful of heavy coins, and belts and daggers strung over his shoulders. Dirken, with a dramatic gesture, laid another doll in his father's hands. It was white.

Brown John held it with trembling, respectful fingers as he turned it over, and over, then said, "Oh, my."

When Brown John and his sons reached Weaver, at sundown, they parked their wagon outside the Forest Gate. Before their feet touched the ground, Robin was heading for them with a crowd of frightened children. Their faces were tearstained; their little hands pulled at her tunic.

Reaching Brown John, she clung to him crying. "You're here! You're here!" Her big feathery eyes, moist with desperation, looked up at him trustingly. "What can we do?"

"What we must," he said quietly.

"Did . . . did Gath try to stop them?"

Brown John shook his head.

"Nobody's seen him." Bone interjected. "Not for days."

Robin sank slightly, then lifted her chin gallantly. "I'll find him. I'll leave right now."

Thirty-six

CHICKEN BROTH

It was night when Cobra's eyes blinked open. Above her, in the golden torchlit ceiling of her bedroom, she could see the strangely elongated reflection of her supine body cushioned by down pillows with soft fur covers. She explored her nose and lips with cold fingertips, found blood, and looked at it. Her eyes were startled, cold, as if her brain had turned to ice.

She pushed herself onto an elbow, and glanced around. A silver tray stood on a nightstand beside her bed. On it was a silver pitcher and cup, and a silver bowl steaming with chicken broth. Behind the stand her alchemist, Schraak, and his two assistants, kneeled in patient attendance. Beyond them the head of the giant snake was upended. Its tangled and twisted body nearly filled the room. Smoke still filtered out of the interior stairway.

The room trembled and Cobra sat up, startled. Across the room, past a curve of the snake's motionless body, silver columns were down. She pushed herself off the bed, and stumbled beyond the toppled columns to a large hole dug into the wall of the tunnel beyond. Guards, stripped to scaly waists, were digging. She turned to her alchemist.

Schraak rose and said gently, "We are preparing a fitting burial for your beloved sentry . . . in the holy fire pits."

Cobra glared at them fiercely. "Madness! Cut him apart, and take him down in pieces. There is no time for tunnels." She dismissed the subject with a wave of her hand, and demanded, "How long have I been unconscious?"

Schraak cowered. "This is the second night you've slept. You were nearly buried in the tunnel under fallen rock, so we thought it wise to let you rest."

She pressed her finger against her brow. "Tell them to stop digging immediately and remove this sickening stench."

Schraak motioned to his assistants, and they, bowing, hurried off.

She turned to Schraak. "Where are you holding the Barbarian?"

Schraak shifted uneasily. "He . . . he's escaped."

"What?" Involuntarily her body changed color and texture. The scales turned crystalline, and snowy white cracks appeared in them as if she were turning to ice.

Schraak stammered inarticulately, then blurted, "Everyone ran. We . . . we thought the mountain was going to explode.''

"Fool!'' she hissed. ''Have you never heard the anger of our god before. Are you incapable of thought? He stole the helmet.''

Schraak gasped.

She snarled, started pacing with a cold stiffness, and from deep in the mountain came a roar. She shuddered. ''It is no wonder he still rages.'' She turned hard on Schraak. ''What time is it?''

''Morning comes within an hour, perhaps two.''

A cruel line lifted a corner of her mouth; it stayed in her cheek as she spoke. ''He won't dare travel at night. That means he won't reach Noga Swamp until tomorrow morning.'' The line pushed a malevolent smile into one cheek, and with rising excitement she whispered, ''Alert the swamp. Before daylight every servant who dwells there must know the Dark One has stolen the Master's helmet and must be stopped. And tell them, when they catch him, he is to be eaten alive . . . finger by finger.''

''But there's only one, two hours at most. We'll never . . .''

''Send water snakes by the underground river,'' she said with authority. ''We will follow the same way and arrive in time to watch the ants feed on his rotting scraps.''

Schraak bowed, and hurried down into the interior staircase.

Cobra watched him, then turned to see his assistants reappear with five guards. Holding axes in their sweating hands, they contemplated the body of the monster like butchers faced with quartering a steer with their fingernails.

Cobra hissed contemptuously, ''Start with the head.''

They bowed and started to hack at the neck. Cobra watched the blood spurt until it had painted the guards red, then reached for her still-warm chicken broth. She lifted

the silver bowl to her dry lips and drank. Her nostrils
flinched at the smell and taste of the potion. When she
could see the silver of the bottom of the bowl, the rose tint
had returned to her translucent cheeks.

Thirty-seven

NOGA SWAMP

Gath sat under an overhanging rock in Panga Pass blinking
at the first light of day brushing the distant night sky.
Behind the slits of the horned helmet, his eyes were
weblike red trails. The searing, stinging lids hammered
each other. But he did not dare sleep.

The helmet had produced an incredible heat, as if his
brains and blood were on fire. He was soaked with sweat
and parched. Earlier in the night, he had thought the heat
would fry his flesh and bones and kill him, and he had
frantically and blindly tried to untangle its cowl from the
chain mail, but failed. Then the heat abated somewhat and
a strange unnatural sensation had coursed through him, as
if the heat had somehow melded his head into the helmet.
He could feel the cool night air on its metal, and at the tips
of the horns. They had become part of his flesh, and they
brought other sensations. He could sense danger about him
as if it were a palpable substance. All night he had felt it:
cannibal ants crawling under the earth he sat on, and
predators hiding behind the tall grass swaying nearby.

The helmet was serving him like an infallible sentry, but
it was also playing a deadly game with him. His eyes
fluttered tiredly, then closed and stayed closed. His head

dropped sideways and the weight of the helmet, just as it had been doing all night, got the better of his neck and tried to throw him to the ground. With a grunt, Gath came awake and yanked his head upright. He gasped with exhaustion, then forced the helmet to behave like a normal helmet and remain balanced on his head.

He looked around warily as his body heaved with heavy breathing and steam drifted through the links of his chain mail. His eyes fluttered and closed again. This time the helmet enlisted a numb elbow as an ally, and dropped him to the ground. His helmet hit a rock, and clanged with mind-splitting vibrations. Metal ate into his jaw and scalp. The pain screamed into the core of his brain, leaving him paralyzed. He lay like dead meat on a plate until a sharp and different pain arrived unannounced, and his eyes snapped open.

Gath was eye to eye with three inches of feisty dragon-lizard. It was perched on his sprawled hand, and break-fasting on his thumb.

The thumb tolerated this only a moment, then punched the lizard aside. The reptile tumbled over three times, leapt up and charged again. The thumb was ready. It had taken hold of a neighborly fingertip and drawn it back like a tiny catapult. It snapped, clubbed the reptile in the side of its blue jaw, and drove it several feet through the air to land in an unconscious lump beside his boot.

Gath picked up the lizard, tore off the head, legs and tail, and shoved the body through the mouth hole of the helmet into his mouth. Chewing and swallowing ravenous-ly, he dragged himself to his knees. The horned helmet suddenly lifted, and his eyes stared at the underside of the overhanging rock. The sense of danger was so palpable it could have grown hair. His muscles rippled and swelled in response, as if instructed by the helmet. His body exploded off the ground, and drove the helmet into the lip of the rock shattering it. He stepped back quickly. The crumbling pieces fell to the ground in a cloud of dirt carrying a flailing, six-foot python. Its mouth stretched wide displaying a parade of toothy executioners. Gath closed it with his boot, flattening it to a bony pulp.

He picked up his axe, strode out and a din of noises greeted him. He could see grass and brush moving, and feel deadly adversaries lurking in the shadows and behind rocks. He trotted down the trail, ready for their attack, wanting it, but they did not appear.

He reached Noga Swamp, in good time. Home waited beyond its wet, murky body, but the local residents had other destinations in mind. Every branch, root and vine was alive with deadly creatures, all hungry to fill their bellies with his meat, and whirlpools of murky water beckoned with the same dread invitation.

He turned along the dirt road with a determined trot, then picked up the pace and began to run. Up ahead, as far as the floating bridge, the entire surface of the road undulated with swarming lizards and snakes. He charged onto the living carpet, his boots crunching and churning. Viper, adder and lizard cracked their teeth on his chain mail as he dodged and leapt past, but others buried fangs in calf and shin.

He made it to the bridge and pulled up gasping with horror. A dozen tiny snakes clung to metal and flesh, pumping venom into them. He ground his teeth, picking and slapping them off, then gave up and waited for the venom to do its work.

The pain came, and he staggered back, blinded. The heat was swept from his body by an icy wave of terror, then death's cold bite tore into him. It did not allow him a flashing moment to review his life, but propelled him headlong into an endless void of emptiness and loneliness. He was nothing. But he still stood on his feet, and still held his axe.

He howled with the crying torment of death. But still he stood.

The coldness abated, then the heat came surging back, like flames searing through his veins. His muscles corded, then bulged and stretched the confining chain mail until it was molded by his body. His bones swelled within his meat until his joints accommodated his weighty mass. He fed on the power of the helmet.

He looked down at himself uncertainly, then strode on through the foreboding landscape to the center of the swamp where the stone bridge spanned the two ponds. Sunlight trickled through the leafy roof. Reaching it, he stopped and bathed alone in its splendor as understanding and exhilaration surged through him. He was a massive horned demon of black metal and sinew graced by golden light, drinking air and holding the bridge with booted feet as if all the elements were personal possessions. The helmet had transformed him. He was death, and he had never felt so alive.

Thirty-eight
COBRA'S EXECUTIONERS

Gath looked up toward the sky, and fire glimmered behind the eye slits of his helmet with an insatiable and unnatural hunger.

High overhead among the branches of the tree cover there was movement, the angular jerking movement of Feldalda tree pythons. Their grey-green color and sharp angles made their long, thick bodies look like tree branches. Suddenly they defied their instinct to hide themselves, serpentined to a position directly over Gath, and deliberately threw themselves into the air. Their bodies flattened, catching the air, and they fell in a controlled dive toward him, with saliva flying from their open jaws.

Flames spit from the eyes of the horned helmet. Gath's body sank into a cocked position, eager to feed.

Fear glittered in the eyes of several of the pythons, as if they suddenly had serious thoughts of turning back.

The axe soared skyward in a sweeping arc. The blade kicked back shafts of sunlight, then sliced through the first wave of pythons to send heads and lengths of body flying. One reptile, eluding the axe, hit the helmet, and its jawbone was driven back into its brain. The mass of swarming snakes, living and dead, fell over him, and he dropped on his back, losing his axe. Rolling over and over, he pounded the tangle of squirming muscle with fists, elbows and knees.

Jaws clamped down on a horn of his helmet, around his metal-clad knees, and over an elbow. Living lengths of thick muscle wrapped around his legs, neck, and arms. In one mass they wrestled, pulled and rolled toward the edge of the bridge.

Gath ripped an arm free, drew a dagger and began to saw. Blood spurted from severed necks and trunks, drenched his chain mail and blinded several snakes. A flailing head drove the dagger from his grip. His legs and chest were wrapped in snakes, being crushed. His only weapons were his fingers. He sank them into snake flesh. The bodies were too thick for the grasp of his hands to hold, but his fingers continued to squeeze relentlessly.

The cold nothingness of death again coursed through him. But this time it exhilarated him. A thundering, cavernous roar echoed out of the mouth hole of the helmet, and his fingers plunged into the meaty bodies, ripping away handfuls of flesh. The reptiles, writhing for escape, dragged Gath's body and axe off the edge of the bridge, and he plunged heavily into the water below.

The helmet sizzled and brought the murky liquid around it to a bubbling boil as flames continued to spit from the eye slits. The surviving reptiles floundered off, churning up the muck to blind Gath. On his hands and knees, and with his lungs aching for air, he probed the muddy bed hunting for his axe.

Moments later, the spike of the horned helmet rose slowly out of the murky slime, followed by the steaming helmet. Gath, gasping, stood shoulder deep in a fetid, black and blood-red pool of mutilated lengths of snake. He waded onto a small island of mossy earth, and stood panting and dripping slime, axe in hand. An ominous, deathlike silence pervaded the swamp.

Suddenly he dropped into a slight crouch and turned slowly in place.

Something large and dark loomed toward him out of the light at the center of the lake. It emerged teeth first. The elephant-sized alligator. Green slime dripped from its rotting jaws. They were parted, showing jagged, sharp stumps, dark with yellow and black holes. The alligator belched, and a pale green mist issued from its mouth.

The Death Dealer staggered back gagging and blinking at the alligator's foul, stinging breath, then glanced about. He had an audience now. A crowd of fair-sized alligators, no more than twenty or thirty feet long, floated on the water not far off. Snakes were gathered in the treetops, dangling recklessly to get a clear view. Cape bulls, wart hogs, lizards and swarms of white ants covered the banks along the raised road and the bridge overhead.

Gath looked back at his latest threat.

Reaching the island, it shuffled forward to do what it, the Lord of the Swamp, had done for centuries: destroy any competitor that invaded its world.

The ancient predator spread its mouth until its upper jaw blotted out the sun, leaving Gath in shadows to contemplate the thick ropes of slime that stretched between the upper and lower teeth. Then he bolted forward, and leapt in between a gap in the lower teeth. He advanced on the two tonguelike slabs of pink muscle blocking the throat, his axe slaughtering the living red meat underfoot. The alligator gagged violently, throwing Gath backwards into a puddle of stinging digestive fluids.

Then the alligator remembered to close its mouth.

The Barbarian, crouched in the bowl of the jaw, watched the upper jaw descend and snap shut. The roof of the reptile's throat was only a few feet away. With all his strength he thrust up to drive his axe blade through the pulpy roof at the back of the mouth and into the brain.

The monster sucked in its breath, and Gath was pulled, tumbling, toward the throat. He spun, bringing the axe handle around in front of him, and it stuck in the sides of the throat like a fence rail, brought him to a stop.

Gath, heaving for breath and with body stinging, looked around. The flames from the helmet cast eerie orange light on the dark living cavity dripping saliva. The whole structure shuddered. Slowly the cavity began to roll over, then flopped upside down, dropping Gath on his back against the roof of the mouth. Saliva puddled around him, then water began to flow between the predator's teeth and fill the bowl as the alligator began to sink.

Once more Gath felt death's cold bite.

Thirty-nine

BOOTED FEET

The giant alligator, after thousands of years of service to the Lord of Death, was dead. It floated belly-up at the eastern edge of the Noga Swamp. Its massive head was moored in mud. It had obviously been used as a raft.

Beside the body were footprints through the mud, and into a stand of tall reeds, some parted and crushed by booted feet.

Rage distorted Cobra's face under the glittering, silver magnificence of her skullcap. She swore bitterly, curses that her attendants noted as substantially more colorful than usual. They stood warily beside her on the road, fearing to comment on the disaster before them. Beyond the group, within the thousand shadows of the swamp, small reptilian eyes glittered and bodies trembled.

Cobra shuddered and hugged herself, muttering, "He will wish he had died here in the swamp. I promise it."

She stepped off the road and followed the footprints toward the reeds. "You will wait here until I return."

They bowed low in reply.

The footprints marked a path through the reeds and around the skulls marking Trail's End, then vanished on hard earth. Instinctively she reached for her Glyder Snake, then remembered her pocket was empty and scowled. Down the trail she found shrubs and brush recently crushed by some bulky creature. Beyond them was a new trail of crushed undergrowth. Whoever made it had no fear of being tracked. She followed it anyway.

Forty

LIVING METAL

Deep within The Shades, Gath of Baal stood alone beside Smooth Pond, a familiar mirror-surfaced puddle of water as wide as he was tall. It was formed by the creek which twisted and curved through the rain forest just west of his root house. His sun-darkened chest was naked. The hair had been rubbed off by the chain mail which dangled from his hips. He rubbed his back against a tree dislodging the leeches still feeding there. Then he stretched, and a low sigh came from the helmet, as natural as the wind speaking as it passes through a cave hollow.

It was time to challenge the helmet again. He tried levering it off using the handle of his axe, then tried hammering its edges to widen the opening. Each attempt to remove it failed. But he kept at it until his body rebelled, and he sagged in defeat.

After a moment he crawled back to the mirrorlike pond, and looked reluctantly down at the reflection shimmering on its smooth surface.

The horned helmet, eerily elongated, looked up at him with red glowing eyes. A breeze brushed the surface, and the eyes moved in haunted ripples. When the water quieted, the red glow had faded. Made of metal and bone, with a hundred nicks and scrapes from sword, mace and axe, the helmet itself looked proud and triumphant. But there was no triumph in the eyes, and they seemed to belong to a stranger.

He touched the dark metal tentatively. Then he dipped a fingertip into a hole and felt the familiar skin beneath. His fingers explored the curved horns and his hand came away trembling. He spoke to the reflection, in an involuntary whisper, "Gath of Baal?"

The reflection did not reply.

He gathered up the heavy chain mail around his waist, slid his arms into its scalloped sleeves, buckled it. Something rustled in the verdant shrubbery on the opposite side of the pool. He turned slowly, sensing an evil presence.

Cobra stepped boldly out of the shaded greenery and posed arrogantly at the edge of the calm pool. The reflection of her emerald and silver presence shimmered ominously on its cold blue face.

Ignoring her, he kneeled beside the pond and once more looked down at his reflection. He took hold of the lower edge of the helmet with both hands and tried again to force it off.

Cobra laughed. "Do not exhaust yourself pointlessly, Dark One. The helmet belongs to the Lord of Death. And it responds only to him . . . or to me, his most beloved and precious servant."

He looked up at her, his contempt defying her own. "If I can steal it, I can remove it."

"Fool!" she snarled, the word reverberating across the water. "You are the helmet's prisoner. Your own greed has trapped you. Forever. You have no power to match my Lord's. Nor magic to threaten me . . . not anymore."

She smiled without humor, then used a tone as resonant as a temple bell, and her words echoed through the trees before fading off.

"You are trapped. The horned helmet cannot be removed. And even if you did, by some miracle, remove it, you could not escape it. It has released your true nature . . . addicted you to its powers. Now you can not live without it . . . and you will not live with it."

"Magic?"

In reply a bitter grin danced in her creamy cheeks. "You've made an irreparable blunder. You should have honored your bargain . . . and understood when I told you the metal was alive. Now you are going to pay for what you have done to me."

He bolted upright plucking his axe from the ground, and turned from side to side again sensing something.

She watched him as she would a caged animal. "Is there danger approaching? Or is it your own evil that frightens you?"

He turned toward her, and took a quick step back.

She smiled with resplendent malevolence and purred, "That is one of the helmet's powers. It can sense danger and evil no matter where it hides. And what it senses and feels and sees, you will sense and feel and see. Nothing that is deadly can you ignore or escape. No poisonous flower, no stinging beetle beneath the leaf, no vermin, no cat, no hound or demon, will be concealed from you. Not even what is base and vile within yourself. You will see the world as we know it truly is. Until you submit to my Lord, you will not have a single moment of rest."

He shook his head, whispered darkly, "Nothing, no man or demon, ever has been or ever will be my master."

"Oh yes," she replied. "You have the power to master and destroy all creatures born of nature. You have found that out already. But you can not master or defeat the helmet. Never. Only I know the magic that can remove it."

The muscles in his back swelled and rippled, and the helmet shifted slightly of its own accord.

"It already grows heavy, doesn't it?" She smiled, then added, "You would like to rest, wouldn't you? But you won't. It will grow heavier and heavier. It will take control of your brain as well as your body, until you understand there is no hope. Then, when you are totally mad, it will rip your insolent head from your shoulders."

She turned, moved back through the greenery, and merged with the shadows beyond.

Forty-one

THEATER OF ILLUSION

Robin Lakehair was running, almost dancing. In the leafy shade of the late day she looked like a dappled fawn. A wild rose was tucked in her red-gold hair which rollicked about her shoulders. Sharn and the she-wolf followed her. Hearing a sound, all three stopped and lifted their heads.

It resounded again, the clang of metal on wood, then stopped.

Robin and the wolves moved down through the trees, then she stopped short, holding her breath.

Beyond the trees at the base of the rise, a huge warrior stood in Smooth Pond splashing water over himself. He was naked except for boots, a loincloth and a horned helmet, and his flesh glistened. He strode out of the water and kneeled facing two birch trees.

Robin, ignoring Sharn's warning growl, moved so she could get a closer look at the stranger.

He forced the two trunks apart, placed his head through them, then released the trunks so they were wedged under the collar of the helmet. He gathered himself, then thrust savagely against the trees while pulling his head back. His massive arms corded like the necks of young bulls. He pushed and pulled until blood trickled between his fingers and ran down the white bark, then sagged in place.

Robin, holding her lower lip between her teeth, looked around the clearing and gasped quietly. The trunks of half-a-dozen trees were hammered raw by the helmet and gouged by its horns. She looked back at the kneeling stranger.

Three more times the warrior tried to force the helmet off and failed, then, gasping and sweating, he tried to stand. But the helmet did not rise with him, and he dropped to the ground with a painful grunt to hang by the helmet. He wrenched and twisted until he finally righted himself, only to discover his head was gripped even tighter by the trunks.

Gasping, he gathered his body in a low crouch. He took a deep breath then tried to force the trees apart with his arms and lift his head free all at once. For a long moment the two birch trees played with him like he was their pet beast, then suddenly they snapped apart and his helmeted head ripped loose with a woody screech. He staggered backward across the clearing, tripped on a fallen branch, and went reeling forward. His helmet maimed a large blunt rock, but the rock appeared to hardly even know it was in a fight and knocked him flat. He rolled over twice, then lay facedown in a crowd of brown and gold leaves.

Robin whimpered with fear, tiptoed forward, and dropped to her knees beside the man.

His muscles rippled under her fingertips. Suddenly the powerful body rose abruptly on its elbows, driving her aside, and crawled in a zigzag manner toward the cool water. Reaching the pond, his fist closed around the haft of the axe which stood beside it.

Robin gasped. She knew the weapon. Wide-eyed, she crawled back against a tree trunk as the helmet turned toward her. The cruel eyes within its shadows could not be Gath's. Seeming not to see her, he dropped the axe, crawled halfway into the pond, and dipped the helmet beneath the water.

While the man-animal continued to drink, Robin rose quietly and braced herself against the tree. He lifted his metal head and glanced about as if she weren't there, then dropped himself in the water, rolling and splashing. When he stood, his dark brown body was steaming.

Robin eased back around the tree, concealing herself, ready to flee. But her feet held and, hardly daring to breathe, she peered from behind the trunk. "Gath." It was only a whisper, but he turned as if to the sound of music.

She stared in disbelief, openmouthed, then resolutely came back around the tree. Reaching him, she hesitated again, trying to reconcile this intimidating giant with the man she knew. Seemingly incapable of anything else, he only looked at her. She blushed, and slipped her hands around the collar of the helmet saying, "Let me help."

He took hold of her slim wrists and held them softly for a long moment. She started to speak but he stopped her. His eyes were studying the surrounding forest.

"What do you see?" she asked. "What's wrong?"

She followed his gaze, saw the wolves beyond the trees high on the rise, and turned back to him. "It's Sharn, and the she-wolf. Don't you recognize them? They're your friends."

He looked at her and the expression in his eyes made her shudder. It said he had no friends. Robin started to protest, but gave up and smiled helplessly.

Robin's smile was the most eloquent argument Gath had ever beheld. He gazed at it, forgetting all about finding answers to why he had not sensed her presence and allowed her to get close enough to put a dagger in his back.

Her nut-brown face with its cheeks the color of budding roses was a theater of soft illusions saying something to him. Or was it the helmet playing tricks on his mind? He could not be sure. What he was certain of was that the two little red dancers were only pretending to perform as lips while actually being much, much more. Tiny mountains of color, the tissue of dreams.

"What is it?" she asked again.

He did not answer. He could not. She would not understand, but now he could see the answer to his questions. There was no deceit within her. She was without his greed. Without Cobra's dark lust. Devoid of evil.

She took her hands back gently. "Please, let me get that helmet off. You need some sleep."

Instinctively he lifted his hands to the helmet to remove it, then hesitated remembering it was useless. She smiled brightly, placed her hands over his, pushed and it rose easily off his head.

Forty-two
NAKED

Cobra was alone in her chambers. Her face was as white as an albino's ghost.

The room had been cleared and the pillars replaced. Behind her a wooden tub of hot water steamed with soapy bubbles. Puddles of water glimmered on the silver floor beside bare pink toes protruding from the hem of her jeweled robe. It enveloped her body completely, glittering obsidian petals decorated with large silver eyes. Her blue-black hair, parted at the center of her head, fell to the sides in a flat shimmering shower past her throat, to cascade over her delicate shoulders.

On an ebony stand a leaden vial waited. Beside it a small open jar held a scarlet paste of female chochineal insects. A tiny brush of horse hairs and a silver mirror rested beside the jar. She let an arm escape her robe, picked up the mirror, and looked worriedly at her reflection. Her heavily kohled eyes were dull and sick. She dipped the brush in the red paste and applied it to her full lips. The color looked garish against her cold, chalky complexion.

Wearily, she set the brush down and picked up the leaden vial. Her hand and arm trembled, as she removed the lead plug. A beam of black light shot forth from the mouth. She stared at it vacantly, then with both hands brought the vial to her lips and drank its smoking contents.

She gagged and staggered back. Smoke drifted past her bright parted lips. Her body convulsed voluptously. The swell of a breast heaved into view above her clutched hands. A sliver of naked thigh showed through the slit skirt of the robe. She clutched at the mirror anxiously, and peered into it as the glorious creamy color returned to her cheeks, then their rose tint.

She faced the interior stairway. Black smoke beckoned out of it, demanding her presence before the underworld altar of her Master. With a languid pace she crossed the room and dissolved into the dark vapors.

At the center of the mountain, black smoke filled the living cone. It swirled and rumbled angrily. Fires glowed within the dark center of its body. The floor of the cone had become one massive lava pool except for a thin path of hard basalt which curved through the vaporous black atmosphere, then vanished. The lava bubbled and spit, sending flames up and around the sides of the path. Cobra clutched her robe around her, and solemnly advanced through them and into the blackness.

She could barely make out the giant saurian skull. The bridge which had risen like a tongue into its spreading jaws was gone. Pieces of skull bone and teeth were broken away. But the brain cavity still boiled with fire. The flaming eye sockets glared down at her.

Cobra bowed once, then parted her robe, letting its weight carry it down off her body to gather in submissive silver and black folds at her feet, a perfect pedestal for an offering of perfect naked flesh. Her creamy translucent skin blushed exquisitely at cheeks and breasts. The thin diamond patch of curling hair glittered at the center of the fleshy setting, a black living jewel.

The devil rumbled. His smoke billowed up around her, stroking her thighs and breasts, arousing her until she trembled. Then without warning he shook the narrow stone path, throwing her down to her quivering knees, and lashed her with stinging flames until her skin was welted and the tips of her hair smoked.

She buried her face behind red lacquered nails. Her black hair cascaded over her wounded breasts. She sobbed, "Oh, Master! Forgive me. I know I have failed you. Scourge me. Degrade me. But I'll make it up to you. Don't . . . don't cast me away! I beg you."

The cone rumbled, spewing smoke over her, and she prostrated herself on the scorching stones, fingers clasped prayerfully.

"At this moment the Barbarian is dying," she pleaded. "I swear it. The helmet will be yours again."

She pressed her face to the floor, flinching as its heat scorched her breasts and stomach. The cone rumbled, shot flames to the ceiling. "No! No!" she whimpered. "It's not possible! It's been three days. The helmet has destroyed his mind by now."

The altar rumbled again violently, bringing dust down on her bare arms and shoulders. She looked up with startled eyes, gasped, "The girl! No! How could she prevail against the helmet?"

Sheets of flame rose up on all sides of her, walled her in as the altar roared and shook bringing down parts of the skull. Then the flames sank away, and the room became quiet.

Cobra, sweating and oozing blood, rose tentatively, her large dark eyes dilated and rigid with shock. "Is . . . is it possible? He . . . he could live with the helmet? Turn it against me? Against you? Oh, Master, what have I done?"

Her head dropped silently, shuddered. Then she lifted her eyes to the altar as her body wilted with total surrender. "Take me, my Lord. Destroy me. I am ready."

The flames flickered and diminished, and a rush of hope straightened her. She cautiously tilted her head, listened intently to the rhythmic drumming rumble rising out of the depths of the mountain as her Master instructed her. She sank to one knee, touched groin, breast and forehead, and whispered reverently, "My adored, my most worshipful Master, I will not fail you this time. I will go to Bahaara immediately. With the high priest there, I will create demons such as there have never been before to send against him and destroy him."

She stood proud and magnificent, her hard full breasts thrusting. Ambition sparkled in her eyes. Her voice was clear and certain. "Your will shall be done. I will not only bring you your helmet, but his head, and the head of the miserable interfering girl as well."

She swayed voluptuously and bowed her head bending gracefully until her streaming, black, silky hair caressed the floor in passionate homage. Swaying and undulating, she retreated in this position dragging her hair the length of the narrow stone path, then vanished in the shadows of the tunnel.

Forty-three

THE WHITE DOLL

Robin, kneeling beside the pond, slowly dipped her hands in the water, then splashed it over her face and scrubbed. She shook and wiped the drops off, then blinked at her reflection in the sparkling surface. Her reddish harvest-gold hair was rimmed with a white feathery halo where the sunlight filtered through.

Smiling at her vanity, she picked up an earthen pitcher resting on the ground beside her and scooped up a pitcherful of water, playfully taking it from the place where her reflection smiled back at her. She laughed lightly as her image came apart in glittering ripples, then stood and, propping the pitcher on left hip, started up the shaded slope toward the root house.

Reaching it, she paused to wave at Sharn and the she-wolf sunning themselves in the clear track, then entered and descended the stairs to the main room. Gath sat on his bed of furs, with his back against the hearth and his hand resting on the horned helmet which shared the furs. He wore his loincloth, and throbbing veins webbed his massive muscles. He was shaved, but there was a white pallor around his dark eyes, flakes of ashen callous on his forehead and cheekbones, and his dark hair was shorter, singed and burned at the ends. There was now a deep crease between his eyes, his mouth was stretched flatter, and his expression was of a man who had lived a hundred lifetimes.

Robin smiled brightly and crossed to the table saying, "You always wake up, don't you? Everytime I go out, or get up to put a log on the fire, or even turn over in my sleep." She set the pitcher down and put her smile on him.

He said, "Habit."

"Oh, I see. Well, it's understandable. It must be frightening to live here alone." She picked up a pair of shears from the table. "Are you going to let me trim your hair now?"

"I'll do it," he said quietly.

"I can do it better."

He shook his head.

She poured fresh water into a waiting cup, kneeled beside him and extended the cup, looking directly into his eyes. He took it and, with lids closed, drank, then let the dripping cup dangle from a finger. Her eyes followed the drops thoughtfully. "Gath, why . . . why won't you let me help you?"

He seemed not to hear her. His eyes wandered to the part down the middle of her hair. His empty hand reached curiously, then quickly withdrew. She shifted uneasily at the warmth of his nearness and size. Even in repose he was threatening. She blinked uncertainly, then boldly extended her hand for the cup. He put it in her hand and held it there, his massive grip enclosing her hand and wrist. His voice was a hoarse whisper, and his words were measured.

"Stay with me."

"Of course," she said lightly. "If I was acting like I was going to run off, I'm sorry. It's just that I don't understand what's happened to you." She tried to remove her hand, but he held on, and she stopped trying. "Aren't you going to tell me?"

He let go of her hand, lifted a red-gold curl away from her cheek, and admitted quietly, "I need you."

Confusion crowded behind her innocent eyes, and she blushed so intently she was unable to speak.

"I am sorry," he said. "But you must stay here."

"But . . . but for how long?" she stammered. "Even after you're well?"

His eyes held an uncompromising yes, then filled with guilt, and he stood. Facing the anvil, he began to putter with a belt buckle; a horned death's-head emblem had recently been hammered in it.

She watched him helplessly, her cheeks still florid, then her words poured out. "Gath, I'm glad you need me. I think that's what I've wanted from the moment we met. But it's all so confusing and mysterious. And I need you." She began to sob. "Oh, Gath, I know you don't want to talk about it, but I've got to. The Kitzakks came again. They attacked three villages and destroyed them." Her head dropped, and she covered her face with her hands. "Oh, Gath, we're all in such terrible trouble."

He looked over her shoulder, asked, "You?"

"All of us," she blurted. "But you most of all. Look!"

She hurried to her bedding, gathered up a cloth bundle, and hurried back. Kneeling, she unwrapped part of it and removed the black doll. He took it from her, grinned grimly while examining it, and tossed it into the fire. Its lacquer burst into flames and crackled hotly.

"Gath," she pleaded, "you don't understand! Brown John took it from a bounty hunter. A man the Kitzakks sent to kill you. And there are more, out there in the forest somewhere. Hunting you. Brown John says they strike from shadows. They'll kill you before you see them."

"I'll see them," he said quietly.

She watched his face darken strangely as he sat back down against the hearth. Boldly she crawled to him and placed a hand on his raised knee. Her eyes found his. "Please, listen. There is a plan, but it needs your help. Brown John has joined the Council of Chiefs, and they're raising an army for you and Brown John to lead. You just have to. They need a champion." Her voice pleaded. "That's why I came. To tell you. You have an army now, just like Brown John said you would. All the tribes will fight, but only if you lead them.''

He did not reply, but an odd, shiny heat of excitement glittered behind his eyes.

"Oh, Gath, you're our only chance." Her voice broke, "You must understand that.''

Tears filled her eyes and he looked away, but asked, "If I help, you will stay here?''

"I could, but it wouldn't make any difference. They'd still find me." She unwrapped the rest of the cloth saying, "I don't know why anyone would bother to take the trouble, but they did.''

She removed the white doll. Seeing the likeness, he sat forward, ripped the totem from her hand and held it buried within his thick, knotted fingers. His body pulsed, seeming to expand, and his heat made her flinch and crawl back.

"What is it?" she gasped.

His hand trembled and the doll dropped to the floor. Robin stood abruptly and backed against the wall staring at the image on the floor as Gath squatted over it.

A faint hot red glow appeared on the face of the white doll. It grew hot and brilliant, spreading over its body to spill on the floor.

Robin whimpered and retreated to the staircase. Her foot found the first step, the second, then stopped and she swayed faintly.

His black mane was lifting. When it looked at her, the eyes were glowing, filled with flames.

Robin screamed, bolted up the stairs and out.

He started after her, then stopped short. Turning with a slow ominous movement, he strode to the back of the fireplace where his chain mail was hanging from a peg. He put it on easily, belted it using his new death's-head buckle, picked up his axe and slung it on his back.

He moved with slow deliberation to the horned helmet, took it in two hands and lifted it above his head. It was slow, hard work. His muscles fought against themselves.

Beads of steaming sweat broke out on his face. Only his eyes were fixed with resolve. His arm pulsed with constricting muscles, and the black metal dungeon grudgingly descended over his head, once more claimed its prisoner.

It was an hour before he found her sign. A small footprint in the mud at the side of Smooth Pond. He found another and part of a third amid broken leaves. The three footprints were each a good stride apart, clear indication she was running wildly.

Forty-four

BIG HANDS

A wagon, with a two-horse hitch and tall red wheels, rolled north along Summer Trail where it passed through the marsh at the southern end of the Shades. In winter the trail was impassable. Now the road was still marked by muddy potholes, but the trees were thinner here and the mud had begun to harden. Streaking low across the ground, the morning sun struck the spokes of the tall wheels and cast moving bars of shadow across the driver, across his light brown armor, and across his long bow which stood in a holster beside him. "Big Hands" Gazul.

Three leopards sprawled on straw spread over the open bed of the wagon. Shallow side boards cast a shadow over their sleek, spotted bodies turning them a cool yellow.

Beside Gazul, dangling from an iron hook, were two black cylindrical pouches he had been issued by the high priest of the Kitzakks, Dang-Ling.

The horses slowed as they began the climb up a grassy

hill. A crack of the whip, and the animals bolted forward to the crest. There Gazul reined up.

The road moved down the opposite side of the hill and crossed an open spread of grassy ground, then vanished into a black hole of shadows cast by a forboding rain forest. The dense growth stretched for miles, rising and dipping between mountains and hills, toward the horizon where white clouds filled the sky. Not a sign of a village or anything human, only the sound of wind playing in the grass, and the occasional hoot or roar of a predator looking for breakfast.

Gazul was without expression. His head was square, but he was not young anymore, and his flacid flesh gave it a long look. His lids drooped over the outside corners of his eyes. His cheeks were sunken, and the muscles and skin hung down over the corners of his mouth. Thin strands of hair drooped from his upper lip and dangled in irregular patches from his jaw.

He felt among the clutter of tiny, colorful totem pouches dangling from his neck and selected a violet stone jar. He uncorked it and poured a thick, translucent glob of sticky, red fluid onto his tongue. Hashradda, an expensive stimulant favored by beastmen who trained animals for warfare. He sucked on his tongue until color blotched his loose flesh, and his eyes brightened, giving him a virile expression.

He looked again at the forest, then flicked the reins. The wagon made a half circle and started back. When it was about to descend behind the hill, the wagon bed lurched and he glanced back. The three cats, tails swishing, were standing with their paws resting on the raised tailgate. Gazul reined up sharply.

A figure had plunged out of the distant hole in the shadowy forest, a short staggering figure with light hair.

Gazul tongued the corner of his mouth thoughtfully, then tied off the reins, climbed down to the ground and removed his waterskin from a hook on the back of the driver's box. He poured water into a shallow pail, then fed it to his leopards and two horses. By the time he had finished, the figure had reached the back of the wagon and stopped there. It was a disheveled and frightened young girl.

She studied Gazul a moment with wary eyes, then looked at the leopards and instinctively smiled, moved closer. The leopards snarled and purred threateningly.

"It's all right," she cooed. "We're friends . . . aren't we?"

They lowered their small heads with their lithe muscular necks, and sniffed her face and hair. She crooned and scratched their furry jaws.

Gazul watched with puzzled eyes. With a show of mild indifference, he sauntered to the back of the wagon, and stopped at a harmless distance from the girl.

He said, "They've never let anyone touch 'em before. That's weird. Real weird."

"I like animals," she said in a tone that explained everything. "And I guess they know it."

He extended the waterskin. "Got a name?"

She nodded. "Robin." She took the waterskin. "Thank you."

"Pretty," he said, careful to make his comment apply only to her name, not to the parts of her he was thinking about.

She drank deep, returned the waterskin and asked, "Could you tell me where we are? I . . . I got lost."

"I'm new to these parts, but some folks back up the way said this road is called Summer Trail."

She sighed. "Thank goodness."

Gazul looked past her shoulder at the forest and said, "They told me there would be good hunting out this way, but I'm afraid I'm not good enough for this kind of country. Looks too wild."

"It is," Robin said quickly. "They shouldn't have sent you out here."

"Well, you know folks," Gazul said in an easy tone. "Maybe I went farther than they meant me to." He smiled. "Need a lift?"

"Thank you," Robin said. "I'd be glad to ride in the back with your cats."

"No," Gazul said firmly. "Wouldn't do. I don't mind you petting 'em a bit, but, you know, I don't want 'em gettin' too friendly with people." Gazul turned his back on her, moved to the front of the wagon, and climbed into the driver's box. Staring ahead, he said, "Climb aboard if you're coming."

Robin hurried forward, climbed up and sat tiredly on the board seat beside Gazul. Gazul glanced back down the road and frowned. A huge wolf had bounded out of the forest and was plunging through the grass headed his way. A second wolf followed but was limping and falling behind fast. Gazul glanced suspiciously at Robin with the corner of an eye. She had closed her eyes and was catching her breath. He whipped the horses hard and the wagon bolted down the hill with a lunge. Robin grabbed the side boards and held on, gasping.

Gazul chuckled, "Might as well enjoy ourselves."

He laughed a laughter which he was certain the innocent girl had never heard before. It was vicious, brutal. She shivered slightly and turned to the leopards. They were standing in the wagon bed with their heads right behind her. Their mouths were open, drinking the air as it whipped past.

She looked at Gazul. "They look hungry. Can I feed them?"

"Nope. Got nothing to feed them."

"I've got some bread," she lifted her satchel.

"Forget it," he said easily. "They only get the best."

She half smiled. "What's that?"

"People," he said. Then he laughed riotously and whipped the horses forward until the wagon was racing along the dirt road and bounding over rises, almost flying.

Robin, clinging to the wagon, shouted breathlessly, "Could you please slow down?"

"Could," Gazul hollered. "But won't. I paid heavy silver for those big wheels, so I use 'em every chance I get." He chuckled, whipped the horses again, then dropped the reins and held up his big hands laughing. "Look! No hands."

Robin moaned quietly, and hung on as the road raced past underneath her. Out of the corner of her eye she watched the colorful pouches bounce on his chest. Without looking at her he answered her unasked question, "Got to have a lot of totems in my trade. They're mostly, you know, teeth and finger bones." He nodded with the back of his head at the leopards. "Things they don't eat."

She frowned with annoyance. "Why are you trying to frighten me?"

"Just answering your questions," he shouted.

"I didn't ask you any question," she shouted back.

"Yes, you did," he said. Then he reached inside his leather chest armor, and came away with a large padded glove. He slipped it over his right hand, and worked his fingers into it carefully. Then, smiling at Robin, he held up the gloved hand. "Nice, huh?"

She did not reply, then shrugged. He laughed, and made a fist with the gloved hand as he hollered over the racket of the wheels. "Had it made special. I just love hitting women, but I can't afford to break their skin. It lowers their price." He laughed again, a wet throaty laughter.

Robin, with sudden panic in her eyes, looked around at the landscape flying past them as if she wanted to jump.

He hollered, "Want me to stop?"

She looked at him with big pleading eyes. He laughed uproariously, then suddenly stopped short, pulling hard on the reins. The wagon skidded to a stop. As it did, Gazul stood up abruptly, and glared with startled eyes past Robin. She turned sharply to see what he saw. Seeing only a clump of bushes, she turned back in time to see his gloved fist coming for her jaw.

It caught her flush on the side of the face, lifted her out of the seat, then dropped her. She landed on the ground like a sack of potatoes. Gazul dropped casually to the ground and toed her unconscious body. "You're one dumb sugarhole, girl. That's the oldest trick in the book." He laughed some more. "But you are special. Real special."

He picked her up, dumped her in the back of the wagon with his leopards, then climbed back into the driver's box and glanced up, then down the road. The road ahead was empty. The back road was the same, but a turn in it blocked his view, so he drove rapidly down to a side trail. He turned down it, then parked behind a tangle of concealing thick brush and overhanging tree limbs, and scrambled onto the bed, squatted over Robin.

Using a dagger he slit her tunic at the middle of the square collar, then ripped it apart all the way to the hem. He pulled her arms out one at a time, then took hold of the tunic and yanked on it hard, rolling her over roughly and pulling the garment off. He tossed the tunic into the underbrush, then rolled her onto her back. A smirk squirmed its way through his flabby face as he stroked her nude stomach, and cupped a firm breast in a calloused hand. After some of this, he said aloud, "Enough of that," and spanked the playing hand with his other one, laughing.

That was when the huge grey wolf erupted from the shrubs at a dead run and leapt for the wagon. The animal landed lightly on top of a side board, bounded over the surprised leopards, and caught the startled Gazul in the chest with his full weight. The impact drove man and wolf out of the wagon.

They landed with a crunch on powdery dirt, and rolled over in swirling dust onto all fours. Knowing this position favored the wolf, Gazul howled, but it only seemed to encourage the animal. It drove for Gazul's throat, just missed, but tore off a strip of shoulder. The man screamed and scrambled back. The wolf whirled towards the wagon and the three leopards leaped at it. Gazul, recognizing their mistake, screamed a warning. Too late. The wolf leapt up into the body of the first cat and his jaws snapped hard.

Cat and wolf hit the ground, and broke apart. The cat's throat was hanging from the wolf's mouth. His fur was raked with claws.

The surviving leopards spun in place, and faced the wolf snarling as Gazul shouted, "Kill it! Kill it!"

In reply, the wolf drew his lips back behind bloody fangs and the cat's meaty throat fell in the dirt.

This only increased the bounty hunter's volume, and there was only one thing on his mind. "Kill it! Kill it! Kill it!"

The leopards hesitated, and Gazul sobbed knowing why. They loved the chase and hated the pit fight, while the wolf loved it. He charged the nearest cat, but it raised up, circling for the wolf's back with its claws slashing. The wolf let it slash, dove under it, found the soft underbelly, and his jaws snapped. His teeth went into the meat up to gums, and hung on as they whirled and rolled.

A fountain of blood spurted from the fight, and Gazul whimpered and went limp, unable to do anything but watch.

The wolf, with its teeth tearing cat flesh, had his muttle drowned in hot blood, then his jaws came away leaving a hole in the cat's belly. But his triumph was short as the third cat raked the wolf's belly, then bore into the belly's wound with its teeth.

Howling, the wolf spun, whirled, and finally tore himself free. In the process his jaws found a cat's foreleg, broke it, and the cat backed away from the fight limping. The bleeding wolf followed relentlessly. The cat tripped and the wolf charged, burying his teeth in its neck. Under him the cat had all three good legs working on his underbelly but the wolf kept his jaws clamped and stayed on his feet. The two animals worked in this position until the cat finally went limp.

Gazul, whimpering, watched the wolf back away from his third kill and turn on him. Transfixed with fear, Gazul looked around and discovered he was sitting on the ground with his back against a tree while his dagger was ten feet away. Cursing his luck, he watched the wolf advance slowly. All the middle of him was gone or hanging. The animal dropped just short of Gazul's shaking boot, shuddered and died.

When Gazul's legs steadied, he got back in the wagon, and squatted over Robin. She was still unconscious.

He whispered, "Well, pretty one, you have cost me my three treasures, but you will buy me six more."

He took henna and umber from his satchel, and mixed a dye with water. Then he colored the hair on her head, under her arms and at her groin a dark chestnut. Using a sticky substance, he made a scar over her left eye, then removed a plain tunic from a bundle of clothing in the wagon bed. As he put it on her, she began to revive. He played with her a little then. She tried to stop him, but was helpless. With one hand he forced her mouth open and poured the contents of a red vial down her throat. By the time he had finished dressing her she was unconscious again.

He threw some straw over her, then climbed back into the driver's box. There he picked up one of the black cylindrical pouches, removed the doll of Robin. He stroked it possessively, then glanced back at the sleeping form and grinned. "They'll never know you, lass. Least not 'til you and I reach Bahaara and have a long hot bath." He laughed, put the doll away, and drove off.

Forty-five

PASSION

Toward noon, Gath found the she-wolf standing guard over Sharn's body. The three dead leopards had been gutted by hyenas and jackels, but the she-wolf had made certain Sharn had not provided anyone with a meal.

When Gath approached, the she-wolf backed off, and Gath squatted over his friend's carcass, deliberately staring into the matted gore of death. But this time he did not allow the helmet to enjoy it; he raged so violently the she-wolf backed away in fear. Gath looked away from the dead animal to the living one and said, "Do not be afraid. He was my teacher and friend, and he will be avenged."

He removed the thin length of violet cloth from his wrist and tied it around Sharn's foreleg, then made a grave in the ground under rocks.

Gath searched the area, and found scrapes of red paint made by wagon wheels on the sides of trees, black dye on the grass, and Robin's torn tunic. Then he moved off at a run following the wagon tracks leaving the she-wolf howling mournfully behind. The tracks led back onto Summer Trail, then south to Border Road. There they turned east and mingled with a thousand similar ones.

Gath followed Border Road until he reached the rubble of Bone Camp. The leveled village was deserted. Five different trails led off the village square. All were marred with countless wagon, foot and horse tracks.

Gath stood motionless over Bone Camp's rubble for a

long time, with the dying orange light of day gracing his metal-clad body, and helmeted head. He looked to the west, and watched the sun sink behind the cataracts. As a child of eight or nine or ten summers—he did not know for certain as he did not know his age—he had vowed never again to ask a human for help, and he had kept that vow. But now he needed help. Nevertheless, his mind refused to change. He stood in place until night descended and he became indistinguishable from the darkness, then his mind surrendered to his passion.

Forty-six

DRUM AND DRUMMER

The small group of elderly men and women sat silently around a fire in Rag Camp listening to the sounds of a massive creature moving noisily through the night. Suddenly, realizing it was headed toward them, they grabbed their weapons and hurried into shadows watching the edge of the clearing.

A massive shadow strode out of the darkness and across the clearing. Moonlight glanced off sharp horns growing out of its black helmet and the cutting edge of a steel battle-ax.

The Grillards, trembling, scurried off, alerting the sleeping village.

The creature ignored them. It leapt up onto the stage, marched across it, kicked open the door of the red wagon with a booted foot and strode inside.

A crowd of chattering Grillards, carrying weapons and

torches, quickly gathered in the clearing, and hurried toward the stage in fear and confusion. The prolonged scream of their *bukko* erupted from the red wagon and brought them to a stop. They stared in rising terror, then angrily surged onto the stage shouting threats at the horrifying stranger.

Suddenly the menacing horned helmet appeared in the second story window. "Quiet," it bellowed, and a hush promptly descended over the crowd as it stumbled to a stop.

Within the red wagon, Brown John sat stiffly on the edge of his bed, a wooden shelf supported by chains bolted in the wall. A candle holder in his hand trembled. Its flickering light cast a glow over a surprisingly simple raw wood room that was as empty as his face. That face's many wrinkles, like his bedclothes, were in disarray. As the horned figure closed the shutters and turned toward him, he lifted the candle, and its light flowed erratically over the metal-clad body.

"Ah, it's you," Brown John sighed. "I thought I recognized the chain mail, but your new headpiece gave me a start. For a moment there, I was certain I was facing my long-awaited and so richly deserved doom." He set the candle holder on a nightstand and took up his normal jaunty tone. "Where have you been? You look extremely well fed."

"Who do you serve?" Gath demanded. "Who is your master?"

"Master? Why I have none but myself. No . . ." he stopped himself, "that's not true. The pleasures of life still order me about, despite the fact that each year I serve them with less ardor."

"Take off your shirt!"

"Undress!" Brown John's voice choked. His mouth gathered primly, then he chuckled. "Well now, I expected you to say and do many things, all of them quite out of the ordinary. But 'undress'? What possible value could you find in looking at my time-battered body? It is a bit paunchy, and . . ."

Gath reached the old man in one stride and ripped the front of his loose homespun nightshirt away. He shoved the startled man back onto his bed, and yanked away the remnant of clothing, tossed it into a shadowed corner.

Brown John struggled upright trying to draw a blanket over his nakedness, but Gath did not give him a chance. He lifted a gnarled leg, upended the *bukko*, then picked up the candle holder and used the light of the flame to inspect between his toes.

Brown John, with his head half buried in bedclothes, protested in a dignified if muffled tone, "I assure you there is . . ." A mouthful of blanket cut him off as Gath lifted him higher and inspected his legs. Brown John removed the blanket and blurted, "I am quite prepared to allow you to inspect me in a reasonable manner, but . . ." He dropped face first on the bed and groaned with shame as Gath spread his legs. Over a shoulder, he shouted, "Damn you, there's no need for this. If there is anything on my person which might be of interest to you, just ask." Gath replied by rolling him over and examining an armpit. Huffing and puffing, the old man mumbled, "You'll find nothing there. My powers are quite mundane. I don't even claim to have a tail." Gath rolled him over to see for himself, then dropped the *bukko* and set the candle holder back on the nighttable.

Brown John, with his head dangling off the bed, gathered his breath, then reassembled himself. When he was properly covered and sitting spread legged on the edge of the bed, he placed his long-fingered hands over the tops of his spindly knees and faced Gath with lofty composure.

"That, my man, was no way to treat the one person in all the forest who has befriended you. You seem to have forgotten that my sons and I have traded fairly with you for many years, and that I personally sent you that chain mail without asking one crogan in exchange! And it was my doing alone that Robin Lakehair was sent to heal you, and then, despite your lack of gratitude, sent a second time to warn you about the bounty hunters." His finger-tips drummed his kneecaps in righteous impatience. "She did reach you, I presume, and tell you about them? And that the chiefs have offered to accept you as their champion?"

"She's been carried off."

"Oh no! By animals?"

Gath shook his head. "A man."

Brown John groaned and his head dropped, suddenly feeling beaten and frail. "Who?" he breathed.

"I found her tunic and some scrapes on the sides of the trees made by tall red wagon wheels . . . and black dye on the grass."

Brown John looked up sharply. "A bounty hunter?"

Gath nodded. "There were three dead leopards wearing collars. Sharn reached them before I did. He killed the cats, but the man got away." There was no emotion in his voice, nor did it sound like there ever had been.

"Ah," Brown John whispered. "And the wolf?"

"Dead."

The old man studied the eyes within the helmet in search of a clue to Gath's feeling, but found nothing. "I am truly sorry," he whispered.

"Do not be. He is free!"

"Of course . . . of course. Now he runs with the summer fire and the winter wind." Brown John shook his head in disbelief. With his elbows braced on his knees, he pressed his long fingers to his brow in concentration saying, "A wild beast of the forest sacrifices his life for a beautiful village maiden." He looked up at the stony figure. "Tell me, Gath, why?"

"He did not share his reasons."

"Ah, yes, and shame on me for asking. The deed speaks more clearly than any words." He sighed. "I would have liked to have known him."

The helmet studied the old man mysteriously, then its

voice, rasping harshly with inner turmoil, demanded, "Help me find the girl."

Brown John, sensing the control of their relationship suddenly shifting in his direction, sat erect. "Gladly," he said. "I am responsible. I sent her to you. I risked her life." He flattened his lips ruefully. "But I can't help you find her. Not immediately."

With one hand, Gath lifted blanket and man off the bed as if they were no weightier than a cream pitcher. The slits of the helmet began to glow. His breathing was harsh, audible.

Brown John's eyes widened, and he began to squirm. "Don't misunderstand. I'll help. But if it is one of the bounty hunters who has her—and I am certain of it—by now he has carried her high into the cataracts to the Kitzakks."

"Will he kill her?"

"No! No! I am sure not."

Gath glared at the old man a moment, then shoved him back onto the bed. Bruised but relieved, Brown John looked warily at the dimming eye slits, but said nothing about them.

Instead he said, "The Kitzakk priests will not kill her, either, as they apparently believe your power is linked to her. They will examine her until they discover the nature of this mysterious connection, then attempt to use it, and her, to destroy you." He smiled with macabre reassurance. "You are their target, not her. Remember this, they are a people accustomed to success. So accustomed that at the slightest defeat they become confused and frightened, and lay all blame on their leader. That is why your destruction is crucial to Klang, their warlord. Entire continents and nations have not been able to delay him, and now one man has not only slaughtered his scouts, but defeated two of his commanders and made a shambles of one of his proudest regiments. That, I can safely say, is driving him mad."

With a sardonic laugh, he rose and fetched a clean tunic

from a wooden hook. Balancing precariously on one foot, he stepped into it.

"Where will he take her?"

"Eventually, to Bahaara, the capital of the Desert Territory," Brown John said, belting his tunic. He rolled his neck and stretched stiffly. "I'll say this for you, sir, I have not been handled so roughly since I purchased my first whore. I was thirteen, and she outweighed me by sixty pounds." The *bukko* laughed delightedly.

His audience did not join in. "How far is this Bahaara?"

"Many days away."

"Then we have time to catch them."

"Patience. Patience. There is an entire Kitzakk army between you and the girl now. If we are to succeed at all, we must have a plan, and a great deal of help."

Turning his back, he picked up the candle holder, carried it to a wooden chest. He rummaged through it and came away with two more totem dolls, one of Gath and one of Robin. He asked, "You know what these are?"

Gath nodded.

Darkly serious now, Brown John spoke with measured words. "The man-hunter who carried these was caught by the Wowells. Being of a curious nature, the Wowells encouraged him to talk before they butchered and cooked him." He turned to Gath. "The Kitzakks have built a base camp at the heights of The Narrows. The bounty hunters were ordered to bring the girl and your head there."

Gath picked up his axe, moved to the stairs and stopped, looked back expectantly at the old man who had not moved.

"You have grown remarkably since our last meeting, Gath. But this is war, not personal combat. You will need an army to take the fort." He hesitated. "And you have one. The Kaven, the Wowells, the Barhacha, the Cytherians and many others have joined forces. They are camped in the forest near Pinwheel Crossing. Ours to command if you are ready to be their champion."

"I only want the girl."

"Then you must have this army." Brown John closed the chest emphatically and crossed with slow deliberate steps to Gath. "The work ahead is far more difficult, and meaner than you can possibly imagine. There are many besides Robin Lakehair who need our best efforts. The Kitzakks have enslaved hundreds, mostly women and children." He placed a long bony hand over the massive fist holding the axe and looked hard and direct into the slots of the helmet at the eyes he knew were there. "So let us begin."

"I will lead the army through the Narrows to the fort, and destroy those who hold her. But that is all I agree to."

"Excellent," Brown John said, then said it again, certain now that he was gaining control.

They started down the stairs, and Brown John began to chatter amicably.

"Now, what precisely did you expect to find on my body? A hidden mark? A sign that I belonged to some secret cult of assassins? Or perhaps that I was a servant of the Master of Darkness?" He chuckled. "Come now, say it. For what reason did you maul me so shamelessly?"

"It does not matter," Gath said as he reached the first floor and moved for the door.

"Come, come," Brown John halted him, "everything matters. Particularly your confidence in me. I am aware that we face the Kitzakks, but what else? Tell me. If I am not aware of all the pieces of the puzzle confronting us, then I cannot juggle them to our advantage."

Gath's eyes grew hot, but he said nothing.

"So, we have another mystery. Well, if you wish to leave it like that, I will be content to play the fool, but only for the time being." He looked up at Gath's helmet admiringly. "Perhaps then you will at least tell me this: Where did you get that spectacular and extraordinary headpiece?"

"You talk too much, *bukko*. Save your breath and use your feet." He opened the door, and strode into the flickering light cast by the torches of the gasping Grillards.

The old stage master chuckled to himself. "Well, this has not been the kind of opening scene I would wish for. But it was a scene, and played by candlelight at that." He chuckled again. "And I do like its possibilities." He hurried after Gath. "You and I, my friend of shadows, now share the same stage. Irrevocably and colorfully, one might even say. Like the drum and the drummer."

He laughed, stepped through the door into the torch-light, and was greeted by cheers.

Forty-seven

PINWHEEL CROSSING

Brown John led Gath through the night to a small camp laid in a clearing to the west of Pinwheel Crossing. A dying fire lit the bodies of Grillard men and women sleeping beside their weapons. Bone and Dirken were on guard. As their father emerged from the trees, they greated him but kept their wary eyes on his massive, metal-clad companion.

The stage master, flushed by pride and the long walk, said, "Yes, it's Gath, and he has agreed."

Dirken's sharp lips curled at the corners, and Bone chuckled grandly. "By Bled, this is good news."

"There is no time for celebration," Brown John said tersely. "Hurry. Tell the tribes and have them gather at the crossing."

The brothers, without delay and with a minimum of explanation, woke the others and sent them off into the forest to deliver the news.

Brown John, watching his Grillards stumble and trip in

their haste, smiled with a swelling sense of prophetic wonder, as if he suddenly could see the future. His Grillards were not merely messengers but heralds of a newborn legend.

The stage master guided Gath down a footpath through the forest that ended at a rock rising twenty feet above Pinwheel Crossing. When they climbed the rock's exposed promitory, they found it flooded with torchlight. Hundreds of torch-bearing warriors massed at the crossing and in the surrounding forest, and looked up at them. Seeing the horned champion, they cheered lustily and began to bang their swords and spears against their shields.

Brown John chuckled to himself and watched with pride as Gath instinctively mounted the promitory to stand in the spilling torchlight. His metal glittered, his arms and legs pulsed with cording muscles as that power known only to men who command armies surged through him. The power swelled, and he lifted his axe like a hammer, saluted his followers.

The army returned the salute, shouting their champion's name. This caused a reaction that Brown John could not have dreamed of or hoped for. The power inside Gath grew so hot and intense with blood hunger that it demanded release, and fire flamed from the eye slits of the horned helmet.

The reaction among the Barbarians was magical. The ragtag horde surged forward cheering, like an army.

When dawn broke, the Barbarians were marching across Foot Bridge at the base of The Narrows. The line of march was organized by long-standing custom, except for two notable exceptions. Gath led, and the stage master of the outlawed and outcast Grillards, grinning with a sumptuous satisfaction, followed close behind.

Behind Brown John marched eleven big, hairy Grillard strongmen wearing scars, swords, iron and furs. Then came Dirken and Bone riding their gaudy wagon. It was crowded with Grillard men and stacks of Kitzakk armor and weapons to be distributed to needy volunteers.

The main body of the army followed jauntily, each tribe marching as units: large, happy, strutting Cytherians with their long spears; dour, dark, skull-faced Kavens with long serpentine knives; Wowells, naked except for fur wraps around lanky hips and carrying stone clubs in their large hands. Then came the Barhacha woodmen hefting monstrous axes, and Dowats in persimmon tunics with longbows and quivers of reed arrows mounted on their broad backs. Most were on foot. Some were mounted on horseback. A few rode wagons. Three thousand, all told.

The tail of the army consisted of heavily laden wagons and carts pulled by draft horses, camp followers, cooks, witches, whores, sorceresses, maidens with healing hands, hunters, woodgatherers, messengers and entertainers. The tribes were not divided here. Everyone rode together, but the Grillards in their bright-colored patches stood out like brave banners, and the Wowell witches in their black robes followed like shadows of death.

Brown John looked over the army proudly. Flurries of fog swirled around its tramping boots, and, up ahead, dense fog hid the cataracts behind a billowing grey wall. The soupy mist was just the thing to conceal the army from the Kitzakk watchtowers. Prospects for success were growing by leaps and bounds, and he had never before seen an army move with such commitment. It marched into the wall of fog as if it were impossible to turn back, like wine poured past the lip of a pitcher.

Forty-eight

BATTLE AT THIN BRIDGE

By midday Brown John looked as if he would never grin again.

The army was not a third of the way up The Narrows. The fog had burned off and taken the army's confidence with it. Now it marched like armies usually marched, sweating and complaining.

Brown John, wearing a frown that looked as though it had been made with a pitchfork, slumped achingly in the Grillard wagon and did more than his share of the sweating. He took a deep swallow from a waterskin and, sighing, lifted his face to the sky. Its pale, translucent blue was graced with billowing white clouds out of which poured golden shafts of sunlight so beautiful they could have been the source of a new religion.

Brown John, not being in a religious mood, mumbled unpleasantly and spat over the side of the rolling wagon. He watched his meager spittle fall a thousand feet into the gorge, then turned away, letting it go it alone for the next two thousand.

Twenty strides ahead Gath marched in the puddle of his own shadow. Apart from sweat dripping from the hem of his chain mail, he showed no sign of discomfort and moved with the same strong stride with which he had started the march. Suddenly he raised a hand, halting the column, and it staggered to a dusty stop.

A distant sound was drifting down out of the massive grey cataracts. A musical sound without melody or rhythm.

Brown John climbed off the wagon, joined Gath, and they walked slowly forward. At the next bend in the trail, they stopped short. A red glow flickered behind the slits of Gath's helmet, and Brown John groaned.

Far up the pass a long, winding, colorful body was surging down the narrow road, appearing and disappearing, a serpentine column of scarlet, rose, crimson and vermilion. As it descended the music grew louder and the instruments became distinct.

"Chains," Brown John whispered as a group of warriors crowded up behind their commanders. They spoke in startled whispers.

"Kitzakks."

"Thousands of them."

"That's no raiding party."

"That's the whole bloody horde."

Brown John turned to speak to Gath, but he was heading for the next sharp bend in the trail. The old man hurried after him, heaving and panting with each painful step, and caught up with Gath just as he started around the next bend. Again they both stopped short.

Up ahead, the road ran alongside the sheer cliff to a wide, deep-sided chasm angling off the main gorge. The chasm was spanned by a narrow wooden structure called Thin Bridge. It was a hundred strides long and wide enough for a single wagon to cross, providing it moved like a cautious caterpillar.

The bridge was guarded by a recently constructed palisade gate and a guard tower that stood on poles beside the main gorge in a small clearing at the front of the bridge. The five Kitzakk archers occupying the tower appeared to be having difficulty deciding whether to look back up the pass at the Kitzakk column or at the Death Dealer.

Gath and Brown John were having a similar difficulty. They were looking back and forth from the Kitzakk column to their ragtag Barbarians. Finally Brown John said, "Our army is not strong enough."

Gath nodded. "But if it comes apart now, we will never get it back together again."

Brown John glanced at Thin Bridge, then his eyes met Gath's. They glittered with the same reckless plan as his own. Gath, moving at steady trot, headed toward the bridge as Brown John shouted for the Dowat archers. But they were frozen with fear and staring openmouthed at the road up the gorge.

The front end of the Kitzakk column was emerging, a Company of Skulls with painted faces, Beetle Red armor and flags. Their tall spears glistened in the sunshine five feet above their marching bodies.

Brown John shouted louder but without results. The Barbarians were behaving like ants standing in the shadow of a falling avalanche. He looked back at Gath in time to see the Kitzakk archers in the tower level their crossbows at him. When Gath was within five strides of the tower, two archers opened fire.

Gath leaned out of the way of one bolt, and bounced the second off his horned helmet, then dropped his axe and charged! The other Kitzakks fired. Too late. Their bolts drilled his dust, and Gath hit the nearest log support of the tower with his shoulder. The log shook with a loud ripping sound, bounced him off, and he hit the ground.

The guards, reloading, stopped and looked over the edge of the tower just in time to see the cracked log splinter and sag. The tower dipped at one corner and threw them into each other.

Gath leapt off the ground beside the splintered log with his legs wide, and circled it with his massive arms. He twisted it and, with his legs driving, pushed it over.

The tower lay over in midair, then suddenly swung around. Its weight ripped the remaining log supports loose, and it crashed through the palisade wall, taking out a large hunk. It deposited two archers on the bridge, then continued its lurching arc out over the gorge where it tossed the other three, along with their wine jars, hard biscuits and signal flags. With one long throat-tearing shriek the archers disappeared into the abyss.

Gath was left on the ground hugging the splintered log. It was still attached to the tower, which was suspended over the gorge and impatient to complete its fall. It dragged Gath half off the road before he could let go. The log ripped free, leaving him a handful of splinters as a reminder of their brief acquaintance, then clubbed him in the head by way of saying good-bye, and dropped.

Dizzied momentarily by the blow, Gath dangled half off the road until Brown John reached him. He helped Gath scramble back, and the Grillards surged forward cheering. The main body of the Barbarian army, still holding its ground at the bend in the road, cheered too. Briefly.

The Company of Skulls, their spears lowered, were charging for Thin Bridge. They were about five hundred strides away and closing fast.

Gath let out a low growl, swept his axe off the ground and strode through the wreckage of the palisade wall, leaving Brown John and the Grillards in his heat. He appeared fresher and more alert than when they started, like a wolf scenting live meat. The Grillards stared in awed wonder, and Brown John clucked with pleasure.

Two surviving Kitzakk archers, swords in hand, stood on the bridge staring down at their falling comrades. When they looked up, Gath had joined them.

He hammered the first archer's startled face with the flat of his axe and the man's head caved in. The other archer swung his sword, but Gath leaned out of the way and kicked him in the knee. It popped and doubled up under him. The archer staggered back, then forward. He was good at staggering, but not good enough. He stepped off the bridge and fell as the charging Skull spearmen burst around a turn not three hundred strides away.

Brown John joined Gath, and they looked down at the

supports holding the bridge. To reach them would be difficult and time-consuming, but a section of the wood flooring was rotting. Before the old man could suggest it, Gath was hacking at it with his axe. Brown John started off to fetch Barhacha woodmen to help, but they had seen the plot emerging and were already hurrying toward the bridge.

With professional skill and ten axes the Barhacha went to work on the five logs forming the span of the bridge. They had cut only halfway through when the Skull spearmen came within thirty strides of the bridge. But Dowat archers, with Dirken leading, had climbed the side of the cliff and opened fire. Their arrows leveled the front rank of the charging spearmen and ate into the second.

The Skull spearmen, however, did not break stride. They charged over their fallen comrades, kicking several into the gorge, then swept onto the bridge. The Barhacha were still chopping when Kitzakk spears found their thighs and chests. Two went down. The others gallantly kept at their work, but the spears only begat more spears. The Barhacha finally fell with the logs severed more than two thirds of the way through.

Gath abandoned the bridge and, with the help of the Grillard strongmen, blocked the charge of the Skull spearmen at the north end of the bridge. They cut up whatever came their way, spears, arms, legs and snarling faces. The Kitzakks dropped in twos and threes in front of the Death Dealer and piled up quickly. Their confederates had to climb the dying bodies to get at the Death Dealer. As they did, Dirken and the Dowats rained arrows on them and Brown John shouted at the bridge, "Fall! Fall!"

At first the bridge refused to behave as the old stage master felt a good piece of scenery should. But all of a sudden the logs snapped apart, and the Skulls departed in the manner they had arrived, as a colorful body. But there was no pleasant music now, only screaming. Some fell with their spears still in their hands. Others clung to falling timbers. Both should have let go. The spears did mean things to their comrades tumbling beside them. The timbers bounced off the sides of the gorge with rock-shattering cracks and dull thuds where a clinging body padded the blow.

Gath remained standing at the end of the broken bridge with his legs apart and his chest heaving. His axe dripped blood, and his heat was so intense that the Grillards backed away. The pile of tangled dead and living bodies in front of him had been sucked back by falling comrades into the gorge. All that remained was one dying Kitzakk. He clung to the Death Dealer's boot. His legs dangled into the ragged gap. Gath considered him a moment, then lifted his leg and shook him off. The Kitzakk fell by himself. His lonely scream echoed up out of the chasm, then was cut off when he joined his silent comrades far below.

The Barbarian Army stared spellbound, barely moving as Brown John, seeing the main body of the Kitzakk column only a hundred strides off, ordered them back out of range.

At the opposite side of the bridge, the remaining Skulls glared with dark, maddened faces at the Death Dealer, and flung their spears wildly. Gath deflected them with axe and horned helmet, as if it were a game. When they were finally empty-handed, they shouted foul curses, then turned to greet the approaching head of the main column, a Hammer regiment.

Brown John, peering around the turn in the road, watched the approaching Kitzakks thoughtfully. Slowly an expression of grotesque understanding began to twist his many wrinkles.

Except for the soldiers at the very front of the arriving column, the Kitzakks had no idea what had happened or that the bridge was destroyed. The surviving Skulls screamed in warning, but the column kept coming. Some of the Skulls fell to the ground, others were forced back onto the remnant of the bridge and began to spill over its broken edge. That brought the front ranks of the Hammer regiment to a stop, but the column behind them kept surging forward. The surviving spearmen and the first five ranks of the Hammer regiment were fed to the gorge, then the officers managed to halt the column.

The column was trapped. There was no space on the narrow road for messengers to ride, or even walk, back along the column and explain what was wrong, so the officers dismounted and gathered in a group, chattering excitedly.

Brown John, with his expression changing to one of grotesque anticipation, was certain he knew the subject of their discussion. They were asking each other what the command for retreat was. One or two of the veteran officers might remember seeing commands for a retreat in some ancient yellowed parchment, but the old man was certain they had never bothered to read it. There would have been no need. The Kitzakk Horde had not retreated in a hundred years. Consequently, the officers, no matter how long they talked, would find no means of turning the column around in an orderly fashion.

When Gath joined Brown John, the *bukko* explained what was happening, and the eyes within the horned helmet darkened with anticipation. The two joined their army beyond the turn in the road, and Gath started climbing a narrow crack in the rocky cliff siding the road. Seeing the jagged break led all the way to the top of the cliffs, a surge of excitement coated the old man's cheeks like fresh paint. He turned to his troops and just as quickly lost his color.

His sons, the strongmen and the rest of the Grillards were joking and laughing with the Dowat archers, congratulating themselves. The army was behaving no better.

Cold panic ran up the old man's spine. He pushed his way to Bone's big, bragging face, and interrupted his laughter by stepping on his foot and shouting, "You idiot! We've won nothing! We've only stubbed their toe. If you

want something to cheer about, get up there. Follow him!''
He pointed at Gath. ''Hurry!''

Bone and Dirken promptly started up the cliff with the
Grillard strongmen following. Brown John ordered the
remainder of the army to wait in place, then set the
Barhacha to cutting timber for a temporary bridge to
replace Thin Bridge, and ordered messengers back to the
forest to tell the tribes that had stayed behind of their
glorious victory. Then, with nothing left to do but collapse
on the road and wait, he did just that. He was wet and cold
to the touch.

Forty-nine
WAY OF
THE INVADER

The horned Barbarian and his strongmen reached the top of
the cliffs within the hour. They had clawed their way up the
crack without a thought to what they might find at the top.
Now they hesitated as the great golden eye of the sun
looked down at them to light their stage. The top of the cliff
was a bald rock tier worn smooth by wind and rain, and
washed clean by the same elements. In the distance, a
massive spreading staircase of similar tiers rose to a world
dwelling above the clouds, the birthplace of thunder and
lightning. The staircase of the Gods.

The huge Barbarian moved his men inland around the
side chasm, then returned to the cliffs above The Narrows.

A tumult of confusion and cursing rose out of the gorge. The sun, looking directly down at the Kitzakks trapped on the pass road, drenched them with bright light, making a perfect target. The horned helmet seemed to watch with pleasure for a moment, then the Barbarian hurried forward, leaping crevices, and the strongmen, like a physical appendage, followed.

High above the cataracts, the sun could see that they were headed for a distant crowd of loose boulders resting precipitously on the edge of the cliff above the rear third of the Kitzakk column. The intense golden eye had never found these Barbarians of particular interest before and could not remember much about them. But something about their horned leader's movements excited it, and it brightened with anticipation, concentrated its attentive light on The Narrows. It had been decades since the golden orb, which had watched the Kitzakk Horde from its infancy and knew it intimately, had looked down on an unfolding drama with such striking possibilities.

The Kitzakk column stretched for miles back up into the narrow pass. The front third consisted of the surviving Skull regiments, the Hammer and Spear regiments, and their supply train. The middle third was made up of commercial companies of Chainmen, Cagemen and a train of huge wagons stacked with empty cages. The rear third was composed of Engineer regiments and a long wagon train bearing precut timbers for a base fort. Each group was separated by a wide interval. Well behind the last group a Wenchmaster led a wagon train of camp followers, a rowdy group of hardy whores, tinkers, magicians dealing in cheap love potions, cooks, gamblers and healers.

Earlier, when the Wenchmaster had seen the tail of the column stop far down the pass ahead of him, he had halted his wagon train. He was now barking orders, organizing a hasty retreat. The horses were unhitched. Both wagons and horses were turned around in place. Then the horses were hitched to the wagons they had formerly followed. This left one wagon without horses. It was unceremoniously shoved into the pass. The Wenchmaster then started his wagon train back up the pass toward the desert.

Several miles down the pass from the retreating camp followers, General Kayat, the commander of the invading column, still sat his horse at the head of the rear third. He had sent orderlies forward at five-minute intervals to investigate the delay, but none had returned. He had also ordered himself some hot tea. As an aide arrived with it, he dismounted and took the steaming cup. He walked casually to the edge of the gorge and raised it to his lips, glancing uneasily over the rim.

He was standing on the section of the pass after which The Narrows was named, a thin stretch of road barely wide enough for the passage of one wagon. The open mouth of the gorge beside the road was no wider. Both road and gorge were walled by sheer rock cliffs rising toward the watching sun.

The road ahead descended gently as it twisted down through the pass. General Kayat could see the entire middle third of the column with its large wagons of cages and chains, but only the rear end of the front third, a regiment of Spears in bright fuchsia armor positioned at a sharp turn. The soldiers were shouting and arguing. He watched several run back across the gap separating them from the middle of the column and gesture wildly to the commanders of the Chainmen and Cagemen. An argument began to roar loudly up the pass.

Kayat tilted an ear toward these uncharacteristic sounds and carefully returned the half-empty cup to the waiting aide. Behind him, mounted and at attention, waited the three successful old campaigners who had advised General Yat-Feng on the raids against Coin, Bone Camp and the village of the Barhacha. Their eyes were fixed on the road ahead. Dedicated Kitzakk invaders in blood, bone and mind.

Kayat remounted and turned his eyes to the front. His head was shadowed under the wide brim of his helmet, a place of grim resolve. For ten minutes he did not move or speak, then suddenly he stiffened with shock.

At the sharp turn in the road ahead, the regiment of Spears had started moving back up the pass. Behind them a Black Hand regiment appeared around the sharp turn and ran wildly in among the retreating Spears. Both regiments promptly panicked, plunged across the wide interval of empty road separating them from the wagon train of cages, and pushed into and over the wedged wagons. Their drivers, showing no skill at backing up, panicked the horses. Several threw themselves, their drivers and the wagons they pulled off the edge of the road into the gorge. As they fell, they ricocheted off the narrow rock walls again and again. Before they had fallen halfway, there was little left of them for the sun to shine on.

The remaining wagons backed up into each other, and into the side of the road. Wheels broke and wagons collapsed, causing a huge roadblock. It continued to grow as more and more soldiers retreated around the sharp turn, propelled by still unseen regiments retreating down the gorge. It was a formation the sun had never seen the Kitzakks use before, but which it knew well. It was designed by panic.

Blocked by the broken crowd of wagons and cages, the soldiers quickly jammed up all the way back to the sharp turn. There they collided with the surging crowd behind them. Fighting broke out, and bodies began to drop away from the bunch like overripe grapes to fall into the gorge. Others dangled from the road edge, clinging to one another. Suddenly the bunch buckled, burst apart and fell in clusters into the gorge.

At that moment the huge Barbarian and his strongmen began to heave rocks down from the cliffs above.

General Kayat, seeing the shadows cast by the descending rocks, stared up in horror as the young commander of the wagon train of cages reached him. The commander, sweating and shaking, saluted, then started to speak, but stopped as he heard the falling rocks arrive and looked back at his wagon train. His cages and wagons were being smashed by huge boulders. His drivers were being crushed and knocked into the gorge. He turned to General Kayat for instructions.

General Kayat's saddle was empty. The general was half buried in the road under a large boulder. A bigger boulder hit the general's boulder and sent it rolling toward the edge of the road taking the Kitzakk with it. Bits of the general's bloody armor were crushed and wedged in cracks of the boulder. He pounded the rock incessantly as it fell into the gorge.

The young commander, aghast, turned in desperation to the old greybeards. The expressions on their faces made it clear that they would not, could not, consider retreating. The commander could only stare in bafflement, but the sun understood. The golden orb had seen and admired such men before, men who had made the Kitzakk Horde strong, who had built the empire. A Kitzakk never panics. Never turns back.

The young commander groaned with despair and fled past the old men. As he did, a boulder flattened him. A moment later an avalanche swept the greybeards out of their saddles and all four sailed resolutely into the gorge.

As they fell the expressions of the old soldiers did not change. Not until they met the rocks far below. But this was not their decision. It was made by the rocks.

Fifty

HIGH BRIDGE

In the late afternoon, a team of four hauled an olive green wagon up The Narrows. It was well above the section of the pass where the Kitzakk column had panicked. The road was empty except for a cloud of brown dust chasing the wagon. Cool shade now filled the gorge giving it a savage unity and size. The wagon was infinitesimal against the sheer rock cliff, like a roach skittering over the wall of a great hall. Nevertheless there was a plunging vitality to it, as if the same forces of nature which had conspired to wrench open the earth to create the gorge had been brought into play for the single purpose of providing the wagon with a road.

The wagon caromed and skidded around a sharp turn, and pulled up short of Bone, Dirken and the Grillard strongmen who blocked the road with their weapons leveled. The dust billowed over the wagon, concealing it and the driver as he roared with delight within its dusty embrace. The hard faces of the Grillards broke with smiles and chuckles, and they crowded forward as Brown John rose up out of the dust with widespread arms, shouting. "Victory! The pass is ours! From here all the way to the forests!"

He bowed, and they, knowing a cue when they saw one, cheered wildly and began hugging, dancing and throwing caps and weapons into the air. The celebration had begun.

Brown John, in a soaring voice, pronounced over the

joyous din, "My brave, brave, brave Grillards, this is a day of days! The world has been turned upside down and we, you, and our champion, have done the work of it."

He pivoted in a dance to the music of their joy and glory. Then a drumming, pounding beat, rising out of the pass below, joined in. The Grillards rushed to the side of the gorge and looked down into the pass.

The Barbarian Army, draped in the fuchsias, scarlets and vermilions of plundered Kitzakk armor, were tramping up The Narrows at a loud steady pace, a confident one. It now carried weapons of hard steel.

Behind the army trailed horses and wagons heaped with plundered provisions, armor and weapons. In the distance new arrivals were running up the pass to join the victors.

Bone and Dirken climbed up beside the old man for a better view. Brown John threw his arms around them. "The Gods are in attendance, lads, and our cast is swelling."

Bone and Dirken turned their awed, flushed faces to their father. His cheeks were apple red and his smile as reckless as an infant's. They had never seen him like this before, and it unsettled them.

"I do not boast," Brown John continued, "but it is as if the birds themselves had played a part, carrying word of our victory to the world. New volunteers were arriving even before we had time to rebuild Thin Bridge. I truly believe that before nightfall our ranks will have doubled!"

The sons, making sure their father could see them, winked at each other playfully, mocking his childish exuberance. Catching their exchange, Brown John's eyes twinkled. Then they sobered as he looked thoughtfully at the whole scene: at his clan shouting encouragement, at the advancing army, at the dark stains of blood around the clearing, at a scatter of Kitzakk dead, at two new graves heaped with rocks. Then, solemnly, he raised his eyes to High Bridge. It was still standing, undamaged. His Grillards, by advancing over the cliff tops, had reached it before the escaping Kitzakks and saved it. He caught his sons' attention and with a calm yet significant gesture, indicated the structure. "You have done a brave piece of work," he allowed. "Not having to rebuild it is going to save precious time. Now, where is Gath?"

Dirken was quick to answer. "He went on ahead, to the fort at the top of the pass."

"Oooh!" Brown John's brow crinkled.

"He's gone after the girl," Bone added.

Dirken pointed at a Kitzakk tower mounted above the pass. "They've got signal towers all the way to their fort."

"They'll see him coming hours before he reaches it," the old man muttered to himself, "but that may be to his advantage."

He stepped up onto the wagon seat with extended arms and in stentorian tones demanded attention. When he got it, his voice resounded through the hushed crowd.

"You are to be congratulated. All of you." Cheering interrupted him, and he paused, smiling, until it stopped. "There is an entire Kitzakk column lying dead back there in the pass. A full sixth of the Kitzakk Desert Army." There was more cheering, but he continued, shouting over the rapturous response. "The Outlanders have not suffered such a defeat in a hundred years!"

The group went wild, hooting and whistling, and he let them. When the hysteria had subsided somewhat, he raised a triumphant finger to the sky and bellowed, "From this day forth, our champion, Gath of Baal, is going to be known forever for what he truly is. The Lord of the Forest! Invincible."

The Grillards cheered and chanted. "Gath! Gath! Gath!"

Dirken frowned nervously at his father, and whispered, "That's crazy. If the Kitzakks are up there waiting for him behind palisade walls, not even a nine-armed god would stand a chance."

"We will see," Brown John replied. "We will see."

There were tears welling in his eyes, and his sons shifted uncomfortably. But they knew why. His Grillards were no longer merely strutting actors, but real men who had worked the brutal stage of life. The equals, perhaps even the best, of all the men in the forest.

Dirken fidgeted, then brought his father's indulgent musing to an abrupt stop. "Are we just going to stand around and cheer, or do something?"

Brown John blinked, then wiped a cheek with the back of a hand and looked sternly at his sons. "You stay here, Dirken. When the army arrives, keep it moving at a steady pace and don't let any of the Wowells, Cytherians or Barhacha get ahead of you. They are desperate to rescue their women and children, but if they race ahead and try to do it by themselves, we are lost. The army must be held together."

Dirken asked respectfully, "What do we do with the prisoners?"

"There aren't any." The *bukko* watched with satisfaction as Dirken's and Bone's mouths dropped open. They both swallowed hard, then Dirken hurried off to meet the arriving army as Brown John hollered at a group of strongmen, "You five, get up in the wagon. The work's up ahead."

The Grillards piled aboard. Bone cracked the whip and the wagon rumbled south across High Bridge waving its tail of dust behind it like a proud banner.

Fifty-one

THE FANGKO SPEAR

Gath stood motionless in the deep shade. He was several hundred feet from the heights of the cataracts. Here the trail no longer followed the gorge. It zigzagged up through rock walls to an opening about twenty feet wide and thirty feet high at the top of the pass. The mouth of The Narrows. It was closed by a wooden palisade and gate that glowed with the orange-gold light of the evening sun.

The helmet sagged heavily in front of his heaving body so that he looked like a bull ready to charge. His chain mail steamed. His eyes, hard slices of white within the shadows of the metal, were active and wary. Sensing danger, yet not seeing it.

A wall-walk formed the top of the gate. It was crenellated, as were the palisades running along the tops of the cliffs on both sides of him. No soldiers stood on the ramparts. No glitter of steel betrayed any hiding behind them. Above the gate and along the palisades poles stood at regular intervals. Dangling from them were smouldering shreds of cloth; charred, stringy remnants of Kitzakk regimental flags. They fluttered timidly on the light breeze. Their modest flapping gave the silence size and weight.

Beyond the gate spires of smoke rose against the yellow sky, caught the breeze and were carried down the pass. Gath sniffed at the familiar cedar aroma, then his eyes focused on the top of the signal tower rising beyond the gate. It was only a small open-topped wooden box standing

on a single tall wooden pole, and there was no sign of
anyone there, either.

He looked back down the pass at an identical signal
tower where the gorge turned away from the road. He had
seen no sign of life in it before, and there was none now.

The prospect of having no one to fight maddened his
blood, and his muscles convulsed as smoke drifted from
the helmet's eye slits. Then his head began to throb with
pressure, and he strode recklessly to the gate with his axe
slightly to the front, eager for blood. He pushed at the gate,
but it was locked. Frustrated, he hammered it with the
blunt end of his axe, then kicked it. No one responded. He
slung his axe on his back, and drew two daggers. Holding
them overhead, he jumped up and drove one into the wood.
With that dagger bearing his weight, he lurched higher,
driving in the second with his other hand. He pulled the
first dagger free, stabbed it higher into the wall. The
muscles of his back bunched; the tendons of his arms
corded with power. The chain mail shirt kicked up like
metallic wings around his hips as he lurched and swung.
Reaching the crenellations above the gate, he hauled
himself onto the wall-walk. Panting, with sweat dripping
from the edges of his chain mail, and smoke drifting from
the helmet, he studied the interior of the fort.

Billowing smoke obscured the center of its large courtyard, but he could make out a second gate at the far side. It
was open, and a section of the palisade beside it had been
torn down to widen it. Beyond it the flat bone-brown body
of the desert spread toward a distant horizon where golden
dust clouds tumbled in the fading sunlight. Former residents leaving in a hurry.

Apart from a few vultures perched on the walls, the fort
appeared deserted and barren. The corrals, stalls and shops
built under the palisade ramparts appeared empty, as did
scattered piles of cages. Abandoned sacks of grains,
baskets of eggs, dried meat, hay and wine jars spilled from
the storehouses. Here and there were hastily discarded
saddles, harnesses and wagons. Fires had been started

under racks of spears and a wagon full of crossbows and bolts in an attempt to destroy them. But they had been built too hastily and gone out. Only the one at the center of the fort smouldered with dense smoke.

Gath waited until the pressure in his head abated, then jumped into the yard and entered a storehouse. He poured a half-dozen raw eggs into his mouth, smearing the sticky mess over the face of the helmet. He pushed in two handfuls of dry meat while emptying a wine vessel. Gorged and sated, he looked around uncertainly for a cistern to wash off the mess, but saw none. Unnerved by the silence and lack of movement, he lumbered impatiently toward the smoke-filled center. A wind swept in through the desert gate and, with a swish, lifted the cloud of smoke like a curtain to reveal a muscular black stallion standing on a dirt mound at the precise center of the yard.

The animal was huge and thick chested, with legs the size of knotty tree trunks. A powerful, rounded neck supported the short-nosed, blunt head. Its eyes were intelligent but wild. Its forelegs straddled a dead Kitzakk officer clasping a pole mounted with two red horsetails.

In a row beside the dead man were four more bodies, Kitzakk officers uniformed in the bright reds of various regiments. They were facedown except for one who kneeled as if praying. Sprawled half off the front of the mound was a soldier of the Skulls. He held the hilt of a bloody dagger in his right fist. The blade was buried in his chest.

Gath recognized the style of spear used for the executions. It was a Fangko, a spear designed with heavy barbs to pull out the rib bones and heart muscle. The spear, thick with the gore of human organs, lay beside the soldier. A ritual killing performed by their own.

The animal snorted and stomped the ground as Gath approached, obviously not caring for his messy appearance and smell. Or was it audaciously and foolishly defending its fallen master?

Gath kept coming.

The stallion reared. Its neck corded with muscle; its distended nostrils blew. Its hooves beat up the sky and plunged down, hammering the earth between the officer and Gath.

Gath halted three strides short of the stallion and looked it dead in the eye. "It's useless to argue. I need your help."

The horse bolted forward, snorting and kicking up dust. Gath stepped in and drove a fist into the side of its head, like a hammer. The resounding impact made the stallion concede no more than an inch of ground. It charged and butted Gath in the chest with its head. Gath conceded no more than the horse had, and grabbed two fistfuls of mane. The stallion lifted its head bringing Gath off the ground, kept charging and drove Gath into a wooden railing. It splintered, and Gath dropped to the ground. Not liking it there, he leapt up and circled the horse's neck with his massive arms, taking a firm hold on its mane. The stallion snorted and whinnied. Gath, with his legs driving and arms twisting, forced the animal backward, then with a growling surge of strength, threw it down on its side beside the dead officer and held it against the ground.

Thrashing and kicking, the stallion tried to rid itself of the man, then suddenly surrendered. The red glowing eyes of the horned helmet looked directly into the stallion's wild eyes. Slowly they quieted, then Gath let go and they stood facing each other. Heat mingled between them until they smelt the same, a pungent but binding aura.

The horse snorted, then lowered its head to the man. Gath pressed his face against the horse's nostrils, and they breathed each other's breath. The stallion neighed softly, pushed its cheek against the rough chain mail.

"You are mine," Gath whispered. He glanced down at the dead officer, looked off at the vultures, then said to the horse, "I will put him in the ground for you."

The stallion slowly lowered its broad-necked head to the body of its former master, then backed away.

Fifty-two

TWO DRAGON TAILS

It was turning dark when Brown John's wagon pulled up in front of the fort. The gate stood open, like a giant mute mouth. Its silence was chilling, unnatural. Bone flicked the reins resolutely, and the wagon proceeded into the fort.

Inside he reined up, and Brown John and the strongmen stared openmouthed at the scene being played at center stage.

Gath of Baal stood in the middle of the yard currying a magnificent black stallion. A black enamel saddle with gold inlay was propped against a pile of rocks from which a horsetail standard protruded. It appeared to be a fresh grave.

Brown John ordered Bone and his men to secure all food and weapons, then drove the wagon slowly toward his champion as he glanced warily at the dead bodies, the empty fort, the stallion.

As the old man reined up, Gath turned and, with an uncharacteristic lift in his voice, asked, "What do you think of him? He's a fine one, isn't he?"

"Fine," exclaimed Brown John, "is not the word. He is superb! And he suits you." He glanced pointedly at the grave. "I presume there is no need to ask how you acquired him?"

Gath laughed roughly, and its hollow ring startled the old man, made the horse bolt. "Hey! Settle down, friend," Gath crooned. "Settle down."

To Brown John's amazement, the stallion returned to Gath, lowered its head and nuzzled the arm of his intimidating new master. Looking at the horse, Gath said to Brown John, "I did not acquire him, *bukko*. These men were dead when I got here. We simply met and made an arrangement."

Brown John looked down and saw the Fangko spear. "Ah, I see," he said, then grinned and shook his head. "You never cease to amaze me. Everything you do seems to have an aura of the miraculous about it, particularly today."

Gath glanced up at him.

"Our ranks grow by the hour. There has never been such unity. You have led our forest tribes to undreamed of success! Now they are not only hungry to free their women and children, but are ready, eager to take revenge." He hesitated thoughtfully. "But what of you? Is Gath of Baal pleased with his new role?"

With the light tone gone, Gath replied, "I will be pleased when it gets me what I must have." His eyes met Brown John's. "She is not here. The fort was empty when I arrived."

Measuring his words the old man argued, "But this is the butterfly fort the bounty hunter told the Wowells about, and we both knew there was small chance she would be kept here." He glanced around. "Nevertheless, I am surprised you found it deserted. Perhaps your reputation now does your conquering for you?"

Gath shrugged and picked up the saddle, set it gently on the steed and began to adjust the cinch. "I saw dust to the south and started to follow it, but then it vanished, and I could find no tracks in the sand."

The old wizard nodded. "They're there, if you know what to look for. It's three days to Bahaara, maybe longer, depending on the winds. So there is still a chance for two riders moving at a strong, steady pace to overtake them. If she's with them, you'll soon have her back." He smiled at the stallion admiringly. "You've provided superbly for the chase."

Gath picked up his axe, slung it over his back and mounted carefully. The stallion shifted sideways, adjusting to the heavy weight. Gath rested an arm on the animal's mane and looked down at Brown John expectantly.

"Oh yes," Brown John said. "I will accompany you and point out the trail. By all means. There are dangers in the sands a forester like yourself will not even see. But first you must understand what has happened here." He pointed at the horsetail standard over Yat-Feng's grave. "The man buried here was not merely a general, but the commander of the Kitzakk Desert Army. The man second in command only to their warlord, Klang. He was no doubt executed because he had been irredeemably disgraced by today's defeat. To avoid a similar fate, Klang will now have to send not only regiments against you, but magicians as well. You will need my skills."

"Just find me their trail."

"Oh no," Brown John protested, "I can be of far more assistance than that. If we find they have already carried Robin to Bahaara, then I will be as invaluable to you as that spectacular helmet. I am familiar with the ways of the cult of the Butterfly Goddess. And I know Bahaara's shadows."

The helmet was silent, but the stallion's hooves pattered restlessly.

"Good," said Brown John. "I am glad to know there is some room within that headpiece for reasonable thought. Because I must also know why you are so desperate to rescue this girl. If they are already devising some method of turning her magic against you, I can not help you unless I know what it is."

"We have no time for that now."

"Come, come, my old friend," the old man coaxed. "It is far past the season for mysteries and shadows."

Gath turned and trotted toward the desert gate. Without

looking back, he muttered brusquely, "If you are coming, come."

Brown John tossed his hands up helplessly, then hurried off and found a saddle. With Bone's help he unhitched and saddled his strongest horse, then ordered Bone to wait for Dirken and the army, telling him that, after the army had watered and eaten, he and his brother were to supply every tenth man with a torch and proceed into the desert following the trail he would mark. Brown John then mounted nimbly and galloped swiftly out the desert gate to join Gath. In the night shadows he looked twenty years younger.

Fifty-three

THE BATH

Dang-Ling glided across the floor through the dense steam, opened the hall door and smiled effervescently under his glossy pink lids. His voice swooshed, "Come in. Thank you for coming. We are bathing her now."

Klang stood impatiently outside the door in the polished black corridor of Bahaara's Temple of Dreams. The commanders of the Guards and Executioners stood behind him. All three wore combat armor. The warlord glanced at the high priest with disgust, as if he were an overly sweet desert, and entered.

Dang-Ling closed the door firmly in the faces of the two commanders, and plucked a large bamboo fan from a hook in the stone wall. Waving the steam aside, he proceeded into it. "This way. She is in the bath now. But watch your step. Before we drugged her she had a terrible fit, splashed water about everywhere."

He guided Klang through the steam to a large, circular, vaporous pool set in the center of the stone floor.

A huge black mute, Baak, stood waist deep·in the water holding Robin's limp body under one hairless arm as he lathered her dyed hair with soapy bubbles. A dark stain swirled in the water around her head.

Klang looked intently at the young, unblemished girl.

Robin's lips were parted. She was breathing in rapid erratic gasps. Her eyelids trembled, sometimes fluttering open to reveal glazed unfocused eyes.

"An absolutely exquisite subject, don't you think?" Dang-Ling asked. "Gazul brought her, and was paid quite well. He is a true professional, that man. He had dyed her hair and dressed her in rags. But I, of course, recognized her immediately."

Dang-Ling motioned with a limp hand, and Baak lifted Robin out of the water with his huge hands. He turned her slowly so that her glistening smooth body could be seen from every angle: slender arrowlike legs, flat brown tummy, high firm breasts with their nipples pinkened by the heat, and luxuriously dripping red-gold hair. As submissive as a glove. Klang was visibly impressed.

Noticing this, Dang-Ling's milky face turned florid, and a tremor ran through his voice. "Have you ever seen such a fabulous creation?"

"She's still a child." Klang snapped turning on the high priest. "What possible power can a child have over this savage killer?"

Contempt curled Dang-Ling's lips, but he disguised it with unctuous words. "My lord, it is a puzzle to me as well, but I am certain she has some magic which will be the key to his destruction."

"Then find its nature, priest. Quickly!"

Dang-Ling bowed stiffly, unable to conceal his bruised feelings. "If you will permit me to proceed, I will take her to my laboratory and begin the examination now."

"Not yet, I am not finished." Klang's suspicious eyes riveted on the black man.

Dang-Ling bowed, saying petulantly, "He can not hear you. Baak is deaf and mute."

Silence was between them, then the warlord said, "I have ordered the army to maintain a position between the Barbarian Army and this city, and delay its advance, but not engage it."

A strained tenseness entered the high priest's eyes.

"I am going to delay the battle until you, Dang-Ling, place in my hands the magic that will destroy their leader. Do you understand? The Fangko spear is not going to rip my heart out. I am going to kill him in personal combat."

The high priest sputtered, "Whatever my lord commands, but . . . but personal combat! There are such risks! Unaccountable risks. An accidental fall, a spill of blood in the wrong place! There are just no guarantees, and your safety is the safety of us all."

Klang placed a hand on the high priest's shoulder, and squeezed it painfully as he drew the soft albino closer. "There will be guarantees, priest. You will see to them. In addition to whatever this child has to offer, you are going to find me an invincible weapon. Do you understand?" There were a hundred nefarious, even sacrilegious, meanings in his tone.

Dang-Ling, understanding the one he meant, suddenly relaxed, but was careful not to make it apparent. "I understand, my Lord," he said evenly. "And fortunately your demand comes at an opportune time. My informants tell me that the unholy Master of Darkness himself wants this demon destroyed."

"Informants?"

"Acquaintances, professional magicians. One in particular, a sorceress, is sometimes able to arrange for his help."

"Then deal with her. Get me the strongest weapon he has."

"Everything will have to be done in total secrecy."

"Of course."

Dang-Ling bowed slightly. "I will inquire as soon as she arrives, which should be shortly. I am sure she will be eager to help, as will he. The Lord of Death will be honored to assist a great and powerful leader such as yourself. But his price can be terribly high."

"Do not instruct me, priest," Klang snapped. "I am fully aware of the nature of his transactions."

Dang-Ling bowed, and Klang strode through the steam, went out slamming the door behind him.

Dang-Ling grinned, rushed to the side of the pool and clapped his hands. The huge mute carried Robin's dripping body up the sunken steps and through the steam to the far corner of the room. Dang-Ling pulled a lever hidden in the wall, and a huge stone lifted up off the floor. Flame-tinted clouds of smoke billowed up, encircling them, and they descended into it. Firelight ran riot in Robin's wet, red-gold hair, then they were gone, and the stone lowered back into place.

Fifty-four

THE GLASS CAGE

The smokey stairway descended to the high priest's workroom. They crossed it and passed through a door beside the workbench, closing it behind them.

The huge rectangular room they entered was a stone-walled underground laboratory. A world of retorts, flasks, beakers, waterbaths, condensers, phials, ladles, crucibles, and corked glass jars holding human and animal organs:

hearts, gonads, livers, penises and tongues. A maze of bottle green vessels were mounted on the tables and connected to each other with glass tubing rising to large colorless crystal tubes suspended from the ceiling by iron bars. Many leaked hissing fumes that dripped to form fuming puddles on the floor.

The crystal tubes wound their way toward a huge, perfectly transparent glass vessel barely visible beyond the clutter of apparatus, the culmination of some mad thaumaturgical scheme.

The neck of the mammoth flask was suspended by iron rings from the ceiling. Its ten-foot bowl dangled into a large circular hole in the stone floor. Baak climbed a ladder to a wooden deck built around its long cylindrical neck. Using a pulley attached to the ceiling, he lowered Robin headfirst down through the neck into the bowl.

Naked, her limp, nut-brown body descended slowly into the crystalline glass. It magnified her to almost three times her normal size, and lust glimmered in Dang-Ling's watching eyes.

When Robin landed on the bottom of the bowl, Baak climbed down the neck and untied her, then climbed back out and pulled the rope up behind him.

Dang-Ling had moved down a stone staircase that circled around the flask and now peered at Robin's enlarged body hunting for a mark, numeral, or tattoo of some kind. At the bottom of the hole, he peered up as Robin tumbled over languidly onto her back, then over again onto her stomach. She half opened an eyelid, saw Dang-Ling's soft boiled eyes glistening wetly only inches from her own, and moaned, collapsed again.

Hours later, after Dang-Ling's priestesses, two middle-aged women named Dazi and Hatta, had induced various vapors and fluids into the retort, Dang-Ling was sitting tiredly on the staircase staring down at his subject's wet, steaming body. Earlier, when snarling red smoke had swirled over her thrashing screaming nudity with its stinging bite, he had expected to see fangs or scales appear. Then, when the amber vapors were induced into the bowl, he had prayed for yellow cat eyes and claws to materialize from her flesh. But Robin had remained essentially unchanged. Then white powders nearly smothered the girl, but no insect wings or antennae appeared. And the ritually prepared saltwater which was designed to expose any relation to sea demons had also brought no results.

Robin sprawled on the bottom of the flask exhausted from pain and terror. Dang-Ling, exhausted from effort and frustration, sprawled on the stone floor beneath her. He sighed, then appealed to the worried faces of Baak, Hatta and Dazi, "This is terrible. Have we no other potions? Am I to believe she's just another pretty girl?"

Fifty-five

CHELA KONG

The vast area between the fort at The Narrows and the city of Bahaara was filled with mountainous sand dunes which moved constantly across the body of the desert. Otherwise it was an empty void as still as death, except for a cluster of upturned rock, clinging to which was the rubble of a village destroyed long before the coming of the Kitzakks. The village had been the desert marketplace for nefarious and dangerous magic totems carved from the rocks. It had been such a successfully offensive market to the ancient rulers of the desert that they had had it destroyed. Since that time its history had long been forgotten except for a few storytellers. All that the Kitzakks and other travelers of the road now knew was that it had been called Chela Kong. The reason underlying the success of the original residents had been forgotten by everyone, but the earth remembered.

The upturned rock was unlike any other in the desert, an eruption from deep in the bowels of the earth. These stones had helped form the surface of the earth before the nature of what was animal, insect, reptile, fish and fowl had been determined, before the nature of what was right and wrong had been considered. Undetected vapors were emitted by the rocks, and they had a peculiar quality. They revealed and magnified the mystical power within the tiniest and weakest totems so that no sorcery could hide in their presence. Instead, it was revealed in all its potential might and terror. This phenomenon was most potent after the midnight hour, when the sands of the desert had cooled and cold winds swept unimpeded across the land to summon forth, not only the nocturnal creatures who dwelled in the body of the sand, but the vapors.

Now, as the midnight hour approached, forty *nomad* slave drivers sat around fires in the midst of the rubble, and drew forth their totems. Descendants of the ancient people who once ruled the sand, they had been privy to the mysterious legends since childhood and, without understanding why, knew that when they camped in Chela Kong the drugs of pleasure they enjoyed were somehow made stronger. As they waited, they stroked and kissed the vials holding them.

They wore desert dust, smears of their own filth, and loincloths over blue-grey flesh. The women had shaggy, filth-laden manes of hair twisted with snakes. All their bodies were distorted by overdoses of Cabalakk. Arms and earlobes were elongated. Here and there a bald head sported short horns, a tail swished, and arms carried webbed, lizardlike fins. The heavy users were dog faced.

Spears stood upright in the soil beside each man. They were long, painted indigo and charcoal, and their blades were serpentined leaf shapes with serrated edges, tridents and axe heads.

The slavers drank a thick dark liquid that bubbled in small brass pans over fires. When midnight arrived, each *nomad* mumbled a short prayer, emptied his or her vial into the pan and drank the hot fluid down in one gulp. The drug made their blue-grey flesh twitch. Hot spots of crimson gathered in their bony cheeks.

Two overfed Kitzakk slave merchants, owners of the company which employed the *nomads* as guides and chainmen, squatted over a small fire in the clearing. They wore expensively embroidered yellow tunics and heavy jewelry. Untouched wine and fresh fruit rested in brass pitchers and bowls at their feet. Every so often the pair glanced at the darkness filling the surrounding desert as if they expected it to rush over and hit them.

Behind the two merchants, better than twenty forest boys shivered in cages stacked on wagons. Their chained sisters and mothers did the same on the ground. At the edges of the torchlit clearing oxen grazed noisily.

The two merchants huddled together until their stomachs touched. Using the ancient Kitzakk dream language, they repeated what they had already told each other a dozen times. That the Kitzakk Army was surely somewhere between them and the Barbarian Army, and that the two riders they had seen far behind them on the trail were nothing more than mercenaries headed for Bahaara. Not the dreaded Death Dealer. Then they glanced at their nomad chainmen, their only protection, and saw again what they could not ignore. Their horns, fins, tails and dog faces had enlarged, and even though there was no sign or sound of an enemy, the savages were preparing for battle, as if their desert-trained senses had heard and seen what the merchants could not.

The moon slowly slipped down the side of the blue-black sky, then sank below the flat endless horizon. Silence and darkness took command of the night.

It began with a soft thunk somewhere along the rubble of the northern wall. The sound was followed by the sudden appearance of a flying rope of blood which glittered against the black sky as it caught the firelight, then disintegrated into red wet jewels before vanishing in the blackness.

The nomads jumped up, spears in hand, as the headless body of the guard at the north wall staggered into view and fell to the ground. Bodies crouched, the nomads nervously jabbed their spears in front of them as if they could draw blood from the body of the night.

Behind their wagons, the merchants found a shadow big enough to hide in, and glanced about trembling. The Barbarian boys rattled their cages, and the girls and women wrestled their chains, then gasped and became silent.

Out of the bowels of the night appeared a menacing living darkness, a warrior mounted on a black stallion. His horse picked its way through the rubble easily, as if it had always grazed on the short, hard growth of destruction. The rider carried an axe decorated with streaming blood that glittered in the slashing firelight. A masked and horned helmet crowned his wide shoulders. The eye slits, like windows to his nature, glowed red, as if his bones and brain were ablaze.

The Kitzakk merchants began to sweat and whimper. The Barbarian captives stared openmouthed. The shouting nomads converged behind their main fire with their spears protruding like the quills of a porcupine.

The intruder dismounted, and strode into the firelight seemingly oblivious to the obstructions blocking his path. He kicked over a low wall as if it were a pile of brush. His shoulder took out a section of still-standing doorway. He pushed a second wall aside with the flat of a hand, and it obligingly fell on its back, kicking up dust which swirled reverently around his tramping feet. He marched up a pile rubble, looked down at the nomads, and raised his axe with two hands over his head. His muscles bunched, and he charged, an avalanche of steel.

A stride short of the waiting spear tips, he planted his foot and, pivoting on it, swung his axe in a wide sweeping arc. The blade carved a half moon out of the spears. The power of the blow propelled his heavy body into the blunted poles. Wood splintered and snapped. Spear tips caught in the Barbarian's chain mail; others gouged his legs and slashed his forearm. He did not appear to notice. His axe was back over his head, coming down fast. This time it fed itself on meat and bone. Slavers fell spouting blood from necks, chests and arms. Blue-grey bodies writhed in wet red fountains. The axe kept at its task as a howl of savage pleasure rang out from the horned helmet.

The Kitzakk merchants watched with spellbound terror, then covered their eyes as the horror took on a new dimension. The black-clad warrior was slowly rising on a growing mountain of the dead and dying. Terror gave way to panic, and the merchants fled.

They raced down a footpath and into the shadow-filled southern desert beyond. They stumbled blindly past Brown John as he was hurrying up the footpath. He stared at them uncertainly, then dashed along the rubble of a wall, reached a rise behind the cages and stopped short. His eyes widened with shock, and he sat down before he realized he had to.

Gath of Baal stood on a pile of dead bodies working his axe. The surviving nomads surrounded him. Splattered with blood, they mindlessly charged up the bodies of the fallen into the Barbarian's slashing axe. Bodies and pieces of bodies tumbled in the air, tossed on fountains of blood, and still they charged. Gath was knee-deep in carnage, slipping on bloody chests and heads. Dying men clung to his legs, bit them, struggled with the last of their strength to pull him down into their mire of gore.

Brown John did not see Bone and Dirken arrive until they, and the group of volunteers they led, reached the clearing. The same thing that made them stop short made the old man relax enough to notice their arrival.

The battle was over, and Gath had disappeared. Nothing remained but bodies stacked as high and wide as a haystack. Shuddering feet protruded from it, and bleeding faces and twitching hands.

There was a slight movement at the top of the pile. A severed tail fell away, tumbled down indifferently to dangle for a moment against a sword, then rolled to the ground and twitched fitfully until it finished bleeding.

No one breathed.

Slowly the stacked gore parted at the top and horns arose, bringing large pieces of carnage with it. The black steel mask appeared with its eye slits flaming. Shaking off bodies, Gath of Baal climbed out of the pile, axe in hand. He ripped spears out of his chain mail, then staggered toward the Barbarian captives.

He searched through the chained women mindless of the fact that he was bleeding on their trembling faces. His blood mixed freely with their flowing tears and splattered against the hair of their bowed heads. Not finding whom he hunted, he growled with frustration, severed the women's chains with his axe, then ripped the cages apart and moved into the night.

The boys fought clear of the wreckage of their cages and fled into the waiting arms of their mothers and sisters as the volunteers broke rank and hurried to them.

Brown John greeted his sons and they pointed with pride at the desert. To the north a line of flickering torches had appeared across the horizon. The Barbarian Army.

The old man smiled with rare pleasure, then saw a dark, horned silhouette moving up a wide path of rubble. Reaching the top, the figure stood against the night sky at the heights of Chela Kong staring south. Whiffs of vapor swirled about his legs. The vapors thickened until they enveloped his body, as if the rocks themselves were breathing. Brown John trembled with a sudden chill. It was not any man he had ever known, but a demon.

Brown John rubbed his arms until the chill was gone, then bravely marched himself toward Gath. When he reached the heights, he found the dark man slumping against a piece of wall. He did not look at Brown John or greet him. The helmet's eye slits still glowed as they stared south.

Anguish and disgust rushed through the old man, but he made himself squat, then asked warily, "What's happened to you?"

"I must see her," Gath said. His voice was a distant, desperate rumble. "I must look on her face and touch her."

A vague expression of recognition crept through Brown John's wrinkles as he watched the red glow die behind the eye slits. He said, "I think I begin to understand, but not nearly enough to help. What is the nature of this magic that possesses you?"

The great metal headpiece dropped forward, and Gath caught it with his hands, held it with his elbows resting on his knees.

Brown John edged closer until his eyes could discern the dark figure, then sat down beside it. He reached to lay a comforting hand on Gath's shoulder but hesitated. He suddenly felt unequal to the task confronting him, unable to draw forth the energy, skill and friendship the night demanded. His wrinkles fell slack, and he felt a thousand years old. It was a long moment before he spoke.

"My friend, we have two choices. Advance with the army and battle the Kitzakks until you are dead of exhaustion . . . or try to find her ourselves, secretly enter Bahaara and take our chances. Your helmet will be difficult to disguise, or perhaps it will not even permit such an adventure, but I believe it's our best chance. What do you think?"

The shadow made no reply.

"I think we must face the fact that if you die, then she surely will."

The shadowed figure shifted restlessly.

Brown John waited, then grunted mockingly at himself. "What an arrogant fool I've been. Two days ago, I asked you to confide in me because I thought that if I knew what the pieces of this puzzle were, I might fit them together. But I had no conception then of the magnitude of the players in this game. This whole affair has gone far past my poor powers of understanding, and if you are as aware of the presence of evil as I suspect you are, there is no way I could expect you to give me your trust. There is simply far too much darkness within me, even a man with only a particle of your powers could see it."

Gath did not move or speak.

Brown John chuckled mockingly. "From the very first day at Lemontrail Crossing I have been conspiring to use you for my own dreams, to make certain my Grillards remained free to practice their frivolous magic. And what happens? I am usurped by a girl of my own choosing. A mere child who will not have the slightest idea of which necks to feed your axe, to say nothing of which nation to have you bring down. I am utterly defeated. And unable to help you . . . the one I would help the most. Yet I will tell you, Gath, whether you trust me or not, I would not trade places with any man. But, if you wish it, I will leave you alone now."

It was a long time before the shadow replied. When it did, its voice came from the depths of a tortured soul. "Stay, old man, and listen."

Fifty-six

ANSARIA & MERALDA ROOTS

Robin Lakehair sat naked and dry on the bottom of the mammoth flask in Dang-Ling's secret underground laboratory. Around her the glass glittered with highlights cast by oil lamps, like a huge jewel with Robin's warm, brown body as the living center.

She was calmly eating brown bread and cheese. When she finished she washed her throat with wine, then curled up against the curve of the bowl and closed her eyes. Sighing long and deep, she cast a suspicious eye through the glass wall and gasped, sat up.

The Queen of Serpents stood regally at the head of the staircase looking down at Robin. She wore full-length armor, a tunic of gold and silver plates that shimmered over her magnificent breasts and sinuous thighs. Her fingers spread over her hips like blood-tipped fangs.

A tiny diamond-and-silver hooded cobra with topaz eyes crowned her raven hair. Her face was polished ivory flushed with scarlet. Her dark eyes glittered with malevolent energy.

Robin sank in a helpless sprawl, her face buried in bare brown arms.

Dang-Ling's obsequious, half-bowed figure crept around Cobra as he said guardedly, "I hope, your highness, that our procedures with this girl meet with your approval. We have worked diligently but she still holds her secret, that is, presuming she has one."

Cobra avoided responding by looking around admiringly at the maze of tubes, bottles and vessels. "I am impressed. I have never seen equipment of such complexity."

"It keeps me amused." Dang-Ling bowed with an unconvincing show of humility.

Cobra humored him, "I would imagine," then asked curtly, "What is your specialty?"

Her abruptness startled the priest. His confidence wavered and he stammered, "My specialty? Well," he rubbed and squeezed his fatty pink hands, "it may not seem very spectacular . . . or even practical . . . but in deference to the Butterfly Goddess who is worshipped through the embraces of sacred prostitutes, my laboratory is dedicated to the pursuit of carnal pleasure."

Amusement coiled in Cobra's cheeks. She asked archly, "And the Barbarian girl, you have examined her only along these lines?"

Without waiting for an answer, Cobra turned back toward Robin. Dang-Ling qualified apologetically, "Well, no, as a matter of fact. It seemed hardly likely that such a child could have any real carnal power. My efforts have been directed more toward discovering her true nature."

"And what have you found?"

"Actually nothing. She is merely what she appears to be . . . a young, exquisite, but inexperienced girl."

Cobra eyed him condescendingly. "You may have misjudged her, priest. For instance, would you not agree that, for one so young and innocent, she wears her nudity quite naturally, even sensuously?"

Dang-Ling peered down at Robin. "Why . . . why yes," he piped with a startled voice. "You're quite right. That is a precocious quality."

Cobra's black-rimmed gold eyes were hard, intense, her voice more so.

"Listen carefully, priest. If the Dark One continues to outwit the helmet, he can turn its powers not only against you and me, but against our master, the Lord of Death himself."

Dang-Ling staggered.

She pushed a trembling curl away from his round ear delicately. "You are right to tremble. A very sinister and deceptive enemy has revealed herself, the most deadly the Master of Darkness has ever faced, a sorceress who can not only counteract the power of the helmet, but remove it with her bare hands."

"No! You can't mean . . ."

"Yes." Cobra directed a long finger to the prisoner. "You have caught an extraordinary prize, priest. Invaluable. She controls the Barbarian, and keeps him alive."

"But I have examined her!" Dang-Ling stammered. "She . . . she has no magic."

"Oh, but she has," Cobra whispered. "You simply were looking for the wrong thing." Her personality changed abruptly. The woman disappeared, and the dark sorceress took command. "Bring me powdered Ansaria and Meralda roots. And barrels of fresh milk. From cows, goats, cats! It does not matter. Hurry!"

A short time later Dazi and Hatta stood on ladders above the mouth of the giant flask holding a large glass tube steady as it spewed white fluid down the throat of the vessel over Robin's body. Baak stood on the floor nearby pumping it out of an underground cistern into the glass tubes.

Cobra and Dang-Ling stood on the circular staircase watching Robin struggle against the torrent of milk. She tossed and flailed as her legs were repeatedly swept out from under her. Defiance animated her small face.

Cobra said, "I should have seen it the first time I saw her. She has extraordinary desire . . . and empathy. An extraordinary combination."

Dang-Ling's cheeks flushed with anticipation. "Her flesh is perfection."

"It is not simply her flesh, priest," Cobra retorted. "Look closer."

Dang-Ling edged down the stairs to the bottom of the hole. He steadied his weight against the glass flask, leaned forward until his nose touched it.

Robin was thrashing wildly against the slosh and spill of the weighty fluid, but her movements had an erotic eloquence to them. It was as if her breasts, throat, arms and legs danced with the moving whiteness. Within her nut-brown body a white glow grew and spread under her smooth, firm flesh. It filled her with light, reaching to her toes and fingertips.

"I see it," Dang-Ling squeaked. "I see it!"

Thin shafts of light began to radiate from Robin, then speared through the glass of the flask and flashed across the priest's animated face. He staggered back against the wall of the hole, grimacing in terror. The light whipped over him with bright bars, holding him prisoner.

The Queen of Serpents watched the light play over the priest, then shivered. "We will all be well advised to remember this lesson, priest. With a girl such as this one, the flesh is merely an outward sign of what dwells within."

Dang-Ling, as much as he now wanted to, could not avert his eyes from Robin.

"That's it," Cobra hissed. "Look at her. What you see is a body singularly untainted by any substance or idea that might impair its spirit. In short, priest, she is the ideal which drives off the brutal realities the horned helmet forces him to see."

A last shower of milk spilled down and Robin rolled

under its impact, then settled facedown as it sluiced out the drain. Exhausted. Half-drowned. Wet, white streaks trailed down her battered flesh. Before she recovered, the inner light was gone.

"There is nothing to fear from her at this moment as she will have no idea of what we saw, and will remain ignorant of her powers."

"She must die." Dang-Ling snapped indignantly. "Immediately."

"No," said Cobra. "Even though it would give me great pleasure to kill her with my own teeth, I can not. The Master has instructed me to use her to destroy the Barbarian and retrieve the horned helmet, and we need her. If she were to die, he might become enraged and do irreparable damage to our Master's work. At the very least I am certain you and I would not survive his displeasure.
But she will suffer, priest, that I promise you."

Dang-Ling looked back and forth from Cobra to Robin helplessly. "How?" he pleaded as Robin stood and stretched tiredly, then lay down in a lovely puddle of brown limbs, giving them her back.

"How?" repeated Cobra. "Look at her. She is going to make a lovely serpent."

Fifty-seven
LOGIC

Brown John, his hands clenched behind him, plodded up the wide, sun-drenched ridge of rubble towards the heights of Chela Kong. At the summit he paused before the only tower still standing and fanned himself with a rag.

The tower had once commanded the corner of a great wall, but now, up to its throat in rubble, it looked like a common stone house. One wall had collapsed long ago exposing the flooring of the parapet. It lay about five feet above the rubble to roof a cavelike shelter under it. Gath's black stallion was tethered beside the shadowed opening.

Throughout the surrounding rubble of the village, the Barbarian Army, now over seven thousand strong, was camped. It cooked, ate and sharpened weapons. Its many eyes lifted every so often to follow the Grillard leader's pilgrimage to the tower.

A warm breeze swept over him. Brown John watched it swirl down the southern slope and roll onto the flat desert floor. There it picked up speed, became a wind, and swept across the yellowish earth toward a dark crescent-shaped formation a few miles off. Spires of smoke rose above the curve. The Kitzakk Army.

Brown John studied this distant adversary for a moment wondering. "Why do they so diligently follow, yet avoid a battle," he muttered. "Ah, well, we can play the same game.'' He felt his way into the cavelike shelter, and stopped short. Out of the pit of his gut an icy chill raced up his back into the base of his skull.

Gath's body sprawled in a contorted heap against the rear wall. He was naked except for a fur loincloth and the horned helmet which rested against a rock. His new wounds were caked with sand and his body twitched involuntarily. His fist fumbled in the dirt for the axe handle lying beside his legs.

Brown John, crouching low, hurried inside and, squatting, peered at the eye slits. Smoke drifted from them veiling glowing red embers within.

''What's happened? What's it doing to you now?''

The black helmet rocked back and forth oddly. The eye slits shot forth flames driving him back.

''Ahhhh!'' Brown John moaned. ''This demon helmet is burning up your brain.''

The old man sighed and dropped back against the wall. He glanced out the opening of the shelter at the distant Kitzakks and sighed again. ''And no wonder. There is enough evil out there to stoke its fire eternally. It is a wonder you did not explode in flames the moment they appeared.''

Gath straightened slightly and whispered weakly, ''Who did you tell?''

''Not a soul! Your army still believes it is led by an invincible champion. And from the way the Kitzakk Army is cowering in the distance, I dare say it believes the same thing. I would be the last man to weaken those beliefs.'' He forced a smile. ''You may be heartened, if that is possible, in the knowledge that the hope you have given them is not a futile one. Our scouting parties have repeatedly challenged and driven off theirs.''

''What *did* you tell them?'' The hollow voice insisted.

''I told them what they wanted to hear. That when you decided the time was right, you would lead the attack, march over their army and into Bahaara, free the rest of the captives, and make the Kitzakks crawl away bleeding into oblivion.''

The helmet uttered a bitter, brutal grunt.

Brown John continued anyway. ''It is my firm conviction that no one be told what you have, to my great honor, confided in me. Not even the girl.''

Gath was not listening or watching. His breathing was a dry heave. His neck, straining to hold the helmet erect, streamed with sweat. Suddenly a chunk of the rock it rested against broke away, and the helmet fell sideways. Gath threw out a hand and caught the ground, and his falling body jerked to a stop. His head fell down between his arms, as if trying to fall off his shoulders. A cavernous moan ripped loose from the mouth hole. He heaved the weighty head up and slammed it back in place against the rock. His wounds began to bleed through their sandy crusts.

Brown John started in horror, then controlled himself and his voice hardened. ''By Bled, I'm not going to let this happen. There is always an answer somewhere. If only I could think of some way to outwit this demonic metal! Perhaps if you lay down?''

''Worse.'' It was a guttural grunt, more than a word. ''The fire enters my veins.''

''Then I will help you stand,'' he leaned forward onto his hands. ''If you move around a bit it might . . .''

''I tried. The helmet is too heavy now.''

''Is that what happens? It grows heavier and heavier?''

A grunt of agreement.

''And . . . and then . . .'' The words did not come.

''It will rip my head off my shoulders.'' There was a ring of insane anticipation in his words.

Brown John's howl rent the stifling heat. He flailed his clenched fists at the ceiling, then quietly his determination returned. He crawled beside the dying man. He forced a smile into his wrinkled cheeks, and, with a jaunty, defiant air said scoldingly, "What you fail to appreciate, my dramatic friend, is that I am the *bukko here*. And I did not put you on stage to perform in a tragedy. Not today! And not tomorrow! Now try and get that clear!"

The eye slits of the horned helmet blazed hotly, as if it, not the man, were replying.

Brown John, wavering, sat back on his heels, then obstinately resumed his lecture. There was a hard edge of authority to it now. He said, "I have it."

The helmet was unimpressed, but the old impressario had played to that kind of an audience before, and he did not falter. "Today," he proclaimed standing as tall as the cave allowed, "despite our awkward situation, is like any other day. And no day, throughout the history of days, was ever ruled by mere gods or demons. No, sir! There are far more powerful forces which rule this protean play we call life. Lust, virtue, greed, passion, these are the ultimate players which daily alter our malleable lives. We can submit to them, and allow them to raise us up or throw us down. Or we can find some means of struggling through so that when tomorrow comes we can take hold of whatever new possibilities these supreme forces have created and use them to our advantage."

The helmet replied to this philosophy by crushing through the rock that supported it and hauling Gath over sideways. He landed facedown. The flames from the eye slits singed the dirt and rock, raising smoke. Gath groaned, pushed himself up onto his knees and elbows, but could not lift the helmet off the ground. He struggled, gasping and sweating. Brown John, devoid of words, watched in terror. Before the old man could draw a breath, Gath collapsed.

With surprising strength, the old man heaved Gath over

on his back dodging the helmet's spitting flames. He
hesitated, gasping, then forced himself to lean over the
monstrous body and look down into the flaming face of the
helmet.

Within the flames, faint at first, he saw writhing,
tortured men and women of hideous deformity screaming with unnameable pain. Then he heard the whimpering of tortured children and maimed animals, and
smelt the nauseating stench of death. From beyond and
within it all came the malevolent melody of demonic laughter.

"So this is the way of it," he murmured, awestruck with
pity, "it feeds on the darkness of the world." He sat back
muttering. "Hold on, old man, hold on."

Avoiding the flaming eye slits, Brown John arranged
Gath's body so that his back was raised and the helmet
propped between two rocks. As he did he kept chattering,
as much to divert his fears as to help his friend.

"I dare say that my old father would tell me that now is
the time to call on a story of such artful magic that it would
make the ugly reality which feeds these flames vanish like
the rabbit in the wizard's cape, and replace it with the kind
of dreams which make children think of sailing ships and
castles in the clouds. But, in all truth, I must admit that I
have found soft fantasies of small use in hard times." He
smiled with resignation. "Besides, I seriously doubt you
can even hear me now."

He sat back against the opposite wall and sighed. For
long minutes he watched Gath lie still, then the red glowing
eyes dimmed a bit and the battered warrior stirred slightly,
muttering unintelligibly.

"Ahhh!" whispered the old *bukko*, "so we still share,
for the moment at least, the same stage. Good." He drew a
deep breath and then, with the light-winged clarity of
sudden inspiration, volunteered, "Perhaps we should talk a
little about this girl, Robin Lakehair?"

Brown John sat forward. Had there been a faint response, or had he *imagined* it? He sneered at his rash excitement, but could not keep it from doing optimistic things to his face. "My, my," he chuckled, "that would be curious, if by the mere accidental mention of her name, if just . . . just the words . . . *Robin Lakehair* . . . could . . ." He waited.

The eye slits flickered, almost went out.

Brown John propelled himself forward on all fours and monitored the dying glow, like a boy discovering for the first time that girls were indeed made differently. An involuntary giggle spilled out of his open mouth. He threw his head back and laughed wildly.

"By gad, I should have thought of it immediately. Here we sit on a battlefield, the ideal setting for salacious talk of carefree girls and raucous fornication, to say nothing of wives and sweethearts! And I nearly forgot to mention her name." He laughed again.

Gath, shifting slightly, pushed his helmeted head up an inch.

"Well, well, Gath, old man, perhaps you and I will play this scene out after all. Tell me, is their something you find particularly fascinating about her? For a man of my years, of course, it is always their legs and lovely bottoms. But as a youth like yourself it was always the breasts. There was never a question of it. Of course, when I was fortunate enough to be involved with a beauty approaching that of the Lakehair child, I admit the face ruled my heart.

"Come, come, tell me. Is it her small straight nose? Or those big feathery eyes. Or perhaps her soft golden-red hair? Come, come, coax your memory. Think of every part of her. Her voice, her laughter, her small perfect hands, her fresh warm scent, those plump soft red lips."

Gath shifted and lifted the helmet another two inches. As he did, Brown John leaned down, uncertain if he had

seen a trace of smile pass across Gath's now white eyes.
Then he laughed and said, "I admit it, I am partial to lips
myself. At least in my more sentimental moments. But lips
are, you must admit it, only the beginning of a whole set of
extraordinary delights." He paused remembering her more
soberly. "There is such a natural loveliness to her, her joy
in simple things, her love of just being alive. And her
kindness, even to lizards and lecherous old men."

Gath muttered unintelligibly, but more agreeably, the
old man thought.

"By Daybog!" Brown John exclaimed, then he laughed
again. "This is truly astounding. The fate of the greatest
army ever to plague our land, and the fate of the Master of
Darkness himself, all that lies in the balance, on whether
you live or die." He mused. "And that balance is now
tipped by the weightless memory of a pair of soft red lips."
He clasped his hands together and wrung them in wonderment.

Late that night Bone returned to the campfire at the
center of the square where Dirken and the Barbarian chiefs
waited and made his report. He said, "They're still talking
about girls."

Fifty-eight

SNAKE FINDERS

A wagon carrying five wooden barrels rolled quietly
through the shadows cast by the torches lighting Bahaara's
Street of Cats. The shops were shuttered and abandoned.
Refuse cluttered the ground. The panting and whine of

caged animals somewhere within were punctuated by an occasional screech. The wagon wound up through the mesa forming the body of the city toward the back of the Temple of Dreams.

It carried the serpent priest, Schraak, and his assistants disguised as nomad traders. They had left the Land of Smoking Skies shortly after Cobra, but their passage had been impeded. The flickering light illuminated the white-eyed panic on their faces.

The reason was the small crowd of ragged, filthy beggars trailing them. Their eyes were distended by cheap stimulants, and they carried torches, poked long, forked sticks at the wagon. They were Snake Finders, and they were gaining on the wagon.

The priests knew that the Cult of the Butterfly Goddess outlawed all reptiles, and that fanatic Snake Finders were licensed to carry out the low, repugnant and dangerous work of destroying reptiles. They were abundant in Bahaara, particularly in times of unrest. So the priests had taken great pains to scent themselves with camel dung. But just as the light revealed their features, their rising fear brought forth the fetid scent of the reptile.

They shuddered as the fanatics broke into a run, wailing and chanting incantations.

Schraak hissed at the other two. "The barrels must be delivered. Give them your bodies! Now!"

His assistants sickened as they looked back at the ragged pack swarming towards them. But when Schraak slowed the wagon, they obediently jumped off. Schraak whipped the horses smartly, and the wagon lurched into the shadows ahead as the two serpent men drew their swords and faced their plunging tormentors.

Seeing the priests' metal, the Snake Finders pulled up short. Their forked sticks trembled as if alive, then pulled them forward, magnetizing their drug mad eyes. Their victims took one step back, then panicked and fled. The Snake Finders, howling, scampered after them, leaping walls, and easily cornering them. They threw them to the ground and stripped their flailing bodies. At the first sight of scales, they squealed with triumph and crushed their skulls with rocks. Then they skinned them.

With their scaly prizes spread on poles, several of the fanatics paraded through the mostly deserted city while the rest resumed the chase, hunting the wagon. They found it parked in a dark secluded alcove behind the Temple of Dreams. It was empty. The driver was gone and so were the barrels.

Deep under the ground, just slightly east of where the empty wagon was parked, the five barrels were lined up on a stone balcony. They were open, and the dark fluids within them bubbled and steamed, with a strong fishy odor that clung to the walls of Dang-Ling's laboratory. Schraak and Baak were shoveling red-hot rocks from a huge fire and dropping them into the bubbling concoction of snake venom, snake blood, and the entrails of tiny molusks.

Fifty-nine

TRANSFUSION

Robin and the five maidens abducted from Weaver were strapped naked to inclined benches lined up below the row of barrels. Thin glass tubes had been inserted in their necks and attached to spigots at the base of a wide trough positioned under the barrels. Similar tubes descended from their ankles to a gutter hole in the floor. The girls were drugged, only semiconscious.

Cobra moved along the line of girls tracing the signs and

marks drawn on their foreheads and murmuring incantations. Reaching Dang-Ling, who stood diligently beside Robin, she bestowed a condescending smile on him. "I commend you. The addition of the five maidens will increase our chances of success greatly. It is fortunate I brought enough blood."

"Your highness has demonstrated again her foresight and leadership." Dang-Ling bowed low. "I am honored to assist the Queen of Serpents."

"If you enjoy watching as much as you appear to," she winked, "you are quite welcome to continue." Ignoring the high priest's reaction, she appraised Robin's sleeping body, and her eyes hardened. "She sleeps very deeply."

"A mild drug," Dang-Ling purred, petting Robin possessively. "Her little body has been overtaxed these last few days. I thought she should look as fresh as possible when he sees her." His lips were prim, but his eyes glimmered.

Cobra addressed his eyes. "You are a weak fool, priest. We must revive her!" Her arm and hand uncoiled, and she struck Robin hard across the face, bringing a moan. "Wake the others! Screaming is absolutely essential!"

Dang-Ling paled, and his eyes narrowed. "First I must inquire about the necessity of screaming in this particular experiment. Is it essential to the process or to you?"

Cobra glared at him, her fury rising. "To both, you simpering lecher."

The high priest's smile returned with the slightest trace of mockery. His eyes met Cobra's, and held them with surprising ease. Cobra glanced warily about the laboratory, then hissed sarcastically, "If you have anymore professional comments, ask them now, priest. Once we begin there will be no interruptions."

"Actually, I do have one question," Dang-Ling said flatly. "Would it not be easier to simply enslave each of them with the bite of the Pawder snake?"

"An excellent suggestion." With regal grace Cobra reached inside her emerald robe, and brought forth a small rose-pink snake. Dang-Ling flushed.

Bestowing a tender kiss on the snake's head, she said, "The Pawder's bite is an essential part of the procedure. But merely to enslave their wills would not suffice. Their nature itself must be transformed, and the transfusion and signs will accomplish that. Not completely. Just enough to allow them to develop a very strong venom which no human can withstand, not even the Dark One."

"Of course," Dang-Ling said hurriedly. "But if you will excuse my impertinence, I think we must consider the possibility that this particular girl," he stroked Robin's thigh, "might serve our Master more effectively without alteration."

Cobra's high cheeks turned crimson. Her fist unclenched and the Pawder snake wound its way up her arm. She said archly, "Your interruptions tire me, priest. Pay attention, and you will understand. All the Barbarian has to do is see this girl. That alone will relax his guard and allow her, or one of the others, to strike. And only one bite will leave him helpless. Now do you understand?"

"Perfectly." Dang-Ling's inflection was so florid it would have humbled an orchid. "Your jealousy and arrogance have blinded you! And it is apparent, if the Master is to be served as he deserves to be, that I must conduct this procedure myself."

Before Cobra, snarling with outrage, could reply, the harsh sounds of scraping rocks filled the room. Four huge stones were receding from the wall; four temple guards appeared in the openings pointing loaded crossbows at the Queen of Serpents.

Cobra whirled on Dang-Ling. "You go too far, priest!"

Dang-Ling said soothingly, "Do not be offended. I have not betrayed you. These four are devoted servants of the Master of Darkness, and will do you no harm unless it is necessary. So do not tempt them. Being Kitzakks, they are unusually fond of killing reptiles."

"They would not dare. I am the Master's 'chosen one'."

"They will dare, sorceress, whatever I dare. Because they understand that what I do, I do in our holy Master's best interest. Now, I must ask you to remember what you have forgotten in your jealousy. If the girl's nature is altered, if she is tainted in the slightest way, the power of the horned helmet will discover it . . . and the Death Dealer will destroy her before she is even close enough for him to smell the enticing fragrance of her flesh."

The bones in the Queen of Serpent's face seemed to pulsate under her creamy flesh.

The high priest delicately removed the glass tube from Robin's throat. A drop of blood splashed on her breast and trickled down the curved slope. He wiped it off fastidiously, saying, "It is only in her perfection that she will be able to subdue the helmet's power and distract him long enough for these maidens, transformed by your formula, to strike."

Cobra's body vibrated under the gold and silver plates, and began to shimmer with opalescent light, fusing her voluptuous flesh and translucent metal. Her breasts were smooth heaving globes of soft gold, her stomach a silver slope of carnal invitation. Her pupils were pools of black magnetism rimmed by irises of radiating gold. The rose cheeks drew in and hollowed. As her scarlet lips parted, they revealed a single drop of glistening blood trickling freely down her alabaster chin.

The temple guards trembled, eyes white with terror.

Dang-Ling observed all this with surprising equanimity,

then, bowing to the Queen of Serpents, he responded,
"Thank you for this spectacular display of the generous and
unequaled gifts our Master of Darkness has bestowed upon
you. It is an eloquent reminder of the sacrifices we all owe
him."

He fastidiously removed the rose-pink snake from her
arm and stroked it. "Now, if you will restore your
appearance so my aides can function, we will begin the
work."

Cobra's magnificent body wavered. Then, like a tide
receding into the ocean, her body drew into itself, ebbing
and flowing back to a less intimidating though still impressive presence that glared impotently at the high priest, as if
she had had her fangs pulled.

The guards carried Robin out of the laboratory as the
maidens were revived. Then Dang-Ling himself applied the
enslaving snakebite to each girl's foot, and the screaming
began.

The process proceeded at a slow dripping pace for
several hours. Then, distressingly, a blood clot formed in
the neck of one girl. Before they could remove the tube, her
skin ballooned and exploded, splattering the room with
flesh and blood, and she was dead. After that there were no
more delays.

Sixty

ESCAPE

The wagon, racing across the flat desert, sent up a tail of dust that boiled with bright golds and yellows in the midday sunshine. Half a mile behind and barely visible through the dust, a crowd of mounted soldiers chased it. Far off to the right, miragelike in the wavering heat, was a thin crescent of reds, the Kitzakk Army. Ahead were the ruins of Chela Kong.

A Cytherian temple maiden drove. Three others sprawled on the bed, clutching the side boards desperately as the wagon bounced and rattled. Robin, still unconscious, tumbled about on a layer of hay between them. A large stack of hay was piled in a corner.

One of the girls, a small, chubby old friend of Robin, crawled over to her. She uncorked a tiny blue jar, and, pressing it against Robin's teeth, poured a clear amber liquid into her mouth. She threw the jar away, then waited anxiously. Robin coughed and sat up abruptly. Her eyes were wide but her body, still weak, was trembling.

"Where am I?"

"We've escaped!" As she spoke, she pounded small fists together excitedly. "Robin, we've escaped!"

"Escaped!" Robin gasped. She rolled onto her hands and knees and through the tumbling dust saw the riders chasing them. She pivoted to the front. A dark collection of black boulders lay ahead.

The chubby girl pointed a plump finger at the rocks shouting, "Our people are there! There in the rocks!"

Robin gasped incredulously, "But how . . . how did we . . ."

The girl hugged her as her words spilled out. "They were taking us somewhere. They didn't tell us why. They thought we were all drugged, like you were. But two of us woke up, and when the soldiers guarding us fell behind, that gave us our chance. We killed the driver and ran." She uncovered the stack of hay revealing the large body of a man crumpled under it. His neck was slit.

Robin recoiled in horror.

"We used his own knife." The girl picked a knife out of the hay. It was wet and red.

Robin, still wobbly, turned to the other girls. They nodded happily. The chubby girl, pressing close to Robin, placed her lips next to her ear. "Don't worry. We'll make it. The Death Dealer will save us."

Realization, then hope, nourished Robin's shaken body. She smiled tentatively, and the girl, staying close, said, "It's true! He's in those rocks."

She pointed ahead at Chela Kong. Robin, fighting for balance, shuffled to the front of the wagon, and stood there holding onto the driver's shoulders. The wind whipped her hair like a red-gold flag. Feeling the pressure of Robin's hands, the girl's lips parted slightly, enough to expose the tips of her tiny fangs.

A raven-haired girl at the rear of the wagon took hold of an iron bar hidden under the hay, and fed it out a hole in the side board. She gathered her weight behind it, and shoved hard.

The iron bar plunged between the spokes of the rear wheel. Spokes snapped with rapid cracks, and the wheel caved in. The wagon banged on the ground and spun, girls screaming and floundering. The horses reared and halted, throwing the driver back into the wagon bed among the other girls. The living pile thrashed about hysterically as its pursuers descended fast.

Terrified, Robin fought free and looked ahead at the dark rocks. A startled joy shone on her tear-stained face.

A horse and rider were charging down Chela Kong toward them. The rider was big and powerful, and wore a horned helmet.

Robin and the girls tumbled out of the crippled wagon, and raced toward him.

The Skulls thundered up to the wagon, and, finding it empty, plunged after the girls. But, when it was clear that the Barbarian would reach them first, they slowed down and held their distance, watching the girls scatter toward the Death Dealer.

He reined up and dropped to the ground lightly, strode toward Robin. Robin, her face glowing, stumbled and raced ahead of the other girls. Undaunted, as if she were unaware of the dark massive figure of brutal destruction which was the Death Dealer, and could see only Gath. She leapt into his arms. His pawlike hands clasped her like a small soft ball and held her against his chest.

A wagon load of jubilant Grillards arrived with Bone driving and Brown John sitting beside him. Dirken and ten Grillard strongmen were crowded in the bed. They scrambled out as Brown John hollered joyously, "My dear child, you'll never know . . . there are simply no words . . ." He was laughing before he finished.

The maidens hesitated five feet short of their target, realizing it was covered with metal except for its arms and lower legs.

Robin lifted her head off Gath's shoulder, and gazed into his eyes. "I'm all right," she whispered. "It's all all right now."

A glint of light showed behind his eyes, a gentle warmth. She smiled and slid to the ground, still within his embrace. Turning to the maidens, she beckoned them forward. "Come on. Don't be afraid."

They giggled, and, as they approached Gath smiling,

their mouths came open slightly.

Brown John and his group were still ten feet off when the old man saw their fangs and bolted forward. "Look out, Gath!"

Too late. The freshly fashioned servants of the Lord of Death crowded around Gath and Robin, lunging at his arms and legs. His axe came up. It caught the chubby one in the chest, stopping her fangs inches short of his arm. The impact lifted her three feet off the ground, and she screamed, spitting blood, as the others buried their fangs in his forearms and ankles.

Robin shrieked. Gath jerked around toward her, ignoring the girls. They still had their fangs in him when Bone and Dirken arrived. They ripped them off, threw them on the ground, cut their throats, then stepped back in revulsion.

The girls were hissing, coiling and writhing on the bloody sand as if their bodies had only spines, their legs and arms no bones.

With a gasp, Robin folded up and dropped unconscious into Gath's arms. He touched her hair gently, then he and the Grillards looked up.

A half circle of eighteen Skulls, two squads, were forty feet off and closing on them slowly.

Gath placed Robin in Brown John's arms, "Take care of her."

He swung up into his saddle and bolted toward the Skulls' line.

Brown John shouted, "No! It's a trap!"

Gath kept riding, and Brown John, groaning, turned on Bone. "Hurry! Get the army!"

Bone started running, waving his arms and shouting, toward the rocks, as Brown John carried Robin onto the wagon. Dirken and the Grillards, already moving to aid their leader, suddenly stopped.

Gath of Baal sat on his horse strangely motionless in the their leader, suddenly stopped.

Gath of Baal sat on his horse strangely motionless in the middle of the circling Skulls. They made no move to attack.

Brown John, holding the unconscious Robin in his arms, watched uncertainly, then glanced down at the fangs on the dead girls and slumped, groaning with dismay. Slowly his eyes lifted and reluctantly watched.

Gath sank wearily in his saddle, then looked down at his hand holding his axe. His fingers trembled, involuntarily released the handle, and it fell to the ground.

Brown John and the Grillards shuddered.

Gath looked down at his weapon as if it were a long, long distance away. He leaned slowly out of his saddle until he fell and joined it on the ground.

Sixty-one

COSTUME CHANGE

The light of a standing torch flickered over the silhouettes of two figures on the heights of Chela Kong. Below them, on the southern slope, the Barbarian Army was gathered in small groups staring south. In the distance, tiny specks of light grew fainter and fainter as the Kitzakk Army withdrew, then vanished and were replaced by the star-filled night.

"Are they retreating?" Robin whispered to Brown John.

"No," he answered tiredly, "I'm afraid they're just moving back to a far more favorable position, Bahaara. There they will ignore our badly equipped army and celebrate their success. Public execution is their favorite amusement."

"Oh, Brown John, what have I done?"

Brown John patted her shoulder and whispered firmly, "Do not despair, small one. Look around you. Not a single man has fled. See!" He lifted her chin with a finger. "The army is more determined than ever now and so am I."

A rush of hope lifted her eyes and voice. "What are you going to do?"

"We are going to do precisely what we Grillards do best. Pit our particular skills against theirs, and change our costumes."

"You're going to Bahaara!" she gasped.

"Of course! Bahaara is now the stage, so we are duty bound to use it." He turned towards two figures moving up towards them and chuckled. "Here is our wardrobe now."

The *bukko* gestured with dancing fingers, and Bone and Dirken stepped into the glow of torchlight. In their arms were heaps of filthy tattered clothes. They tossed them in front of their father with a flourish surpassing his own.

Bone, holding his nose, pronounced, "There has never been, nor will there ever be, a filthier bunch of rags. You can count on it."

"Whew!" Robin wrinkled her tiny nose. "How can you call them costumes. They're disgusting!"

Dirken, profoundly offended, thinned his eyes at her. "Because filth, young woman, is the most convincing adornment in the theatrical profession. And this is the real thing." He threw a hand at the tattered clothes. "Those slavers rubbed camel urine in them to drive off scorpions and evil spirits."

"They'd drive off anything with a nose, that's a fact," she replied jauntily.

Brown John laughed. "Robin, I believe you will find these garments to be priceless. In Bahaara, we will not only be ignored, we will be avoided." He winked at his sons. "Well done, lads. Good thinking."

Exchanging I-told-you-so nudges, Bone and Dirken grinned broadly.

Brown John turned to Robin and, with deliberation, bowed. "Now child, as you have the principal role, you get first pick."

Robin choked. "Me?"

"Of course," said Brown John. "Rags are the only clothing the Kitzakk reptile hunters wear. With some simply made forked sticks, we can enter Bahaara without suspicion and move about freely. No Kitzakk willingly associates with such disgusting characters."

Robin nodded. "I understand, but . . . but you know I'm not an actress. I won't know what to say."

"You, child, will not need to say anything," Brown said with flat confidence. "You are, for reasons I have sworn not to reveal, essential to him. If he can get a glimpse of you, we have a chance."

"We . . . we can save him?"

"We can try."

Robin hesitated, then bent over tentatively and picked up a rag. She considered it solemnly for a long moment, then said, "Well, if I cut my hair, I think I could look like a boy!"

They all chuckled, then laughed out loud in a warmth of companionship Robin had never shared before. It was as if she were one of them. A Grillard player about to take the stage.

Sixty-two

THEATER OF DEATH

Bahaara's place of execution was an outdoor arena at
the eastern extremity of the city. Its dirt stage was backed
by a stone wall, and a red-carpeted staircase ascended
the center of the wall to a landing with two tunnels. The
one at stage right had a red arch, while the one at stage
left had a black and orchid arch. At the sides of the stage
were ground-level access passages linked to the stage by
ramps. Facing the stage was a semicircle of empty, tiered
seats.

Skull soldiers were dragging the Death Dealer's
weighty, unconscious body across the stage to a whipping
post. He wore only a fur loincloth and the horned helmet.
His flesh was shiny with sweat, and blotched with bruises.
Several leaked thin trails of blood.

After chaining the dark Barbarian to the post, one
soldier took hold of the horned helmet and pulled on it
repeatedly without success. He cursed and moved back into
the passage following the other soldier. Moments later he
returned with a hammer and wedge and began to hammer
the bottom rim of the helmet. Blood promptly started
running down the Barbarian's back and chest.

Dang-Ling emerged from the black and orchid arched
tunnel and stopped on the landing. He clapped his hands,
once, and the soldier looked up in embarrassment. Dang-
Ling waved him off brusquely, and the soldier backed
quickly down the ramp into the access tunnel. The high

priest looked down smugly at the captive's limp body, then turned and bowed as Klang's black-robed figure emerged from the red arched tunnel.

"Why did you stop him?" Klang growled.

"I thought it best, my lord," Dang-Ling replied in a carefully cordial tone, "that his distinctive helmet remain on his head so that when the people arrive tomorrow they will have no doubt that the man whose head you remove is the true Death Dealer. It, of course, will be taken off before the execution begins."

A tense silence passed between them. Dang-Ling whispered, "I have made all the arrangements. Come tonight, at the midnight hour. You will have your request."

Klang watched the high priest with the corners of his eyes. "There's no need now. I have decided not to fight him, simply execute him."

Dang-Ling bowed obediently. "The decision is yours, of course, I would not presume to direct you . . ." He paused artfully.

"Yes?" demanded Klang.

With a troubled tremor, Dang-Ling whispered, "This demon is very unpredictable, my lord. Nothing with him turns out to be simple. If you will allow me to advise you," he hesitated, "I would take every precaution, and use the strongest weapon available."

A look of contempt came over Klang's face. He pushed the priest aside and moved halfway down the staircase, his eyes fixed on the prisoner. The whipping post began to shudder. The dark helmet raised and the Barbarian's sinewy mass of bunched muscles and hot nerves thrashed powerfully against the wood and chains. It ceased suddenly, momentarily spent and pacified, but still menacing and upraised. A red glow burned at Klang behind the eye slits of the helmet.

Klang involuntarily stepped back. Self-consciously he stiffened and rolled his shoulders, flexing proudly. Then he turned away and slowly returned to Dang-Ling.

The high priest said quietly, "You will have reactions like quicksilver, and the strength of the Master of Darkness himself."

"The price, priest, the price?"

Dang-Ling smiled innocently. "A trifle. In exchange, the sorceress merely asks for the horned helmet."

"She'll have it." He strode through the red arch, and his cape swirled behind him blending with the shadows.

Dang-Ling held his breath as the warlord's booted feet tramped down the tunnel. With a sigh of relief, he started to leave but paused at the sounds of excited voices, running feet. The sound grew and a filthy, babbling, scratching group of scavengers surged through an entrance tunnel on the opposite side of the arena and clambered down the tiers of seats.

Dang-Ling clapped his hands sharply.

Skull soldiers trotted up both ramps and spread out in a line around the edges of the stage. One carried the Death Dealer's axe and chained it to the front edge of the stage. Seeing it, a group of the scavengers howled raucously and surged forward to stroke its awesome steel. Others sat down chattering in the front rows. They wore rags, and crude decorations on their naked parts; arrows, bolts of lightning and numerals were the most popular. Several were stark naked and stained bright vermilion or yellow. They all had a drugged glint to their eyes. There were several women, ragged, bangled and unwashed. The mongrel trash of Bahaara. Among them were numerous forked sticks.

Dang-Ling covered his nose and mouth with his cape and hurried under the black arch almost colliding with Cobra. Her cloak was clutched tightly about her, the hood pulled low. Her face was fraught with fear.

"Snake finders," she rasped.

"Are you suprised?" Dang-Ling asked indifferently. "They're everywhere these days, but usually only a minor irritation. I told Klang the helmet would be removed tomorrow at the third hour, just before the execution begins."

She looked at him vindictively, but spoke respectfully. "I will gladly remove the helmet, but not in the daylight. I will not expose myself to that crowd of vultures."

Dang-Ling frowned. "Then you will do it tonight, when the city sleeps. Only my guards will be on duty at that time. They will see you are left quite alone with him."

She nodded agreement, and looked down at the Death Dealer's chained body. "Klang must understand that he has fed on the helmet's powers for many days now. Even without it he will be dangerous."

"Klang has been informed, and is ready to accept your assistance."

"What did you tell him," she asked warily.

"As little as possible. Just make certain the magic potion you prepare is more than sufficient."

She smiled disdainfully. "Nothing can withstand the strength of our Master, but it will only last a day and drain most of his own resources. After tomorrow he will be only the shell of the man he is now."

"That cannot concern us. All that matters is that the execution goes smoothly, and the helmet be returned."

She turned sharply so his milky face was within inches, and snapped, "No! That is not all. I will be revenged." Her eyes were as wavering as arrows in flight.

Dang-Ling blinked behind his wet lashes, then turned, and she followed him back down the tunnel.

At the opposite side of the arena, four more Snake Finders huddled against the back wall watching the Skull soldiers drive off scavengers trying for a closer look at the chained prisoner. One of them was a young boy with short reddish hair, dressed in shapeless rags. There were tears in his eyes.

Sixty-three

COBRA'S BITE

Baak conducted the striding warlord through the dimly lit corridors of the Temple of Dreams. Klang's eyes were without light or warmth, as confident as tombstones. Reaching a heavy wooden door, Baak knocked, opened it, and Klang strode in.

Dang-Ling, waiting just inside, bowed in welcome. A single torch in a silver embrasure lit the room. The shadows on the far walls expanded and shrank at the touch of the orange light.

"Where is she?" Klang demanded.

Dang-Ling bowed again. "We are alone, my lord. The sorceress says that the potion works more effectively without the presence of a female."

"Potion?" Klang asked abruptly. "If that is all there is to it, give it to me."

Dang-Ling spoke cooly. "It is not simply a potion."

"Then what?"

"It is a fresh venom, my lord."

Klang went white. When he finally spoke, his voice was dry. "All right, priest, venom. Just so you are certain of what it will do!"

"Absolutely."

Klang extended his hand, waited. Dang-Ling hesitated, looking at the empty palm, then up with professional candor into the warlord's expectant eyes. "There is one more thing. It can not be swallowed. It must be . . . administered."

Klang said nothing for a moment, then, "How?"

"Injected, my lord."

Again the warlord paused, and again asked the same question. Dang-Ling indicated the pool. Klang peered over the edge and jumped back, drawing his sword.

The pool was drained but not empty. Lying on its bottom in a neat coil was a ten-foot, emerald-green cobra. Its head lifted, and the black balls at the centers of its yellow eyes stared at the warlord.

Klang turned on the priest, growling, "Fool! How can you let filth like that creep in here? The Goddess's own temple?"

Dang-Ling replied calmly, "It is not an accident. The sorceress placed it there herself."

Klang looked down at the green serpent, and his breath came in harsh gasps.

"The serpent's fangs are the instruments which will inject the venom."

"No!" growled Klang. He turned on the priest. "That is madness! I can not, I will not submit my flesh to such filth. What kind of foreign practice is this?"

"An extraordinary one," said Dang-Ling quietly. "With the venom comes the strength of the Lord of Death himself. You cannot fail. With your people watching, you will destroy the Barbarian and regain their absolute confidence."

Klang looked down at the menacing snake, "All right!" he said quietly. "I will let it bite me. Once." He started down the steps into the stone bath.

"Wait," Dang-Ling requested. He indicated the sword

in Klang's hand. "You must leave your sword behind, in case your natural instincts betray you and you attack as it strikes."

Klang shuddered, but set his sword and sheath down on the stone rim of the pool.

"One more thing," Dang-Ling said quietly. When Klang looked at him, he added, "The reptile is a very carefully cultured species, and while its venom is extraordinarily powerful, to obtain the best results, it should be injected as close as possible to the genitals."

Klang turned white again. He swayed, then brought himself erect. Defiantly, he struggled out of his armor and clothing, and tossed them aside. With a deep breath, he advanced steadily into the tub, white from forehead to toenails.

Dang-Ling, impressed by his reckless bravery, clasped his hands in excitement and held his breath.

Klang reached the floor of the stone bath, and stood, legs astride, at the center. The reptile uncoiled languidly in front of him, as high as his eyes. Its hood spread wide, a brilliant black and yellow-green. Its tongue darted. Its jaws parted displaying rows of sharp teeth, and two upper fangs of curving white porcelain. As Klang waited, the sweat drained off him and puddled at his feet.

The snake dived for his genitals, and buried its fangs deep.

Klang screamed and staggered back ripping the head away, and flung the snake across the hole. He dashed up the stairs and snatched up his sword.

"No!" screamed Dang-Ling. "If you kill it, the magic will be turned against you."

Cupping his wound, Klang glared from the reptile to Dang-Ling, and back to the reptile. Its hooded head floated three feet above the ground. Suddenly Klang's hands stiffened, his fingers trembled, and his sword dropped with a clatter.

Dang-Ling retired quietly to a corner to watch.

Klang looked down at his trembling hand in wonderment, as if it belonged to someone else. He squatted over his armor and clothes, and a tremor ripped through him, dropping him to his knees and fists. His body convulsed, rippled with growth, and blood trickled from his nose and ears. It was bright against his suddenly alabaster flesh. He shuddered again, then, defying the pain and blood, he stood and dizzily picked up his things. Two inches of scaled tail protruded from his flesh just above his anus.

Klang had grown a good five inches taller and six inches thicker. Like a man asleep he forced his massive arms through the sleeves of his tunic. The sounds of ripping cloth cut the silence. Oblivious, he continued to dress with similar results. Finally, he turned his dazed eyes to Dang-Ling.

The high priest smiled. "Excellent. You are superb now."

Klang smiled back, as if not certain why. A dull acquiescence glazed his normally bright black eyes.

Dang-Ling picked up Klang's sword and sheath and guided him to the door, patting him soothingly on his hard rump. "Get some rest. I will see you tomorrow, at the third hour. You'll be just fine."

Klang nodded, took his sword and sheath, and numbly shuffled out the door as Dang-Ling closed it behind him. The high priest threw back his head and laughed deliciously, then stopped himself short as Cobra's voluptuous, armored body emerged slowly from the empty pool. She looked exhausted. Dang-Ling composed himself and hurried to help her, murmuring praise.

In the corridor outside, Klang headed back the way he had come. The halls were empty, dark and silent except for some slight ripping sounds. There were beads of sweat on his face, his eyes swam, and he felt sick to his stomach. It rumbled, and he passed gas with a sound like rolling thunder. He stopped, looked about, uncertain as to just what had happened, then moved on. As he stumbled out the temple door, he hiccuped and smoke drifted past his lips.

Sixty-four

DEAD YELLOW

Torchlight greeted the temple guards as they moved swiftly onto the stage to relieve the Skulls. Casual words were exchanged, and the Skulls strolled away chatting amicably. Their crude laughter echoed out of the tunnel, then silence rejoined the night.

In the front row of the tiered seats a small group slept entwined in ragged blankets and each other, fanatics, idlers and veteran soldiers more than willing to relinquish their own flea-ridden cots in order to obtain the best seats for tomorrow's entertainment, or perhaps turn a nice profit for those seats in the morning.

The temple guards frowned with distaste at the crowd and at the chained man sharing the stage. He slumped in his chains. Blood was gathering at the end of his right thumb. It glistened brightly, then dropped, hitting the dirt stage with a silent splash. Another drop began to form.

Four shadowed figures on the highest row of seats also watched the chained man. A tear glistened within their darkness, then fell and splashed as silently as his blood. It belonged to Robin. She rubbed her wet eyes with the butt of her hand, whispering, "Can't we bring him some water?"

Brown John hushed her. "Shhhh. We can not risk being discovered."

Robin choked back the tears. "But he's dying."

"Shhh!" The old man lifted a finger to his lips. "Wait! Just wait!"

"But what are we waiting for? What's supposed to happen?"

Brown John took her small hand in his and patted it. "Trust me, small one. Our chance will come."

The torches suddenly went out, and darkness swallowed the arena. Robin buried her face against Brown John's chest, and he gathered her close. When their eyes adjusted to the darkness, they could see the doused torches smoking in their iron crucibles at the corners of the stage. The temple guards had vanished.

Brown John whispered, "Something's up. Listen."

They heard a faint rustling at the back of the stage. A phantom figure was descending the red staircase. Moving with supple grace, it glided like a living shadow to the stage and started toward the chained prisoner.

Brown John pressed a hand over Robin's mouth.

Reaching the sagging body, the dark slender figure pushed back the hood of its black cape.

Robin reeled, mumbling through the old man's fingers, "That's her. The snake woman! She . . . she was there in the laboratory . . . with their high priest."

"The Queen of Serpents," Brown John muttered.

He motioned to his sons, and the group crept silently down the steps until they could hear Cobra's soft, mocking voice.

"Do not disdain me, Dark One. I have come to save you."

Cobra stroked a red nail sharply across Gath's chest, letting it linger playfully in a wound, then ran it across the steel of the helmet, making a nerve-splitting sound. The eye slits began to glow with heat, but he did not move.

Muttering ancient incantations, Cobra drew obscure signs on the helmet. Then she gripped the horns with her fingers and thrust her thumbs into the eye slits. The helmet jerked away from her. She held on and began to lift it humming softly.

Robin shuddered, and Brown John began to sweat. Suddenly he reached down and brought up his forked stick. He commanded Robin, "Stay here."

She nodded, hugged her knees to her chest, and rocked silently as the *bukko* turned to his sons. They held their sticks in hand. Brown John whispered, "Dirken, you sneak around behind her. Bone, you take the right corner. I'll take the left. Wait until I give the sign before you show yourselves."

The brothers nodded, then the three moved down through the shadows towards the stage.

Cobra smiled as a grunt of pain escaped the helmet. She pulled harder, straining, and her eyes glazed slightly, turned dead yellow. Torchlight splashed across the helmet. She jerked around toward the light and shuddered, dropping her hold on the helmet. It sank back into place.

The torch at the far corner of the stage had been relit and a figure stood in its light, a ragged old man waving a forked stick. The stick lifted as if with its own life, and aimed itself at Cobra as the old man's resonant voice chanted, "By fang and by venom. By the days of nine and the nights of ten, deliver the reptile, great goddess, to thy servant."

A torch burst into flames at the opposite side and another forked stick emerged from the night, aiming itself at the Queen of Serpents. Cobra recoiled hissing to reveal needle-like fangs.

More torches blazed to life in the hands of the front row fanatics. They rushed forward rubbing their sleepy eyes as Brown John continued his chant, then saw Cobra, shrieked and charged onto the stage poking their forked sticks.

Cobra whirled for the red staircase. Dirken cut her off. The fanatics swarmed at her and struck her to the ground. She twisted, slithered, hissed. A forked stick pinned her ankle, another her wrist. She convulsed, snapped and spewed hot venom that drove them off with rags and flesh smoking. Amazed, they watched as her entire body opened up, emitting a gush of yellowish smoke; they backed away coughing, their eyes confounded. One screamed out fanatically, and they plunged into the concealing smoke pounding and prodding with their sticks.

Brown John stood at the corner of the stage waiting. His eyes darted around until he saw it. At the feathered edge of the yellow smoke, probably no more than two inches under the earthen stage, something was wriggling towards the ramp. Brown John jumped off the stage into the shadows.

The slight bulge of earth reached the edge of the stage, and the head of a small Skink snake emerged, looked around, then slithered down to the ramp. For a moment torchlight revealed its shovel-shaped head, enamellike scales, and muscular tail. Then it vanished into the shadowy ramp toward the access tunnel. Out of the darkness a forked stick descended over its neck and pinned it to the ground. The Skink's shovellike head dug into the ground. Half of its body was under the earth when a hand grabbed the tail, pulled it out of the earth and deposited it in a leather pouch. The hand tied the pouch securely with a thong, then picked up its stick, and the owner, Brown John, returned to the stage.

The Snake Finders were still floundering in the dissipating smoke, scratching the ground and each other with their sticks. When the smoke was gone, they saw no sign of Cobra. No wet stain. No shedded skin. They grunted and cursed appropriately, then turned to the chained prisoner, leering. They peered around, saw no sign of guards, and, taking courage, advanced excitedly on the helpless Death Dealer. They circled him in stumbling confusion, then timidly cursed him, and spit on his legs. Then a bold one stepped in close and poked him with his stick.

No response came. But as more sticks flayed him, the helmet lifted and the attackers jumped back. The shadowed eyes were on a small dirty-faced boy standing empty-handed directly in front of him.

Gath rose within his chains. His eyes cleared, and he turned on the fanatics. Obviously shamed by the small boy's courage, they were advancing again. Suddenly the Death Dealer thrashed against his chains. The fanatics, trampling and tripping over each other, fled the stage.

The Death Dealer turned back to the boy, the red glow died, and a voice, low and far away, demanded, "Come closer."

The small figure marched boldly forward wiping off a damp smudge on its face. The massive pawlike hand of the chained arm opened, and his voice whispered, "Robin."

She placed her small hand in his, and the strong bloody fingers wrapped around it, held it as she looked searchingly into the eye slits for the man she knew.

"I won't leave you," she moaned, "never again."

He straightened, pulling his head erect, and let go of her hand. "The army? Where is the army?"

Hearing the weakness in his voice, she trembled. "It . . . it's camped to the north, outside the city."

"Bring it," he gasped. "Tomorrow, at the third hour. I will give it this city."

Her eyes widened with the shock of comprehension. "But you're chained!"

"I will be all right now. Hurry!"

She nodded stepping backward, feathery eyes welling with tears. Then she turned and ran off the stage into the shadows.

Brown John started after her, but backed off the stage at the sight of the Temple Guards trotting up the opposite ramp with whips cracking.

The rabble fled up the tiers of the seating area, and

Brown John joined them. When he reached his seat, only Dirken was waiting for him. The old man dropped beside him exhausted, but his voice was elated. "Did you see her? She was superb. And she thought she would not know her part!" He laughed.

"I saw her," Dirken answered. "Gath told her to go get the army, and Bone followed her."

Brown John frowned thoughtfully, then his cheeks cracked a smile. "My, my, and she takes a cue as well!"

Dirken shot a tired but approving smile at his father. "What happened to the snake bitch?"

Brown John's eyes twisted, and he patted his pouch possessively.

Sixty-five

MARCHING ORDER

The Barbarian Army marched south across the moonlit desert in scattered pieces, each tribe following a separate trail, like the tentacles of some great sea monster reaching out of a dark body hidden in the inky depths of the ocean.

When a tribe, moving through a depression or passing behind a ridge, was swallowed by the enveloping darkness, the other tribes would falter and whispers heavy with rumors would spread through the ranks. Yet no tribe turned back. And each time the vanished tribe reappeared, the entire army would surge forward with new energy.

Occasionally one tribe would take the lead dramatically. They would parade ahead into a spill of moonlight so their armor would glitter, quicken their pace, and spur the other tribes to jealously pick up theirs. Inevitably all the tribes would surge forward until the army was again in line.

In this erratic but effective manner, the Barbarian Army, now nearly eight thousand strong, traveled through the night.

When the cool grey glow of dawn began to rise above the eastern horizon, the army saw remnants of the retreating Kitzakk's regiments discarded in the desert: broken wagons, spears, pieces of heavy armor, and dead ponies, their lips crusted with caked foam.

As the grey light grew brighter, the mists floating above the flat landscape lifted to reveal the large, brown city of Bahaara lying directly south. A massive eruption of blunt rock articulated with a thousand windows, doors, streets, towers and tunnels, as if hand carved with spoons by gods.

The Barbarian Army, intimidated by its first sight of a great, civilized city, faltered. But the colorfully patched Grillards at the center of the march, bravely pressed forward, and the Dowats in their persimmon tunics and golden brown leather belts followed. The Kavens, in their triple-belted umber robes, came alongside, and the others moved up until there was again a single front.

They were two to three hours' march from the city.

The cool glow of light at the eastern horizon gradually ignited with intense white, announcing the arrival of the great orb that ruled all deserts. At the first hour, the tip of the golden fire appeared, and spears of white-gold light slashed across the desert. They flew past rock, tumbleweed and thornbush, climbed the city's walls, and splashed among its tangled buildings turning Bahaara into a city of gold. Magnificent. Brutal. As if the desert were an empty void for no other reason than to focus everything that was living, vital and exotic into one stone structure. The muscle of the desert.

The soft murmurs of morning prayers rose up out of Bahaara's shadowed causeways and streets, and lifted above the thousand rooftops. They drifted across the sand to the ears of the advancing Barbarians. But they kept their pace, wiry, browned men and women glittering with metal and pride. Then drum beats and chanting pounded out of the walled citadel, and floated across the desert. Mighty cheers followed, rising to a roar. Bahaara was welcoming the strangers, in the manner the lion king welcomes its meat.

The Barbarian Army came to a clattering, stumbling stop, and stared in chilling wonder as the sunlight melted over this intimidating citadel of mysteries. A ripple ran through the front ranks of the army, and arms pointed up ahead.

Two tiny figures, racing alongside their long shadows, were moving toward the army.

Sixty-six

BAHAARA

The cheering, laughing crowd was drunk with wine, beer and expectation. They swayed, pushed, fell down and drank in the cool morning shade of the Theater of Death. The arena was packed. Bodies were still spilling through the tunnels fed by the crowd outside. They all waited for the morning sun to descend the wall behind the stage. At the third hour it would fill the stage and the entertainment would begin, blood would flow.

On the walls of the city, soldiers not privileged to attend the execution, paced and also watched the sun. Only a few bothered to glance at the desert where, in a distant line of glittering metal, the Barbarian Army advanced cautiously.

Dang-Ling stood motionless in his orchid robe within the shadows of the black and orchid tunnel above the stage. Sweat dripped from his milk-white cheeks and chin. Cobra had vanished, leaving the horned helmet in place, but the high priest was telling himself that Klang, with the powers of the Lord of Death in his body, should easily be able to remove the Death Dealer's head. He told himself this two more times, but it did not stop the sweating.

In the seating area of the Theater of Death, Brown John and Dirken sat in front row seats. The old man was binding a thong around a small earthenware jar with air holes and a wooden plug in it. He tied it off, and held it up to Dirken. "That will hold her. I put a bit of mandrake root in the jar. It should make her behave."

He chuckled and secured the jar in his pouch. Dirken scowled skeptically, and Brown John winked cheerily at his youngest son.

"Put up your scowl, lad." He lifted his arms, palms up, indicating the arena. "Look at this spectacle and enjoy it. It's a splendid affair. A show, I tell you, like one you may never see again. And so exquisitely human. Look at them. The deadliest soldiers ever to hold swords, and here they sit waiting to be entertained while our amateurish troops approach. While the future of their empire, to say nothing of their lives, is in the gravest danger." He chuckled with light-winged cynicism. "Even a dumb weaver would know to man the walls at such a time as this, but not these proud lads. They are too smart for that. Too civilized." He laughed aloud. A perceptive ear would have heard the mockery in it, but on that day there were few perceptive ears in Bahaara.

Dirken muttered, "When they get a good look at the walls, they'll turn tail."

Brown John shook his head, "You underestimate them . . . and her."

Dirken shrugged thoughtfully, and they looked back at the stage.

Gath, by twisting around within his chains, had noticed their presence earlier, but now did not look at them. He watched the sun advancing down the wall at the back of the stage. It was close to the stage, then it touched it. The third hour was at hand.

He looked down at his axe chained to the front of the stage, and the children touching it scattered off. Behind them the crowd suddenly held its breath. Gath looked sharply back at the stage.

Three Kitzakk officers had emerged from a tunnel and now marched up the ramp on the opposite side. They carried their warlord's weapons, a large black-handled axe, a spiked ball-and-chain attached to a short handle, and a longsword and triangular shield. The commanders sat on stools at the landing of the ramp and waited. Their faces were as unperturbed as stones.

As the sun moved steadily across the stage, Temple priestesses, dressed only in silver jewelry, appeared and followed the sunshine sprinkling the dirt with perfumes, sandalwood and myrrh. Where they spilled too much, the puddles began to steam in the sun. When light filled the entire stage, the priestesses scattered out of sight as the crowd stood and roared.

Klang had emerged from the red tunnel, and stood at the top of the red staircase. He was noticeably taller, wider and thicker. His dark brown, hairless flesh glistened with oil. Black lacquered armor heaved on his throbbing body. It was barely able to contain it. His wide cheekbones were wider and blunter within his narrow skull. His eyes were angled black cuts. His hair, lank and thick, lay flat against his skull. It fell below his shoulders when yesterday it had only reached his neck. The backs of his hands and elbows were scaled crusts.

The crowd hushed with a collective gasp as it saw the alterations in his body, and a wild blood lust swept over the sea of faces. They murmured prayers, then began to chant their warlord's name over and over, faster and faster.

The three commanders rose and echoed the crowd.

Brown John and Dirken shared a nervous glance, then joined in spiritedly.

Klang started down the red staircase holding his helmet proudly in the crook of his arm. Greaves of black steel guarded his shins. His feet were booted in black leather and fur. Not knowing their new strength, they crushed the steps, breaking bits of rock off the edges. At the fourth step from the bottom they came to a hard stop.

Klang's cheeks were aflame, his eyes wild.

The horned helmet was still in place. The eye slits flickered with the same red glow of consuming rage. Something had gone wrong. Where was Dang-Ling? As the warlord glanced around, his face snarled with confusion. To hide it he put on his helmet.

It was black and polished, with a round bowl, long cheek guards and a wide convex brim. There were no corners, or flat edges and surfaces. It was awesome. Intoxicated by the crowd chanting his name. He strode onto the stage.

Sixty-seven

THE EXECUTION

Gath set his legs apart as far as the chains allowed and braced his buttocks hard against the whipping post. With the muscles of his outstretched arms bunching against the steel links, he stared hungrily at Klang.

The warlord's arm bands, breast plate, and steel cod-piece rose and fell on his heaving frame. Fumes drifted from under the steel-studded straps of his kilt. His right arm hung loosely; in its crusted fist was a short, black handle. A taut chain hung from the handle to a spiked steel ball.

Gath leaned forward. The tips of the horns, as sensitive as fingertips, could feel danger of a size and strength they had never felt before. His breathing quickened, sucking in Klang's rank body odor. It smelt of smoke and flaming lava, the acrid scents of the Master of Darkness.

A dark thrill roared through Gath. His blood grew hot. He faced a demon spawn that was his equal, or better, and the blood hunger within him was becoming insatiable.

Klang advanced a step, and the chained body flexed and swelled. With a roar, arms and torso surged forward, ripping free.

The rabble screamed and stumbled back from the seats they had worked so diligently to obtain.

Gath and Klang took no notice. They were rooted to the stage, the unholy scent of the Lord of Death swirling over them. Their blood boiled through their brains, melting reason into passion. Two churning, massive bodies ready to erupt. Animals. Demons. Men.

Gath gathered the chains dangling from his arms into his fists. Klang grabbed his shield from an aide and lunged forward. Gath whipped a handful of chains at him. They clattered against the shield and looped around Klang's legs.

As he staggered to a stop, Gath slammed the warlord's upraised shield with the remaining chains and drove him stumbling back, his chain flailing relentlessly.

Klang, his face a smear of savage red meat, fended off each blow as he played his spiked ball out along the ground. As his attacker stepped closer, he whipped the ball out low with a vicious snap. The chain caught Gath's ankle, and the ball spun back around it to plant its spikes in his calf.

Stunned by the pain, Gath threw his head back, gasping. Klang pulled hard, ripping his legs out from under him. The ball ripped free, taking ropes of blood and flesh with it. Certain of victory, Klang swung at Gath's face. The Barbarian caught the ball with his chains, pulled violently and threw Klang on his leering face. Gath rolled up and raced for the front of the stage. When Klang untangled himself, he glanced over his shield to find the Death Dealer facing him, his axe overhead.

Sweat, pink with blood, trickled from the steaming interior of the horned helmet. Klang swung his ball in a wide horizontal arc. Ignoring it, Gath stepped forward, and the spikes ate into his chest, bounded off taking slivers of red meat. A great roar echoed from the helmet, and the axe raced down.

The blade met Klang's shield flush, and bent it back at a right angle. The scalloped edge caught Klang in the throat, and drove him stumbling backward, howling.

The Death Dealer moved in for the kill.

Klang, crouching, gagging, desperately whipped the spiked ball at the Barbarian's feet. But Gath pinned the chain with one foot and severed the links with a blow. He picked up the ball in his fist and threw it. Klang lifted his shield instinctively, but it was shorter now. The ball caught him in the shoulder and ricocheted into the air over the crowd, and sank into howling pandemonium.

Klang discarded his shield and held his axe in two hands as he circled away from the advancing Death Dealer. The warlord's shoulder was a red sponge, stitched with splinters of white bone at the center and crusted with scales. They were pulsing, growing over the wound to close it. Scales had also grown up the backs of his arms, and the tip of reptilian tail had appeared below the skirt of his armor.

The crowd hushed at the sight of the foul appendage and withdrew from the first two rows to stand in a crouch, openmouthed.

The combatants studied each other, wary now.

Gath's eyes glowed red, and his heaving body had expanded. He waited, and Klang stepped in hard, took Gath's blow with his armored chest and hammered Gath in the helmet. Seemingly content with this exchange, they repeated it, hammering each other like men in a dream. Mindlessly, they met blow with blow striking only each other's steel. Klang's armor began to look like a moving heap of scrap metal, and Gath reeled dizzily like a performing drunk. Blood streamed down his arms onto his hands and the axe handle flew out of his grip, leaving the horned helmet as his only defense. He lowered the horns in front of him and waited.

Klang peppered it with short jabs and slashing blows, herding the Barbarian's staggering body around the stage. Fighting to keep his feet, Gath caught each blow with helmet and horns. Blood began to fly from the helmet's mouth and eye holes. Klang, excited by the sight and smell, licked his lips. His tongue was black and forked.

Gath gaped, the crowd screamed, and Klang swung hard, caught the face of the helmet. The blow knocked Gath flat, but cracked the axe handle, and the weapon went spinning across the stage. Klang dove on top of Gath, and his helmet was knocked off, revealing weblike growth connecting his ears and scaled neck.

They rolled and tangled, jabbing and kicking and cursing. Klang buried fanglike teeth in Gath's shoulder. Gath's hands found the scaled flesh of Klang's neck and buried his fingers deep. Klang's eyes bulged open. His lips crawled back over his fangs, bare to the gums. His forked tongue whipped out and wrapped around a thumb. Then, with a wrenching convulsion, his limbs serpentined around Gath's chest and legs, suddenly boneless, pulsing muscles, and his scaled tail whipped from beneath his kilt, curled around a thigh.

The crowd screamed in horror.

Gath's mouth gaped open, straining to suck up air. Klang's reptilelike limbs kept crushing. Tighter. A rib snapped in the Barbarian chest.

Hard scales were forming in Klang's thick neck, resisting the Death Dealer's fingers, and Klang snorted triumphantly. Smoke, then flames, flared from his nose and scorched the Death Dealer's wrists. A growl of pain leapt from the helmet. The eye slits brightened and spat flames, scorching Klang's metal and flesh. Like one huge pulsing fire-breathing beast trying to devour itself, they held on.

The shuddering crowd backed up, leaving blotches of steaming urine on the tiers. Bunches pushed through the exit tunnels in panic.

Covered in blood and dust, Gath and Klang continued to thrash and roll in one piece. Blood poured from the eye and mouth slits of the horned helmet. It was on fire, and spilling over Klang's scaled hands and arms, setting them ablaze. Klang hissed with pain, and scales emerged on his brow, nose and cheeks. As the flames reached his shoulders, the scales grew down over his eyes, nose and mouth, diminishing his sight and breath.

Gath's world, seen through flaming blood, had once more turned red. But this time it was the real world. He saw horror flash across the demon warlord's eyes, as if he had suddenly recognized the foul thing he had become. Klang howled with human torment, and the greenish-grey crusts covered his eyes, blinding him.

Their bodies ripped apart and rolled away from each other gasping, bleeding and flaming. Gath doused his flames with dirt and leapt up. Klang rose mindlessly, body aflame and jerking as a thick crust of scales formed on his back and chest to force off his confining armor. His fingers had turned to claws. Fangs descended below his jaw. His tail whipped about the ground as he groped blindly in front of him.

The tips of the helmet felt the danger riding on the air,

and Gath lowered the helmet in front of him, charged like a primeval bull. Thunder roared from the horned helmet. Tongues of flame spit from the eye slits, then cracking flashes of white lightning.

Klang turned toward the sound and clawed the air blindly.

The horns of the helmet caught him in the chest, driving through his thick crust of scales like they were soft bread, impaled the reptilian warlord, and lifted him off the ground. Klang hissed and howled, his arms, legs and tail flailing wildly.

Gath threw his head back with a roar, and the warlord flew into the air. He turned over twice in midair, and landed with a moist thud in the empty front row.

The remaining crowd screamed and pushed through the tunnels to escape, trampling on its own convulsing body.

Brown John and Dirken finally fought free of the flowing crowd, raced back down the tiers, and raised their eyes to the stage. It was empty of life except for the victor.

He held center stage, erect and alert, listening. Cries echoed through Bahaara as the Barbarian Army stormed through the streets chasing the Kitzakks as they fled out the gates into the desert. His knees slowly bent, and his monstrous smoking body cocked. He lifted his axe and held it across the bloody thighs. Liquid red dripped from its cutting edge.

From within him rumbled a demonic thunder, like the blood lust of a sweeping fire. His attitude was plain. He wanted more.

Brown John cried out in despair, "We've lost him!"

The great helmet turned slowly toward the pair, then looked beyond them. As father and son watched stupified, the huge body straightened. The red glow behind the eye slits began to fade. They twisted around to see what he saw.

A group of Grillard warriors were spilling into the arena led by Bone and Robin Lakehair.

Sixty-eight

BURIAL

On a shelf in a silent chamber deep under the noisy confusion in Bahaara's streets stood a huge swallowtail butterfly carved from soft lead and enameled orange and black. Dang-Ling, old of eye and using both hands, plucked its heavy body from its perch and set it on a stone pedestal beneath the shelf. Slowly it began to sink into the floor.

His eyes avoided a door at the opposite side of the buried room. Heavy steel bars locked it shut. He could picture Baak, Dazi, Hatta, and Cobra's servant waiting for him beyond that door in his hidden laboratory. But they would never see their priest again, or anyone else. He had no doubt that it was the Queen of Serpents' fault, that her lust for the Death Dealer had been the cause for the current calamity. But what more could he have done, or what more could he do now than he was doing? He could not afford to trust anyone.

He pattered over to a side stairway and listened. Loud grating sounds came from within the surrounding walls where weighty stones began to shift and slide. A stone receded in the ceiling of his chamber releasing a stream of sand. It began to flood the room. Faint cries came from behind the locked door where the same thing was happening, then there was a heavy pounding on the door. His unfortunate servants had finally realized their fate.

Dang-Ling eased his ample body up through a dark hole

at the top of the stairway. A large stone descended behind him and the rising sand piled up against it.

A short time later a wagon with tall red wheels rattled out a postern gate in Bahaara's north wall, and rolled southeast into the desert hidden behind its own dust. "Big Hands" Gazul drove. Dang-Ling was ensconced comfortably on thick cushions in the wagon bed accompanied by six young leopards and several chests of jewels and gold. The road ahead was clear. A great deal of what he had cherished lay buried under Bahaara, but a promising future waited ahead, and he did not look back.

Sixty-nine

MIDNIGHT STAR

For five days the Barbarians looted Bahaara, and each night there was a great feast held in the Court of Life. At each feast, the meat and cooking were provided by a different tribe. Rumors said that one night they were served the roasted body of the warlord Klang. But the way in which the Kranik savages charred their meat left it unrecognizable, and since the rumors had started after the meat had been consumed, the impropriety could not be proven, and the after-meal belching was particularly loud and raucous.

The Grillards provided songs and dances for each feast, and they all told the same story. But the hero had a plethora of names: The "Dark One who dwelled in The Shades," the "Savior of Weaver," the "Defender of the Trees," and the "Lord of Forest." But to each description was added "Death Dealer."

On the sixth night there was no celebration. Instead, the Barbarian chiefs sat in council and, after much deliberation, came to a radical conclusion. Gath of Baal would be their king, the first king the tribes of the Forest Basin had ever set over themselves. The decision was unanimous, and Brown John sent Robin Lakehair to fetch him.

Delighted to be the carrier of such good news, she hurried to the altar room in the Temple of Dreams where Gath was quartered, but he wasn't there. After searching the temple without success, she found him in a torchlit courtyard at the rear of the temple, but hesitated to approach, holding her little hand pressed against her heart.

The dark warrior was dressed in black chain mail. A curved Kitzakk sword hung from his belt by a glittering brass chain. His huge axe stood in the black stallion's saddle holster. The horned helmet was tied to his belt. He was clean shaven, but his singed hair was crudely clipped so that it hung to his neck in wild disarray. His face was scabbed and burnished with callouses. He turned to her expectantly, and Robin, frightened and flustered, ran over to him.

"You can't leave," she gasped. "Not now, Gath. Please."

His hand reached out to gently gather in her short red-gold hair flickering in the torchlight. "I must, little friend."

"But why?" she pleaded. "Why? Where would you want to go? And . . . and the people love you. The tribes want you to be their king."

Gath shook his head. "I am not a king, and I have been too long among men."

She trembled at the uncompromising tone of his voice, then, breathless, she gazed up into his eyes. "Let me go with you then?"

He shook his head, swung up onto his saddle.

"Please," she begged.

He leaned down, took hold of her under the arms and lifted her to face him, holding her as easily as a flower. A rush of hope burst through her, and she smiled. He kissed her smile where it moved her cheek, then pressed her lips against his, and she melted, moaning blissfully.

He held her away. "I will come see you, in your village, but I can not take you with me. Stay with your friends where it's safe."

"But it's you I feel safe with." He set her down, but her eyes still begged. "Gath, please, don't you still need me a little?"

His eyes turned towards the distant northwest. "Where I go, I must go alone."

"Then I'll be waiting! I don't care if it's a year or ten years. I'll be waiting for you. I . . . I belong to you."

He shook his head, saying quietly, "People do not own people, Robin."

His eyes were warm and tender but resolute, and something hid behind them, a new wound that was deep and active. Her head dropped. It was a wound she could not heal, because, even though she could see it and feel the terrible pain it brought him, she could not imagine its nature.

"If ever you are in danger," he said softly, "look for me. I will come."

Her face lifted, a beautiful mask hiding all that was inside. "And you, if you are ever hurt or in need, you will let me find you, and come to you. Promise me that, at least that."

He looked away in silence.

"Then good-bye, Gath of Baal," she whispered. "I won't watch you go."

She headed for the door of the temple. Gath watched her figure disappear, then he and the stallion moved across the yard and under the shadowed gate.

At the rear door of the temple, Robin met Brown John

coming out and fell into his arms, sobbing, "He's gone. He doesn't want us."

Brown John patted her head. "Now, now, child, we'll see about that. You wait here."

She slumped to the door stoop and sank back against the jamb as the old man hurried off.

Brown John found him riding slowly down the road that twisted along the western side of the mesa. In the distance was the northern gate, and beyond it, the desert: empty, silent and dark. The old man, wheezing from his short run, looked up accusingly. "This is not a very civilized way to bid good-bye!"

Gath smiled ruefully. "Have you been trying to civilize me, old man?"

"Never mind that. I told you they would make you king. Surely you'll at least stay the night to consider it!" Getting no reply he sighed. "All right, all right. But tell me what it is that you think you're up to?"

"The Master of Darkness hunted me. Now I hunt him."

"That's madness, and you know it!" Getting only silence he grunted. "I suppose then, you're not going to give up that headpiece?"

"Never." It was low and deep, from another world.

"But the Master of Darkness! It's impossible to . . ." he stopped himself and sighed with resignation. "Oh, what's the use. You'll try this thing regardless of what I say."

Gath smiled, and the old man laughed at his own defeat. "Well, I will tell you this, my friend, there has never been such a futile quest, never one of such size and nobility, and never one so reckless." A familiar twinkle flashed across his eyes. "However, if you were to become king, even if only for a short while, you could build up your resources for the hunt. And there would be no chains to bind you to your throne. You might appoint me as your minister. I would attend to all the routine nonsense, and leave you to live however you wished to live. You'd be loved and respected. You could even return to your forest if you wished, come and go undisturbed and unchallenged!''

Brown John stopped short. Flushed with embarrassment, he confronted Gath's stony countenance. ''Built my own trap, didn't I? And blundered right into it. Well, I'm me, I guess, and you surely are you. There's no changing that. Go to your challenge, Gath. But whether you want it or not, the gratitude and respect of the forest tribes go with you.''

Gath didn't appear to hear him. He said, ''Look after her, *bukko*. We will meet again.''

''Yes,'' Brown John's voice cracked. He paused and cleared his throat. ''But one moment, I have something for you. A gift.'' He reached inside his pouch and brought out the small earthenware jar with the tiny air holes, handed it to Gath. ''This may be a useful tool of barter, or a toy. That's up to you. It houses the Serpent Queen.''

A rare look of surprise and delight lit up Gath of Baal's solemn features. He put the jar to his cheek feeling the imprisoned reptile's movement, and his eyes smiled at Brown John.

''You did this?''

Brown John, swelling with pride, nodded several times.

''Well now, I expected you to say and do many things, Brown, all of them quite out of the ordinary. But never this.''

Brown John laughed uproariously at the mimicry of his own dialogue. Gath put the jar in his saddlebag, squeezed the old man's raised hand, and moved on down the road.

He trotted across the moonlit clearing just inside the northern gate, and galloped out into the waiting desert shadows. The moonlight gleamed on his broad shoulders for a long time, then he became part of the darkness.

Brown John found Robin sitting on a stone watching, and gathered her in his arms. ''I'm sorry, little one,'' he murmured. ''I could not talk him out of it.''

She looked off at the spreading desert. The dark night sky was wearing one radiating white jewel, the midnight star. After a moment, she said softly, "Brown John, someday, somehow, I will find a way to be with him. I will, I swear it by the midnight star."

"I think you might, Robin. I think you just might." She gazed up at him, comforted, and saw the reflection of the star twinkling in his eyes.

Seventy

COUNCIL OF CHIEFS

The Barbarian tribes were angered by Gath of Baal's refusal to be their king, but it did not blunt their resolve to become organized and possess a champion whose magic was contagious for times of emergency. To resolve the problem, the Council of Chiefs argued and consulted throughout the night.

The next day the council announced their decision. As the *bukko*, Brown John, with his foresight and possible magic, had compelled the Death Dealer to act as their champion during this last, great emergency, and as his Grillards had organized and supplied the Barbarian Army, they invited Brown John to sit permanently with the Council of Chiefs. In addition, for the duration of any emergency, the *bukko* would serve as their leader. It was assumed by all, of course, that the old stage master still had the power to compel Gath of Baal to serve as their champion, and Brown John did not offer to confuse them with the facts. As no one considered Robin Lakehair to be more than a momentary romantic distraction for Gath, her name was not brought up at all.

Brown John formally accepted the offer, and made no mention of her either.

After hearty congratulations all-around, the tribes packed up and moved out the northern gate heading for the Great Forest Basin. They left Bahaara in flames. It burned brilliantly for hours, then the flames died leaving a blackened, smoking skeleton city to be ravaged by the sands and time.

The Barbarians were no longer an army. They were tribes again, and traveled on separate trails. All, that is, except for the Grillards. They accompanied the Cytherians. They followed them across the desert, down through The Narrows and across Foot Bridge. There they said their sentimental good-byes, and Robin turned east for Weaver. The Grillards continued north on Amber Road back to the Valley of Miracles.

Seventy-one

WEAVER

Reaching home, Robin and the Cytherian warriors were greeted warmly and with great honor and celebration. Robin was given a place of honor at the feast, annointed with incense and garlands of flowers, and, even though she was wan, pale and stood out vulgarly in her short hair, was praised as a daring and courageous girl of virtue and beauty.

During the following weeks, the children came flocking

to hear her tell of her adventures. Their adoration, along with a steady diet of milk, hardy bread and fresh fruit, quickly nourished her back to health and lifted her spirits so that once more she began to echo the melodies of the birds and the laughter in the ripple of the brook.

But when the wounded veterans of the campaign dragged their crippled limbs back into the taverns to tell their version of the war, things began to change. The soldiers relieved their aches and pains with quantities of hard wine and wildly exaggerated tales of their battles, laying dark emphasis on all that was unnatural, mysterious and brutal: the satanic appearance of the Queen of Serpents, the devil fire within the horned helmet, the horrible transformation of the warlord into a hideous reptile, and the long, unexplained and intimate visits Robin Lakehair had paid the Dark One in his secret home in The Shades, a place where strong men feared to travel, yet a place from which she always returned unhurt and in remarkable health.

As these tales, along with those of the unholy carnage done by the Death Dealer and his axe, circulated, they grew uglier and more sinister according to the appetites of both the tellers and listeners. Consequently, many of the villagers who had suffered loss of loved ones during the conflict, were uncomfortably reminded of their unhappiness, and disturbed by unnatural fears. The stories, after becoming old and revolting, stopped. But Robin was an ever-present reminder of times best forgotten. And, as she herself had suffered no ill effects from her very questionable adventures, rumors began that she was in some way tainted by them.

If she was, of course, she could contaminate the holy work and spoil the cloth, so her spindle was taken away and given to another girl. Robin tried to bear up under the hurtful insult, believing that time would eventually restore her tribe's belief in her.

But it was the gossip that was fed by time, and Robin, who could not comprehend these attacks against her, did not know how to argue against them. The situation compounded. She was shunned at the well, and the children were led from her presence. She spent much time in the forest, but too much time alone brought on a deep melancholy, and it became more and more difficult for her to return to her room in the evening.

Then one night she dreamed of the children themselves reviling her. She woke up drenched in sweat and sobbing. Panic made her heart pound and showed in her eyes. She jumped out of bed, threw on her bone-white tunic and slipped into her soft leather boots. With her belongings packed in a bedroll, and tied to her back, she dashed out of Weaver before first light. Her sacred whorl was held tight in her fist. But there were shadows under her eyes, and no lilt in her stride. There was no longer a friend to whom she dared say good-bye.

When she arrived at Pinwheel Crossing, the morning sun was beating down on her hair and shoulders. She studied the many signs marking the roads: Amber Road which would take her she did not know where, the road to Coin and the Kavens, then the road to Dowat territory. But they only made tears well in her eyes. She glanced back down Weaver Road, and looked at the sacred whorl in her fist. Defiantly she flung the whorl into the surrounding foliage and started down the Way of the Outlaw.

She had no other choice. She was an outcast.

Seventy-two

RAG CAMP

Robin reached Stone Crossing when the sun was low in the western sky. She climbed to its heights and paused there, gazing down at the camp spread out among the apple trees in the clearing beyond the river. A tentative smile lifted the corners of her small pert mouth, but before she was halfway down the slope, the smile was moving with abandon into her cheeks.

There were children playing on the ground under the trees. Seeing her approach, they stopped their game, and crowded around her, bombarding her with questions.

"Who are you?"

"What's your name?"

"Did you come to see the show?"

"Are you going to stay?"

Robin listened with delight, then covered her ears playfully and they laughed, quieted. She considered them for a moment with warning eyes, then asked, "Are you going to let me say something, or aren't strangers allowed to talk in Rag Camp?"

They smiled shyly, and nodded.

"All right," she said, then squatted facing their small active faces. "Now, I am looking for a man called Brown John, is he here?"

"Oh yes," they squealed.

They took her hands and led her across the clearing

toward the stage where the three colorful wagons served as backdrops.

"He's over here."

"In the red wagon."

"That's his house."

"Really?" Robin gasped admiringly, "I thought it was just part of the stage."

"Oh no! It's his wagon."

"The best in the whole camp."

"He's real important."

"And bossy."

"But don't be frightened."

"He'll like you."

"Because you're pretty," put in the littlest one.

Robin laughed, picked her up with a squeeze. They all hurried to the raised stage, and the children pushed Robin up onto it. They began to shout at the upstairs window; Brown John stuck his frowsy head out and shouted right back, "What is it now? I told you not to bother me during my nap. Do I have to . . ."

He stopped abruptly seeing Robin's face smiling up at him, then said quietly, "My, my." He turned on the children shouting, "Let her in, you noisy imps. She's late, very, very late!"

After the evening meal, Brown John held court on the stage to determine Robin's status with the Grillards. He sat on a large thronelike chair facing Robin. Gathered around them, sitting on stools and the floor, were the tribe's principal players: Mother Drab, Krell the Rubber Man, Bone, Dirken, Nose the Fool, and Belle and Zail, the lead dancing girls.

From his prominent position, he listened patiently to the speeches, all of which were rich with opinion and style, and lengthy. Then he presented briefly his conclusion. Robin Lakehair would be accepted into the camp and given a bed, a blanket and an equal share of wine and food. Then

the arguments began as to which craft she would pursue.
But, as these entertainers and thieves had no experience
with such an abundance of virtue and beauty, they had no
idea what trade Robin was suited for, and their disagree-
ments became loud and hot. By tradition Brown John was
only to speak when the group was out of words. But
knowing that rarely happened, he interrupted firmly,
"That's enough. The discussion is ended. Robin will train
as a dancing girl."

Mother Drab, Belle and Zail laughed riotously, then
Mother Drab arched a wicked eye at Brown John and said
with a wry chuckle, "Her! A dancing girl! Why she's got
nothing up front and less behind, and even if she did she
wouldn't know how to toss it, or who to toss it at!"

Brown John waited until they all ran out of laughter, then
fixed an eye fiercely on the troop.

"She will dance," he said conclusively, "because she
has other attractions which are suitable to the dance. And
the stick and hoop will not be her teachers, but the white
water splashing over the rocks of the stream, and the
swallow in flight, the tree in the wind, the shooting star
dashing across the night sky." He raised an acknowledging
hand to Mother Drab, Zail and Belle. "Do not misunderstand. I do not underestimate the extravagant wealth of your
bouncing breasts and thundering hips. These are profound
and sacred contributions to the dance, and I respect them
as profoundly necessary and highly inspiring. But . . . I
have a different vision for Robin. She will not dance as you
dance. She will not perform "The Pregnant Virgin" or
even "The Wicked Wife."

He leaned forward, gathered Robin's hands as light
glinted in his warm eyes. "No, child, your dances will tell
the tales the animals and elves tell, and speak of far
pavilions, and of gods and goddesses riding the wind,
bathing in the sky, and building castles out of cobwebs and
clouds."

He paused and directed her eyes to the floor of the stage

as if it were the whole of all the earth. He whispered, "You think now, Robin Lakehair, that you are an outcast, but you are not." He looked into her moist eyes. "You have come home."

A month later, when many visitors from the forest tribes had gathered in Rag Camp to celebrate midsummer, Robin Lakehair performed for the first time. It was the opening number, a dance designed to distract the little children so the main entertainment could begin. It was titled, "Tails Up." She performed as a dragonfly, and wore pea green tights, small yellow wings and a long red tail. Some of the adults had no idea what her dance was about, while others imagined it meant strange and significant things. But their children howled and rolled about with delight, and the tiny ones kissed her nose and petted her tail, so the parents applauded appreciatively.

A massive armored figure standing in the night shadows at the edge of the forest also watched Robin's debut. As she moved among the children laughing and hugging them, his body shifted in place as if he would approach her, but he did not. Instead he turned and strode back into the forest night.

Seventy-three

THE QUEST

That night Gath of Baal rode slowly up a narrow gulley toward the top of Calling Rock. About him the darkness held an eerie hollowness and echoed with the soft plodding of the horse's hooves. At the summit, he dismounted and led the animal through the shrubs and boulders into the clearing beside the naked thorn tree. A lonely silence oppressed the area. Not even the wind spoke among the leaves.

Within the circle of small blackened rocks that Robin had once gathered for her fire, he placed a few logs and dry leaves. They lit easily. He spread his blankets below an outcropping of rock, and removed his armor. After feeding the stallion, he ate some bread and cold meat, and drank some wine. A breeze moved softly through the rocks, but its faint whistle only enhanced the magnitude of the silence and solitude.

He lay down on his blankets using his saddle as a pillow, and picked up his helmet, studied it for a long time, fascinated with every detail of its powerful construction and the pulsing life in its steel. Tomorrow he would head for the Land of Smoking Skies to begin the hunt. But not tonight. He set the helmet down and looked at the fire.

Demons and ogres began to take shape within the red and orange dancing tongues. All the spawn of darkness that the Master of Darkness could send against him seemed to writhe in the red heat to the sounds of night predators creeping and slithering in time with the noisy flames. For a moment he glimpsed an old frowsy wrinkled *bukko* with laughter in his eyes fighting at his side, and he smiled. He peered past the flames at a small huddled shape sleeping in the embrace of the exposed roots at the base of the thorn tree. When it moved, he could see the long red-gold hair of a girl, and when she turned her face to the firelight he could see her soft, plump lips, stretching and sighing like little red dancers.

Later, during the darkest hours of the night, when the fire had turned to glowing embers, his sleeping body shifted slightly and he muttered contentedly, like a man in the middle of a dream.